Also by the same author:
THE RAGGED CLIFFS TRILOGY . . .

Ragged Cliffs
Inheritance Lost
An Equal Judge

The Bent Brief

Julian Ruck

DINEFWR
PUBLISHERS

First Impression: September 2012
Reprinted: November 2012

Published in 2012
in the United Kingdom by
Dinefwr Publishers
Rawlings Road, Llandybie
Carmarthenshire, SA18 3YD

The author would like to stress that
this is a work of fiction and no resemblance
to any actual individual or institution
is intended or implied.

A catalogue record for this book
is available from The British Library.

ISBN 978-1-904323-24-2

Cover illustration: Jeff Kirkhouse

Printed in the UK

For Lynney,
with all my love – when I can get a word in!

Yet each man kills the thing he loves,
By each let this be heard,
Some do it with a bitter look,
Some with a flattering word.
The coward does it with a kiss,
The brave man with a sword!

Oscar Wilde,
*The Ballad
of Reading Jail*

CHAPTER 1

Her Majesty's Prison, Pentonville, London.

"Slop out, fella!"

The prison officer's verbal assault smashed into my mind and forced me to open my eyes and read the 'Thought for the day' that had been scratched into the wall facing me.

'Don't fight the system 'cos you're the knob 'ed for bein' 'ere.'

Ah well, at least someone in here had a sense of humour.

These gems of foresight had been scratched into the green wall that ran alongside my bed, a metal-framed apology for comfort and rest – and ha-ha to that! The graffiti always ensured that I smiled at least once a day though, so I was grateful for this crude mercy. It definitely beat looking at the unsavoury lout who had just disturbed my sleep. My escape.

On second thoughts, 'sleep' is perhaps the wrong word to describe a constant state of sensitivity. More often than not I simply floated in and out of my senses; sometimes they were acute, at other times far too blunt.

I stayed where I was, so to hell with him! I knew that I was fooling myself yet again, and that sooner or later I would have to shift my backside. Prison was like that; there wasn't a lot of room for 'choice', Her Majesty's Pleasure being exempt from the 'choice' that pious politicians kept banging on about.

Another 'Slop out!' insulted my eardrums along with a couple of violent kicks to the cell door. I had been spotted enjoying a temporary release from punishment, which wouldn't do at all. I looked up at the distorted face staring down at me and noted the contempt. 'Thinking' was frowned upon in clink; the screws hadn't forgotten their history. For a moment I felt decidedly uncomfortable. 'Thinkers' I knew were always the first to be put up against a wall and shot.

Slopping out was, without doubt, one of the more stomach-wrenching highlights of the day. Ignoring the order of navy blue authority to dispose of my now cloudy and unappetising waste, I treated contempt with contempt and stayed beneath the prison blanket that was so thin I could almost see right through it. I needed, nay demanded, these few minutes to allow my little world to adjust yet again to its new and exciting environment.

My jailer observed, snorted, then disappeared. Perhaps I had managed to retain some dignified defiance after all.

I continued to observe the décor of my new home. Naked females grinned and laughed at me from every wall. I couldn't understand why my fellow inmates kept plastering their 'homes' with unobtainable bosoms and eye-watering rumps. What was the point, for God's sake? But then prison had its own rules – a unique society with its choked insults and resigned madness.

I had inherited the papery pornography from my predecessor and had yet to decide what to do with it. The odd furious nipple did have the virtue of reminding me that I was still alive and still a man, so to date the walls had remained untouched.

Having finished my morning ritual of cell study I finally got up and began to dress. The blue-pinstripe shirt reminded me of other, less offensive days. I used to wear them to the office; they always made me look suitably lawyerly and professional, especially with a yellow tie. Were I ever to be liberated from this prison of human misery I doubted I would ever wear a blue-pinstripe shirt again. You know I do believe there is a song in there somewhere. Anyway, the prison tailor obviously wasn't up to much, neither were the laundry facilities. The collars and cuffs were frayed and loose, no starch being used for certain. Single cuffs, so cufflinks were out of the question. Bad form all round, really. Must have a word with the Governor at teatime.

As if all this wasn't enough, the real abomination and total insult to my dignity were HMP's underpants. These white monstrosities should have had a sign printed on the front saying, 'HOP IN!' My pale muscle-free legs made me look like a malnourished stick insect or worse – a strutting Superman without the body, perhaps. The rest of me wasn't too bad, but the legs . . . well, the less said the better. In the past some women had actually envied them, if you can work that one out. The coarse blue denim trousers I slipped and slid into completed the sartorial battleground. Now I looked just like every other con in the place. Uniformity and cheapness had thus been achieved.

On the outside at least.

CHAPTER 2

At 7.30 a.m. the prison officer was back with another shout of "Slop out, fella!"

Why couldn't the unimaginative bugger use another word instead of 'fella'? 'Fellow' wouldn't have been so insulting, and neither would it have made me feel like some dejected animal in a circus being called upon to perform for the titillation of a band of disreputable and overindulged urchins.

I picked up the piss-pot without rancour – resistance was futile – and began my journey to the toilets and washing area. As I joined the disappointed surge of other blue-striped bodies, I noticed that some of them had managed to acquire a more conscientious and bespoke tailor than I since the prison garb seemed to hang better on them than me. On the other hand, of course, it could have been the diet – they were fatter and probably more disposed to starch and haute cuisine bilge.

As I closed in on the cesspit my nasal passages were blasted with a stench as angry as any of those characters around me who cursed and groaned at their misfortune. This was one of the more subtle punishments I would never get used to – I'll spare you the details. I did what I had to do and almost ran back to the blessed sanctity of my 'Peter' (or cell, for the uninitiated).

Amazing how one's values are devalued in prison.

My cell had become a refuge, a place of peace, somewhere I could shut out the reality of my present existence. My body might be 'banged up', but my mind was as free as the pigeons that crapped on my window ledge. Windows? Prisons? Well, barred they might be, yet at least I was able to distinguish night from day – not that it mattered.

I won't describe the morning's breakfast. It isn't worth it.

At 10.00 a.m. a shout of "fours" echoed along the corridors. I was on level four. I had been summoned.

The highlight of the day had arrived.

An hour's exercise.

An hour of air.

An hour of social intercourse.

One hour snatched from twenty-four where life could be confirmed and the skies above stared at for no particular reason.

The prison yard was a triangle enclosed by Victorian wings of strict bricks and mortar. Everything about this hour was strict. No running. No independent travelling. Everyone traced the exact lines of the triangle; after all there was nowhere else to go.

"'Ere mate, 'ave you got a minute?" A man who looked as if he hadn't seen a decent meal in years suddenly appeared at my side along with a fatter version of criminal recidivism.. The thin man's eyes bulged and couldn't keep still, while his partner shuffled his feet from side to side and kept his head firmly tucked into his chest. Crime had obviously bent his ambition and, it seemed, his neck. I quickly concluded that life had beaten him into a scrunched-up nonentity and that the overloaded starch of prison grub had become his only escape.

The thin man smiled whilst his long nose sniffed me up and down. Then his fat friend lifted his head for a brief moment and looked at me with eyes that had seen too much guilt and teeth that had seen too much nicotine – those of them that were left anyway. The sensible fellow had shrewdly avoided the avarice of Denplan, who emphasised how good their services were for all who signed up. Not that dental insurance would have been much good to him in clink; even the namby-pamby State wasn't prepared to go that far – private dentists for the criminal classes, heaven forbid! His lower lip trembled for a moment, so I took this for a smile. There was certainly no threat in the

11

man's eyes or indeed his ragged teeth; frankly I couldn't imagine him threatening a handicapped kitten, let alone anybody else.

"Now then, me and my mate 'ere have been thinkin'," the thin man said. This one had to be the Laurel of the team, and I'm not joking either. "You must know lots of toffs, being one yourself, like."

"Well . . ." I muttered. I had never considered myself to be a 'toff', but then everything in prison was arse over tit. Middle-class upstart would have been more accurate. I hated being called 'mate' but wasn't about to start complaining. Not that it would have made any difference as Laurel didn't really give me much of a chance to reply properly.

"Anyway, we thought you might think about goin' into partnership with us." Partnership? The only partnerships I had ever known were of the private practice variety. "It's like this, see. I bet your pals have big 'ouses, you know plenty o' dosh like antiques and stuff. Well, me and my mate 'ere was thinkin' that maybe you could case the places, you know, find out alarm codes and all that stuff. You must 'ave plenty of inside knowledge like, being a brief. We could work as a team. Very profitable. You provide the info and we do the business. Split the proceeds, fair and square, like. What d'you think?"

I looked at Laurel then at Hardy, who so far hadn't said a word. They were serious and I had to admit that they had a point. I rubbed my chin. My future as a lawyer was a trifle in doubt at the moment, so perhaps I ought to be thinking about other avenues of gainful employment. I smiled.

"I'll think about it, gentlemen. Though I'm not promising anything." And ha-ha to that. I may be in prison but I wasn't a villain for God's sake, grim future prospects notwithstanding.

"Good," Laurel beamed. "You do that then. Let us know – oh you 'aven't got a match, 'ave you?" I was about to hand him one when Hardy suddenly confirmed that he was a living organism.

"Jesus, don't give 'im a match! 'Ee's in 'ere for arson. We'll all go up in fuckin' smoke!"

Prison had its moments.

A few minutes later I was accosted by another inmate. There was something different about this man. There was an isolation in his eyes similar to my own. There was also desperation and yet he looked so normal, the local authority clerk or middle-manager type. No doubt on the 'out' he always wore short-sleeved shirts and ties that didn't match, and jeans and trainers on the weekend. I don't know why, but I immediately felt sorry for him. His girlfriend was getting ready to jump ship apparently, so could I write a letter for him? Refusal wasn't an option, his eyes saw to that, so I agreed to have the letter ready by the following day.

You may be wondering why I was receiving all this attention. Well, the answer is simple – I was a celebrity. I had also been given a new name, the 'Bent Brief', which I found rather amusing as my present rather inconvenient housing problem had nothing whatsoever to do with my practising law.

My suspect stardom was due to the fact that I could write a competent letter or compose a sweet love sonnet for those cons who were either unable to write something appropriate to their women on the 'out' or were incapable of writing anything at all. Now and again I was also buttonholed for the odd bit of legal advice too – not that I knew much about criminal law; not my thing, but I would try anyway. Not likely to be sued for negligence, was I?

'Dear Johns' were a daily threat to the delicate balance of prison life. Such a letter could cause rebellion and mayhem. It seems my pen was sometimes able to calm the threat, or at least sweeten it. In any event, it ensured a constant supply of my only succour – tobacco. Two decent roll-ups per letter was my fee. Everything had a price, even brains and literacy. Not so sure about the brains though; wouldn't have got myself into this mess if mine were in plentiful supply, would I?

I continued to push my body into an aimless nowhere, wishing as I did so that its more infamous Bermuda counterpart would transport me to sunnier triangles, or at least to a place amongst less troublesome aliens.

I enjoyed my lonely hour.

My whole condition was lonely, but this hour allowed me to at least place a few yards between myself and the unknown equation of which I was now a part. Here I was. Different. Apart. The occasional conversation was childlike, the careful laughter that accompanied it always soaring with outrageous obscenity. I rarely enjoyed participating.

Before continuing with my precious moments of exercise I decided to imitate my fat friend. I shoved my chin as far down into my chest as I could and dropped my shoulders until they started to ache. Hopefully my beaten demeanour would deter any further interruptions on my alfresco thinking time.

My feet hadn't tramped more than a few paces before my secluded mind was hijacked by a vision of incarcerated beauty – a single yellow rose. How it had managed to survive and blossom in such human darkness, rancid misery and profound ugliness, God knows, yet it prompted me to whisper, "Oh Jaz, where are you?" But my question went unanswered as my eyes misted over.

'Banged up' once more, I looked in the partly demolished plexi-glass mirror. At forty-five my face remained handsome – although I say it myself – and refined, if not a little too lived-in. The lines had deepened and had been ploughed a little more thoroughly in recent months – a mossed-up sheet of corrugated tin immediately came to mind, God knows why; I was hardly Oscar Wilde after all, and writing the odd 'Ballad' wasn't really my thing. Yet my hair was still thick and auburn, although some grey yelled 'age' here and there. My green/brown eyes had lost some of their humour, but not their humanity. Overall, I decided that my worn-out chops were gentlemanly or even versatile, certainly not unkind or primitive anyway. For a few moments my eyes seemed to speak in many tongues as my lips searched for a woman's touch. The warmth of a female finger-tip.

A woman named Jaz.

I turned away from my own reflection. There was an unmistakable stamp and footprint of prison on it. It happens. My own face offended me; it was an affront. I lay down on the excuse for a bed and allowed my mind to return to the events that had brought me to this hell-hole.

It all began about six months ago.

CHAPTER 3

I signed the mail of Hillyard, Ducane & Co., Solicitors of Bury St Edmonds, and left the office. The flaky gold lettering of the ancient and now outdated 'Commissioners for Oaths' still hung around underneath the name on the frosted glass window of the office. As a Commissioner, my clients made me swear and curse on a daily basis – didn't they just! The name by the way: Edwin Hillyard. David Ducane had died years ago, but his goodwill remained eternal, in name if nothing else.

It was the end of a usual day.

My evening I knew would be filled with emptiness and frustration, so there was no rush to get home. Warm doorstep kisses and a loving smile or two had become figments of a disappointed imagination. These days I didn't look forward to going home as there was no longer that lovely feeling of contented release at 5 o'clock. In fact I didn't look forward to anything, only backward. Memories and the past had become my cloak and dagger, my laughter and my protection.

As was now my habit, I walked slowly out of the office; these days each step seemed unsure of itself as my feet had become instruments of gloomy indecision. What to do next? Where to go to kill some time had become a major early evening problem. No one would be disappointed if I was late arriving home, no lovingly prepared food would be spoilt, so my footsteps were always soft and begging for direction.

As I started the car I finally made a decision. It would have to be a pub again, a pub where no one knew me, the anonymity always so comforting.

I found a suitable drinking hole down a drab country road – town pubs were out of the question, too many viruses (take that for clients) – one of those worn-out places where brass horse-shoes and pictures of eighteenth-century gentlemen sucking on empty pipes were the order of the day. Like pubs all over the country it was a secretive place, a place where shallow and betrayed friendships festered and falsehood ensured an empty immortality. The establishment had enjoyed some character back in that century, but right now it looked dishevelled and thoroughly bankrupt, like most of the clothes that were sent to Third World countries. Not surprising really, as who in their right mind was going to pay three pounds a pint when you could get the same stuff for fifty pence at Tesco? The breweries had overpriced themselves, so serve them right.

I bought a double whisky with a drop of water, no ice, and sat down in a corner. The bar was quiet, no intrusions. Covering the matrimonial and criminal stuff all day had left me at a low ebb.

As I took a sip of whisky – I felt like gulping it but exercised restraint instead – I cursed my partner Tom (or Uncle Tom when I felt like exercising some colonial superiority – apart from this he was one year older than me, so the avuncular nick-name was quite appropriate) who usually did all the dubious crime and tear-soaked divorce cases while I stuck with the more arm's length and less traumatic nonsense of commercial con-veyancing, company and civil litigation.

Tom was a big black sod whose parents had made a few bob from property in Brixton, so the story went anyway. He was always smirking when he repeated it, so I was never entirely sure where all the bucks had come from. In any event, the parents had made sure that all their children received the best education money could buy.

He was a fat-free, good-looking brute who firmly placed me in the shade anyway, God forbid, with huge, gentle brown eyes that always made me feel so bloody apologetic. He was ex-Harrow, Savile Row chalk-striped, bright red polka-dotted pocket handkerchief and more English than the English, whoever the hell we were anyway. His blood was probably purer than ours, as he kept on reminding me on a daily basis. I was 'white trash' and shouldn't forget it; after all he hadn't been contaminated by a mishmash of European barbarity, had he?

Apart from matters relating to me personally, Tom was wonderfully multicultural in all things, including his love life (like me in many respects – for example I had tried to pay him in Libyan dinars, but he wouldn't have any of it). Two ex-wives, one German, one Irish, both white.

Like my good self, Tom had seen more peachy buttocks than a toilet seat in his time, but once again his uncontrollable addiction to wedding cake had prevailed and he was now on his third marriage. His current wife is a charming black woman whom I've always described as brown or even permanently tanned, if you like. (I've never quite worked out how someone whose skin is overlaid with the colours of autumn is always described as black, even though there's not a spot of blackness to be seen on her.) Having finally tamed his wanton ways she has hauled him back screaming to matrimonial bliss. It was that huge slice of wedding cake being dangled in front of his eyes that finally did it for him.

Anyway Tom was in hospital at the moment following an operation to remove his piles that were like Mediterranean tomatoes apparently, so that the poor sod could hardly sit down. His excessive intake of red wine had helped the ripening process along his doctors had told him – and his wife.

One thing about his operation though that pleased me was that his stitched-up anus would make him think twice before blasting me with winds from the Caribbean. Christ, some mornings the whole office smelt like a West Indian takeaway in West Brom. Cajun chicken and jerk everywhere; I certainly wouldn't miss that.

I took a longer sip of my whisky and couldn't help laughing to myself. I had to admit I'd be glad when the sorry devil was back in harness. There were too many echoes in the office when his humour and laughter were absent. It was too much like home.

I was about to go up to the bar for another drink when a "Hello, Mr Hillyard," stopped me in my tracks. Oh God, no. It couldn't be. I knew that voice. It had been plaguing me for a couple of years. Bloody Sniper Sam. This was all I needed.

Now before I go any further, let me explain. Samuel Langton Fitzgerald (I'm serious) had been one of my more irritating clients for quite a while. Trained as a sniper in the Royal Marines (and thus the nickname) Sniper Sam had yet to earn a respectable living since being honourably discharged. He had done numerous tours of Northern Ireland in his time (during the 'Troubles'– now there's a euphemism if ever there was one) and was without doubt a brave and decent soul. The problem was that Northern Ireland was still in his blood. So much so in fact that he had been thrown out of every cinema in the area for leaping up with an imaginary sniper's rifle and yelling at everyone to dive for cover every time some villains on the screen started shooting.

There were also the frequent arrests for being drunk and disorderly; well, not quite disorderly perhaps, more the Northern Ireland Syndrome again as I liked to call it. Not so long ago he had been arrested for lining up a few unsuspecting shoppers against a wall and searching them for concealed weapons. There had also been the umpteen occasions when he had been discovered up in a tree with a broom handle trying to shoot at terrorist pedestrians walking into Boots for a can of inoffensive hairspray or the odd packet of Durex – ribbed and multicoloured, of course.

"How you doin' Mr Hillyard?" Sniper Sam asked with that endearing grin of his.

It had been that blasted grin that had made me take him on in the first place. Having given up on his Legal Aid, I usually appeared in the local magistrates for nothing, not all lawyers being money-grabbing thieves by the way – well, maybe. . . .

Anyway the man still didn't realise that court work was outside my area of expertise, but then the occasional appearance for a boozed-up ex-soldier was hardly court work, was it? A few words of hopeless mitigation, a silly fine (which I always paid) and a humble smirk from Sniper Sam was all that was ever required.

"I'm fine, Sam," I replied, unable to stop myself smiling. "I'm going up to the bar. What do you want?"

"A pint of Best, Mr Hillyard, gent that you are. What are you doin' round these parts anyway? Bit far out for you, isn't it?"

I looked at the smashed-up face. A face that had seen so much and yet still managed to laugh. Sam's dark green eyes whispered many things.

"Mind your own business, Sam. . . . Now, I'll buy you a pint, but that's it and don't ask me for a sub. You're still owing me for all the fines I've paid for you. Anyway, how did you get in here? Like the cinemas, I thought you'd been banned from every pub from here to John O'Groats."

"Fuck 'em, Mr Hillyard. Films never get it right anyway."

"Is that so? Never mind. Right, come up with me to the bar then and collect your drink. You're not sitting with me all night getting plastered on my hard-earned cash by the way."

"Perish the thought, Mr Hillyard, perish the thought. I'm with some mates anyway."

"Good."

A few minutes later I handed him his pint and went back to my seat. I couldn't resist slipping a tenner into his coat pocket as I left him to his own devices. He would never learn, but who was I to judge? The stupid idiot had the vote too, a 'fearsome thing' as Churchill would have put it. God and Country, the two most demanding and bloodthirsty blots on the landscape of mankind

CHAPTER 4

Having attained an appropriate level of alcoholic protection
in the pub I made my way home. 'Home' was an eighteenth-
century thatched cottage in Lavenham, Suffolk. All straw, crazy
ivy trying to play havoc with the masonry and intermittent
bouts of peace. Time had distorted and bent a great many of the
buildings in Lavenham, and the cottage was no exception. The
village certainly excelled where the bucolic idyll was concerned,
but I was still trying to work out how the pancake flatness of
the Suffolk landscape had so inspired Constable, although to be
fair to the man, there were more trees and wooden carts around
in his time.

What he painted was not what we see today; wheat and
people had changed all that. Now the landscape clung like a
black invoice from an undertaker's hand. In these vast tracts of
emptiness, the treeless fields were unable to escape the soulless
assault of massive combine harvesters and industrialised farm-
ing. Like Norfolk, there was no new silence about the place, no
liveliness either. (Well, I suppose I can forget any East Anglians
buying my story now.)

The car tyres made the gravel on the forecourt crackle and
moan. I knew as I walked through the front door that I would
soon be receiving some of the same. It was rare these days for
my return home to inspire anything else. Lights shone everywhere like some cheap seaside resort on a Friday night as Clare
didn't care much about my pocket or saving the planet. I have
to admit, though, that I had some sympathy regarding her apathy
toward climate change. As far as I was concerned, mankind had
bought itself a one-way ticket and pressed the self-destruct
button years ago. In the not too distant future our species will

be as extinct as the dinosaurs (and a good thing too, I suspect), so what difference did the odd light bulb or two make?

The cottage (although I have to say it was more of a house in size, a big house, I never really knew how to describe it) had taken three years to restore and a great deal of money. I was proud of it, its warmth, its comfort and its inviting texture. It would have been a perfect family home, but without even a semblance of love or childish nonsense it was just another 'With love' postcard dropped on some stranger's doormat.

Clare's propensity toward employing people to do things (like Fanny Sparks, the woman who came in 'to do') and her avoidance of anything remotely resembling physical labour had allowed me a free hand. There were no brash or vulgar colours. No 'show house' furniture or pretty wallpaper borders. I had hunted the antique and second-hand shops and restored everything where I could. Art Deco joined with Victorian and Regency, all the different styles lingering together to create a meal of interesting and absurd harmony. I thought so anyway.

The place would have been as welcoming as an up-market Salvation Army hostel had not a permanent matrimonial ice-cap settled on its roof (and this one wasn't melting either).

The house had always been my area of operations, at least in respect of its physical appearance. Clare was happy as long as it imparted an aura of wealth and materialistic well-being. The woman had never even picked up a piece of sandpaper. I often wondered when the services of a professional arse wiper would be required next. Sorry, I forgot that Clare was too perfect to indulge in a good old-fashioned bout of toilet action; she just didn't do things like that – like most women I suppose, they always seem to be constipated most of the time anyway.

Upon entering my domain I went straight upstairs to the master bedroom. 'Master' bedroom? Presumably all the other bedrooms in the house were for servants, so work that one out if you can.

I removed my jacket, put it on a hanger and went into the en suite bathroom. Note the 'en suite'; a home isn't a home without an 'en suite' is it? Rather like the 'Master' bedroom.

The cast-iron tub with its clawed feet gave off a hopeful picture of watery romps. The tub had actually been bought with randy exploits in mind. That was in the days when Clare and I couldn't leave each other alone. It's always like that in the beginning, isn't it? A quick one over the arm of the sofa or on the bonnet of a car. Location never seems to matter or be a problem. Lust is incredibly inventive. Where the tub was concerned, my fantasies had yet to be fulfilled. These days Clare rarely allowed me to see her naked, let alone anything else.

I knew only too well that once sexual intimacy flew out of the matrimonial window a marriage wouldn't soar for long until it crash-landed. Sex is critical to joyful union, not everything perhaps, but have you ever considered how sex can actually keep two people together? It's more powerful than money and when it really shifts into top gear everything else becomes tolerable. I looked again at the tub, used now only for washing not slippery bouts of rumpy-pumpy. Remarkable what a bar of soap could do, I thought. Never mind.

I washed and changed into my slops. These were my house clothes. All scruffy items of cloth that sobbed with misery and dejection. Holes everywhere. Even the charity shops would turn their self-righteous noses up at them. Damn it though, they were comfortable. Having checked in the mirror that I looked admirably tramp-like I braced myself for the entrance into matrimonial hell.

I opened the sitting-room door and headed straight for the booze. As usual, the idiots' lantern, i.e. the television, was slithering around in its own feculent slurry and slop. The hideous thing was always on. Clare hated anything that informed or enlightened, like one of those funny things called a book.

"The dog's dead," my dear wife declared without looking up at me.

"I beg your pardon?" I replied, somewhat bemused by this sudden announcement of canine tragedy. We didn't have a dog, so what the hell was the woman going on about?

"Jack, the dog, is dead."

"Oh, is he? That's a pity then," I replied again, not having the faintest idea what she was talking about.

Having noticed a tear or two well up in her eyes, I felt obliged to treat her trauma with the sympathy that it obviously demanded. A few more words from the screen explained my wife's grief. A repeat of some soap opera was showing her the reality of life's little ups and downs, I concluded. Bloody moron. Televised grief was everywhere these days, mass hypnotic gnashing of teeth and tearing of hair at its most insidious. Princess Diana had started the process with her untimely death and my wife was still grieving over that. God knows why, she had never known the self-indulgent neurotic – tut tut, Edwin, you're forgetting that the pitiful Princess nearly stepped on a land mine and kissed a bowel basher.

"You're early," my wife remarked as I sat down. She was wearing one of those yellow 'designer' tracksuit things. 'Easy living' clothes so I had been informed; she hadn't bought the thing to run in, that's for sure. Clare run? The only time she ran was to the bank to withdraw another bundle of my cash.

It was 9.45 p.m. so I ignored the sarcasm. I was tired and refused to be drawn into yet another row. The idiots' lantern was continuing to make my eardrums creak, but who was I to spoil the fun? Clare enjoyed her 'soaps'. She would.

"Yes," I answered. "I'm sorry, things to do." Like keeping your glorious arse (which I rarely, if ever, got my hands on) in the lap of luxury I nearly added, manfully resisting the urge.

Clare was playing with her mobile phone as she viewed. She refused to play with anything else that vibrated, the narrow-minded twot. So far I had resisted the urge to have my privacy bombarded twenty-four hours a day. Besides, talking a load of complete rubbish every five minutes wasn't my thing.

The intrusion of Clare's excuse for communication irritated me, as if the soaps weren't bad enough. I felt like grabbing the mobile and shoving it right up her rear end, beautiful as it was. All I wanted when I came home was some peace and quiet. Fat chance.

"Two bills arrived today," she announced in that wonderfully sour way of hers, only just managing to tear her eyes away from the obscene object in her hand. "One from the decorators and the other from your precious landscape gardeners."

"They can wait. Right now I want to have a drink and unwind a little."

"Haven't you had enough already?" she stated. "No doubt you've spent all evening in the pub as it is."

"Come on Clare, I'm not drunk; I rarely am and you know it. Besides, alcohol gives me more comfort than an expensive wife." Here we go I thought, my tongue getting the better of me. No matter how hard I tried to avoid conflict, the damned woman would manage to provoke a few words tinged with acid.

"Oh go to hell, Edwin. Now shut up, the telly's far more interesting than you."

As usual my arrival home was a fraught affair. My tongue, usually weighed down by imaginative expletives, tended to lift when women were around. Even my wife. No foul mouth, no chancy innuendo, no male filth. Clare sat in her armchair like some precious gift from hell. At thirty-two her body still chased my sex drive into sordid sexual fantasy that was fuelled now only with memory. My rare glimpses confirmed her body's perfection.

"Why have you insured me for so much money, Edwin?" Clare asked as she actually tore her eyes away from the television or mobile, I could never be too sure which. Where money was concerned Clare always adopted my Christian name, at other times it was usually 'Bastard' or 'Shit'. She loved the two words more than me. Her question took me a little by surprise for once.

"Pardon?"

"A letter from some insurance company arrived this morning, a statement or something. Anyway, it said my life is insured for one million pounds." Her tone of voice was accusing, "Are you thinking of having me bumped off or something? I wouldn't put it past you. You can be such a shit."

I didn't think it would take her long to get round to one of her pet names for me.

"Don't be silly, Clare," I replied. "Firstly, you are 'assured' not 'insured' and secondly, no doubt if you had read the correspondence properly you would have seen that we're jointly assured for the same amount. It's a question of who dies first."

Not me if I can help it I thought, at the same time reminding myself to review my Will. Although my dear wife didn't deserve a dime, I would look after her, come what may. She was Mrs Hillyard, after all.

"Talking of bumping you off," I continued, "how do I know you haven't got a hit man lurking in the bushes waiting to send me to an early grave?" I started smiling now at the farcical nature of our conversation. "We can have a competition if you like. The first one to knock the other off wins a bumper-size box of Bassett's Liquorice All Sorts. How is that for incentive?"

"Why do you always have to be so boring and facetious, Edwin," Clare snarled in that beautifully operatic way of hers. "Have you got some kind of incurable disease or something?" Jesus, she was good. I had nicknamed her 'Snarler', to my friends anyway.

" 'Facetious' – now that's a big word for you, Clare. How did you manage to get your tongue around that?"

She was rising to the bait in her usual magnificent way, at least as far as make-up, personal trainers and beauticians allowed. Her bosom was rising and falling along with the ebb and flow of imminent temper which reminded me that I needed to check whether my 'new for old' insurance policies covered my wife's tits.

Recently she had been hinting at the need for a pair of silicone jobs. These were next on the menu, yet I knew full well that I wouldn't even get to sample the soup, let alone the main course. I didn't know why she was bothering anyway. The present pair were formidable and firm enough to withstand the most violent of grips. At least neither had given up the ghost and started to attack her kneecaps. I didn't have any complaints anyway. Besides, these false numbers always reminded me of American porno stars with their unnaturally large and grotesque plastic jobs. Not that Clare was into pornography. Fanatical about 'image', she drew the line at the pornographic genre. More's the pity.

She wasn't going to allow my last remark to go astray,

"Do you have to make a joke out of everything, Edwin? You really are such a bastard!" Pet name number two hadn't taken very long either.

"Don't I know it," I said. "You remind me every day."

With that she returned to her mobile phone and some mindless activity. God, I thought, it must be great to be so easily entertained, so empty. I decided that these bitter exchanges served no one. As usual I adopted the line of least resistance. I would soothe and placate.

"Clare, you've nothing to be concerned about I promise you. These policies are simply there to make sure that we're both financially secure if something happens to the other. Prudent financial planning, that's all it is. A lot of husbands don't bother, believe me, so quite frankly you should be grateful that I am making comfortable provision for you should anything untoward happen to me. After all, we men have a tendency to pop it first. Stress of work and so on." I felt like exploring the word 'work', but refrained.

"Please don't fret," I continued, "and let's not quarrel over such a silly thing. It's nothing Clare, all I'm trying to do right now is to have a quiet drink after a trying day. Please allow me this modest indulgence. Now, can we at least be civil to one another if nothing else? We are husband and wife after all." I didn't know whether my words were registering but at least I tried. I was about to leave the room when life beyond text message and television was confirmed.

"God, listen to it!" Clare was alive after all. "The voice of reason. You amaze me, Edwin, you really do. All I ask is that you settle some bills. Then I ask about these 'assurance' policies. Next thing you're treating me like a child."

"I didn't mean to sound pedantic, Clare. I apologise."

I meant it. I really had had enough of these nightly skirmishes. This seemed to soften her. Victory was hers. She was unable to see how easy it was to manipulate her anger. She was so predictable; she always took my counterfeit weakness for her strength. She was a simple child in many respects, and like a child she could only see things from her own small world. Clare was the centre of the universe. Her universe at least. I changed the subject.

"Is there anything to eat?"

"There's some beef in the fridge," came the blunt reply.

"Thank you," I said and walked out in search of some sustenance.

I opened the fridge door with my usual pathetic optimism. There was nothing to tickle my curious palate. Not even the standard lump of mouldy cheese so celebrated by desperate TV sitcoms. I found a packet of Asda's best processed beef. What had got into Clare, I wondered? Asda's? Bit too downmarket for her, I'd have thought. It was usually Waitrose carrier bags only. Then it occurred to me that, of course, Asda's was closer to the house. Even Clare could rough it where less effort was the reward.

I made up a couple of watery beef sandwiches and took them to my study. I put on some Puccini – ever the hopeful romantic, that's me – sat down and allowed the music to massage my anger.

My study was me.

My sole creation.

A stuffed brown bear stood in one of the corners. I had found him in an auction house I frequently visited. Covered in cobwebs and spiders I had rescued the poor old bugger and given him a new lease of life. At least his yellow glass eyes sparkled with more enthusiasm these days and his snarl didn't look as ferocious as Clare's. One of my old felt hats sat on his head reminding me of who I was, minus the violent disposition it has to be said. The outsize black dildo I had attached to his crotch made me laugh on a daily basis whenever I thought of Clare's face at being confronted by my artistic genius. At one point I had even thought of entering the noble monster for a Turner prize. He would win hands down, I was sure of it.

The walls were lined with books on philosophy, cooking, history, eastern religions (I bet that's got you – wouldn't have believed it, would you?) politics, sex and just about everything else you can think of. They composed my own personal library. Books were my passion and addiction; besides a home wasn't a home without books. Nothing compared to the hunt for knowledge through the turning of pages. The Internet could rot in hell together with its virtual delusion, its fraud and insidious prohibition on innocent thought. Besides, I was quicker finding what I wanted in a book. The whole process was more dignified and more fulfilling than the artificial and gaudy search through electronic colour and impersonality.

My study was my own world. Somewhere where I could think and allow my mind to wander at will. It had become my freedom, my nurse, my lover and loyal companion. It didn't change. It didn't betray.

Chinese porcelain sailed from other worlds with the maritime pictures that blew and struggled across the walls. Antiquarian books lorded it over modern paperbacks, but for me the mixture in some ways decided my character. Old and new, all thrown together and fighting to remain apart.

My sensitive side responded to the romanticism of the composer as the tenor touched my anxiety and hidden tears. My vulnerability and fear could enjoy release within the privacy of my books and music.

I thought about Clare. Our marriage, how destructive it had become.

We had been married for three years, having known each other for a year before. I was thirteen years older than my spouse. Marriage for me had been a late arrival, not from any particular intent on my part; it had just never happened or been an issue. 'Living' with a woman had somehow always seemed more convenient and less demanding. Commitment had never bothered me and I had certainly never been anti-marriage, but like I say, the whole institution had never seemed necessary – until Clare, that is.

There had been many women in my life, a legion of meaningless sexual encounters and one enduring love before Clare. The love of my past had been true and strong. There were no bitter memories. No hatred. I had always considered myself a lucky man by escaping the misogyny of middle-aged failure. Even now I tried with a desperation that surprised me to avoid any feelings of anger and poison toward my wife. I wasn't made to hate; I adored women. I had enjoyed relationships with the loveliest and kindest of female kind. I had known the sweetness of loyal companionship and the post-coital touch. I had no regrets of the past. None of the women in my history had been bitches – until now.

Night after night I would ask myself, 'Why? How?' I couldn't reconcile my experience, my knowledge, with such crass idiocy as my dysfunctional and issue-bloated marriage to Clare – mind you, being dysfunctional and having issues are essential facets of the human condition, so where would we be without them one may well ask? Even so, how could I have been such a fool? I never thought I would be asking myself the questions repeated a trillion times a day throughout the history of the mulched-up union of men and women.

My mind, as it often did these days, went back to that flight to Paris some four years ago. I didn't know it then, but the jet was taking me to disaster – not of the aviation kind either.

Perhaps such a death would have been kinder.

CHAPTER 5

Clare caught my eye as soon as I walked into the cabin to find my seat. She was one of the air stewardesses.

Her lipstick-splattered lips smiled with airline goodwill at all and sundry. The bright red blended with her short brunette hair. There was something different though. The smile didn't seem to be forced through screaming lips of frustration. It lacked the fraudulent picture of glamour and pretty, insincere welcome. I fooled myself that it was all for me and that her lips twisted with genuine interest and not chronic boredom.

She was a petite vision.

Small hands, small feet.

God knows why, but where women were concerned I always looked at the face first, then the hands and feet. Was the face one that I could wake up to in the morning? This was always the real acid test. Believe me, I have received some hung-over shocks in my time. I'm sure some women use a catapult to put their makeup on – splat! And here's a shovel to make sure you don't forget the stuff that's missed the target.

I came to the enlightened conclusion years ago that the reason some women wear pints of perfume and layers of make-up is because most of them are smelly and ugly. Jesus, when I think back I've woken up to a few porcine surprises in my time. It's true, you know. Women look better the more inebriated you get, which just goes to show how boring sobriety is, doesn't it? Drink on, alkies of the world, and live your dreams – you probably get a damn sight closer to them than the rest of us.

Now where was I? Clare, her face, small hands and feet.

Her face definitely demanded being slobbered over. Every feature was just right. Nose, lips, eyes, chin, all fitted together perfectly. Her body was the sort that created dreams of sexual athletics and bouncy castles, she being the bounced. I watched her bum wiggle down the aisle and wanted to leap up and grab the cheeks until they blistered. Some women have rumps that just plead to be squeezed, kneaded and pummelled, don't they? Hers was one of them. The tight uniform accentuated the curves and overall sexiness.

I had already joined the mile-high club, but my membership had lapsed. I decided to renew it as quickly as possible with Clare as the proposer. As I've already said, her hands and feet were small and in proportion. Always pick a woman with small hands, you male readers – they make your willy look bigger. In my case this principle doesn't apply – blessed are the well-endowed and so on. Though thank God I don't have big ears. Some women are obsessed with oral sex, but imagine having a couple of handlebars attached to your head. Dear God, it doesn't bear thinking about!

Back to my flying beauty.

Believe it or not, when I look at an attractive woman or at least a woman whom I feel may be a serious contender for my favours, sex is not the first thing that crosses my mind. My middle years had brought a maturity of attraction, if I can put it that way. I looked for more than bosoms like train buffers and grabbable bottoms.

I was forty-one at the time and, perfectly content with my single status, felt no urgency to immerse myself in some kind of explosive or tumultuous love. There was no fear of an uncertain loneliness in old age either. Indeed, quite the opposite. From what I could see we all died alone one way or another, and children were hardly a safe bet. Experience and observation had taught me that all most offspring did was hover around death beds grinning gleefully as their eyes begged the surly nurse to administer a merciful overdose of morphine. Another day meant less money in their bank accounts, for Christ's sake! Bloody nursing homes cost a fortune!

I had never understood why people always seemed so obsessed with being *with* someone, men in particular. After all, men had never been put together to be monogamous. Evolution had seen to that. We are conditioned to go out there and copulate ourselves to death. The more mates the better, keeping the species alive paramount.

No, as far as I was concerned, if some kind of lasting love came along that was fine by me, but I sure as hell wasn't going to go looking for it or indeed spend my life worrying about being 'alone'.

Life had lowered my expectations. Love didn't have to devour anymore. It didn't have to shout and yell in order to attract my attention. As for sex – well, that had become a necessity, a simple fact of life that couldn't be ignored. An ejaculation didn't move the earth, it simply added another layer. Another stitch.

When I looked at Clare, I admired the physical perfection with my eyes while my mind asked, could I love that face, could I adore the personality behind it without having to clap my hands every morning? The cerebral phallus no longer dictated. Age had forced the important questions, yet it had also, unknown to me at the time, brought delusion. Youth has its virtues, its pleasing, uncomplicated ignorance.

As I buckled myself up our eyes met again, then crashed when she handed me a gin and tonic. Look out, that confounded 'It' was in the air, the 'It' that surpassed the inane and nervous chatter of my fellow travellers. There are no words to describe these momentary impacts of male/female union, they just happen. The woman was disturbing me and upsetting my ordered life of independence, my individuality and my detached weekend companionships and sex. This pretty little bag of unknown tricks in a smart blue uniform and impertinent hat was ruining me, yet I couldn't take my eyes off her. She made me want more in my life.

At least I thought she did.

When the plane landed I made sure I was the last to get off. Clare hovered around the exit door. We both knew. The pheromones had done their work. We could smell each other at fifteen paces.

I walked up to her and said, 'Thank you'.

I took her hand, it was warm, welcoming even. I looked directly into her eyes as I placed a piece of paper in her palm. A few seconds stood still, it's true I'm telling you. Mills and Boon doesn't have the monopoly on a bit of romance, you know.

I said, "Goodbye . . . for now," and left. The note said, 'Ring me please – Edwin Hillyard.' I had written down my office and home telephone numbers underneath the words. I hadn't placed an 'x' after my name; that would have been presumptuous and cheap like some painful and screaming object from a Clinton card shop, all noise and pink tat.

The rest of my weekend was spent thinking about the air stewardess from nowhere. So much for my intended cultural break. I didn't bother with any of the Parisian sights, the museums, the art galleries – I had seen them all before anyway. I didn't even bother going for a wander around the red-light districts, not that I had ever paid for sex or ever intended to. Watching the tarts ply their trade was an education, though. I could never quite make out who the diminished fools were, the tarts or the punters. Still, I had always considered prozzie watching an enlightening experience – it was life at its most sordid or at its best, depending on which way you looked at it. In any event the anticipation of seeing Clare again used up most of my thought processes. The woman wouldn't leave my brain cells alone. Her prodding and tickling never stopped.

I had no doubt at all that she would ring. In these days of female emancipation women often pushed the dating agenda as they saw fit. Gone are the days of masculine hunting – the prey now did the catching and the killing. At forty-one I was still getting used to this wilful element of extreme femininity. I had not yet accepted its aggression, its unattractive character. I didn't enjoy having my spear and net taken away from me. Forward women usually made me run in the opposite direction. I enjoyed seduction. Playing the game. Some women might have seen their overt display of strength as their emancipation. I saw it as a bloody great turn-off.

A week passed before the expected telephone call.

Her voice was as alluring as the rest of her, despite the unnatural distortions of cables and fibre optics. Clare seemed bright enough on the telephone. She responded to my ribald wit and laughed unconditionally. All good signs. I did go easy with my foul mouth; I can exercise restraint when I have to. After all, we weren't even on farting terms yet.

We arranged to meet in London the following Saturday.

Another five days of frustration and fantasy.

CHAPTER 6

I travelled down from Suffolk and eventually arrived at one of those glamorous coffee houses just outside Victoria Station; you know, those places where all on offer was froth, wart-infested muffins and pictures of exotic coffee beans. It was one of those normal summer days – blazing sunshine one minute, belting down the next. Do I take a brolly? Do I wear a raincoat? The usual petty indecisions.

I had arranged to meet Clare here in order to avoid the possibility of missing her on some overloaded station platform. My middle-aged eyesight wasn't too clever either when it came to looking at all those huge electronic timetables that hung in the air like hostile UFOs about to crash-land.

I had taken longer than usual to dress that morning. Sartorial perfection was important to me. In other words I was a bit of a dandy. More so when I was meeting a lady for the first time. I was still one of those anachronistic fools who considered attention to dress plain good manners. I expected exactly the same from the other side. I have my standards and they are non-negotiable. Unkempt slappers were not for me, even as a last resort and face down.

I ordered a cup of crushed, gold-plated coffee beans – they must have been, judging by the price – and sat outside at a chrome and glass table stuffed with tubes of brown and white sugar, not to mention, of course, artificial sweeteners. Coffee drinking was an 'experience' these days; frankly a cup of Nescafé would have done me, but there was no chance of that. Profit margins were everything and an essential part of the whole 'experience'.

I smoked and waited.

I didn't blend into my surroundings as well as the espresso, latte, cappuccino or otherwise. These days the rigid faces and curdled lips of café culture has replaced the torn-up beer mats and smoky mirth of filthy pub humour and heresy. Everyone in these places always looks so dull and up themselves, suicidal even. There wasn't even a suppressed giggle to ripen up the superior atmosphere.

I wasn't trendy enough, either.

My shirt that didn't hang out of my trousers (I usually remembered to tuck it in after enjoying a good old-fashioned bowel movement); the Irish linen jacket that didn't look as if it had been stuffed at the bottom of my bed for months; the sparkling brogues (handmade of course – after all, a good woman will always look at a man's shoes before anything else) that hadn't been made to go tearing around race tracks, not to mention the cufflinks, collectively placed me outside the new coffee-drinking loop. And as for wearing a tie on a Saturday morning, well, God forbid. But as far as I was concerned, a man who doesn't care about his clothes doesn't care about much else. Actually no, not really. 'Fashion' was for glossy magazine fantasists and the 'Hello I've arrived' demented brigade. I had no time for it. Apart from anything else, I had yet to discover where all these 'fashionably' dressed people were, as all I ever saw were waves of charity shop rejects, washing machine-abused gym shoes and bulging born-again Levi jeans. 'Designer' stubble is the best; dirty buggers who are too bone idle to shave more like.

I looked at my cufflinks for something to do. Simple gold studs. I then examined my watch – a wafer-thin affair. Its name was expensive and I'm not going to tell you, but it wasn't a Rolex. I wouldn't lower myself, neither had I ever fancied having a ship's anchor attached to my wrist with a sign saying, 'Look at me, I'm rich – ignore the tattoos'. I was well off but restrained about it. Image meant nothing to me, certainly not the consumer variety anyway. So, there I was, drinking coffee and all fagged up.

I glanced around, looking at my fellow customers and keeping my nerves under control. Nerves? It's true, I was nervous. My stomach gurgled. First dates had never bothered me before. This one did. I wanted success with Clare. I cared, thus the chaotic stomach and chain-smoking. I had been on a few blind dates in the past and I don't recommend them. Thank God, at least I knew what Clare looked like. There would be no hideous surprises, no 'Oh Jesus, what have I done to deserve this?'

I remembered my last 'blind' encounter. On that occasion I had worn a sign on the front of my jacket saying in big, bold print, 'IF YOU BARK, SOD OFF' (my idea of fun going a bit off piste again). The woman didn't appear, so either her sense of humour was in short supply or her face would have scared the hell out of a top-of-the-range JCB. Either way, I considered the rejection a blessing. Her loss, etc. etc.

The one I love is, 'Looks are not important'. Where do these people come from? What would you rather kiss, a cow's arse or a face to die for? 'Looks are not important.' What a load of unmitigated tosh! The only people who adhere to this noble principle are the ones who haven't got any 'looks', so no wonder they 'are not important'. What else can they say, for God's sake? "My face and body need a re-fit, but my mind is a bloody good shag." Give me strength!

Back to my first date with the venerable Clare.

Oh, I forgot to mention that I always wear a hat. I was old enough now to get away with my stubborn affectation and had become immune to people calling me Dr Who or looking for a lasso every time I walked into a room.

My hat wasn't a bowler or a homburg, but just a plain, old brown felt hat, the sort that are worn by men at the races. A wider-brimmed trilby I suppose. I remember some reputable hatter telling me the purpose behind the design of a man's hat. The brim I was told, which was always made of the best material, was there to cover the ear holes. The top of the hat, apparently made from inferior quality material, was there to cover arseholes. I still wasn't sure which category I fitted into. I had married Clare, hadn't I? Anyway to hell with it, my hats are me. I look good in one, and at least all the women I have known like me wearing one. One of them even insisted I wear a hat whilst I rogered her into the following week (have a high opinion of myself, don't I?). Can you imagine it? Talk about being under starter's orders – hat an' all! She had a thing about doing it with Humphrey Bogart if I remember correctly. Ah well, takes all sorts.

Sixteen minutes had passed the arranged meeting time.

Not good. I was a fascist where punctuality was concerned. Untidy timekeeping meant an untidy mind. I ordered another coffee, at the same time asking the young counter assistant if their coffee beans were crushed by the sweaty thighs of women workers in Colombia – the things cost enough. The young assistant didn't smile, humourless little tyke, but then judging by the vacant expression on her face she had no idea where Colombia was anyway. Typical. Counting out my change hadn't helped her surly mood either it seemed.

I continued to wait.

Twenty minutes late now.

I was starting to twitch with anger. I cannot bear inconsiderate timekeeping. It is one of my pet hates – amongst many you will have already gathered – and one that I do not usually tolerate. Had it been anyone else I would have left after five minutes. Punctuality is another one of my 'non-negotiables'.

I waited and smoked.

"Will you please sit somewhere else? Your disgusting smoke is harming my little boy."

"I beg your pardon?" I replied to this voice from nowhere, my irritable meanderings disturbed by some female Pol Pot, or at least a female version of gargantuan proportions. In other words, the women was a big fat slob with over-extended jowls who had the temerity to intrude upon my refined thinking-space. Her snot-faced offspring didn't look much better either.

"You heard!" she wobbled back.

"Madam," I retorted coldly. "There are no-smoking seats inside – that's assuming, of course, you're able to find enough of them to accommodate your offensive girth. Come to think of it, may I also suggest you enrol on a crash dieting course as soon as possible before you draw attention to yourself? Oh, and take that Burger King Whopper of a son of yours along with you; he looks as if he could shed a couple of stones too!"

I thought the monstrous lump was going to clout me. Instead she spluttered and blustered, realised that I had the law on my side and took off, dragging her slab of lard with her. I carried on smoking. Blessed are the meek; they will certainly not inherit the earth.

Thirty-three minutes.

By now I was beginning to seriously consider the prospect of my being stood up. Unthinkable. My arrogance would not allow this to happen. How dare she? Stand me up? Not possible. No woman ever did that. Ever. I was too much of a catch. Forty-one, no attachments, no belligerent ex-wives or truculent offspring, affluent, good looking etc. etc. etc. What was the woman playing at?

Thirty-eight minutes

Right, that's it. I'm off.

I started to walk to the underground. I was incensed. The only woman in recent years who had seriously interested me and she had stood me up! She had sounded so enthusiastic on the phone, too. Just as I was devising a lexicon of the most imaginative insults I could throw at her answering machine I heard footsteps rushing up behind me and a shout.

"Edwin!"

I turned and saw Clare running towards me. She ran into my arms, gave me a kiss and said, "God, I'm so sorry. Trains. Signals out or something. I really am sorry."

Now show me a pretty face, a genuine apology and I'm a dribbling idiot. Like most men, I suppose. All my anger vanished in my smile and her lovely face. I was completely undone. The rush into my arms and kiss totally disarmed me. Her natural affection took me by surprise and her kiss was outstanding.

I smiled, still holding her I said, "Oh, that's all right, Clare. Don't worry. Trains can never be relied on. I was just going to buy a newspaper. I thought something like that had happened. Anyway, you're here now. No harm done. Your kiss was worth the wait."

Smooth or what? All lies, of course. A few seconds earlier she'd been on her way to the index of one of my history books. And who is the weaker sex? You may well ask.

She took my arm, "Where are we going then?" Forthright, that was fine by me as long as it didn't domineer. Stuff equality and liberation. I was the boss – and forget the 'at least I liked to think I was' bit. Domination and control, that's me.

"Let's find a half-decent bar somewhere. Have a drink and a chat. Then we can go and have a good lunch. I've booked a table at a place I know. The grub will give you multiple orgasms."

Clare laughed; the sound travelled right up my spine.

"Fine by me. I could use a drink. The train journey seemed to take forever."

"From Reigate?"

"That's it, near the airport."

"Well, considering you've been stuck on a train you look remarkably well-ironed. You look as if you've just stepped out of a dry cleaner's. Amazing."

She giggled this time. Not in one of those loud, imbecilic and childish ways. Her giggle was all sex and promise. Her looking 'well-ironed' was an understatement. The light green trouser suit and white blouse she was wearing bulged in all the right places as they pushed and punched my eyes into a depraved stupor. She had the whole lot: sex, élan, panache . . . and all the other adjectives that annoy book reviewers so much. (You know, I've often wondered why these perfect overseers of literary endeavour never seem to churn out Nobel prize winners themselves being as they always seem to know exactly what makes the faultless novel.)

My memories of her hadn't let me down.

This, as they say, was going to be the mother of all dates.

CHAPTER 7

I led the way to an elegant bar in the West End, not far from the restaurant I had booked, Wheelers.

Before going inside I dug into my pocket for some smokes. It had been more than an hour since the last one, my nerves were shot and I was well and truly gasping. I had been smoked up for most of the morning, but was on a roll – literally. I rolled my own cigarettes you see, deluding myself that my lungs would be better served by the absence of preservative chemicals and so on. Roll-ups didn't smell as much as tailor-mades either. Besides, I rather enjoyed the contradiction: well dressed, refined lawyer smoking a roll-up. A concession to my working-class roots I would always tell people. Another load of eyewash. I was preppy through and through.

Before pulling out the Golden Virginia it suddenly occurred to me that my 'disgusting' habit could blow this romantic adventure into never land. Pol Pot's female doppelganger had already had a go – I was on my guard. Blossoming love could only take so much after all. Before actually rolling up I remembered an encounter with a lady solicitor. She had been a looker too, that one – a rare commodity amongst the female of the legal species, I can tell you. Don't believe all these glamour pusses you see on the idiots' lantern. That's fantasy television at its best. All those producers and directors have never been members of the legal profession, that's for certain, because if they had they would know what a motley lot the female contingent is. It's all the years of shoving legal tomes up their learned backsides in a vain attempt to smash the legal glass ceiling that does it. Anyway back to the exception. The woman had pounced on me for sexual favour. I obliged, and notwithstanding her Rampant Rabbit, committed myself with admirable dexterity and lust. Satisfied and replete with casual sex she had pulled on her black suit, said "Cheerio" and made a quick exit.

I was left feeling used, bemused and insulted. Apparently she didn't like the smell of tobacco. If a smoker's willy was fine, a smoker's breath was intolerable. Women! They're all unhinged. Do you know that there are more women in secure mental health units than men? I rest my case.

Everyone is so mind-blowingly sensitive these days. Hell, I don't jump up and down with righteous indignation every time some fat bastard squeezes the life out of me on a train or aircraft. We smokers may well annoy and irritate, but at least the undertakers won't have a hard time pushing our arses into a coffin. Actually I take that back. Some misguided fatties smoke as well as eat. I wasn't one of them though. Lean and mean, that's me. Anyway, back to my darling from the skies.

I pulled out a packet of baccy,

"Do you mind if I have a smoke before we go in?" I asked, not really giving a damn whether she did or not. If she had minded, then she could get back on the train to Reigate – and sharpish. There are some things that even women are not worth. Love me, love my nicotine sticks.

She looked relieved – which rather surprised me – and then smiled. "No, not at all. I'll join you," she said, pulling out a packet of Bensons & Hedges and lighting up. Well, didn't this take the wind out of my self-righteous sails!

"I must say you being a smoker too is a relief," I remarked. "I was worried that you may be one of those women who hated the habit – you know, run a mile as soon as a whiff of tobacco hits their nostrils. I can't bear intolerance." (Nothing like a bit of blatant hypocrisy, is there?)

"No chance of that, Edwin. I do try and smoke as little as possible though."

Here we go, I thought. Why does every smoker defend and virtually apologise for their right to light up? I had to live with the mass stupidity and feckless intellects of pernicious *Sun* and *Mirror* readers every day of the week, but did I complain?

"I've tried to give up I don't know how many times," she continued. "No success though. Once a smoker always a smoker, as they say."

"How very true," I replied, "I gave up trying to give up a long time ago. I love nicotine. Adore it."

She smiled. God did she smile! She was better than my own exaggerated memory. I wanted to kiss her there and then. Instead I absorbed, all grins, teeth and charm.

As I started the ritual of tobacco, paper and miniature tampon (these are tips by the way) packing, I noticed a slight movement of eye that conveyed an element of disapproval. I could have been wrong, of course, but I don't miss much. Perhaps my concession to supposed working-class roots wasn't fully appreciated.

I let the thought pass. My imagination needed to concentrate on other things. Like the goods hidden inside the wrapping. She moved a leg. She moved a hand, an arm. Everything was elegant, refined. Her clothes were expensive. I knew about women's clothes. Had bought enough of them. I put her down as a size ten. Her height was a perfect 5 foot 4 inches. Her body was slim but with enough roundness to cuddle last thing at night and when all the work had been done. At least she wasn't a bag of bones. Like most men I couldn't stand skinny women as they grate too much when things start to get lively. MEN LIKE CURVES (and a hell of a lot of women too), so when are all these damn fool magazines and TV producers going to wake up?

We finished our smokes then went into the bar. Surprisingly not one anti-smoking passer by had spat on us or grunted superior disapproval.

I ordered two glasses of dry white. The next hour was spent exchanging careful pieces of innocuous information. Rattling skeletons were kept firmly in their cupboards and all bad habits kept under wraps. Like me, Clare had never married, there were no children. Trans-Atlantic Boeing 747's had always got in the way apparently.

Another glass of wine later I suggested it was time to eat.

"I hope you like oysters and lobster. Before you say anything, I'm not trying to get you randied up on the oysters." She didn't seem to catch my sexy little quip but took my hand anyway. My insanity was progressing with each of her smiles.

As we waited for a taxi she asked, "By the way, what do you do? You haven't said anything." The classic question came easily. My answer would reveal all. Or so most people thought.

"I sort out people's legal problems."

"You're a lawyer."

"Yes, unfortunately."

"Unfortunately? I wish I had your job. Must be more interesting than mine and better paid. All I do is pacify uncouth drunks and stuck-up little kids. They're the worst, I can tell you. Spoilt brats. Thank God I don't have any!"

Now this response shouldn't have gone unnoticed, but it did; at least I failed to give it the attention it deserved.

"You must earn a lot of money," she persisted.

"Not really. I'm not complaining,though. Truth is, I would get out of the law tomorrow if I could. It's not the same anymore. Too mercenary. Too uncouth. Like everything else I suppose." She looked at me and seemed slightly confused.

At last a taxi responded to my thrashing arms. I opened the door for Clare.

"After you."

"A gentleman. That makes a change."

Gentleman! All I wanted was a bent-over view of her bum and to hell with the manners. I didn't tell her that though. I must confess, however, that I am still one of those men that opens doors for women. It's only the sad, inferiority-complexed women who don't like it. To add insult to their injury I still insist on walking on the outside of a pavement too.

As we drove to the restaurant in Soho, Clare's curiosity deepened. Her probing became more serious. I still remember the next question even after all this time.

"What car do you drive?" she asked with an intensity that would have made Sigmund Freud dive for cover.

"A clapped-out Ford, why?" I replied, trying to hide my disappointment.

"You liar!" she laughed, "you're teasing me."

She really didn't believe me.

A solicitor driving a heap of rubbish? Impossible. It was true, though. I did drive an old Ford, back and forth to the office anyway. Kept the good stuff in the garage, but I wasn't going to tell Clare that. By the look on her face if I'd told her about my pride and joy she would have wet her knickers there and then.

Nothing like mystery in a man is there? What car do I drive? Was that all she cared about? I shouldn't have been surprised. There are enough women out there who will love a car – and money of course – until death us do part. They will even honour and obey them.

If any of you male readers haven't recognised by now that women have all the ammunition, then pity help you. There I was, radar picking up all the missiles, and still I pursued. I leapt in feet first, penis quickly following. I was hers for the taking. Had been from the moment we had first met. I was allowing the things I didn't like about her to be washed away by a smile, an expensive cut of cloth and a fantasy of the best sexual experience known to the human condition. An intelligent, well-educated man (at least I liked to think I was), experienced in the art of womanising, was not really being fooled though – and this makes my offence even worse. I was 'In Denial' you see – God, don't you just love those two words. God bless America!

So much for my purported middle-aged sophistication and wisdom where sex and love were concerned. I was allowing my primitive lust to bombard my brain into a state of comatose oblivion. Nothing new there, I can hear all you women declare – in which case, come to think of it, why are you always trying to be so mind-numbingly equal? Or should I say 'liberated', which apparently is the latest take on female emancipation, if you call being drunk, loud, pissing on the pavement and fighting in the streets liberated. Your victory, I suspect, would have caused even Pyrrhus to think again. There is no competition, if only you had the intelligence to see it.

We eventually walloped the oysters and lobster. I like eating lobster on its own with a bowl of melted butter; Clare ate hers with some kind of sauce that cost five pounds a drop and mutilated my credit card. In fact, she chose the most expensive items on the menu, not to mention the wine at twenty-eight pounds a bottle. None of the House stuff for her. Best bit is, I was sitting there lapping it all up.

She was the best looking woman in the place though, I'll give her that. All the men leered, slobbered and dreamed. At one point I wanted to turn around and say, 'Here we are boys, she's all yours,' and send her off with the bill attached to her tantalising tits. Talking of bills, ours duly arrived, or should I say mine.

Now, these days this can be a delicate moment.

Emancipation, sorry liberation, has brought tension into the payment of a restaurant bill. In other words who coughs up? Male or female? Me being the gentlemanly, dinosaur type, I usually reach for the plastic first. This can apparently insult. Feminists feel 'demeaned' or 'diminished'.

What do you do then? Don't forget, not all women are feminists. I rarely meet them it has to be said. All the women I have taken out have been far too smart. Why spend money when you have a generous fool like me around? Anyway, the answer to this payment conundrum is to do nothing and see what the woman does. Stick to your manly guns and just let the bill sit there sweating. If she's a good 'un she will say, 'I'll do this or let's go halves.' If she's a bad 'un she will say bugger all apart from, 'nature is calling' whereupon she will disappear into one of those ladies' havens and not return until your plastic has taken a bashing.

Equality does have certain virtues, however. Half and half or 'I'll pay next time' is fine by me. Trouble is, I never seem to experience this liberated leaning toward fairness and equality. Needless to say, once the demand for payment arrived, Clare's chops required buffing and she disappeared.

When I look back, this one calculated departure should have told me all I needed to know, as if the 'what do I do?' and 'what car do I drive?' wasn't enough. Fool time again. No excuse is there? The point is, deep down I knew exactly what sort of woman she was, deluded denial notwithstanding . Her refined speech had started to slip too, particularly as the booze began to massage her vocal chords. Her upbringing was emasculating her consonants. Add this to the way she held her knife and fork and I knew everything I needed to know about her personal history.

It soon became obvious that Clare was not the most intellectual of characters. No harm in that. A woman who wallowed in philosophy, biology or theology or any other equally enlightened pursuit could be a thorough bore. Clare was sharp, bright and intelligent and this was enough. I was happy. However, I was forgetting two of the most important qualities in a woman – honesty and integrity. For this crime I was to pay dearly.

It was obvious that for Clare image and money ruled. She was ashamed of her background. She constantly covered her tracks. The truth is, I didn't give a damn who her father was. Drunk, villain, working class, middle class, aristo, who cares? I sure as hell didn't. She did though, and that was her problem. She was a brutally ambitious working-class aspirant. The finest and most vicious of all snobs.

Clare eventually returned from the Brasso Emporium, duly polished and buffed from head to toe. She sat down. Funny, isn't it, how every time a woman returns from doing her thing they always look different? An extra coat of lipstick. A stroke of eyeliner. Complicated lives they lead, women.

I sat opposite her, absorbing again. Apart from my own observations the meal had travelled without event. There had been no harsh words or awkward sentences. No hostility. Many first dates can end in a fireball, or maybe it's just me. Too outspoken and rude. On this occasion I had restrained myself. It's all in the incentive. I wanted Clare, 'image' or not.

I had no idea where we were going once the coffee was done. Actually that isn't strictly true. Our eyes were talking. Our reserved hands touched. Our words spoke that language so unique to the mating game. Language that is indirect, aimless and yet knowing. Neither of us wanted the day to end. Neither of us, I believed, would allow it to end.

"I don't want you to go just yet, Clare," I said, all thoughtful and 'my universe is you' claptrap.

"I don't either, Edwin. I really have enjoyed myself."

I reached across the table and held her hand. All romance and love. All we needed was the demented fiddler and his moustachioed sidekick.

"Let's go somewhere else then. It will start to get very busy in here soon. We've caught it at a quiet time. There's still the whole evening to go."

I stood up. Doing my demonstrative bit again.

Women prefer the strong wilful types, believe me. They don't like wimps, although many twenty-first century men are losing their grip on their own masculinity. Too much hair gel, anal hair removing, baby changing rooms and disastrous counterfeit tanning. Have you seen some of them? Babies strapped to their chests, feed bottles and teats protruding from their arse pockets and quaint little nappy bags hanging from their shoulders. It's enough to make you puke. The fudge-packing side of the fence is becoming more alluring, too. Not surprising perhaps. Not me though, I am glad to say. All manly stink and malodorous fart, that's me. Well, I do use the odd whiff of deodorant but believe me, women adore the primitive, natural aroma of man. Makes them horny.

"Let's find somewhere quieter then," I said, "more salubrious?"

"More what?" Clare replied, with a puzzled expression on her face.

"Healthy," I translated.

I had already noted a certain lack of versatility where her vocabulary was concerned. Like an imbecile I found it charming. No doubt it had something to do with my feeling superior. Having the upper hand. Being the professional chauvinist. Great, isn't it?

As we walked through the restaurant door Clare took my hand and looked at me. Her green eyes contributed her share of the bill as she said, "That was lovely, Edwin. Thank you."

"Not at all. My pleasure," I smiled. "Perhaps we could do it again sometime."

We both knew there were going to be many more 'sometimes'.

That night we 'made love'.

I use these two words in an attempt to satisfy the romance-loving brigade. What I really mean is that we banged ourselves silly. At least I did. You know I can only just bring myself to write these two supremely idiotic words 'making love'. Since when do human beings, when they revert to their most primitive instincts, 'make love'? How can grunts, indignity, sweat, obscenities – depending on your verbal inclination in times of passion – smelly bodily fluids and a finale that would do the apes proud be 'making love'? You tell me. Romance? Forget it.

Genital flatulence is the best. Now these violent expulsions of wind really add a sense of comedy to the proceedings. There you both are, all lost and emotional, speechless with love, orgasm and exquisite euphoria, the Earth has just been blasted off its axis and a flatulent fanny announces its objection to such rude and crude intrusions. 'Making love'? You either die laughing which, in the woman's case usually results in a further fanfare, or say bugger all and suffer from chronic embarrassment. There is, of course, a possibility that the wind has blown in from another location, in which case you really do have problems for God's sake.

The hotel room had been designed to serve a purpose. It was a typical, brief respite for the weary traveller. Shampoo, bath salts, fluffy bath robes, all helped to make his or her (notice how non-sexist I can be) stay a night of lonely convenience. Everything matched. The room excelled in triteness and consumer demand. There was no humanity or inspiration in the empty air that sprawled around the air-conditioned perfection.

As soon as the door closed I pulled Clare to me and kissed her.

At times like this a gentle approach is the order of the day. Neck tweaking, earlobe nibbling, nose nudging, all have to be part of the seduction repertoire. My first kiss was modest. I didn't bite lip or tongue. My hands held her face and my lips hovered. My tongue probed. Reactions need to be noted, a catch of breath exploited and used. I unbuttoned her blouse and threw it away. I undid her trousers. Suspenders. My fingertips stroked the hairless flesh between stocking top and knicker line, the softest part of the female anatomy. My lips moved from neck to thigh. My tongue floated, never quite touching. I was in control.

I undid her bra.

Sheer delight. The pair I fondled were tight and acrobatic with just enough slack to squeeze through my fingers.

My hands held and cherished.

I knelt down and pulled her knickers to the floor.

My tongue licked from foot to navel, crossways, sideways and a few nibbles in between. I pushed Clare onto the bed and kneeled beside her. I leaned forward and finally went for the big kiss. The woman could kiss, I'll give her that. We kissed for quite a while actually. This pastime can be more erotic than sex itself, you know.

Never underestimate the power of tongue to tongue.

Believing that Clare was now aroused to a point of insanity, I went for the 'rosy, moist and honied' fig between her legs (I've pinched that from D. H. Lawrence, the pervert, but if it's good enough for him, it's good enough for me) or the tastiest cockle on the seashore for those of you who have a penchant for sea food.

Now, 'yodelling in the canyon'– damn, I'm getting a bit carried away with maritime imagery, aren't I? The best bit is I get sea-sick lying on a lilo in a swimming pool – is hard work. But before long the inevitable happened; a pubic hair inserted itself in between two of my teeth. I tried discreetly to remove the offending item but it wouldn't budge. Clare was lying there, all demanding and excruciatingly female, and all I could do was huff, puff and keep my tongue on the move whilst at the same time trying to evict a pubic intruder. The swine moved from my teeth to my throat. I started coughing and spluttering as it insisted on trying to choke me. God knows what pubic shampoo she used – presuming there is such a thing – but these days women's cosmetics can fly them to the moon, so who knows.

"What's the matter, Edwin?" Clare asked, all concern and blossoming love. "Are you all right?"

"No!" I yelled, "I'm not all right! A bloody pube is stuck in my throat!" See what I mean? 'Making love!' God help us.

Eventually the offending item disappeared down my throat and I was able to return to the job in hand. I bet my digression has upset some of you. It was all getting quite sexy, wasn't it? Makes me feel frisky writing the stuff – and I'm the writer! Dear me, really won't do, will it? Now then, where was I? Ah yes . . .

I have to say that our first bout was not the best I have known, but then, to be fair about things, they rarely are. Fiction in the form of film sets and novels would have us believe that a first sexual encounter is something beyond reality. From my experience this is rarely the case. When two people copulate for the first time it is usually a tentative, blundering occasion. Both parties are on a crusade of sexual discovery. Movements are cautious. Does the other party like this or that? Will he or she howl with indignation if I allow my fantastic sexual proclivities to run riot and so on. All in all it is a particularly fraught business, in my view anyway. Accomplished sex takes time. Knowledge. We are all different, particularly where sex is concerned.

Clare was one of the 'lay back and let the man do all the work' types. She kissed well but that was about it. Her orgasms were uncertain. Unqualified. At the time I put this down to nerves and shyness. Not unusual. Even so, she was obviously inexperienced to some extent.

My instincts told me there was something not quite right about her sexually. As I have said, her orgasms didn't inspire; they weren't true. I knew about orgasms. There were the warm-up ones, the little ones, the big ones, the ones in between and, of course, the tidal waves that went on for ever. Clare didn't even fake the ones in between.

Eventually the post-coital blur arrived. I was spent.

Clare slept. There was the odd snore; I put it down to the booze. I hoped.

As I too fell asleep, I knew deep down that I was falling in love with a money-grabbing witch who didn't even know how to handle a willy properly. Yet ever the passionate romantic, I felt that love would conquer all. Clare was worth my best shot. She was young, healthy and pretty. Good baby-producing hips too.

What more could a man want?

A damn sight more as time was to reveal.

CHAPTER 8

Puccini and the tenor brought me back to my study.

I loved this room.

It was a nerve centre of refined passion and tactile warmth. Only here could I allow my natural inclinations towards tenderness and compassion to run riot. In three years Clare had killed those feelings I had once felt when looking at her. She had destroyed my inherent kindness toward her. It disturbed me that my own heart could become so cold. It wasn't me. I hated myself for allowing Clare to make me feel so inhuman. So detached.

In a vain attempt to distract myself, I switched on the portable television which didn't even have a proper aerial and was hidden in a far, dark corner of my study. Then I sat back down and thought, dear God, I must be down in the dumps: the idiots' lantern is on. I was looking for the pugnacious Paxman and *Newsnight* – one of the few news programmes that demanded at least a modicum of concentration and a tweaking of the intellect.

Too late for Paxman, I switched to BBC 1 in the hope that there might be at least something, anything, that would challenge my tired brain. In vain. BBC 1 had become as irritating as the commercial channels. It was all mass sound bites, entertainment for the masses and news headlines telling me that Beckham was about to have another tattoo etched onto his arse, Helen Mirren's bosom was about to be awarded a BAFTA and some people who could run around London until they were half dead, swim a length or two and row a boat a bit sharpish were about to be made 'Knights' and 'Dames'. Oh, and I nearly forgot: they were all 'heroes' too.

The annihilation of honesty had become the Holy Grail of news reporting whether in print, on the radio or on the idiots' lantern. People's brains were being killed by exaggeration, ignorance and manic commercial gain. Execution by media.

I soon gave up on the fairground waltz of mind-numbing trivia and unlikely dreams. In any event, Clare did more than enough 'viewing' for the pair of us. For relief I turned on the only semi-reliable media vehicle left, Radio 4 (allowing, of course, for public relations and news agency distortion). The voices calmed and the information informed – well, at least I kept my fingers crossed that it did. Ever the optimist, that's me.

Eventually the shipping forecast came on and I switched the radio off. Possible shipwrecks, swirling storms and a dodgy Dogger Bank would only exacerbate my own emotional storms.

I reached for a book; safe territory and the only object left to calm my miserable mood. After a while my eyelids started to fall across my eyeballs, so I closed it.

I was alone, wonderfully dejected and not knowing what on earth to do about my destructive marriage. Deep inside me I knew there was only one way. Divorce, with its betrayal and failure. I didn't want to think about these things. Not now. Going to bed was hard enough. My dear wife would be all 'back' as soon as I entered the room, and she had a lovely back too. The rejection would hurt, it always did, but I had become used to it. We still slept in the same bed which was something I suppose, although one of the guest rooms interfered with this harmonious arrangement from time to time.

Every night the words of a Jewish sage came back to me.

"When love is strong a man and a woman can make their bed on a sword's blade; when love is weak a bed of 60 cubits is not wide enough."

Why we carried on this pretence of matrimonial well-being was a mystery. There were enough spare beds after all. Our sleeping arrangements were a tired fraud. Most of the time I used a guest bathroom to do my ablutions, as waking Clare could cause another outbreak of war, so why not a permanent guest bedroom? I had been bullied into my own bathroom due to my hostile toilet action and the intense stench that was its aftermath or finale, depending on which way you looked at it. I prefer the latter, more polite and complimentary. My defecating outrages certainly merited an orchestral accompaniment I can tell you.

I brushed my teeth, washed, changed and rammed on a tee-shirt. No pants. Ever hopeful. The days of going to bed fully naked were well and truly over. The slightest touch of bare skin was enough to make Clare nauseous. I slipped into bed, careful not to knock the concrete wall that had been erected down the middle of the king-size mattress. The only consummation of our union that took place these days was through the medium of conflict. The bed was cold, and no matter how long I lay in it never warmed up. I closed my eyes and eventually dropped off, a troubled and unhappy man.

A man who had forgotten how to love.

The following morning I left for the office at my usual time. Clare still slept. Or at least she pretended to sleep. She didn't fancy doorstep kisses. I said, "Goodbye," received no response and made my way to the office.

It was my habit to stop off and enjoy the fare of a greasy café now and again. The place was always lively. Real. It stank of burnt fat, but at least I could smoke myself silly without it being seen as a declaration of war, outside and when it wasn't raining anyway.

The radio told me it was a 'National No Smoking Day', the misleading creation no doubt of some anti-smoking lobby with a cooked 'survey' to back it up, you know the sort of thing: 'Here's a luxury weekend for two at Benidorm if you answer just a few questions. It will only take a few minutes of your valuable time, we promise'. Well, big deal. Why couldn't some-one think of something more imaginative and less damaging to my health? How about a 'National Write a Letter Day' for example? Can you imagine it? All our under-25s would be having nervous breakdowns while I could sit back and enjoy the fun. So much for 'education, education, education!'

As I drove I winced at all the trendy chocolate-coated mothers driving their armoured cars. Now I know our roads are not too clever, but they are not as bad as tank training terrain either. We don't even have any snow to speak of. Do we really need tanks and off-roaders to take our charming little monsters to their violin lessons? It's all about status you see, success being judged by your 4x4. I couldn't believe it, but one day I saw a couple of wrinklies driving one. Where were they off to then, I wondered? A trek across the Sahara perhaps? No, down to Tesco's more like for a pint of skimmed milk and a bullet-proof crate of laxatives – Jesus, I'm sounding worse that those bloody silly grumpy old 'celebs' now. Really, what next! Bugger it, the odd rant never did anyone any harm, and who reads these days anyway?

I dodged the manic mothers and their smug offspring and, believe it or not, continued to regret the fact that I wasn't a father myself. That's got you, hasn't it? You weren't expecting this confession of frustrated fatherhood, were you? It's true. I wanted a child. Not a 'kid'. I'm not an American, I am happy to say. My derogatory remarks about little folk are a front. It is my way of hiding from disappointment. It may also be jealousy. I don't hate children at all, at least I wouldn't hate my own, I would love them beyond words. I would be their father, but never, never their friend.

I had wanted children when marrying Clare. We had even discussed it. The crafty cow had told me she wanted a brood after all, in spite of her negative comments on our first date. At least, this was her position during the run up to my earnest proposal. As soon as contracts were exchanged and completed my ambitions for fatherhood were quickly demolished. 'What! *Babies*? Horrible! Horrible!' was Clare's response to an abandonment of contraception. I remembered our first date. Fooled again. Clare didn't want her body stretched and distorted. She loathed children and, it soon transpired, my willy.

As planned, I stopped off for my breakfast – a bacon sandwich, white bread an' all – and an easy smoke. At least the sun was shining and I enjoyed every fat-filled crumb and inhalation. Smoked up and full, I made my way to the office for another day of legalised tripe. I was a married man, a lonely man who had lost his way amongst the 4x4's and his vows.

CHAPTER 9

Thomas Winston Smith-Twiddy (the 'Twiddy' bit of the double-barrel had originally belonged to some disgraced English slaver apparently) crept through the hospital exit doors gripping his buttocks for dear life. His backside was killing him, any slight movement resulted in a sharp pain shooting up from his feet to the top of his head.

"Serves you right, you stupid man," Lucretia Smith-Twiddy admonished in that lovable way of hers. There was never any real combat or aggression in her voice. "Don't expect any sympathy from me and don't think for one moment that I'm going to rub that cream the doctors have given you onto your stitched-up anus either. I'm not a nurse. Thank God!"

"Well, thank you for that, Lucretia," Tom grimaced. "I won't be asking you to, so don't worry."

"Good. Ugh! The very thought! That backside of yours is possessed by the devil, I'm sure of it! At least there won't be any flatulent outrages from you for a while, because even Satan has had enough!"

"Very funny. Now, where's the car? I need to sit down."

Lucretia looked at her husband and smiled. He was such an oaf – a lovely one, but nevertheless an oaf. Big, soft and most of the time incredibly stupid. Certainly where his back passage was concerned anyway. One thing was for sure though, he wouldn't be reaching for the red wine as soon as he walked into the kitchen and neither would he be ravaging *The Times* in the toilet for hours on end. *The Times* had been part of the pile problem, all that reading and heaving so the surgeon had maintained anyway.

"Come on, it's over there. Do you think you can manage it? I mean the stitches aren't going to rip or anything, are they?"

She did care, of course she did. She loved her Tom, but he needed to be taught a lesson. The red wine had been getting out of hand lately; that was the law for you.

"If they do, Lucretia, you can re-stitch them, being as you have such an affinity with arseholes."

"Very good Tom, very good. God, you're so crude sometimes. Now come on and stop being such a martyr." She put her arm through his and gently nudged him towards the car. As she walked alongside him she stumbled. Tom managed to catch her before she fell. His wife was a lightweight, so it wasn't difficult.

"Are you all right, Lucretia? You haven't been on the booze, have you?" Tom managed one of his *Blitzkrieg* smiles. The stark white teeth clashing with the obsidian black could blast the unprepared into eternity.

"No, I'm fine. My heels again. Come on, let's get you into the car."

It wasn't the heels at all. It was the second time that month that she had somehow lost control of her balance. Lack of sleep, worry about Tom, the children always playing up. She wasn't the only one who needed to take things a bit more slowly.

Lucretia had given up her career in public relations despite heading for the top. It had been a difficult decision. Children or career. Independence or dependence. The children had eventually prevailed, but she still wasn't too sure about the 'dependence'. How some women managed to do a full-time job and bring up children was beyond her. Someone had to suffer, and she suspected that, as with most things, it was probably the children, although she would often slyly admit to herself that giving up work hadn't been easy. The intellectual death warrant of motherhood and housekeeping still terrified her from time to time.

The school gate congregation was the best. Gaggles of persecuted mothers whose lives had become an infinite cycle of competitive birthday parties, competitive schools, swimming pools and piano lessons hung around school gates comparing lipsticks and gyms in the hope that some day or another something exciting would happen – like their worn-out and sexed-out husbands dying from boredom perhaps. It all made Lucretia shiver with fright and enrol herself as quickly as possible on another degree course in the arts. Botticelli and Dostoevsky beat the tedium of school gate irrelevance any day of the week.

Of course, loving Tom had played a part in her decision. She would love him until the day she died, and of this there was never any doubt.

She and Tom had three children altogether. Two girls and one boy. All under ten and all from previous entanglements. The boy was Tom's and the two girls hers. A fourth one was under discussion but Lucretia was beginning to wonder whether she was turning childbearing into a hobby; apart from anything else she was now thirty-eight, not a good age to be thinking about another child. Three of the little brats was enough to contend with, surely. All the same it would be nice for she and Tom to have one together. 'Nice'. She hated that word, so sterile, so pathetic, but like most people she just couldn't help using it.

Lucretia parked the car outside a squashed Georgian house down one of the side streets of Bury St Edmunds. A Residents Parking permit ensured that she was just about able to cram the car into a spot the size of a wrinkled postage stamp. Tom crept through the gate and up to the front door, one hand stretched out and the other gripping a buttock as if it had just been thrashed by some Harrovian headmaster. Not that headmasters thrashed the boys anymore; they were too busy providing pastoral care and empathy.

"Hurry up Lucretia, will you?! I'm dying here."

"Oh, do be quiet Tom and stop being such a baby," Lucretia replied as she put a key in the door lock. "Fortunately all the children are still at school, so you'll have a couple of hours peace and quiet."

"Good. Have you any idea how noisy hospitals are? They're a disgrace. An absolute disgrace."

As Tom walked into the hallway a yapping Yorkshire terrier tried to jump up his trousers.

"Oh no! Now go to hell!" Tom yelled. He hated the dog, if you could call it that. A long-haired rat would have been more accurate. "Bloody hell Lucretia, why is this objectionable mutt still here? I thought your sister was supposed to have picked it up a few days ago."

"She was, but she didn't. I'm not happy about it either. Anyway you didn't seem to complain the other morning when the dog jumped into our bed and started licking your nether regions.

"What! Are you accusing me of bestial tendencies, Lucretia?" Tom laughed. "Mind you now you come to mention it— "

"Oh God, Tom. You're disgusting, do you know that? Disgusting."

"Come here, my treacle-coloured beauty." Tom leered as he made a grab for his wife. "Come on woman, upstairs. It's been a few days and the children are all in school."

"Tom! Stop it! What about your operation. I mean—"

"It's my backside that's stitched up, not my manhood. Now come on, stop your nonsense!"

Lucretia demurred, there wasn't much else she could do; besides, she had missed her husband's warm body beside her at night. Piles or no piles. As he dragged her up the stairs she just about managed to say.

"Talk all posh to me while we're doing it then. You know that public-school voice of yours turns me on. Oh, and no wine afterwards, Tom. Agreed?"

"What! What! White man's poison! Those days are gone. Gone!"

An hour later Tom pulled the duvet cover over his wire wool head. God, he loved the woman. It may have taken him a good few years of trial and error, but he had got there in the end . . .

wedding cake notwithstanding. Lucretia was the best of them all and smart too. Beautiful and sensitive with teak-coloured eyes that tripped and caught everything that wandered in their wake. She was affectionate and loving in all things and yet she enjoyed a deep inner strength, a strength that he knew he personally lacked. All in all she was enough to destroy any man, in the best possible way, of course. What would he do without her? He knew she had made sacrifices, he knew how important her career and independence had been, he also knew that he couldn't have asked for more love than she gave him. He was indeed a lucky man.

As he dozed off to sleep her familiar scent gave him a feeling of security and well-being. Yes, it might have taken him time to finally settle on the right one, but 'he had got there in the end'.

CHAPTER 10

We had been invited to one of Clare's 'smart set' parties.

You know the sort. 'Professionals' (these days the word can mean anything from an estate agent and 'cleaning engineer' to a brain surgeon), big mouths, big new houses and big landscaped lawns. Personally I had never been able to see the attraction in these new-build warehouses. Have you ever been in one? Vast rooms that echoed desperation from one DFS cut-price sofa to another, rowdy wall-to-wall laminated flooring and kitchens built to make sure their owners never had to do anything. They were glorified public conveniences, plenty of human litter but no soul, no being. Voices became loud-speakers, but there was no character or tempo to their music. They were 'homes' without anything homely about them, always on the edge of shrieking for some injection of honest-to-God life.

On this particular occasion the middle agers were on the second level of priority. It was both a daughter's twenty-first and a celebration of her recent graduation, First Class Honours, of course – it couldn't be anything else, could it? Two ones, two twos and, God forbid, thirds went out with failure and red pens years ago. I was still trying to work out what there was to celebrate; after all one only has to be as thick as pig shit in order to obtain a degree in the first place these days. Even Clare could graduate if she put her mind to it.

I didn't know the parents particularly well. Clare played tennis with the wife, thus the acquaintance. I had vague memories of the husband, a District Judge. In other words a long-serving, trumped-up solicitor with delusions of grandeur who can't cope any more with private practice. I knew it was going to be one of those occasions where I would get legless to lessen the boredom, insult a few people just to have some fun and generally annoy the blazes out of my dear wife. I would have thought by now that she would have noted my resistance to these 'do's' but not Clare. It was a 'must go' party.

Where she found these people I had no idea. Thank God they were not my friends. I have always found people who aspire to be something they are not a sorry bunch. They would stand around sipping the Chardonnay, talking about house prices (that's a good one these days), expensive holidays and private schools. They would boast about how much they had spent on a new kitchen or a couple of pots they had bought for their Chelsea Flower Show gardens – all on credit, of course. It was enough to make you puke.

Some of them had yet to evolve beyond reading the *Beano* or worse still the *Daily Mail*. At least the *Beano* was honest about its character and personality – it was a comic and not to be taken seriously. Desperate Dan didn't really go around beating people half to death. The *Daily Mail,* however, excelled in vindictive falsehood and racist distortion, 'the voice of Middle England' the imperative, the bigoted middle-class everything.

In spite of all the above I would try not to wince every time someone talked to me, superior smart-arse that I am, and try to keep my dear wife happy for the sake of her 'appearance'. I would attend, dislocate my tongue, be sociable and not get drunk. All lies of course. A party wasn't a party if I didn't upset some stupid devil dull enough to fall for it.

When I arrived home Clare was in one of her jolly moods even to the point of being civil; she was wearing one of her negligee things. It both revealed and in my case tortured. She knew what she was doing, the crafty minx. Warm up time. Be nice to Edwin and he might just behave himself. She was making coffee in the kitchen. Cafetière, of course. What was wrong with Asda's best and a stained mug you may well ask?

"Who is going to this party then?" I enquired, all smiles and shotgun enthusiasm.

"Oh, the usual," came the uncommitted reply. The 'usual' meant the 'smart set' whom I have already described in my own contemptuous and derisory little way. She noticed the tired expression on my face.

The shotgun was moving out of my rear end.

"If you get bored Edwin, don't drink too much . . . please. You know what you're like. You can be so offensive. It surprises me that our friends still invite us."

"Your friends," I corrected. I didn't give her a chance to respond, "I'll be on my best behaviour, I promise, darling. So don't worry." She looked at me and gave me one of her smiles. I didn't often receive them these days, but when I did those brief seconds reminded me of why I fell in love with her. She could still transfix me.

"You really do promise?"

"I do."

"Good and don't sneer either (that was a good one coming from her). Or put on that superior look of disgust of yours. I know you consider them all to be your intellectual inferiors but do try not to show it, just for once."

"I'll try. What time do we have to be there?"

"Around nine. There's plenty of time. I'll be another hour getting ready. Make sure you change into something suitable. . . . I don't have to tell you really, I know. That's one of your saving graces, I suppose. You know how to dress." And with that tortuous and covert compliment she disappeared.

Another hour, I thought. She had probably started preening herself at 9 o'clock that morning. No doubt there had been the statutory visits to the gym, the beauty salon for a quick turn under the sun lamp and the hairdresser's for a £100's worth of character assassination and airhead discourse.

Her body cost me a fortune. I wouldn't mind if I was able to reap the benefits, but it was all hard-earned money. My money.

Apart from anything else I was starting to forget what her lovely body looked like anyway. Some investment, eh? Worse than Northern Rock. My 'preening' cost damn all. A shower, a shave, nail clippers and that was it more or less. My only extravagance was a few paltry drops of Chanel, and even a bottle lasted me years.

I wasn't offered any coffee so I went into my study for a drink.

There was no point in my changing yet. I would only end up ready and pacing whilst Clare farted around with her priceless hair and face. When I think about it I must have spent half my life waiting for women. God knows what they do in a bathroom. They certainly don't spend hours on the toilet, because, as I have already said, they just don't do things like that, do they?

When I had finished my second drink (I was developing a bit of a thirst) I went upstairs to get showered and dressed. I walked into our bedroom. Clare was standing in front of a mirror – her favourite location – glancing fore and aft. She was ready.

"How do I look, darling?" she asked.

I wanted to say 'like London after the Blitz' just to get her going – Clare was highly sensitive when it came to her physical appearance, like most women – but thought better of it. She stood up all grace and endearment. It would be back to 'bastard' and 'shit' by the end of the evening. Guaranteed. As you know she loved the two words, simple but effective. Like her.

I have to admit she was a sight. All sex. I could have bent her over there and then and given her a right royal seeing-to. I wanted to say "back onto this, my lovely" but refrained. She was wearing suspenders too, and no knickers, to add insult. She didn't like 'knicker lines' apparently

I told her she looked delightful, which she did.

CHAPTER 11

We arrived at our host's home.

As expected, a modern monstrosity with a long drive, out-houses and snorting horses to announce our arrival. I convinced myself that they were snorting with distaste, so at least someone was on my side.

We were greeted by District Judge Aeron Mycock (it's true, I'm telling you, imagine having a name like that and a judge too; I almost felt sorry for him). He held out his hand while his long face grinned from head to toe. He was a good-looking man in a quaintly androgynous sort of way, too good-looking maybe, thus the 'androgynous'. There was a female certainty to his face which always made me take a step or two back every time I met him. You know, do I kiss him or do I shake his hand? He may have been gay on the quiet, but who knows or even cares?

"Hello, DJ Aeron," I said whilst shaking the proffered appendage and knowing full well that the pompous little prig hated the familiarity. He was a 'judge' now, so 'DJ Aeron' was off limits. He scowled for a moment then 'blew' some kisses at Clare. I nearly vomited. This was going to be an evening of sickening proportions where pretension was concerned.

We walked in.

The place was stacked with young 'uns. Stunning nymphettes blasted the eyeballs. I took one look around the room and had my fears confirmed. The local business community was out in force. I nodded, smiled, shook hands and wished them all to hell. Clare went off to do her usual prancing and teasing. The 'little black number' she wore rammed her body into the eyes of every man in the place. Even the nubile beauties in the other rooms would have had a hard time competing. In another life I would have been proud of her and enjoyed the impotency of the leering men. In the here and now I too was as impotent as their fantasies. Not in the failing dick sense though, I may add. It didn't need scaffolding yet or Viagra.

As I stood and felt uncomfortable I was pounced on by a few of the wives. Clare wasn't the only one who could attract attention. Up they came with eyes that said, 'Come on, let's have an affair, my husband is a boring bastard and can't keep a hard-on for longer than two minutes.' This is middle age for you – frustration and floppy necks for the women, stiffies that are no longer so stiff for the men, excluding my good self, of course.

I ignored the not so subtle advances. Not that I had anything against vintage models. The older woman had many virtues. Virtues that younger, slimmer models could never hope to aspire to. The age difference between Clare and me had certainly presented problems. Her lack of maturity, experience, hadn't helped. We didn't share the same time scales. Our language was different. We hadn't grown up in the same social environment.

A middle-aged woman can be as beautiful as a youngster but in a kinder, less raw way. One or two of them did catch my eye though, and my regret. Affairs were not for me. Never had been. Infidelity and betrayal were cruel masters. If I was tempted and wanted to pick the flower I would end things first. My eyes were incapable of deceit.

I had a conscience.

My introverted state was interrupted by a tap on the shoulder and a, "Hello Ed, how did you get press-ganged into this poncy charade then?"

Only one person called me Ed. I hated the name, but good friendship permitted a certain offensive familiarity – or at least it ought to. If you can't insult a pal with impunity then he or she isn't much of a pal. I turned and there was Alistair Latham

GP, all fat, crudity, laughter and pathological irreverence. He was a kindred spirit. He was also my doctor, although I never saw him in the surgery; I was banned. Apparently our unrestrained laughter undermined his professional image and upset the patients who were in for a good moan. Not that he cared much about 'image' – most of the time anyway. His classic cars were the exception. Daimler Darts that needed plenty of hands to project them down the road, ancient Rolls-Royces that required a crowbar to open the doors, Bentleys that clanked instead of swished and Aston Martins that did one mile to the gallon all ensured he never failed to be noticed – as were the convoys of RAC rescue vans that were rarely far behind! Yes I know, ladies, boys and their toys – note the 'ladies', just thought I would get that in to annoy the feminists of the species. Daft bloody lot.

We shook hands.

The last time we had seen each other had been at a stag party the week before. All I remembered was four of us falling out of a lap dancing club and a consultant obstetrician wailing, "Ten quid for all that!! I've given my wife bloody thousands and she won't even give me a sympathy blow job!"

Before I could say anything he said, "I see all the 'I'm successful and rich' brigade are in. God help us."

"Indeed they are," I replied. "At least you've turned up to save me from making an insulting fool of myself."

"I'm not saving you. I'll egg you on and have a good laugh. 'Snarler' laid down the law, has she? Same with me. Wives, eh?"

"You can say that again."

"Oh, no progress then?"

"None."

"Need to talk?"

"Not now."

"We'll meet up next week then. We can both enjoy a bit of wife bashing."

"Fine, I'll give you a ring."

Alistair knew me and my troubles. He had known matrimonial war himself. He puckered his jowls for a moment, then let them go into free fall. He loved being fat, considered it a medal of honour. It was his human right to scoff as much as he wanted to, and who could argue with that? It was my human right to smoke too, so at least he didn't try lecturing me about it. Everyone else had human rights these days, so why should scoffing and smoking be excluded? God knows how he managed to explain all the pounds of lard he sported to his patients though. Every time his wife put his pants on the line there was an eclipse; either that or his house looked as if it was about to accommodate a United Nations summit.

"I hear Ivor is providing some sort of entertainment tonight, Ed." The doctor's eyes squinted through the fat as he looked at me. He couldn't stop calling into the baker's shop every night on his way home, his wife had informed me. "He just loves pies," she had despaired. Steak pies, pork pies, you name it, oh and custard slices, were the main cause of all the mischief apparently – and the odd Big Mac. I'd spotted the empty cartons of these last hidden in the boot of his car a few months before. "I love the fat bastard," she had moaned, "but what can I do?" Keep feeding him had been my answer, and you'll enjoy a nice fat pension from the NHS when he pops his clogs. That little remark had soon stopped her moaning about my friend. We men stick together. We're far more loyal than you women. Think about it.

"Is he?" I said. "Look out then. He'll stir things up if anybody will."

Ivor Jones was a Welshman, not that he could be anything else with a name like that. God knows how he had ended up in Suffolk. He was a fallen public schoolboy who had, in another life, known how to be a serious spendthrift. His arse had gone bang at the same time as the steel industry's and his inheritance, but he had landed back on earth with a guitar, a sharp wit and a doped-up understanding of the Divine. No more bank accounts, no more credit cards, no more respectability. He was happy, or at least he hoped he was.

The doctor and I continued to exchange expletives, humour and warmth. He was my best friend, always there, always available and never angry when I buggered things up. We were close. We were joined by another member of our sane community, Don Jameson aka Jameson 'One Kidney', a businessman who didn't take the law or life too seriously. We were all on the same street. Like Alistair he was big but not as rounded, much to his annoyance. The weight reduction had been imposed on him following the removal of one of his kidneys, thus the 'One Kidney' nickname.

"Come on, let's go outside," Alastair urged. "The propriety in here is setting off my arthritis. Got any fags on you, Ed?" He could only smoke on the sly.

"Yes, don't panic."

"Good. Come on then, I'm gasping. Can't show the wife. Quick while she's off yapping. Too many patients in here, too. Bastards get everywhere"

"You shouldn't smoke," I replied. "Come to that, all your blubber doesn't help your arthritis either." Don was quiet, he was only a notch or two below Alistair.

"Stop nagging Ed, you're sounding like that bloody wife of mine. Now let's get out of here for God's sake," Alistair persisted. "There's a lot of healthy gym-obsessed people in here tonight. Makes me feel uncomfortable. Come on, I'm on form tonight and the booze is on Judge Mycock. I want to drink the stuck-up twat bankrupt!"

"Good thinking," I said. "Come on then. There's bound to be a few sheds or something somewhere."

We pinched a couple of bottles of the good stuff – making sure no one noticed – and slunk off. We were like schoolboys creeping around the bicycle sheds trying to sniff saddles. Eventually we found a tack room and settled down on some saddles

– of the horse variety. We didn't try sniffing them either. Middle-aged or not, none of us were quite that perverted

We were drinking ourselves stupid and smoking our lungs out when Ivor turned up.

"Hello, boyos! Thought I'd find you all hiding somewhere. Have you seen the totty in there? Give me a large one quick!"

"We have," we all said in unison and despair. The Welsh lilt continued.

"I said to one little beauty as I was looking for you lot, 'Have you got any Welsh in you?' She said 'No' so I said, 'Well, do you fancy some?'" I cracked up and so did she. Her father didn't though – he was standing right next to her. It won't be long before I'm kicked out and I haven't even started the cabaret yet. That's age for you, boyos, when you start fancying the daughters. I'd kill to get my hands on one or two of those delicious bums, do you know that? In my dreams, eh?"

"Wouldn't we all," Alistair agreed.

"Want a puff?" Ivor asked. He was holding a damn great spliff between his teeth.

"Go on then," I said and reached for the baccy with a difference. I took a few pulls and passed it on its merry way. Ivor always had good stuff. Next thing he pulled a small polythene bag out of his pocket.

"Excuse me boyos, but I'm on tonight. Need a livener."

Next thing he disappeared for a few minutes. When he came back he was full of the joys of spring; in fact the daffodils had never been known to spring up so quickly.

For an hour or so we smoked, drank and enjoyed ourselves. The party passed us by. We were 'professionals' being our human selves. We 'engaged' with our sadness and our laughter, we shared our 'issues' and the self-evident hacking away of our 'self-esteem' and concluded that the government should 'do the right thing' by setting up an agency to 'support' middle-aged men in coming to terms with their 'emotional inertia' – 'absolutely!'. And if you believe that load of old bollocks, you'll believe anything.

Eventually Ivor declared, "Have to go now boyos, earn a few quid. I'll be a rock star yet. Hey doc, before I go give me a script for some pethidine will you?"

"Fuck off."

"Fair enough," and off he went.

Soon, manners demanded that we return to the party.

Being all veterans, our drunken states didn't seem too obvious. The old remained on one side of a huge room, the young on another. Men and women of my own age mixed polite conversation with indulgent smiles as their offspring fell about drunk – mostly the girls it has to be said, whom the young men seemed to be ignoring. They preferred to jig around with themselves. According to Ivor, who was more up on these things being a musician and entertainer, the young fellows these days were all gay. I couldn't understand it. Good luck to them and all that, but all those pretty girls that didn't have boyfriends? At their age by 10 o'clock I would have tumbled a couple of them in the bushes and been about to make a play for a third. It was odd. Could it be that young women intimidated the boys, or were the boys too feminised to resist and return fire? Were they over-concentrating on being good future fathers as previously derided, or was the 'in your face' method of female spooning just plain too much?

I searched the rooms for Clare. No sign. Well, actually I didn't search too hard. When she was out of the way I could smoke to my heart's content and drink myself stupid. I would have done both anyway, but it was more enjoyable without the caustic nagging. I found a table and sat down.

Alistair and One Kidney joined me.

"There they are," I said, pointing to the makeshift dance area. All our wives were dancing round with other husbands. None of us seemed particularly perturbed.

"I can tell you one thing, boys," Alistair announced. "There aren't many low-slung bums around here tonight, or tits for that matter, look at 'em – all tight and smooth. These young 'un's have waists! Can you imagine it? A waist! When was the last time you got your hands around a small waist and tight pair of buttocks? Jesus Christ, when my wife takes her bra and pants off there's a bloody great bang. Her tits and arse know all about gravity, I can tell you. Newton would never have needed an apple. One look at her with the bra off would have done the trick. And another thing, have you noticed how women's knickers get bigger as they get older? Thongs? My wife goes to Millets for her underwear these days. Memories eh? That's all we sad middle-aged bastards have, isn't it? Memories." One Kidney and I nodded our agreement, both desisting in reminding Alistair that he probably wasn't far behind his wife when it came to her excursions to Millets.

Clare didn't fall into Alistair's flabby pigeonhole though, I gave her that. I watched as she enticed and manipulated the men. She flirted, allowed a grope now and again and threw her body into the faces of all the women who were middle-aged, thread veined, fat and looking at her with expressions of longing and hatred. My wife watching was soon disturbed by some young girls trying to drag us up to dance.

We were all for it. Forties and early fifties we may have been, but we could still show 'em a thing or two. The three of us piled in. No inhibitions. The girls loved it. Having got nowhere with the boys of their own age they had gone for the next best thing. Us.

The disc jockey finished and Ivor and his crew started. All music from the seventies and eighties interspersed with his foul humour. Some of the parents turned their noses up. We laughed and excreted more sweat. I had the dog-end of a spliff dangling out of my mouth which didn't impress the architects, business-men, lawyers, doctors and God knows who else. The youngsters? . . . Well, they enjoyed. We were more fun than their peers. We showed them that life goes on after forty and that it can be a good life. Not one of us tried a grope. We knew our place and, it must be said, were quite happy with it. The girls were so young. They were babies, vulnerable and untested. Their cots weren't even cold. At twenty-one we know it all. At forty-one we know nothing. I was forty-five and knew less than nothing, if you can work that one out.

As I held and jived this lovely little brunette, a sudden revelation kicked me hard in the stomach. The sexual dreams of latter years, the middle-aged quest for firm flesh, the longing for pristine fantasy were all a farce. As I danced, I felt only paternity. A fathering. There was no desire in my hands or my eyes. I held the girl as a father would. It occurred to me that a woman twenty to thirty years my junior could never be taken seriously. Her childhood would intimidate and frighten me. At that age a young woman was too precious for my worldly, corrupted touch. I had been given my time. I had enjoyed it. My only regret now was that I was not mature or experienced enough at the time to appreciate what I had – were this the case I would never have got out of the bloody bedroom!

Ivor harangued my huddled peers to join the fray, but they remained in their groups for fear of dislocation. Their status was at risk if they made fools of themselves, you see. Eventually I slumped down in a chair and joined the other wheezers.

"I'm knackered," I said, "can't hack it anymore."

The doctor was in a worse state than me. It was all the fat he carried. One Kidney was in between.

Their two wives came over to join us. Foul mouths clamped shut as men stopped being men and subjugated themselves to the tyranny of female domination. It was time for reasonable, colourless dialogue. They talked amongst themselves. Alistair was having his balls minced for smoking and lusting after 'children' and One Kidney was having cocktail sticks shoved into his leg for being a drunken pervert. As they were getting theirs, Clare came over with another woman in tow.

"Edwin darling, I would like you to meet a very dear friend of mine, Jessica Howard." I stood up and held out my hand.

"How do you do, Jessica Howard?" How I hadn't noticed this woman before was a mystery. She was striking, yet I wasn't too sure in which way. Her grip was firm. Too firm for a woman. Her handshake was almost a warning, or so it seemed.

"I've heard a lot about you, Edwin." The woman smiled in an uncertain way that I wasn't sure was genuine or not. There seemed to be an icicle or two hanging from her lower lip – either that or my imagination was running riot again. "Oh, there was no need to get up. I'm not royalty."

"Glad to hear it," I replied as I remained standing all the same. "My wife has been singing my praises, has she?" I looked at Clare who seemed to be on fire with enthusiasm. She was gripping this Jessica woman's arm as if frightened to death that the woman would take flight.

Before Jessica could confirm my wife's enduring love and respect for me she quickly interrupted. "Jessica and I are old friends," she enthused. "We flew together. We were great friends as well as working colleagues. We lost touch, but here she is. Isn't it wonderful?"

It had been a long time since I had seen Clare so . . . happy. I was bemused. I had never heard Clare mention any Jessica Howard. In fact she hadn't mentioned anyone in particular to me from her star-gazing days – ever. Whenever she spoke about the people she had once worked with there had always been an edge of contempt in her voice. Come to think of it, whenever she spoke about anyone there was always an edge of contempt.

I took a more serious look at this old friend from the past. Early thirties, long auburn hair that threatened an electric shock if touched without permission. Her face seemed beautiful, and yet there was something unexpected about it; a riddle or two seemed to be knocking about the eyes and lips. There wasn't a line out of place, an eyelash out of kilter. Even so, her imme-diate expression seemed to say that she didn't belong anywhere as her deep blue eyes wandered and refused to stay still for even a cursory appraisal. Where Clare was pretty in the extreme, this woman was profound. I could have looked at her for decades trying to work out who she was. There was something odd about the woman. I know the word 'odd' is difficult to define, let alone being a meaningful adjective, but it was the only word that first came to mind. Anyway, no doubt you get my drift.

There didn't appear to be one layer of concrete on her facial skin, or even the odd brush of paint either. A stroke or two of lippy perhaps, but that was it. There was strength in the eyes and jaw too. A wilfulness. Spirit. There was also compassion. It was hidden and secretive, but it was there.

A Rubenesque glow danced around her body, reminding me of one of those lounging sepia-coloured nudes in an old Victorian photograph, sexy and mocking, and yet like the rest of her I just couldn't be sure. It was hard to tell exactly what her body shape was as her clothes were loose and plain. She was wearing a dull green-coloured tent. In spite of all this and her obvious disregard for designer affectation, she enjoyed a unique style. Her clothes said, 'Fuck fashion, I am me, take it or leave it.' She wasn't far off my own height of 5 feet 11 inches and yet her hands were quite small in spite of her grip. Her understatement placed her apart and her lack of colour only enhanced her beauty, if in fact that is what it was. It would take a lifetime to find out, I was sure.

Our eyes touched.

"Won't you join us?" I asked and pulled out a chair.

"Thank you, but I can manage."

Oh, oh, I thought. Watch it. She's one of those women who is offended by having a door opened for them. Her few words blew my growing admiration right out of the nearest window. I was beginning to fancy her too.

"Only trying to be a gentleman, I assure you," I said as she sat down. "So you're a lady from my wife's dark and murky past, are you?" I asked.

"A woman from Clare's past, yes." She emphasised the word 'woman'. Oh God we've got a right one here, I thought. What have I already been saying about 'ladies'? "Oh and would you mind blowing your smoke somewhere else? You really should give it up, you know." Oh no, another one. They were everywhere. Why couldn't these non-smoking tyrannical twats worry about their own bodies instead of everyone else's?

Alistair and One Kidney had gone silent. They were enjoying the show – and the looks. The lines on Jessica's face changed with each word. She antagonised. Provoked. Well, no-one intimidated me but this woman was particularly irresistible. I loved a fight, the smarter my opponent the better. Clare was dithering around getting a drink for her long-lost friend.

I ignored the smoking rebuke and continued to blow. "What has Clare been telling you about me then? What a wonderful husband I am, no doubt."

"Not quite," she smiled, "but then Clare was always on the diffident side."

Don't overdo the charm will you, I thought. She had good teeth. Her eyes went into intense mode. The ambition saw straight through me.

"You're not from Suffolk," I stated, as there was too much neutrality in her vocal chords for her to be Suffolk born and bred.

"Correct. London originally. I live in Norwich now."

"You work there?"

"Yes."

And that was it. Obviously not the talkative type, I concluded. She wasn't giving much away. Well, I wasn't going to lower myself by showing too much interest either. A little more prodding was in order though.

"Are you a 'Mrs' or a 'Miss'?"

"Neither."

"A hermaphrodite then?"

"Muz will do," she replied a little too precisely, the smiles having vanished as quickly as a bullet from her self-aware gun barrel. The conversation was getting as brittle as a feminist's elongated tongue.

"Muz?" I grinned. "Sounds like a bumblebee with a chronic speech impediment or some new fizzy drink. All sugar but no spice and certainly no substance." I paused for a moment deciding that I wasn't really in the mood for mortal combat after all, humility instead of provocation was perhaps the best policy.

"My apologies," I said with a more sincere smile. "I don't mean to be rude Jessica, but 'Muz' does sound rather comical, you have to admit."

"There's no need to apologise Edwin, really." The Mona Lisa smile was back and I have to admit it was quite beautiful, although once again I couldn't be sure. "Perhaps the apology should have been mine. I didn't intend to undermine your fragile masculinity. Clare told me you were the argumentative type. I was expecting a more worthy opponent. Someone more original."

I nearly accused her of being judgemental but desisted. I would have been getting as bad as her. Instead I said, "Never mind, Muz Jessica. I'll endeavour to undertake some practise before you join us for supper one evening next week."

That's got you, smart-arse, I thought. Kill 'em with kindness; works every time. My lips and eyes were all welcome and hospitality, forgiving even. Her response was not so fast this time. Remember I had age and experience on my side, not to mention the lawyer's art of excelling at abstruse verbiage (I'm still trying to work out what 'abstruse verbiage' means myself, so don't worry if you don't get it – and bugger dumbing down, it can stay, I like it!) and learned bullshit. Why do you think we have so many lawyers in Parliament?

She looked at me for a few moments, narrowing her eyes, analysing. Finally she said, "How kind. I'll look forward to it."

"Good. You and Clare arrange something then. Don't expect home cooking though, unless you enjoy a dried-up baked bean on top of a burnt piece of toast. No butter in between either."

"I won't. Clare was never a Delia Smith if I remember correctly."

82

"You remember correctly, believe me. I'll get something in. What do you like? Indian, Chinese, Vietnamese?"

"Chinese will be fine. I'm vegetarian though."

"At least you're not a vegan. Now that would be challenging. I'll bear it in mind." She bristled for the briefest of moments, but had obviously decided to accept my cautious olive branch, notwithstanding the grudge attached.

"See you next week then. A pleasure meeting you."

Not waiting for a reply I went off to the makeshift bar for another drink. I needed one after that little encounter. I also needed some air, so I helped myself to a large whisky and went outside to find somewhere quiet. The thump-thump of young music was making my eardrums do the same.

I found a spot under one of the many manicured trees, parked my backside down and leaned back against the top-of-the-range trunk – it had to be this, didn't it? A full moon lit up my torpor and made me feel a little guilty. I knew I had been far too combative with Clare's friend. It wasn't me at all. Not the real Edwin. In a quiet sort of way I was quite the liberal, each to their own sort of thing. I looked at the moon with its simple patches of grey and tried to work out whether I was feeling intoxicated or miserable. Moons do that, they always demand melancholy and introspection; no wonder so many astrologers are always squinting and so bloody humourless.

I thought of Jessica Howard again. Her unattractive sense of self-worth. Her hidden insecurity. Any woman who feels compelled to be so bold is lacking something. Either this, or she is suffering from a chronic bout of inferiority complex. What man could desire such brutal ego and megalomania?

Women should celebrate their femininity and strength, stop sacrificing their beauty and charm to pathetic and outdated martyrdom and celebrate what they have always been at heart: strong, wise, gentle and female.

The cause is dead.

The chains have rusted and fallen apart on the railings.

No one gives a damn anymore. The children have suffered enough. The war has been won. Do not suffer a lonely victory. Resurrect your love. Return to what you do best – being women. Being mothers.

I mingled the rest of the night away, nearly crying when the father gave a speech outlining the deification of his daughter. The moment she was born, etc., etc. She was going to take the legal world by storm of course, House of Lords here she comes. As if anyone would have expected anything less.

Towards the end of the night I stumbled about the place whispering insulting inanities to anyone dull enough to listen. The drink hadn't helped my 'zero tolerance of fools' moods, and neither had Jessica Howard. Not a sociable condition, I can tell you. I listened to all the politically correct jargon and drank more to anaesthetise myself. All the irritating words, crap and polite euphemisms evading the truth, flew around my head and my mind, making me want to shake the orally stunted into some sense of reality. Our language was losing its unique power to diversify, to be dynamic and yet direct. To offend and insult. A blackboard was no longer a blackboard, as it might just upset someone from Africa. As if they cared. People no longer said what they meant.

When the endurance test finally finished, Clare drove us home.

In a hurry and with a face that would have shamed a tropical thunderclap.

Naturally, that night I was evicted from the matrimonial boudoir. It was one of the guest rooms – again. I'd popped my head into our bedroom on my way into exile and said, "No chance of a shag then?"

I won't repeat the reply. Very unladylike.

That was Clare for you, a woman so cold and frigid that every time she opened her mouth and exhaled the electric fires in the house started to boot up.

CHAPTER 12

"You disgust me!"

Clare was hot and grim. So grim in fact you'd swear I'd been farting in bed all night (notwithstanding the post-party eviction from our bed, I'd always felt women were unreasonably sensitive about nocturnal flatulence and Clare was no exception).

"Well, surprise, surprise. What's new?" I responded with my usual slippery sarcasm. The woman was in one of her virago states. All hostile and warlike. I kept calm which annoyed her even more.

"You sit there calmly drinking your tea, not giving a damn about the way you behaved. You were drunk, rude and objectionable to almost everyone. Apart from your precious friends. And they were just as bad. I'm surprised Jessica didn't hit you. Fortunately for you she tolerated your terrible manners. God, you didn't even know her!"

"Well I do now, so calm down. I wasn't that rude anyway. On the contrary, I thought I was rather restrained. You're exaggerating. I invited her over for supper, didn't I? What more do you want?" As Clare started to froth at the mouth I added, "Actually I think she rather fancied me."

"You! . . . You! . . . You're such a bastard!" I loved it when Clare became so angry that she could hardly speak. Mission accomplished. "Fancy . . . fancy you? In your dreams, Mr Edwin Hillyard, in your bloody dreams. She wouldn't go near you in a million years. She hates old men."

"But I bet she loves their money. Just like you really. Two peas in a jewel-studded pod. Anyway, I'm not going to sit here listening to your neurotic insults. The milk is beginning to curdle and so am I. It's a Sunday morning, and I don't like my

Sundays being disturbed as you well know. I'm off out, so go and shout at one of your designer dresses."

"Don't you dare walk away when I'm talking to you!"

"Shouting would be more accurate, I think."

I folded up the *Sunday Times*, rammed it under my arm, stubbed out my cigarette and made for the back door.

"Edwin, I'm talking to you. Don't you turn your back on me!"

"I'll see you later. Now fuck off and leave me alone."

I walked out.

A crash of tea cup against the kitchen door followed me. A few plates came after it judging by the noise. Clare was certainly in a mood. A crockery-smashing one. They happened from time to time. She could be a ferocious bitch when there were a few plates hanging around. I was lucky this time. The kitchen door protected me from her Grecian dancing. There had been other times when I hadn't been so lucky.

Women do not have a monopoly as victims of domestic violence, believe me. I had been stitched up once or twice by Alistair. Kept it off the record too. I was being a protective husband for all the good it did me. Come to think of it, why is it that I am reluctant to use the word 'husband'? Why do I feel that I may offend someone? For some the word stinks of control or a property-owning inclination. Dear God, aren't our relationships messed up! We don't seem to know who we are with anymore, or what to call them if we do. Crazy. Perhaps I ought to employ one of these lifestyle professors. They can also show me how to wipe my arse properly.

Sunday was my day. Edwin's day.

I went to the garage and smelt my pride and joy. A Bristol Continental. She cost me a fortune, but it was the one thing in my life that remained untainted by Clare's touch. Sometimes I would just sit in it and intoxicate myself with its unique odours as the leather and walnut held me in their arms and protected me from the outside world. The modern world. 'Hi-tech' had not invaded my Bristolian paradise – and before you say anything, my 'classic' drove like a dream and I hadn't had to call out the RAC once. Neither was I worried about image!

I drove the car onto the drive to let her warm up. Some foreplay was needed to coax her passion juices into a gentle flow. I got out to make my usual inspection of her bodywork in the sunlight. If there was even an unobtrusive scratch I would have to have it seen to. As I looked here and there my concentration was interrupted.

"Mr Hillyard? Mr Hillyard?"

I turned to see where the voice was coming from. Dominic Brent, my next-door neighbour, was leaning over the wooden fence that partly separated our properties, "Do you think I could have a word?" he asked. Being the gentlemanly sort I obliged and walked up to the fence.

"Certainly. What can I do for you, Mr Brent?"

"About this fence, Mr Hillyard." This was all I needed. Brent and his bloody fence.

"What about it?" I replied, all innocence and charm.

"You haven't changed the colour even though you're legally responsible. We've exchanged solicitors' letters on this and I would have thought, you being a solicitor yourself, that a more responsible and mature attitude would prevail."

I wasn't in the mood for this. Brent, an officious petty bastard, was the chief executive of the local authority. (No surprises there then I can hear all you readers wail.) I stared at him for a few moments before saying anything. Eventually, I let go a tired sigh.

"Mr Brent, why do you insist on being such an inconvenient and irritating trumped-up little turd? Please be so good as to fuck off and tend to your compost heap or something. Thank you."

I walked off. Two down, how many more to go, I wondered? Now, I agree that my response was a little inappropriate as they say – but hell, my wife had only just tried to brain me. What did the man expect? He had picked on me at an inappropriate time. I love the word 'inappropriate'. It's the best cop-out yet for saying what you really don't mean. Brent was being a turd and that's all there was to it. So what? I am called that a hundred times a day and worse by my clients and my friends. I don't mind. How can I? It's true.

I drove off leaving Brent requiring an ambulance and a bit of heart massage. He had been bothering me about that sodding fence for years. Didn't like my shade of brown apparently.

My passionate Bristol took my mind off Brent and Clare as I sat back and lost myself in her touch.

CHAPTER 13

"Where do you think you're going, Tom?"

Tom stood before his wife and waited.

Savile Row tweeds were the order of the day on Sundays, ditto the rustic green polka-dot pocket handkerchief. Edwin Hillyard wasn't the only tart on the block. The rough wool wasn't helping Tom's anal inconvenience though, at least when he sat down, which was why right now he remained standing.

"The office. Edwin must be tearing his hair out."

"But it's Sunday, for heaven's sake, and you're supposed to be resting for another day or so at least. Edwin has been managing well enough without you; actually the other day he told me he was enjoying the peace and quiet. The law doesn't stop just because Thomas Smith-Twiddy is having his over-indulged posterior sorted out."

Tom looked at his wife.

She was sitting down at the breakfast table looking her usual lovely self. Not far off forty she still looked her best first thing in the morning, 'sexy' and 'wanton' being the two words that always came to mind. Her autumn-brown skin and deep brown, sometimes black, eyes which constantly changed colour always made him love her more, if that were at all possible. She was pinning him to the wall now with those eyes of hers. Only this time there was an accusing glint in them, a glint that usually had no truck with argument. Tom knew his wife. He also knew about Lucrezia Borgia.

"Now don't get all worked up, Lucretia." Tom never called his wife 'Lucy' as some of her friends were inclined to do. 'Lucy' was a frivolous name and Lucretia was never frivolous, at least not in a silly frantic sort of way. "I'll only be a couple of hours. Just need to check my mail and stuff. I won't be long."

Lucretia stood up from the table and straightened her cream fluffy dressing-gown. Her movement was graceful even in the M&S dressing gown, her perfect legs and firm high breasts always demanding his full attention. He was sure that if she put her mind to it she could walk on air. Lucrezia Borgia again. The spelling of their names may have been different but they had a lot in common, although he had never regarded his wife as some *femme fatale*. She was quite the opposite. Too damned soft, particularly where the children were concerned.

Tom looked down at her, not in any superior way; forget that where Lucretia was concerned. Her personality more than made up for her slight build. She was an average 5 feet 3 inches and small boned, almost delicate. There were times when he could have bounced her around on his knee; indeed he did quite frequently bounce her around too, but not on his knee it has to said.

She stood in front of him hands on hips. "I've told you Thomas!" Lucretia almost shouted. This was serious. She only called him 'Thomas' when a spat was in the air. Her face had tuned into a nasty glare too; he had never seen such anger before. "You're supposed to be resting! Why do you have to go to the office!"

"Hey, steady on girl. I'll only be out for a couple of hours, I don't intend doing any 'work' as such. I just like to keep my eye on things, that's all."

What the hell has got into her? Tom quickly thought. She was never this temperamental or aggressive. She had always been feisty but never threatening; there was a difference. For a moment he wondered who was standing in front of him. It sure as hell wasn't his wife.

As quickly as her temper had erupted, Lucretia calmed down.

"I'm sorry, Tom . . . I don't know what came over me. I'm feeling so tired and irritable these days. I don't know what's the matter with me, I really don't. I'm sorry, ignore it." Tom took her hand and pulled her to him.

"Not having a period are you?"

"Oh God, isn't that typical. Men. Every time a woman has the vapours about something it's her period. You men. You're all the same. I also suspect you've been listening to that partner of yours again too." Lucretia thought she knew all about Edwin's views on the female kind, but she could never be too sure. Even so, she couldn't help being fond of the man. She even felt sorry for him, as having a wife like Clare couldn't be easy.

"Now do I have permission to leave?"

"Don't be sarcastic, Tom, it doesn't become you. Of course you do."

"Good. I'll see you later. I won't be long. Promise. Back in time to take the children out somewhere. Where are they by the way, the house is far too quiet."

"Two of them are on a sleep-over – not that you'd have noticed as you were out cold – and the other one is up in her room sulking."

"Again?"

"Again. It's her age. Pre-pubescent insanity. Ignore it."

As Tom walked to the office, with some difficulty it had to be said, Lucretia's outburst still disturbed him. He had never seen her like that before. In the five years they had been together he had never encountered this darker side to her nature, periods notwithstanding. What had got into her? What was so unusual about him going to the office? They rarely fought, at least not in any terminal way. Like most couples they argued and disagreed on things, but this was perfectly natural. A relationship that slid along with constant nicety and sickening lovey-dovey absorption wasn't a relationship at all; apart from anything else such perfect union would have been mind-blowingly boring. Her outburst had actually frightened him for a fraction of a second as he had seen violence in her eyes, something he had never seen before.

As he turned a corner he decided in his usual easy come, easy-go way to forget Lucretia's outburst. It had been an aberration, that's all. After all she was human, and the children were bound to wear her down from time to time. He knew that the loss of her career still prodded her from time to time, so maybe she ought to think about some part-time work. He would suggest it when he arrived back home. She was an intelligent woman and he fully understood how frustrated she must feel. Aimless days of childish stupidity, supermarkets and spin dryers were enough to kill anyone's mind. He couldn't have done it, so why should he expect his wife to?

As soon as Tom had walked out of the house, Lucretia made herself another cup of coffee and sat down. Her long fingers touched the handle of the china mug and for a moment refused to leave the certainty of its cool texture. Her eyes concentrated on the yellow china with its everyday handle. The mug, such a silly thing, brought her a few moments of comfort even though she didn't know why. She lifted the mug to her lips and prepared her taste buds for the hot liquid, but just as the rim of the mug touched her lips her fingers jerked the mug away. Again she didn't know why.

She carefully put the mug back down on the table. Fortunately she hadn't spilt any of the coffee, but only just. She leaned forward and bent her head into her hands. What was wrong with her? First Tom, now disgust at a mug of coffee if that's what it was. Was she going insane? She couldn't stop the tears, she couldn't stop the unpredictable frustration, she couldn't stop being who she was.

CHAPTER 14

I found myself having to travel to London for a Law Society conference. This conference would be like every other. All talk, all opinion and no decisions.

I arrived at Liverpool Street station annoyed and predictably late. Electronic wizardry had screamed at my attempts to enjoy the gentle tap of wheel on track. Mobile phones epitomised nonsensical rubbish while headphones leapt from mindless heads. I sat and fumed. Not being able to smoke encouraged my mean mood. Whatever happened to silver service, erectile napkins, food straight from the soil and dumped in a frying pan? Have you ever tried to eat one of the railways' micro-waved monstrosities? Don't. Their toilets aren't big enough. That's if you can get into one. Trains? Forget it.

Old habits die hard. I chased around the underground as if my arse was on fire, at the same time not quite knowing why. I was not in any hurry; mass hypnosis I suppose. I ran and shoved like everybody else as I forgot who I was.

The conference came and went. A non-event in every respect. The young breed of lawyers disappointed and dismayed, many of them sounding as if they had spent all their sorry lives on a building site. 'Equal opportunity' – in other words 'fuck merit' – was everywhere. There was no style or class in the profession any more. No status and no respect. Hardly surprising, we were only getting what we deserved. Solicitors solicited only money and themselves in a street that was crammed with painted fish-net competition. My profession had sold its dignity to uncouth smiles of modernity, exaggerated personal injury and outstretched sweaty palms waiting to grasp the next inflated buck.

No wonder I had had enough. I was ashamed. Believe it or not, in the distant past the law had been about helping people and their families.

I eventually escaped from the conference. I wandered around Leicester Square for a while and had to admit that there was still an excitement about the place. A danger. I was in no hurry to return home. Clare hadn't spoken to me since her last smashing outburst, and I had no doubt that her sulking would last a few days longer. I decided to treat myself to a decent supper and a good few drinks. I was drinking too much, but what else was there? Like the ciggies, I was smoking far beyond my normal levels, but didn't care. The drink and smokes were my comforters. My reliable companions. They loved me and I loved them. I had found requited love after all. Sitting right under my idiot nose.

I treated myself to an expensive curry at Veeraswamy's in Regent Street.

While I was picking my way through spudded-up spinach and Madras and in a moment of delirious nostalgia, I contemplated returning to a massage parlour I had once patronised many years ago as a student.

'The Fingertips Massage Parlour' it had been called. Five pounds for 'hand relief' – God, I love some of these sexual euphemisms, nearly as bad as 'making love'. Don't worry, I'm not going to start on that one again.

Doubt if the place was called that now or even if it was still in business. The building would still be there though, and the sex. The young would have replaced the old, but the sex would be the same.

Anyway, I had been plastered at the time and even the wanton efforts of a black beauty hadn't been able to pump my willy into some semblance of rigidity. I remembered being my usual sadistic self and making the poor girl tug away like some demented bell-ringer, if only to get my fiver's worth. Her wrist finally gave up, as did I, but I had value for money I can tell you. My bank manager was none too pleased with my thriftiness though. Those were the days when banks used to return all your cheques and when managers paid personal attention to your spending habits. Mine, a Quaker at that, actually rang me up at college.

"I note, Mr Hillyard, that you have been patronising a place called the 'Fingertips Massage Parlour'," he commented. "Not a place of serious legal endeavour I suspect." He was enjoying every second of my discomfort and sober embarrassment. He told my father too, the bastard. So much for extra-curricular activity, eh? I never did go back there, but I'm pretty certain my old man gave the place a go. No doubt the Quaker went with him too for some silent shagging. The pair of them probably paid for the 'De Luxe VIP' treatment as well. The old duffers could afford it.

I eventually finished the food and wine and decided to make my way home. Massage parlours were best left to memory. Besides, some worn-out strumpet was unlikely to solve my emotional problems. I would only feel guilty anyway.

As I walked through the West End I allowed my mind further memories and laughter. My student days had been a happy time. All booze, dope and young expectant lips. No worries. No complications. No technology and no AIDS. Love had found me in my first year and dropped me in my third. Callow blubbering had taught me my first lesson. I still remembered the girl. My first love. The innocence. The terrifying and bungling sexual discovery, but more than all this, the incredible tenderness. Time abuses and mocks our efforts to return to what was. What I would have given to hold that girl again in that time and that place, when the years had yet to fold and drop my face and body into itself. Disappointment and hurt is forgiven but not forgotten. Our faces tell our stories; we can't hide behind pristine youth for ever.

I looked in a shop window and ignored the goods on offer; instead I saw again the girl I had once loved. I remembered her prettiness. Her kiss. Her love. I walked away and realised that I was still the loser. Time didn't always provide every answer. I consoled myself with her taste. At least I had known.

Yes, I admit it. I was lonely. So what? I am human, indulge me. At least I'm not saying I was 'depressed' – whatever that is – or that I am trying to write a tear-smothered book on how hard done by I've been in order to make few quid on the backs of all the other sorry buggers too dejected and worn out to get a life. On the other hand of course, if I was some unfairly maligned celebrity who couldn't read or write but was able to cajole some deluded fool to write about 'My Hell', then this story would probably win an award for literary excellence and earn me a couple of million to boot. No justice is there? Anyway, I was thoroughly enjoying my snivelling weakness in front of that shop window, so nuts to you. I don't feel sorry for myself for long, so don't worry, I'm not one of those who makes a career out of discord. No harm in a modest bit of loneliness now and again, though. It brings balance.

As I entered the Underground my mind went back to that first date with Clare again. Derek and Clive's lobsters up Jane Mansfield's bum immediately came to mind. If I had exercised any sense at all that's exactly what I should have done to Clare. Shoved her lobster right up her bum and made a quick exit. A laugh creased my wrinkles for a moment, confirming my release from this chronic bout of self-pity (you see I don't wallow for long). After all I am the only one who knows how to show myself genuine sympathy. It's my mind and no-one else's. Only I know how it ticks. Hold on – I wonder how many fruitcakes have said that. I take it all back.

The escalator hauled me along with everyone else as we all gazed at fresh air and wondered why it was so fascinating. I had never quite worked out what was so intriguing about underground air. We could all have looked at ourselves I suppose, but then that would probably have been too frightening. Posters claiming this and that moaned for attention from distracted eyes that really didn't want to look. The advertising people earned a few more bob from our mindless aspiration. Take your time people, I thought. Death collects us quickly enough, and what good will a new car and the latest television be then?

I stood on a platform and waited for deliverance. An occasional rush of air tingled my memory banks yet again, but only for a moment.

I noticed a man hovering a few feet away from me. He seemed lonelier than me which was saying something. There was a feeling of concern about him, an anxiety. God knows why he caught my attention. He was in his twenties, young anyway. His eyes were searching for something, they didn't dart, they weren't excited, they just seemed intent on discovering something. There was a depth that I couldn't fathom, it almost disturbed. He stood upright and didn't move. There was an air of the military about him, the polished shoes, the cleanliness of his skin and clothes, his neatness. His posture was constrained, there was nothing casual in the way he stood. His face remained still as if soaking up his own special intent, and yet there was purpose in the way he looked. Determination even.

After a few moments my eyes were distracted by an Asian woman who had moved alongside my military mystery. My eyes stuck to her like enemy limpets about to explode; it was really quite disconcerting. From the secretive and mysterious to the obvious and transparent in a split second. The woman was bloody gorgeous. Knocked Clare off her whitey pedestal anyway. I had always had a thing about these dusky maidens from the East, their beauty always seemed so benevolent and retiring. White women could be brash and primitive by comparison. Not surprising perhaps, considering that the Kama Sutra was written at a time when most Western women, while being yanked about by their hair, thought sex was just another form of mortal combat.

A train started to pull in and distracted my Asian-watching.

The man I had been looking at threw himself in front of it.

There was a violent shriek of brakes, a few sparks and instant death.

Screams.

The Asian woman had seen it all.

She stood still, hands raised to her face as her body swayed. I ran to her, fearful that she may fall, at the same time trying to keep bite-size pieces of Veeraswamy's extortionate king prawn Madras in its rightful place. She started to fall but I caught her. Her eyes were closed so she must have gone into some kind of faint. I stood there holding the woman and not knowing what the hell to do. Before I had a chance to work out my defence to sexual harassment she opened her eyes.

"I am so sorry . . ." she mumbled, "will you help me to that bench? . . . My legs are a little weak." I disengaged myself. Our eyes met. Hers punched mine. Dark brown with blue and yellow speckles. Indescribable. I cannot begin to express the power in that look, you will just have to take my word for it. There was an instant of complete union. A force. I had never before experienced anything like this, not even with Clare. My breath laboured for a few seconds as I quickly gained control of myself.

"Never mind a bench," I said, "a stiff drink is in order here. Hold onto me if you feel unsteady." Here we go, natural-born leader time, that's me, Aries and masterful. With that I pushed through the panic and led the way to the nearest bar which, thank God, was only a few footsteps away, one staircase notwithstanding. The woman didn't object. I put this down to shock and had every intention of exploiting her vulnerability. I couldn't let her slip away.

I sat her down in a quiet alcove and went off to buy two large brandies, looking over my shoulder as I did so just to make sure she was still in situ as it were. I had no idea whether she drank alcohol or not. That's multiculturalism for you; these days one never knows what people drink or eat – Muslim, Chinese, Afro-Caribbean, Hindu, etc. etc., the list is endless.

Oh and not to mention chick-pea eating tree lovers; you have some idea if they wear traditional dress, but if it's Western attire, forget it. Alcohol drinker or not, sneaky serendipity had just arrived in a blaze of blood and guts and I wasn't going to ignore it!

She was still sitting down when I returned. I had half expected her to bolt; after all I was a total stranger. A well-dressed, handsome one, nevertheless a stranger. She took a sip of brandy and I noticed her hand shake. I also noticed the delicacy of her fingers. Remember my thing about hands? I can't say that the colour had drained from her face. She was Asian after all, but she didn't look quite so brown.

"Thank you. You've been very kind," she said. I strained to hear her words as they were so soft.

"Not at all. Take your time with the brandy." Fat chance of that, she swallowed the rest in one gulp. And there's me worrying about cultural sensibility.

"Another?" I asked.

"Yes, please." This was getting better and better. The woman was a boozer. Right up my street. I returned with another double. This time she sipped it more slowly.

"What is your name?" she asked. Those eyes. They were killing me. I was at her mercy.

"Edwin. Edwin Hillyard."

"Thank you once again, Mr Hillyard," she smiled. It was only a moment. A moment that couldn't be forgotten and one that I wanted repeated ad infinitum.

"Edwin will do. Are you feeling better? It was a horrible experience. You must have seen more than me."

"I'm used to blood and gore but not violent death. The poor man. Whatever could have driven him to do such a thing?"

'Used to blood and gore'! What the hell have I got here, I quickly thought.

"God knows," I replied calmly. "Cowardice or courage. Suicide knows both. Tragedy certainly."

I have to say that I wasn't feeling too grand myself. Witnessing a violent death close up is not to be recommended, neither is eating a curry beforehand. Fortunately, I wasn't close enough to see the actual impact or the dislocation of body parts. Thank God. Even so I was shaken. My own hands were trembling as I drank my brandy.

"Never mind me for a moment . . . er . . . Edwin, are you OK? It's an awful shock you know."

Her fingertip touched the back of my hand. It had been a long time since a woman's touch had meant so much. Her fingers moved and pressed into my wrist seeking a pulse. It was a small hand, yet one incapable of a thoughtless grasp. After a minute or two she said, "Not too bad, considering." What's this I wondered? A medico? She noticed the curious expression on my face, "I'm a doctor, trust me," she smiled. God, her face as she smiled, it was rich, decadent even in its beauty. My stabilisers crashed to the ground as I began to wonder whether my shakes had anything to do with the accident at all. She took her fingers away from my wrist, finished her brandy and stood up.

"I must go," she said as she looked at her watch, "I feel much better now. I'm on duty at the hospital and I'm already late."

"Er . . . no. I mean you can't! Damn, that sounds stupid. Look, I don't even know your name."

"Jaspreet. Jaspreet Kaur Shemare. Most people call me Jaz." Her lips moved into more of a grin this time, perhaps it was shock. I didn't know what to think. Her teeth were whiter than me and that's saying something. No staining, no fags or red wine here I thought.

"You're a Sikh?" I stated rather than asked. Her interest was piqued.

"Yes. How did you know?"

"Your name, Kaur – lioness. Singh – lion. The male."

"I'm impressed, Mr Hillyard. Sorry, Edwin."

"Good, well allow me to impress you further over supper." Straight in that's me. Without another word she dug into her handbag, actually it was more like a rucksack, took out a pen and a piece of paper and did some scribbling. There was no pause. No wary look. Just instant decision. She handed me the note and said, "I'll look forward to talking with you in less strained circumstances. You can continue to impress me." With that she turned and disappeared.

I watched her lithe body move toward the doors as long black hair fell down her back. She moved with the certainty of a highly trained athlete waiting for the starting pistol to crack, her perfect buttocks tight but with enough wobble to make any man's lust dance. She wore black trousers, a cream jacket and cream blouse. There was no Asian gold on her hand or body. Unusual.

Her immediate acceptance of my invitation had surprised me. While Sikhs were more tolerant and integrated than many ethnic minorities, the older school could still adhere to the more traditional mores of their culture: in other words, white men were off limits. Could she be a fallen Sikh I wondered? An apostate? This Sikh doctor hit the booze like a real pro too. Again unusual.

When she had gone I needed a few minutes to collect my thoughts. The woman had unsettled me. I have already said I had always found a certain uniqueness in the charms of Asian women, a femininity that could not be matched by their Western counterparts. There was a perfect peace about her. A calm and wise peace. I looked at the scrap of paper. A telephone number, all the numbers neat and exact. I found a gentleness even here. I knew she was a healer, a medicine woman and immediately I wanted her to touch me, to feel me. I wanted her to eat me alive, bones and all. Somehow, I felt certain that she could bring me back.

I tried to decide which of the two had shocked me most – the suicide or the westernised Jaz as she preferred to be called.

I wanted to know this woman. It had been such a long time since any female had battered my interest and this one had done so without even trying. I knew nothing about her. I had barged in and asked for a date. Caution had been shoved right up my arse. Husbands? Boyfriends? What had I cared? I didn't give a damn. I didn't know how old she was. I guessed early thirties, but I had always been a disgrace at judging a woman's age. With Asian women in particular, time didn't seem to savage them as much as it did white women.

I was still dazed when I was sitting on the train. What was I doing? I was married to a wife from hell but that wasn't the point. I was cheating. Not yet in any physical way, but my mind was fornicating my sacred vows into oblivion. I kept looking at the telephone number. Was it genuine? Of course it was. The woman was too honest. Her eyes told me that. Her sincerity had broken through my marriage-hardened cynicism too. I knew my instincts were right. I had always trusted them and they had never let me down. Even with Clare I had known. I had taken a risk and lost. There was no risk with this Jaz though, I just knew it. She was an absolute certainty.

As the minutes passed I realised how much was missing in my life. Love had become an emotion that I could only talk about. I had become a verbal voyeur, I had forgotten how to kiss, how to absorb.

I had forgotten me.

CHAPTER 15

There were no taxis waiting at the station. It was too late.

I pulled my personal mobile phone out of my briefcase and started to fiddle about with it. Eventually when I managed to turn it on, at least it buzzed and a picture of my darling Clare suddenly appeared. She must have put it there, no doubt in an attempt to torment me even when I was away from her.

I rarely if ever used mobile phones before all you readers start screaming about my blatant hypocrisy. I only carried one when I was away, you know, for emergencies and such like. I still couldn't understand peoples' obsession with the things. Who in their right minds wants to be contacted all the time, particularly by seething wives intent on discovering masculine peccadilloes? Each to their own, I suppose. And as for 'text speak' and all those bloody silly photos, God help us. What twisted and diminished buggers we've become!

I dithered around with a few buttons on the thing, got nowhere and made a bee line for a phone box. Believe it or not, they were quite reliable these days. I have to admit it's remarkable what a bit of competition can do. There was no point in ringing Clare for a lift as she would only have told me to go to hell. I didn't want to see her made-up face anyway; such a confrontation would have spoilt the strange feeling of well-being that seemed to be enveloping me. Or was it hope?

I arrived at the house. All the lights being on was no indication of Clare being either up and about or at home. Since our last altercation she would use as much juice as possible just to irritate me. Revenge through the medium of an electricity bill. She had no originality, and sometimes would insist on hiding my car keys, childish idiot. As I walked through the front door I noticed an unknown car hiding at the side of our triple garage. Thought I would mention the 'triple' bit just to show you how posh we were. How I had 'achieved'.

As I disposed of my hat and coat I heard the high pitched tirades of female chatter. I walked into the sitting room. The Jessica woman sat facing Clare. Her chaotic mass of hair looked as if it was about to have an orgasm. Either that or its redness was about to give the National Grid a supply crisis.

"Hello, girls," I said, all friendly and bending lips. "Eaten dinner without me?" I remembered my invitation. Jessica obviously didn't.

"Oh, hello Edwin," Jessica smiled as Clare tried to hold back the snarls.

I had interrupted their 'girlie' talk. 'Girlie', whoever thought that one up? Well, not me before you Boudiccas start creating. I hate the word as well. So demeaning. I am being sincere here, so don't knock it. As I have said before, I like women with brains (believe it or not!). 'Girlie' makes you all sound like brainless *Bunty* readers.

There was something about the way Jessica lit up when I walked into the room that gave me pause for thought. Was it a release from chronic boredom or was it just me? Either way I was surprised. After all, I hadn't been particularly friendly at our last encounter, had I? I went straight for the bottles.

"Are you ladies all right for a drink or can I get you something?" I asked.

"I'm fine, thank you Edwin, I'm driving," Jessica said. "Enough of the 'lady' though." She wasn't being oversensitive this time; I could tell by her tone of voice that she was teasing. I turned around.

"You women then. That better?"

"Much."

"Good. No fights tonight then?"

"None. A truce OK with you?"

"Fine with me," I agreed and sat down next to her.

She was dressed in one of her flowing numbers. I have to admit I was curious as to what lay beneath the fabric. It was still hard to tell. There was no fat; her arms told me that as her dress didn't cover them. There was no flesh hanging from shoulder to elbow. Age could do that to a woman, but Jessica was presumably the same age as my wife or thereabouts. She didn't look any older, anyway. Hanging mounds of skin had yet to take their toll. I was still unable to work out the bosom situation though. Again the damned dress. Going on her general build I would have said there was a fair handful, but I couldn't be certain. Her hips looked sizeable, so I had no doubt there was a big arse in the equation. All in all Jessica was all woman. No mistake. If you liked 'em big and fatless then she would have fitted the bill admirably. Petite was my territory and I was happy remaining there.

I couldn't quite understand the sudden change in attitude though. The woman was actually being friendly.

"Where have you been then, Edwin?" she asked, beaming one of her best. "Anywhere interesting? Clare won't tell me."

Clare didn't tell her because Clare didn't know. She never knew where I was, but only because she never asked.

"London. Law Society conference. Boring as hell. Anyway, never mind about me. The last time I asked what you did, you virtually told me to get lost."

"Yes, I'm sorry. I don't really like these social event things. Not me at all."

I finally decided she was indeed a beautiful woman. She was not my type though. There was too much overt strength. Jaz was the opposite, at least where the display of her feathers was concerned. As she talked to me Jessica looked straight into my eyes. I thought I caught the odd finger of flame brush across their blueness. Not a woman to duck an issue or a fight for that matter. There was clearly little if any reserve. Very unladylike and I liked ladies – as long as they didn't take it too far.

This Jessica enjoyed a fight to the death. Contention. The smiles and indulgence were a front, I was sure of it. She was playing a game, but I didn't know why. The woman was being sly.

"So, what do you do?' I asked, 'Clare isn't talking to me at the moment. Annoyed at missing her targets. Not work targets you understand, targets of a more human character."

I enjoyed watching Clare squirm. I was sure she wouldn't have told her friend about our falling out. Clare was all sweetness, light, harmony and bullshit to everyone except me. Her friend must have noticed the icicles hanging from the ceiling, but had chosen to ignore them.

"I run a law centre; like you I'm a lawyer." Oh no, I might have known.

"Really? That's quite a career change. From air stewardess to lawyer. You can't have been practising for long."

"Long enough. I prefer the not-for-profit sector to private practice. More rewarding."

It would be.

"Free impartial advice, etc., etc?"

"That's it."

"The Legal Services Commission funds you now, doesn't it?" I stated. God, I was being polite. What was it that Edmund Burke had said about manners? 'They vex or soothe, corrupt or purify, exalt or debase, barbarize or define us.' Right now I was being 'purified' by this do-gooding lawyer all right.

"Yes, they do. We have to satisfy their auditors too, otherwise we lose the funds."

"Same for private practice. Those that do legal aid anyway. Don't touch the stuff myself. Too much paper work and not enough money." This comment hit a nerve.

"Well, Edwin, we in the NFPS try to fill the gap. We're not as . . . how shall I say? . . . er . . . profit conscious as you in private practice. We don't charge for our legal advice. A good thing, surely?"

"Mercenary was the word you wanted to use, Jessica, and I have to say I couldn't agree more. Great, isn't it?"

I was off again. The woman always seemed to bring out the worst in me. I was antagonising and being a thorough bore. The truth is I had a certain sympathy for law centres and what they were trying to do. But I wasn't going to tell her that.

Jessica shifted her buttocks around for a moment and tightened her face before taking a sip of wine. I could see her thinking 'Do I or don't I'? I decided to make up her mind for her so I said with a note of sickening sincerity in my voice.

"Well, good luck to you. Your social conscience is commendable. I mean it. Are you sure you won't have another drink?"

This seemed to iron out her face. I already knew she could do a good sneer, so no wonder she and Clare had got on so well. I could see by her expression that she wasn't too sure whether I was taking the piss or not. I was of course, partly anyway. She declined the offer of a drink and our conversation remained polite. We talked about the LSC, her time in the mile-high club and friendship with Clare. Throughout Clare laughed and joked and I wished I could have had that effect on her.

Jessica, it transpired, had never married, neither had there been any 'long term' relationship or 'living together'. At thirty-two this was not unusual. Babies were a definite no-go area. In fact she was more vitriolic on this count than me, but there was a difference. She seemed to genuinely hate the little brutes. I didn't. Apparently, the woman's diary didn't allow for relationships or child bearing. She was a committed woman, committed to ambition and career. There was no room for love or even an appointment 'window' for it. Her life, I suspected, allowed only diarised love and sexual encounter as and when required. A man's heart and penis had to work flexible hours and be on call twenty-four hours a day, seven days a week.

Eventually our visitor went home. It was late after all and there was work in the morning. Clare went to bed and I went to my study. I poured myself another drink. I was drinking too much again. It was 1.30 a.m. It had been a long day, but sleep was the last thing on my mind. I was excited, tense. Jaz, suicides, an unnerving Jessica, all in one day.

I took the slip of paper out of my wallet and looked at the telephone number again. I was tempted to dial but resisted. Apart from the unsociable hour, there was the deceit to consider. What journey of betrayal was I embarking upon?

I thought of Clare sleeping and for a few moments I felt for her. She always looked so beautiful when she slept, as if her eyelids had been touched by the angels (you see I can be soppy when I want to be). She was an innocent in her own way. The law had taught me a long time ago that some people couldn't help the way they were made. Sometimes I would feel only sadness for Clare. Was she truly responsible for what she had become? Perhaps I was partly to blame. There are always two sides after all, and God knows, I was hardly a perfect husband. The only thing in my favour was the fact that I tried. God, did I not try to bring some semblance of contentment, even happiness, into our marriage? Clare was happy but the marriage was not. She was mentally incapable of distinguishing between the two.

She simply didn't think.

Contacting Jaz presented me with a moral mountain. Try as I might, I couldn't move my mind away from the fact that I was being unfaithful. I was betraying, there was no other word for it. I knew that so many men and women enjoyed infidelity at no cost to their conscience or their integrity. I wasn't one of them.

As I have said before, I had made a promise. A vow. How could I lie? How could I look Clare in the eyes? How could I snatch her smile and throw it away? I tried to reconcile my extra-marital intent with the knowledge that Clare cared little for me. She certainly didn't love. At least, that was the only conclusion I could draw. Then I remembered the early days. Was her love an infatuation, a passing fancy? I would never know. She didn't speak of such things.

The legal 'empty shell' of marriage passed through my mind. Mine was now a shell that had cracked beyond repair. I knew it was over, finished, but I didn't want bitterness and hatred. Even now I had managed to avoid these most destructive of all emotions in spite of my occasional rants and insults. I knew Clare would be happy with a generous cheque, her love bought with the quick swipe of a pen. For her there was no such thing as competition between a heart and money. The reality of her indifference to me hurt, likewise the fact that she could walk away so easily, but I knew that there was nothing I could do to change her. One can divorce and still feel a kind of love, for a while anyway or at least until the next spouse comes along. But I knew that this wouldn't apply to Clare. She would say 'Goodbye' with one of her eye-shattering smiles, touch my cheek with an endearing fingertip, throw her hair back and disappear into some hairdressing salon never to be seen again.

I finished my drink. Turned off the lights and made my decision. I had shared all my material possessions with Clare; I would no longer share all the love that was inside me. Jaz may not be the answer. She could remain a brief fantasy for all I knew, but either way I wanted my life back. I wanted to love and be loved again. By someone.

I would make our parting as painless as possible. Whatever happened with Jaz I would not humiliate Clare. I would not shove her body into a pit of sordid deceit. Even she didn't deserve this. Divorce was the only way.

And fast.

CHAPTER 16

The following day I struggled.

Files were annoying and aggravating me. I was too pre-occupied and I couldn't evict the Asian vision from my thoughts. It was madness of course. A chance meeting had sent me into a state of obsession; the woman wouldn't stop slapping my brain as the piece of paper with her telephone number on it perspired and wrinkled in my pocket. A night of confused sleep hadn't helped my stubborn tension either.

My guilt.

Lunchtime had calmed the telephones. I sat at my desk. "Get on with it, man," I kept saying to no one in particular, "ring the bloody woman!"

I felt like a bumbling teenager on a first date. What do I say? What do I do?

Despite being retired from the dating game for some time, I was still a veteran. My womanising techniques just needed a little polishing. I stared at all the familiar objects in my office, kept moving my backside from one cheek to the other, smoked like a demented squaddie and finally picked up the telephone. She was probably saving some poor devil's life and wouldn't be at home anyway.

My fingers pushed the buttons and the nerves in their tips jumped slightly. Four rings, and for a change my call was answered by the reality of a human voice and not the counter-feit fraud of a pre-recorded guarantee to infuriate.

"Hello." It was Jaz. I knew. Even the one simple word made my stomach leap.

"Hello, Jaz. It's the man from the underground, Edwin." (I nearly said it's 'Our Man In Havana', that's how nervous I was – I don't know why but the two sentences sounded distinctly similar.) "I hope I'm not telephoning at an inconvenient time?" Edmund Burke, not Jessica Howard, ruled now.

"Oh, hello! Thank you for calling Edwin, I wondered whether you would or not. Funny way to meet someone after all." She giggled. "How I allowed you to drag me off like that I just don't know. I trusted you somehow. Most odd." There was laughter in her voice now. "I've never heard of a suicide being the catalyst for a date before. Not even at the movies!" Her voice was enthusiastic and natural. "It's not inconvenient at all, don't be silly. I actually managed a full night's sleep last night. I've spent the morning tidying up my flat. Looked as if a bomb had hit it. God, I'm terrible and now I'm talking a load of nonsense. I'm sorry!"

I swear I could hear her smiling as my stomach popped and gurgled. Her voice was making me feel so utterly juvenile. I couldn't stop grinning; you'd think someone had just told me I'd won the Lottery or something. There were no harsh tones to her voice. No sandpaper words. Her vocal chords simply cruised down the telephone line.

"Charming nonsense though," I replied, meaning every word. "So how are you, have you recovered from that awful suicide yesterday?"

"I'm fine. I was shaken at the time. Thought I had seen it all. Thank you again for being so kind. I don't know how I would have coped. I'm supposed to be a doctor, used to death. Not that kind of death though. Anyway, how are you? You were shocked too. You'd gone white."

"I'm fine now, but I don't mind telling you that I've had to gird my loins in order to make this call. I'm as nervous as hell."

"I don't believe that. You seemed very confident to me. In control."

"Not always, I assure you."

"That's nice to know. It means you're human."

"Human?" I had forgotten my humanity over the years; it was refreshing to be reminded that I did in fact possess at least a modest amount of 'humanity'.

"Yes, perfectly natural by the way. You have a lovely voice, Edwin, do you know that? Incredibly sexy." This took me aback. Dr Jaz was a spicy one all right and I'm not making any puns either. She was making me grin again.

"Glad you think so."

"God, I could listen to it all night. Looks and voice. So when are we going to meet?" Straight to the point, see what I mean? So much for we men setting the agenda. Not any more, boys, but then perhaps female wilfulness does have its advantages; at least there is no messing about.

"You're not slow in coming forward, are you?" I replied.

"No. There's no point. I'm sorry though if I seem a little forward. I mean it. I know I can be too forthright sometimes. It's a fault of mine. Just tell me to shut up. I won't mind, really." This spontaneous recognition of her perceived shortcoming impressed me. She was an honest woman and delightful with it. This was getting better and better. I wanted to leave the office and jump on the next train to London.

"How about Saturday?"

"When?"

"Well, how about afternoon tea at Claridges?" I wasn't out to impress, I had given up on those antics years ago. However, doing something different, well that's another matter. Besides I had a feeling that 'impressive' overtones wouldn't cut any ice with the good doctor. She was one of those women who obviously took everything in their stride. "If we don't like each other, at least tea and cakes don't take too long to finish off. There's a quick 'get out clause'. Full-blown dinner, now that's something else. Nothing worse than having to be polite to someone one doesn't like for hours on end."

Jaz laughed. Come to think of it, there probably wasn't much else she could do.

"Well, I must say your enthusiasm certainly knows how to charm a girl, Edwin. Claridges for afternoon tea? It's different though, I'll give you that." See what I mean?

"I don't mean to be rude. Sorry. Damn, I'm at it now, apologising."

"Don't worry, afternoon tea is fine. Besides if we do like each other, and I know we will, then we'll have more of the evening together."

"You know, do you?"

"Oh, yes. You Westerners do not appreciate the power of karma." She was smiling again. I could feel her lips moving.

"No, you're right there, Philistines the lot of us. You'll be telling me next that Vishnu was hanging around the underground making sure neither of us jumped off the wheel . . . Oops, sorry, I forgot you're a Sikh not a Hindu. One God and all that if I remember correctly." She laughed again, the sound drawing me closer. She had a sense of humour, crucial in my book. Also she didn't appear to be too precious or sensitive about things, which was just as well as you may have already noticed I don't tend to hold back where my opinions are concerned. If people don't like what I say – tough. Freedom of expression and all that, arrogant bastard that I am.

"Ah, I remember, you seem to know a bit about our Sikh culture. I'll have to watch my step."

"Not that much. A little knowledge and so on. Right, never mind about all that, I'll see you Saturday, three o'clock sharp in the main foyer at Claridges." Time for me to take control.

"Great. I'll look forward to it."

"Good. Just one thing. How can you fit in so easily with my demands? You're a doctor. I thought they never had time for anything, particularly hospital ones."

"Where there's a will, Edwin."

"And where do you live anyway? I know it's London, but where?" Funny how we forget to ask the most obvious questions at the beginning of a courtship dance, isn't it?

"Baker Street – at least one of the roads that leads off it."

"Marylebone village just around the corner."

"That's right."

This set off some more stupid conversation about nothing. Neither of us seemed to want to disconnect. Jaz didn't question me about my marital status. She allowed me to tell her what I did for a living and didn't ask what car I drove. None of her questions were intrusive. It was as if she wanted my personal details to be divulged under my own steam. There was no interrogation.

Sometimes one can meet a woman and the chemical reaction is perfect. On my first date with Clare there had been doubts, with Jaz there were none. The woman lifted me with her voice. She was so natural, nothing about her character seemed forced. There was no coercion. So far I couldn't find any fault. And despite my cynicism warning me I was prepared to ignore it. Clare had taught me to never ignore anything again, but on this occasion I was inclined, like Jaz, to put my faith in the wily ways of ancient karma (mind you, everyone these days bangs on about 'karma', yet it hasn't done the human race much good though, has it?).

There was something so truthful about the woman. That is the only way I can describe it. There was humour, intelligence and physical beauty, but most of all she was true, which more than anything else drew me to her. Her acquiescence to the time and place of our meeting had been immediate. She hadn't demanded a 'pencilling in' or a 'let me check my diary'. I knew that her love would never be 'by appointment only' or worse still, by text or email.

When our telephone conversation finally ended I sat back in my chair. A few minutes of dramatic meeting through the medium of untimely death, twenty minutes of conversation and I was smitten. So much for my hardened cynicism. I felt warm, not hot. Hopeful, not passionate. Here was a woman who knew how to return. To give. There was a certainty in her nature that demanded my pursuit. I wanted her more than even my fantasies would permit.

When I had finished for the day my reluctance to return home had become even more intense. There was nothing there.

I knew that Clare would have to be confronted. I would propose a two-year separation and a divorce by consent. I would need Counsel's opinion on a financial settlement figure first, just to give me a rough idea if nothing else. Clare wouldn't be fair about anything, I knew that. Expected it. Thank God we didn't have children, I didn't dare think about that. I had already decided to pay whatever it would take, regardless of legal fairness and equity.

What price peace of mind, after all?

CHAPTER 17

The following morning I felt unwell. Hung-over would be more accurate. These shaky mornings were becoming more and more frequent. Even I was beginning to worry. I didn't bother to dress, but instead went downstairs to the kitchen. Remarkably Clare was up and enjoying her coffee. No caffeine of course, it might have given her too much energy. She sat at the oak table all Olay, Elizabeth Hard-on (or not where I was concerned) and expensive cloth.

"Good morning," I said in an attempt at civility, "how are you today?"

There was no reply. Her mobile phone got in before her tongue. David Cameron was ringing for some urgent advice, no doubt. She turned her back on me for a moment, mumbled something and then actually spoke, "Aren't you going into work today?"

"I don't think so. Bad stomach. I'll work at home. Get one of the girls to bring some stuff over for me."

"Oh," she seemed disappointed, not that I expected an 'Oh good, we can spend the day together. I'll make you a nice lunch. Something to help your stomach. Sit down darling, I'll find you something to ease the pain.'

"Is there a problem?" I enquired.

"No, not really. Jessica thought she might take a day off. She said she might call over later for some coffee."

"Well, I won't put you out. I'll be in my study. Won't know I'm here. In my own home too. Aren't I considerate?"

"Very." There was no snarl, which surprised me. "I'm going out shopping this morning. Forgot to get something yesterday."

"Did you? Forget, I mean? Not like you at all, you must be getting senile." So much for my attempts at civility, my hangover was getting worse, more toxic.

"That's good, coming from you. Remember, you are thirteen years older than me darling, but I have to admit you don't look it." The woman actually smiled at me. She meant it too. She wasn't even snarling or trying to compete with my general unpleasantness. Something was up. She was after something. Had to be.

"Do you want anything while I'm out?" she asked with yet another smile.

Something was definitely up, I nearly fell off my chair. What the hell was going on?

"What? . . . er . . . No, I'm fine. Thank you for asking."

"Well, I'm off now. Ring me if you think of something. You might need me to go to the chemist for you. The smoking won't help your stomach, you know."

With that she was gone, leaving me in a state of shock. I rolled another cigarette. My hands were trembling and it wasn't nerves. I had had a few too many late last night, I was having 'a few too many' most nights. It was catch-up time. The mornings after were getting worse. Missing work was a bad sign. The beginning of an alcoholic end. It had to stop and quickly.

I couldn't help it, but my alcohol-soaked brain returned to my dear wife's unexpected concern for my welfare. What was wrong with her? Or 'right' would be more accurate. She was always a moody cow in the mornings. Particularly first thing. She had asked after my well-being, for God's sake! Had even smiled! I decided it was normal female madness. You know, faulty wiring. A hormonal frolic. They're all prone to them. Sane days and insane days. The former were a rare event where Clare was concerned, unlike most women who at least managed to achieve a more respectable fifty-fifty average.

I rang my secretary and asked her to bring some files over, the ones that needed my urgent attention. I didn't want Tom on my tail. I was surprised he hadn't rung. My tongue went into immediate Afro-Caribbean bashing as was my habit, and then I quickly remembered Jaz. Like the drink, my 'blick' (as the whites in South Africa like to call their black brethren) bashing was another offensive habit that would have to stop. First thing to do that morning was to give Tom a call. Apart from lying about my troubled stomach – he knew I was drinking too much so he wouldn't believe a word – I wanted his opinion on my matrimonial intentions. He was the expert on these matters, not me.

The files duly arrived and Tom was going to call late afternoon. We would hide in my study and he could give me the good news in private.

At 11.30 my concentration was interrupted by a knock on the kitchen door. I only just heard it. Usually people went up to the front; only close friends came around the back. It was too early for Tom. The intrusion was welcome – any excuse to get away from the files – and besides, my head was starting to win the war with the painkillers. I opened the door and who should be standing there but Muz Jessica Howard.

"Hello," I tried to smile, with difficulty. "Clare isn't in. I thought she was going to telephone you or something. She mentioned you might drop by." I didn't ask her in.

"I haven't heard anything from her," Jessica looked puzzled, "my mobile's on the blink, so perhaps she tried and couldn't get through."

"That's technology for you, always reliable." We stood there for a few moments. There was still a tension between us. The other night had been polite, but that's all. It had been hard work for both of us. There was something different though this time, the woman's smile being broader, more sincere. There was enthusiasm in her face too, even expectation. This was the second woman I had encountered that day who was acting totally out of character and it was beginning to genuinely disturb me. I was still pissed, that was it, what other explanation could there be?

My foul humour softened as I asked her in, "Well, please come in anyway. You can use the phone here. No doubt Clare is only a short distance away. Rummaging around Bury I expect." I waved my arm at the kitchen telephone, "Please feel free. Would you like some tea or coffee?"

"Do you have red bush tea?"

"I do. Have one myself while I'm at it, the anti-oxidants will do me good." Her eyebrows lifted in surprise. Smart-arse probably thought I'd never heard of the stuff.

She went over to the telephone and started dialling. She knew Clare's number straight off, I noted. There must have been a fair amount of communicating between the two.

I also noted that there were no tents today. Jeans and a tee shirt. I had been all wrong. She was well proportioned and no big arse as I had previously thought. In fact the woman had one hell of a body, too tall for me, but nevertheless . . . For a moment I imagined her in one of those sado-masochistic porno films, you know the sort, all high heels, leather boots up to the buttocks, whips, chains and some poor bugger about to get a lamping. My eyes went from sizeable tit to toe in a split second and quickly collated all the filthy things I could have done to the woman. That's men for you. Still Neanderthals the lot of us and I'm no exception, believe me.

I heard her tell Clare where she was, there was a 'see you in a few', the receiver went down and then she turned around to face me.

"You were right. Clare's in Bury. She won't be long."

"Good, here's your tea."

"Thank you."

"My pleasure."

"I didn't expect you to be here, Edwin. Lucky you were."

"Working at home today. Bad stomach. Day off?" I nearly said that every day is a day off for you lot in the not-for-profit sector but thought better of it. I was warming to her body.

"Yes. Clare and I thought we might do something. Lunch perhaps."

Now I am no fool when it comes to recognising the female signals of 'I want to shag you'. Jessica was all eyes and lips. She was going into 'I want sex with you' mode. I was certain of it and I wasn't surprised either. The face at the door, her whole demeanour. I also knew that the emancipated – sorry again, liberated – brigade made no bones about making a pass. Subtlety was not their thing. Her hand had touched mine when I gave her the mug. There had been a few moments of silence. Eyes. It's always in the eyes. There had been too many smiles and grins. Had her phone really been on the blink? Had she expected Clare to be out? Funny how mutual dislike between a man and a women can often be the harbinger of sexual attraction, isn't it?

"Edwin, may I ask you a personal question?"

"You may, but whether I answer it is another matter." My guard was up.

"Fair enough. You and Clare are not happy, are you?" The presumptuous sod. I didn't even know her!

"Is that what she told you?"

"Yes."

"Well, good for her." I couldn't help it, but my voice started to grate with irritation. "Actually, I'm a happily married man (no, don't laugh) – not that my joyful state has anything to do with you. In fact nothing about my marriage has anything at all to do with you. So please stick to other people's business, not mine."

The woman ignored my warning tones. "You admit there is a problem then?"

"Oh, for Heaven's sake, Jessica. Take another day off will you? Mind your own fucking business. Now is that clear enough?" I can be straight to the point, too.

"Very."

"Good. Now I have work to do, so if you will please excuse me?"

"Wait a minute Edwin . . . please." She hadn't reacted to my insulting behaviour as expected. Full of surprises, I'll give her that. Now she was being humble. "I'm sorry. I was too blunt. You're quite right, it's none of my business. Clare is my friend and you must know that she talks to me. I really am sorry, I should have kept my mouth shut."

"Perhaps Clare is the one who should keep her mouth shut," I conceded. The woman's sudden bout of unexpected contrition had caught me off guard. She was actually allowing her feminine side to take over. I was softening far too quickly.

"Edwin, can we please try and get on? I don't want to fight." She held out her hand. Her face was making all kinds of invitations. I had no idea which was the genuine one. I took her hand and shook it. Firm grips all round.

"Now, I really do have work to do. Clare won't be long. Help yourself to another tea if you want one. Enjoy your lunch." I went off to my study and carried on with the hateful files. Jessica had foxed me yet again.

Later on I heard Clare shout, "I won't be long Jess! Quick shower. Couple of minutes!" Clare 'a couple of minutes' in the shower? That will be the day. The woman did her origami practise in the bathroom. 'Jess' was in for a long wait. Much later, I heard the door close and women's voices crash-land on the gravel as they walked to their cars.

I managed to do most of my work by late afternoon. I was about to throw the dictaphone through the window when I heard another shout.

"Edwin! Edwin! Where are you?"

"In here, you bloody coconut!" came my polite reply.

It was Tom.

My study door opened and in rolled Tom – well, not exactly 'roll'. Alistair 'rolled', Tom was all grit and muscle. "Ah, there you are. Hard at it I see. Bad stomach, my glorious black arse. Hangover more like."

"And 'hello' to you, Tom. Well, are we? How is the arsehole?"

"Grand now, thanks. Just grand. It's healed up nicely. Not happy about the red wine restrictions though. Can't have everything I suppose. Claret or piles the size of tennis balls. Not much of a choice, is it? Never mind." He parked himself down into one of my leather armchairs. It howled in agony at the impact. "Right. So what's up Edwin? You know I don't do home visits."

"Bugger off, Tom." I went to sit down on the other leather armchair. This one sighed with relief. "I want to get divorced. You're the expert. I want to know how much. Don't give me the Matrimonial Causes Act bit, I know enough. I need to know how much it will take for Clare to go quietly."

Tom rubbed his chin and then ran his hand through his hair, with difficulty it must be said. Tungsten steel wire didn't lend itself to thoughtful intrusions.

"I'm sorry to hear that . . ."

"Never mind the bleeding heart crap, Tom."

"Right, fair enough. Well first of all, Edwin, I need a list of all your assets. You know the form. Bank accounts, policies, property, etc., etc. Once I have all this I'll get Counsel's opinion."

"I thought you would say that."

"I'll need to know everything that Clare has as well."

"That's simple enough. Nothing."

"Are you sure?"

"Sure."

"What about interests in Wills and so on. Hasn't she got any family?"

"None."

"Oh well, that keeps things simple."

"Look Tom, we keep this to ourselves. All I want is a yard-stick. A rough idea. I know you can't act on the divorce yourself, you're too close. I'll do that bit unless it gets complicated then I'll have to instruct someone else. To hell with solicitors, they cost too much."

"You're right there," he couldn't help smiling. "I'm glad you're keeping me out of it. Granted I don't really know Clare all that well, but it could be embarrassing."

"I know. Don't worry. I won't file any petition until I know what kind of settlement I'm looking at. I haven't told Clare about my intentions yet. I won't either until I know the price tag." He looked at me with his huge brown eyes as he put on his serious face. We were close friends. He had rights.

"Edwin, to hell with your 'bleeding heart crap', I'm sorry about all this, you know. I really am. I know it's been coming for a long time, but even so. Divorce is never easy. Believe me I know, I'm a bloody master at it. I appreciate it's a difficult time for you. You may laugh and joke on the surface, but I know what's going on underneath. I know you, you old bastard. I'm not going to judge who's right or wrong, only you can do that. Suffice it to say I'm here if you need me. You know that. And Edwin, one thing as your friend: lay off the booze. I hit it when I last divorced. Drunk for two months – mind you, it sure as hell beat the anti-depressants and tranquillisers. Had a great time really." Tom started to laugh then quickly checked himself. He was always laughing, but right now he was trying to be serious. "I don't recommend it though. It took six months for me to feel human again."

"I know, I know," I said. "Thank you."

"Right, well I'm not going to get all mawkish, you know where I am. I'll get that opinion for you and we can go from there. The courts are always up and down on matrimonial property. Ought to put the whole troublesome mess on the statute books once and for all, if you ask me. Bring some certainty for clients. Anything else?"

"No, no thanks, Tom. I'll see you tomorrow. You're right about the alcohol. Already made up my mind to do something about it this morning." There was Jaz too.

"Good. I'll see you tomorrow then . . . Oh and try and make the divorce as clean as possible. Not sure if Clare will oblige from what you've told me in the past, but try. Makes life easier, believe me. Slanging matches don't help anyone. Fortunately you don't have children."

"I realise that."

"Good, because some women turn them into lethal weapons; when I think of some of the divorces I've done, doesn't bear thinking about. There's some evil bitches out there. Known one or two of them myself. I had enough of a war over my own boy. Where would I be without my Lucretia I ask . . .? Anyway, I'm off, so take it easy Edwin."

As Tom walked to the door he paused for a moment as if something was bothering him. I had already noticed a slight strain in his laughter, or at least there was something I couldn't quite put my finger on. Tom and I were close, I knew my partner inside out and something was up, I was sure of it.

"Everything all right Tom? I asked. "Nothing else you want to talk about is there?" He stood still as if deep in thought or trying to make up his mind about something.

Then he turned around and said, "What . . .? Oh no, nothing Edwin. Just trying to work out the best way forward for your divorce."

"OK, if you say so." I wasn't convinced. "Come on Tom, what's up? Spit it out. I won't tell anyone, I promise."

"Oh bloody hell, Edwin. As if you haven't got enough on your plate . . . But you know, after two 'previous' as it were and umpteen bouts of 'in betweens', you'd think I'd know some-thing about women, wouldn't you? Like hell. That wife of mine is playing up, God knows why. The thing is it's out of character. Sorry to bring it up bearing in mind present circumstances, but you did ask. I don't fancy any more wedding cake, that's all."

I couldn't help laughing. Bloody wedding cake again! 'Playing up'?

"What do you mean, Tom?" I asked, not knowing whether to laugh again or cry. As far as I was concerned it was a woman's prerogative to play up. You know, the natural order of things, etc., etc. "She isn't having a ding-dong with anyone else, is she?"

"God, no. Not as far as I know anyway. Her moods are all over the place, that's all. One minute as nice as pie, the next daggers in the eyes."

"Look Tom, sorry and all that, but what's new. That's women for you. Come on, you're an experienced man, you know what they're like. Nuts. All of them. Lucretia is just being female. Don't worry about it."

"If you say so."

"I do. I suspect you are being a little too sensitive, that's all. Maybe you've become allergic to wedding cake or something. Who knows? Take no notice is my advice." This was good coming from me. Edwin Hillyard, bloody relationship expert and ha ha to that!

"Yes, you're right Edwin. Still, needed to get it off my chest. Women, my God where would we be without them, eh?" At last the old smile was back. "Right then, I really am off now. Keep things calm with Clare and let me have that information as soon as possible. I'll see you in the office tomorrow?"

"You will. Now bugger off. I've got a bad head."

When Tom had gone I realised that up to now divorce had been an inexact science. Now it was becoming something I could smell and touch. The rushing Rubicon had been crossed.

CHAPTER 18

It wasn't far off 5 o'clock and Tom's anus was still playing up, in spite of his telling Edwin how 'grand' his anal condition was. The medic who had removed the stitches hadn't been too gentle, the racist incompetent having yanked them out with a pair of pliers, at least that's what it had felt like. As he opened his car door he laughed at the thought; playing the race card now and again always amused him.

Before driving home he rang the office just to make certain that nothing urgent had cropped up. Apart from one of his Legal Aid clients marching in and demanding the use of a telephone so that he could discuss his misfortune with God (he had a direct-line number apparently), all was quiet according to his secretary, who couldn't stop giggling.

Half-an-hour later Tom walked into open warfare.

The seven-year-old Annie was receiving a hot backside from her mother along with a few screams of outrage and yells of "Why don't you do as you're told, you little shit?" His son Rupert, aged nine, was cowering behind one of the kitchen-table chairs not knowing what on earth to do as the whites of his eyes tried to take it all in. He had never seen anything like it as his mum had finally lost the plot. As far as he was concerned, if his new mother had always been loopy, his old mother hadn't been much better, but that was mothers for you. He didn't want to think about his female teachers; that lot really did take the biscuit. As for his two sisters, well . . . According to his father it all had something to do with particular days of the month, including school holidays!

Tom stood in the doorway and quickly took in the chaos. Orange juice was creeping along the floor, a chair had been tipped over and his son's head was covered in pasta with a lump of bolognaise on top, just to finish the job off by the looks of it.

"What? What . . .?" Tom managed to splutter. His previous denouncement of his anus was a minor thing in comparison with the violence and destruction presently confronting him. "What . . . what the . . .?!"

"Don't *you* start, Tom!" Lucretia shouted. "Just don't you start! Don't you dare say a bloody word!"

Tom kept quiet. He had never seen Lucretia in such a temper before and the language . . . dear, oh dear; he had never known her to hit one of the children either. The other morning came back to him with a vengeance. Annie continued to howl with the shock of it all while Rupert tried to remove dangling bits of spaghetti from his face. Like his father he was keeping quiet.

After a minute or so Tom said quietly, "All right . . . all right. Now let's all calm down. Come on Lucretia, come and sit down for a minute, I'll pour you a glass of wine. Annie, you go up to your room and Rupert, go to the bathroom and clean yourself up."

"But Daddy, Daddy, I didn't do anything!" Annie wailed, tears flying about everywhere. "I didn't do anything! Mummy just hit me, she just hit me! Nasty Mummy and . . . and . . . I've got a sore bottom."

Tom squatted down and took the little one's hands. He had to be careful not to undermine his wife; children were good at dividing and conquering.

"Now I'm sure Mummy had a good reason for smacking you," he said gently, "so go up to your room and I'll come and see you later. Will you do that for me, please?" After a sniff or two Annie concurred and walked out of the kitchen. No one argued with Tom; as for Mummy, now that was a different matter. Tom looked at his son who was still cowering and unsure of what to do next. "Go on Rupert, go and clean yourself up, please."

A minute or so later all that could be heard was Lucretia's sobs interspersed with slurps of red wine.

Tom sat on a chair facing his wife. "OK, so what's the matter, Lucretia? This isn't you. It really isn't. You're not pregnant are you? I mean we haven't been too careful lately, have we?"

"Pregnant? Oh dear God, Tom. Whatever gave you that idea? If I was pregnant you would be the first to know, trust me."

"Sorry, just thinking out loud."

"Well don't!" Lucretia was still angry about something, but what? The tears were still falling and the wine was still being gulped.

"Why are you so angry, so upset." Tom was keeping calm, what else could he do? "I mean the other morning you flew off the handle over nothing."

"I don't know, Tom!" Lucretia was starting to shout again. "I just don't know!"

"Calm down, please calm down, Lucretia. I don't want to fight you. I'm only trying to help." He took one of her hands and stroked her fingers. "Maybe you should see someone. The GP or something."

There was silence for a few moments as Lucretia finally started to gain control of herself. Eventually the tears stopped as she sniffed and dabbed at her face with a paper handkerchief. She looked at Tom, who could only see confusion and pain in her eyes. It almost broke his heart.

"Oh yes," she mumbled. "I suppose it will be a shrink next, or Prozac. Well you can forget all that. I'm not depressed or anything, just a little bad tempered . . . emotional. Look Tom, I'm sorry. I know I shouldn't have hit Annie but she asked for it, she's been at me all day. School holidays are a nightmare, the child never stops from the moment she gets up to the moment she goes to bed. She's incredibly demanding. A little angel in school apparently, but at home – and you're not here all day – she's a monster, believe me. The other two are no trouble but Annie, well . . . I just don't know . . ."

"All right, all right . . ." Tom murmured quietly. It wasn't all right at all, something was definitely wrong, and there was a lot more to this than simple juvenile torture. Even so; he stood up and put his arms around his wife. He hated seeing her so distressed, so troubled, but it seemed there was nothing he could do. She wouldn't listen to anything he suggested, and he knew how stubborn she could be. Hell on earth wouldn't budge her. If she wouldn't see a doctor, then that's all there was to it. What was he supposed to do, hold a gun to her head? Not all the love in the world would make Lucretia do something she didn't want to do. Tom loved his wife desperately, so much so that he had to give in. For now anyway.

A few moments later Lucretia stood up and kissed Tom on the lips. The smile that had caught him hook, line and sinker was back. The sudden transformation was extraordinary. "I'm being stupid Tom, I know it. Probably just the menopause. I have been a bit moody lately I know, and my periods have been a bit erratic – and no, I'm not pregnant." This time she started to laugh. "You should be so lucky! Now where's that little monster of ours? I'd better go and say I'm sorry or something, she didn't deserve having her backside spanked."

Suddenly all was well in the Smith-Twiddy household as if nothing had happened, but for a moment Tom regretted not speaking with Edwin when he had had the chance.

CHAPTER 19

I stood outside Claridges smoking, pacing and contemplating the mellifluous clouds of cigarette smoke as they swirled around my head and reminded me not to drop my dog-end on the pavement outside one of London's best (so much for the poetic prose, eh? I always ruin it).

A top-hatted flunkey gave me a warning sniff, but I'm not sure that he really cared that much. After all Claridges didn't own the pavement, did it? At least I didn't think it did, although these days anything was possible.

Jaz was on time. Punctual almost to the minute, early if anything. This was a good start. Remember my views on punctuality?

After we had exchanged polite greetings and reminders that neither of us looked like shit after all (sudden death can distort one's memory, you understand) I followed her through the revolving doors observing bum and general body shape as I did so. Everything was as I remembered. The woman looked as if she had just stepped out of the Taj Mahal and I'm not talking about an Indian restaurant either. Don't misunderstand me, she wasn't all flowing sari, gold bangle and red dot stuck on the forehead or anything, she was just unmistakably Indian and wouldn't have been out of place sitting alongside some Mughal emperor as he dispensed the odd bit of charitable largesse.

When she walked into the foyer a few heads turned – male and female. She was wearing a cream suit, skirt just above the knee. Her long black hair still fell freely down her back. Damn, did it flow. Like Clare she was small boned and petite, the type that always caught my eye. Everything about her was delicate, feminine.

I allowed my hand to touch her waist (wouldn't do to be too tactile at this point, might be accused of invading her space) and guided her in the direction of a semi-circular pale green leather seat big enough for two.

"Thank you Edwin," she smiled as she gazed into my face a little longer than was usual and sat down. I'd forgotten how white her teeth were; they were perfect and aligned in all the right directions. This was another area where black and brown folk have the edge on we pale faced whiteys. Their dark skin accentuates the brilliance of their gnashers.

She wasn't the only one refreshing her memory.

"I still look the same, I assure you," I said.

"Oh dear, I'm staring. I do apologise."

"Don't worry. You merit a stare or two yourself. Some of the men in here seem to think so too. You do look lovely and punctual with it. It's my turn to be impressed."

"Thank you again. I don't do the lady's prerogative thing. No excuse for bad manners."

'Lady'. Thank God she didn't insist on the 'woman' word, another Jessica would have ruined everything.

"Well, I just hope your recollections are not too disappointing. I did have a shower before leaving the house, I promise. Even put on a clean shirt especially." A few sparks jumped off her lips as she grinned and eyed me up and down.

"No, not at all. Quite the opposite I assure you. You dress beautifully I must say, not like a lot of men. I like the tie and shoes."

"Now it's my turn to say 'thank you'. Now then let me order us something. Do you mind if I order for us?"

"Not at all. Carry on." The brilliant smile was back. "It will make a change having someone else make the decisions."

"Jolly good. I won't order Assam tea I promise." Strangely for a first date there didn't seem to be any tension between us. We were oozing into each other rather well.

As I tried to attract a waiter's attention I noticed some chap come in and slip one of them a fifty-pound note before he had even sat down. Milton's 'bowings and cringings of an abject people' immediately came to mind. The fifty quid could have fed some poor bugger for a year in Africa, yet we in the West couldn't understand why our affluence was causing so much resentment and even hatred among so many non-Western cultures. You have to laugh, don't you?

Eventually I managed to order a champagne tea. Only the best for my Asian beauty. In due course the Taittinger Millesime 2002 arrived along with smoked salmon finger sandwiches and scones that were so light they nearly flew off the plate. Jaz made the first stab with a hungry fingertip. Her nails were clean and polished not varnished or despoiled with those false white tip things. At forty pounds each for the afternoon tea I was beginning to be mindful of a certain hypocrisy (yet again!) where my good self and the generous patron were concerned.

When the waiter had eventually stopped fussing about with the white and green striped crockery (he sure as hell wasn't going to get a fifty-pound tip out of me, hypocrisy notwithstanding, and could bow and cringe his way to Mars and back for all I cared) Jaz took a sip of her champagne and said. "It is beautiful here, Edwin. A good choice if I may say so. All this Art Deco is fascinating. Look at the strong lines and sexy curves."

'Sexy curves', that was a new one.

"Basil Ionides had his finger in the Art Deco pie if I remember correctly," I replied. "Mixed it up with a bit of Art Nouveau, Cubism and Futurism. It's all quite striking, I have to admit. Odd name though, 'Basil Ionides', bit of a mix there too. A Greek Brit maybe."

A giggle cavorted with the champagne bubbles for a moment which made me move closer to her. I couldn't help it. There was a natural warmth to her, a pleading to be touched.

"Sikhism, art and design?" she teased. "You are a well informed man I must say. Whatever are you going to come out with

132

next?" Her own body was starting to move closer now. We were thinking along the same lines – I hoped so anyway.

"Not at all," I replied as I fiddled with a smoked salmon sliver of nothing. Half a bite was enough to see it off. "I did my research before meeting you, thought that being a know-all would impress. But I've now come to the conclusion that it won't cut any ice at all. You're not that daft, Jaz."

Out of the blue she took my hand and held it in hers. Her dark brown eyes with their blue and yellow speckles looked into my own and for a few seconds neither of us said anything. There was mischief, coriander, cumin and a good dose of Scotch Bonnet pepper in those eyes, make no mistake.

"I'm glad you think so, but believe me I can be amazingly reckless and self-willed from time to time as my extremely patient father will confirm." She didn't let go of my hand, which was fine by me, I was enjoying every minute of it. Clare hadn't held my hand for years. Jaz's fingers were long but not skinny and nobbled. I could easily imagine them healing.

"No harm in that. I like spirit in a woman . . . within reason, of course."

It was my turn to smile now and look rather stupid I suspect. There we were, sitting in Claridges filling our faces with scones and champagne as we nigh on ate each other alive with our eyes . . . so how juvenile is that then?

I decided to change the subject. Apart from anything else I was rather curious. "So, you are a Sikh, Jaz?"

"Yes, I only wash my hair on Monday and Thursdays. You know, ritual and all that."

"Do you?" I wasn't sure whether she was joking or not. I still hardly knew her, although I was getting there quite rapidly. She didn't seem the sort of woman who hid behind an iron-clad veil of 'hung up and bust up' relationships.

"Don't be silly, Edwin. I'm only joking. Some Sikh girls do stick to the traditions and rituals quite rigidly; I don't. I'm not at all orthodox. Not even religious full stop. I only go along with the saris etc. when family occasions demand it."

"So Guru Nanak doesn't rule then? You're a fallen Sikh girl, Westernised beyond repair. I thought as much when I met you at the Underground station. Very bold, um . . . outgoing. Bet your old man loves it."

"Not fallen, exactly. I stand on the sidelines. I have to keep my dear father happy though, you're right about that. I love him, but he still likes to play the Asian patriarch. Doesn't work of course, but I've found that sometimes it's better to humour him. I am certainly 'Westernised' as you put it. Born and bred here, British through and through, but with a few pints of Punjabi blood in my veins just to ensure balance. I enjoy the best of both worlds." She looked at me for a moment and smiled – well actually, it was probably more of a cheeky grin. Then she added, "You see I have the mysticism of the East and the vulgarity of the West in me. Good, isn't it?"

I returned the grin. Her East and West collision was fine by me. Mysticism and vulgarity. A heady mix indeed.

"Not quite a true coconut then, not like my partner," I said. She laughed in that delightful way of hers and I looked straight into her eyes again. I couldn't help it, they demanded and bullied attention even though her voice was gentle and measured. "Your generation of Asian women are more . . . er, how shall I say . . . independent, more as you say yourself, 'self-willed'. You're not so prepared to toe the traditional line."

"Up to a point, Edwin. Only up to a point." This was getting interesting.

"What do you mean exactly? I thought young Asians, or should I say young Sikhs, were freeing themselves from tradition and historical observance, particularly you women. After all many of you are now doctors, lawyers, accountants and so on. Look at you."

"Yes, I know. Some of us have managed to break away, but believe me, we're in the minority. Many Sikh girls will go to university, drink themselves into a stupor, discover all there is to know about sex, obtain a degree, then return home. At this point they'll go back to being the dutiful daughter and play by the rules. The parents will arrange a suitable husband and that's it. Either she will live with the in-laws, as is the custom, or if the couple are lucky enough they'll own their home. Or be given one by one of the fathers. Believe me Edwin, Asian women are not that liberated, Sikhs in particular. Most enjoy themselves for a few years and then knuckle down. The man still calls the shots. The father is God. Mine certainly likes to think so." She paused and smiled, "I must be boring you to death."

"No, not at all. I went out with a Sikh girl once. Like you say, she had done all the university bit. Had recently qualified as a solicitor. She was living in one of her father's houses. She was always terrified that we would be seen together. The Sikh network apparently. She was extremely liberated in more ways than one, and yet when it came to the crunch her father had the last word. She wouldn't defy him. Or her brothers. I remember having to drop her off a couple of streets away from her house so that she wouldn't be seen with a white man."

I also remembered how her nether regions had tasted like an inebriated Friday night Vindaloo but kept quiet, no point in lowering the tone, not yet anyway. I just kept my fingers crossed that Jaz didn't consume umpteen bowls of fiery curry.

"Ah, so that's how you know so much about we Sikhs. Anyway that's exactly my point. Lots of Sikh girls will tell you now liberated they are, but deep down this isn't the case. I've seen the most incredible hypocrisy. Most will always do as they're told. As for mixed marriages, well most Sikh fathers will just about tolerate a white man – just about – but a black or Muslim are definite no-go areas, believe me. Partition in 1947 hasn't been forgotten."

"So, are you going against the grain by seeing me?" There was genuine concern in my voice. I had experienced the power of racial disharmony before with a Sikh girl. I didn't want the episode repeated.

"Oh, don't worry Edwin. I'm most definitely my own person. My last boyfriend was white. My father didn't jump over the moon, but then he has enough sense to know he can't stop me. He still tries now and again, though. He sees me as a wilful brat, but loves me just the same. Only daughter. I can usually bring him around on these things. He knows I'll make my own choices, not his."

"I hope so," I said quietly, "but I have heard similar words to those before and . . . well I don't mean to offend, but they proved to be extremely empty." She looked at me and took my hand again. The movement seemed natural to her, a normal physical expression.

"I'm not that fickle, Edwin. Or that dishonest."

I believed her. English rose? Give me the dark-skinned mystery of the Punjab any day of the week. White women were cruder, less polished. When it comes to women I am the consummate racist. Proud of it too.

"Talking of relationships Jaz, you haven't shown any curiosity where my own relationship status is concerned."

"Oh, you're married, I know that. But not happily married. Separated perhaps. If it were otherwise you wouldn't be sitting here now. There is too much integrity in your eyes for you to be a deceiver, a betrayer. Besides, I can tell these things. My karma is at work again."

"I thought you didn't believe in all that stuff."

"When it suits, dear Edwin. Only when it suits." She gave me another of her white and brown smiles and dear God, these alone were enough to make me fall in love with her. Her karma knew a hell of a lot, I had to give it that.

"Yes, I'm married. I won't lie to you. And you're right, cheating is not my game. Even this innocent drink doesn't sit easily. I'm not going to go into a tirade of wife hating and how much 'my wife doesn't understand me' garbage. I've no doubt you've heard it all before."

"True."

"Well, I'm not one of those men. Neither is it my desire to have a 'bit on the side' or a mistress. I'm in the process of seeing about a divorce. We still live under the same roof – but that's all. There is no marriage to speak of, believe me."

"I do."

"God Jaz, you are a trusting woman. Don't you have any reservations at all? You hardly know me."

"Edwin, I know all I need to know." And with that she kissed me on the cheek. That one small kiss finally did it. I knew where I was going. I had to take a deep breath before being able to say another word. The obvious seemed the best exit from this rather lovely revelation.

"I'm older than you by a fair bit I suspect. I'm forty-five, how old are you?"

"Thirty-four." She didn't look it. I would have believed twenty-four. "Eleven-odd years is an interesting age difference. You can baffle me with your superior wisdom, Edwin. I will enjoy that. Oh, and no divorces or particularly horrendous and tragic love affairs for you to worry about either, at least no more than the usual bearing in mind my age and single status. I realise that you've been too much of a gentleman to ask."

Stuff the wisdom and gentlemanly exterior, at that moment all I really wanted to say was 'Get 'em off!' Bloody men again, we'll never change.

Instead I said, "Thirty-four and no marriages or fatal love affairs. How have you managed it, a beautiful lady like you? There must be a legion of disappointed men out there with their tongues hanging out."

"I believe there is a compliment in there somewhere, Edwin, which is gratefully received, but the truth is I'm extremely fussy. Marriage was close once, but frankly I didn't love as much perhaps as I should have done. My fault I'm afraid; as I say I've always been far too fussy."

"Well . . . er . . . I like a challenge," I replied, not knowing what else to say and wondering whether I should bugger off right now. Truthfully, what would a charmer like this want with

137

a cantankerous old curmudgeon like me? I mean I might well be admirably turned out, charming, intelligent, etc., etc., but even I didn't presume to be in Jaz's league – you see, I can be sincerely modest now and again, even self-effacing.

She noticed how my chops had fallen ever so slightly and there's me thinking I was good at hiding my feelings.

"Oh, now don't be put off by my fussiness Edwin, I'm not that bad, really." And with that she kissed my cheek again. Her lips were bloody gorgeous, all marshmallow and inside-out oranges. What would the real thing be like I wondered?

When all the grub had been eaten and the champagne had worked some of its magic (I had ordered another bottle, a definite boozer Miss Shemare) we decided to go for a walk. We ended up wandering around the Wallace Collection in Manchester Square. It seemed we both enjoyed some titbits of culture now and again without being too pretentious about it.

'*The Laughing Cavalier*' smooched with Rubens, while Watteau's '*Harlequin and Columbine*' and his ideas on courtship and love reminded me of myself, particularly the randy Harlequin trying to keep his willy in his pants as he makes an unrestrained lunge at Columbine's ample bosom. At that moment in time it was me all over, without the multi-coloured Harlequin's patchwork suit though, it has to be said.

As we walked around the various galleries we held hands and talked, the familiarity growing as we discussed art, music, the Upanishads, the Bhagavad-Gita, medicine and law.

Jaz enjoyed a thoughtful mind and a powerful intellect that demanded respect and admiration, things I had been missing out on for quite a while. She wasn't a smarty-pants though, she didn't constantly try and be clever, she didn't have to prove how bright she was every five minutes. It was there and that was enough. She was all the things that neither Clare nor Jessica could ever hope to be.

She was a registrar at the Royal Free Hospital in Hampstead. She was studying for her membership of the Royal

College of Obstetricians and Gynaecologists. Crack mechanics in other words. She was already a senior registrar, but a consultancy was the real goal. This could take a long time she knew, it all depended on the consultant mortality rate. Vacancies were few and far between unless all the consultants were suddenly to die at the same time. A vain hope.

Our conversation explored and exploited. We were both eager to know as much about the other as possible. Every word counted. Jaz was dedicated but not driven, ambitious but not overbearing. She was a capable woman and yet incredibly feminine with it. Her soft voice made me want to hold and protect as she somehow inspired unhindered masculinity. There was no strong-arm threat or female angst. My testosterone was allowed to flow more freely than a sixteen-year-old lad's as he viewed his first porno film, I was allowed to be a man, and a gentleman at that.

She mentioned her desire for children one day, insisting at the same time that they would not be 'pillar to post' orphans. She would mother them and no-one else. I absorbed and regretted; I couldn't help it.

My foul mouth made her laugh too. Our humour was on the same wave length – toilet variety. She enjoyed the refined and dignified delivery of my verbal profanities and accepted my obscene outbursts. My smoking didn't bother her either. She enjoyed the odd cheroot herself apparently. Even a cigarette now and again. The woman was human, bright and as sexy as hell.

The day came to an end. Jaz was on night duty in the hospital. We said our goodbyes and touched lips. I would ring her the following evening. In one afternoon we had come to know each other. There were no secrets. No boundaries.

We were falling in love.

CHAPTER 20

Why are we men so obsessed with the manic pursuit of female kind? I bet a few of you have asked this question time and time again. We have given up kingdoms for that one stolen kiss in the dark, or more recently a quick blow job behind a presidential door. We have cheated, died, killed even, all for women.

Still we go back. Every time we go back.

Our lives seem so meaningless without them. We destroy ourselves over the delightful creatures, fight to the death for them and then what do we do? Even when we love and lose, we make supersonic efforts to start all over again. Who have I been saying suffers from faulty wiring? We enter into the game of love and kisses, hope to God our dicks will perform (at least we middle-agers do) according to demand, knowing that we will probably end up with smashed hearts and every time we never even flinch. Unbelievable. But here's the best bit – some women want to be like us. They must be mad (or at least they must all suffer from learning difficulties).

I was sitting in my study, red bush tea next to me (Jaz had given me plenty of incentive to cut down the drink). There was a new urgency to my divorce intentions. Clare would have to be told. I doubted there would be any drama, it would all come down to 'How much?' With Jessica the Warrior Queen behind her I would be shown no mercy, of that I was certain. Somehow none of it seemed to matter anymore. There was Jaz and she was all I cared about. The sooner I received the Decree Absolute the better.

When I had arrived home Clare was nowhere to be seen. I was glad. After a wonderful day in London, Clare's face would only have ruined it. Strangely my present plight hadn't made me say 'Never again'. How many times do you hear divorcees saying these two final words? Well, I wasn't one of them. I still believed in the institution of marriage. I would be happy to marry again. Not for emotional security or any other kind of security for that matter, no, I would marry as an expression of my love. Nothing more, nothing less. I would be saying 'There is only you. You alone. No one else has a grip on my heart'.

As I had already discovered to my cost, the twistable bliss of marriage eats up sacrifice at the best of times. Both sides had to give more than they would sometimes take. This is the nature of 'I love you'. If we could all understand this, then voracious lawyers, incompetent family courts, quarrels, violence, childhood destruction, but most of all, excruciating pain, could all be avoided. 'I love you' should never be taken lightly . . . in a perfect world anyway (and a romantically deluded one perhaps!).

The problem here is which spouse is prepared to be the selfless victim? There are no answers, are there? I decided that I could spend all night devouring these quaint and unedifying riddles of the heart and get precisely nowhere. Virginia Woolf believed that if women only existed in fiction written by men then they would be a glorious and awesome mixture of contradictions. She would have no trouble pointing her tragic pen at me now, would she? Suicide was her way out. Contradictions? I rest my case.

My mind finished its infinite helter-skelter on the understanding of women. Jaz was here and now. Clare was gone. Our hearts had died together a long time ago. My wife had never appreciated that understanding was more important than knowledge. That love, if strong, will endure.

The following morning I realised there was no Clare – just goes to show how much touching we didn't do. For all her faults she didn't normally stay out all night without letting me know. As I brewed my tea I concluded that the shrew was up to something. How dare she! After all it was fine for me to meet someone on the sly, but my wife? The bitch! It all started to fit together. The smiles, the caring, the sudden change in attitude toward me. Guilt. The harlot was being serviced by another man. No doubt that Jessica was behind it.

To be honest with you, I wasn't unduly perturbed. And I'm not really that much of a hypocrite either, Claridges notwithstanding. If Clare was debauching herself in some extra-maritals then my job would be that much easier. Adultery, and bugger the two years separation. Apart from anything else, the 'two year' fact to prove irretrievable breakdown was becoming more and more unattractive. It was still also possible that Clare would kick up nasty and make me wait five years. In fact I knew this would be the case if she found out I was seeing someone else. Certain of it. She could be such a vindictive devil. 'Nor Hell a fury' and all that, or as Cyril Connolly puts it so well: 'a woman's desire for revenge outlasts all her other emotions'.

No, all things considered, if Clare was having an affair it would play in my favour. Good reason to divorce and I wouldn't have to wait for years, not to mention having to cope with all the bitterness and anger. I wanted a clean break as fast as possible. If Clare was receiving a good seeing-to elsewhere I would be a gentleman about it. Forgiving. I would still write out a generous cheque. My fountain pen would twitch on the moral high ground though, just to make a point. So far I hadn't touched Jaz. My conscience was clear, if a trifle murky in places.

Before I left for the office to do some overtime – it was a Sunday don't forget; it shows you how desperate I was to get out of the house – Clare's 'unreasonable behaviour' crossed my mind. If I divorced on this one, then I really would be starting a nuclear war.

As I drove into town it never occurred to me that Clare might have been involved in an accident. Clare was above such human tragedy.

I rang Jaz from the office. I knew I had promised to ring in the evening but I couldn't wait that long. The fact that I was ringing from the office had nothing to do with privacy or indeed deceit either; in some ways it would have given me great pleasure for Clare to have found out. She might even divorce me for my adultery. Don't worry, I had already thought of that ploy. But I knew Clare; she would cope with a wandering husband provided he continued to keep her indulged arse in the lap of luxury.

Jaz was as lovely as ever. I was still under her spell from the previous day, my lips unable to stop parting as I sat at my desk shaming an idiot Cheshire cat. We arranged to meet the following Friday night at her place just off Baker Street. She wanted to cook something 'special'. It had been a long time since anyone had done anything 'special' for me.

I had made the arrangements with Jaz without even thinking about Clare. She hadn't bothered to concern herself with my movements for a long time. Why should she bother now? Besides, another man may now be the pencilled victim of her diary. I didn't merit a scratch of lead these days.

After a few hours of legal deliberation I put the files back where they belonged and tidied up my desk. I hated clutter. I liked to see a smooth, open-spaced desk. Order. An untidy desk suggests an untidy mind.

The sun was in one of its more belligerent moods as it tried yet again to fade the red leather desk top. May had arrived and summer was starting to fine-tune itself. I looked at the framed cartooned Law Lords hanging on my office walls; some of them smirked, some of them joked, they had all existed in times gone by in a legal world that was gentler and less bullying. I wasn't so sure whether they would smirk and joke so much if they were judging today. Everything has become more dangerous, more imminent. The world needs a glove filled with iron, not putty.

I stood up and looked out of the window. The Green opposite was quiet. No one was walking a dog and no one was dropping litter. People didn't do that in Bury St Edmunds. Even the Saturday night drunks exercised restraint. It was the only cathedral 'town' in the country after all.

My view of the Green was unspoilt. Pretty houses dressed it, and prettier occupants watered and manicured their small spaces of self-serving paradise. Watering cans and hose-pipes erupted water on a grand scale; it was there to be used and abused after all. Flower pots and baskets, bedding plants, lawns and floral medallions came first in this happy town along with smug smiles and shifty self-importance. Misery and unkempt emotion were kept behind curtains that were drawn to protect the velvet covered furniture and hand-me-down antiques from sun damage. Insecurity and terror of the great unwashed were alarmed and fully armed. Intruders were entitled to be shot.

My perfect view was interrupted by Mr J, the last bastion of freedom and unspoilt reality. The only hope. The local denizens had tried desperately to nose him out – after all he was a man who fouled their shiny pavements and pristine lives. They had failed. They had been unable to lower the angle of their noses, their laudable nostrils having become too accustomed to sniffing.

I watched as Mr J – he had no other name as far as civilisation was concerned – sat down on the only bench available. Too many benches encouraged smokers, which wouldn't do at all. His footsteps were careful, fastidious even. Shoe leather, or in his case rubber, was not allowed to blemish the luxuriant mattress of green. In this town, turf and bowling greens were holier than the blessed cathedral itself. Mr J would have been arrested had he transgressed the holy laws. The police had not given up, neither had the council, the people's corrupted champions and voice of bye-law. In this respect at least, Bury St Edmunds was no different from all the other councils nationwide.

He sat back on the bench and pulled his Tesco bags into himself. Waitrose bags were beyond him. Besides, he had been banned from the most bespoke of all multi-choice grub emporiums. His bags were his children. His own unassuming off-spring and reality. He never stopped cuddling and soothing his guarantees of immortality. The bags were crammed with mould-peppered editions of *The Times*, as yellow as the tip of his beard. He pulled out an ancient copy, placed a thick-lensed pair of battered National Health spectacles on his nose and read. He sat alone in the past. Content. Harming no one.

Mr J had always been available. Much to the embarrassment of many. I had spoken with him at length many times. He was an erudite and perceptive man who had once occupied a senior position in the Civil Service. Many years ago he had chosen not to ignore the warning signs. Avoiding responsibility for a great national mistake he had closed his office door and never returned. He had given up the world of others to live in his own world. The news of the past was preferable to the news of the future.

I had never been able to determine his exact age. Grey hair stretched from the top of his head to his stomach. He wore a long black coat at all times; no seasonal dress code for Mr J. He didn't smoke and he didn't drink. His fingernails were always white with scrubbing. There was a whiff about him – of age, or a room that has allowed years of dust to settle and staleness to keep the air out. He claimed nothing from the State. He claimed only his self-respect, his right to choose and his right to life.

Before driving home I stopped to have a word with this stubborn rebel. His selfless insanity was always uplifting. He looked up as I walked across the Green. I was able to smell him before being within hearing distance.

"Watch out, Mr Hillyard!" he shouted. "The Green is feeling somewhat tetchy today. She is always a little temperamental after a long sleep. Your feet will irritate her gentle repose."

"Oh, don't worry Mr J, the Garden Committee can handle it. The odd footstep or two won't harm her." I sat down next to him. He was stale in smell certainly, but not in mind. "How are you then, Mr J? I haven't seen much of you recently. I thought you may have moved on."

"No, Mr Hillyard. Not yet. My old bones will prod me forward when the time is right."

"How did you manage through the winter? I kept an eye out for you."

"Oh, the local churches offer a parsimonious if draughty warmth. That's if the particular man of God practises what he preaches. Or should I say woman of God? I've noted an unusual change in the clergy. Women, I believe, now sit at God's right hand too. I always thought women had more sense than that. Never mind, eh? Not all of them practise what they preach it has to be said, and that includes the female of the species.

"I am not always welcome. The clergy fear the unusual, as does God it seems to me. Some of them are more wary of their congregation's wrath than that of their heavenly master. Capricious animal Christian charity, you know. My memory fails me Mr Hillyard, but who defined religion as being 'that vast, moth-eaten, musical brocade created to pretend we never die'?"

"Larkin I think," I replied.

"Yes, Mr Hillyard, I think you are right. Your memory is a more reliable servant than mine, sadly."

"I doubt that Mr J. You seem as sharp as ever." I smiled. "By the way, how old are you?"

"Now, now Mr Hillyard, you know better than to try and make me reveal my secret." His old face wrinkled into a whispered grin. "I am older than you, young fellow. Wiser? Who knows? Age merely furnishes us with a different wisdom from youth. Both are fickle and fraudulent."

I stood up. The man's speech was as correct and perfect as ever. It was always a refreshing experience just talking with him. His spoken English was accurate and true. As rich as it was versatile. His words and pronunciation were exact, not flippant and cheap. He had refused to 'downsize' to the poverty of verbal criminality. For him, grammatical heresy was for fashionable fools and the pseudo-educated. Speech still said who you were. It was still the calling card, the key to open all doors. It was the difference between being listened to or ignored. It distinguished the true gentleman.

"Well, I have to go now Mr J. I saw you from my office window. Thought I would come over and say 'hello'. See how you are."

"That's extremely kind of you, Mr Hillyard. It is always a pleasure to speak with you."

"Cheerio then."

"Goodbye, Mr Hillyard."

I started to walk to my car wondering when I would see the learned tramp again. Sometimes he would disappear for months on end. He would return eventually. He always did, if only, as he had once told me, to remind himself of his wisdom in closing a door all those years ago. I hoped my white envelope containing four five pound notes wouldn't be missed. I had placed it carefully underneath one of his Tesco shopping bags. Mr J would never accept overt charity, but I knew that a beautifully hand-written note would be pushed through my office letterbox by the following morning. It would read the same way as all the others,

> Dear Mr Hillyard,
> May I thank you for your kind consideration.
> Sincerely yours,
> Mr J

Mr J's ability to remain independent of the state confused and angered his detractors. I was the only person who knew how he managed it. His six-monthly cheque came to my office. An old family trust continued to maintain him in a begrudging way. Old money. Old values. Old embarrassments better paid for even when the pennies were few. He could not afford the trappings of twenty-first century greed or its credit, but he could afford himself and who he was and this was all that mattered. He was an extremely happy man. His bed may have been hard and windy, but he slept the deep sleep of an innocent child.

CHAPTER 21

When I arrived home that damned woman Jessica Howard was waiting for me. The woman was everywhere.

"Hello, Edwin," she enthused, all lips pulled back and 'hail-fellow-well-met' as she sat on one of the kitchen stools, "Clare is having a shower and getting changed. We're off to the theatre in Bury." Theatre? This was a new one for Clare. The only theatre she knew about was Bill and Ben.

"Oh, how nice," I replied all sarcasm and grit, "I thought Clare had gone off to Tuscany to hand-pick some Italian herbs for my supper. You know how she adores cooking." Jessica ignored the grit. I thought it was quite amusing. She was good at ignoring my permanent state of rancour. The woman was getting right on my tits. In fact she was pinching them with a vengeance.

"Didn't Clare tell you?" she grinned, obviously amused at my outrage.

"No, hardly surprising is it? I haven't seen her lately. Was she with you last night?"

"Oh . . . did she not say anything? She stayed with me in Norwich. We both drank too much, I'm afraid. A taxi would have cost a fortune."

"No, I had no idea where she was."

"I'm sorry, I really am. I think she tried to ring you, but you don't use a mobile, do you?"

"No, I don't. Anything wrong with that is there? And what's wrong with the landline anyway? They do still take messages you know. I was in last night and this morning." You've got to admit I had some front. I was on the attack and being extremely unfriendly.

"Calm down now, Edwin. Calm down. There's just been a misunderstanding." She looked straight at me. She was serious, brimming with not-for-profit empathy. The Great Understander. I have to admit her kissable face did have a calming effect. I fumed for a few more seconds then made some red bush.

"All right. I'm sorry. Bad day. I've been in the office working. Not a good idea, particularly on a Sunday."

"Don't worry about it. No problem."

Why is it that everything has become 'no problem'? 'No problem' this, 'no problem' that and worse still 'no probs' to every other thing on the planet. Well, I had genuine problems right now and Jessica Howard wasn't helping. I didn't trust the woman and never would.

"Truth is, I would get out of the law tomorrow if I could." Now don't ask me why I was opening up to the woman because I haven't a clue. She had that effect. The Jessica effect. I didn't even like her. I quickly changed the subject as the last thing I wanted was to discuss my disillusionment with the law. "So, what did the pair of you do last night anyway? Grooving around the hot spots of Norwich, were you?"

"No, not my scene. I will not demean myself by allowing my body to be put on display for the lurid fantasies of sad, inadequate males . . . I prefer the real thing."

As she said these last few words she seemed to uncoil and slither towards me. Her eyes were stretching across the table and boring straight into mine. She was using a diamond-tipped drill. I didn't like where this was going. The woman was unsettling me.

"Do you now?" I replied. "So you're not into knickerless and braless prancing around on the dance floor then?"

"Well, I'm usually knickerless . . . I go commando. Not braless though, I like my boobs too much." Her eyes remained attached to mine. There was no getting away.

"Really? Very gratifying to know I'm sure."

The air between us was beginning to spark and for once the electricity wasn't coming from Jessica's hair either. I never thought the day would come when I would actually will my wife to walk into a room. Jessica was making a blatant pass. There was nothing subtle here. She had just said to me 'I want to screw you.' At that moment Clare walked in, thank God, wafting shower gels, perfumes and God knows what else. The anti-ageing body beautiful had arrived.

"Oh you're back, darling," she gave me a kiss on the cheek. "I hope you aren't angry about my being away last night. Too much to drink, and you wouldn't have wanted me to spend all that money on a taxi from Norwich now, would you? I did try and ring you on the landline, left a message but you probably didn't check." She was right about that, I hadn't checked. So much for my outraged bout of pique, I kept quiet while Jessica looked at me and smiled in that superior way of hers. The conniving sod. "You are terrible, Edwin. Anyway, there's some game pie and salad in the fridge. I brought you back some nice lemon cheesecake too. We're off to the theatre. I won't be late. Come on then Jess, let's go."

The woman was all loving and caring wife. Decidedly un-natural where Clare was concerned. I was used to sneers and snarls for Heaven's sake. My wife had turned into someone else. Maybe some aliens had kidnapped her and given her an outer space make-over. She would have gone for it. Darling? Food in the fridge? Game pie? Clare's idea of 'game' was a snakes and ladders set. All this I knew was for the benefit of Jessica. Dutiful, faithful wife syndrome. Clare was always inflicted with this particular 'syndrome' when other people were around. On these occasions it became almost fatal. Her insipid grins and wifely bleatings made me want to smack her right in the chops. Stupid bloody woman.

Clare went out of the kitchen to put on a coat. Jessica leapt up to the pad and pencil that was always on one of the work tops. She scribbled something then quickly passed the note to me. It read, 'Please ring me and let's have some fun'. A tele-phone number was next to it.

I can't help it, can I? This effect I have on women. Baffles me sometimes, it really does. Just goes to show though that even the feminist Jessica required a good male length from time to time. Women do without us? Rampant Rabbits are all very well, but they ain't flesh and blood and they don't twitch like an honest-to-God throbbing penis. So there.

I had been generally offensive to Jessica, but still she pursued. Odd, isn't it? The empowered feminist 'I am' still demanding the most basic of masculine benevolence. You see what I mean? They can't do without us and we can't do without them. We men may not be multitask aficionados, but by God we have one thing that women do not! Long live the cock and all who sail on him!

The two women walked out of the kitchen. I took out my own pen, wrote something on the back of her note and went out after them.

"Oh Jessica, before I forget, here's the name and address of those solicitors you wanted." I gave it to her just as she was opening her car door.

"Oh, thank you Edwin, that's very kind of you." She caught my ball of bullshit with the dexterity of a test match cricketer. Sly bugger.

"Not at all. Any time Jessica. Please feel free." I smiled.

I had written 'FUCK OFF' in bold black print. Not one for messing about, me, as you know. She looked at the note then at me. Her eyes changed and added a new dimension to the words 'looks can kill'. In a split second they hanged, drew and quartered me and fried my testicles and penis on a white-hot brazier just to add insult to injury.

The woman scared me, I mean it. What had I been saying about rejection and Congreve's 'Nor Hell a fury like a woman scorned'? Revenge? These words would soon come back to torment me. Her hatred trapped me for a few seconds, then she got into the car and drove off, her passenger oblivious to the declaration of war.

I took my tea into the study.

I had made a serious enemy of Jessica Howard; a woman who seemed to hate male kind but also needed us. A frustrated feminist, she loathed babies and wallowed in her calculated destruction of maternal instinct. The woman had lost her way. She no longer knew her place in the order of things. Her life had become a televised tragedy; it wasn't real, but she had yet to face up to the fact.

I thought of Clare.

She couldn't keep a husband, neither .could she keep a friend. For a second or two my heart went to her. Love? Does it ever die? I wondered. Once given, can it ever be taken back? Can it ever be forgotten? Perhaps the last rites are never fully realised. We simply learn to love again. To relive something we once knew so well, but in a different body. The spirit, the soul of love, stays with us until our eyelids close for the last time, and when they close maybe we finally realise in those last few moments of life that love is the true insanity. The most irrational of all religions. The one condition that is beyond verbal expression. It is a state of flux that is beyond colour, beyond reason, but most of all beyond my insignificant pen.

CHAPTER 22

"We must stop meeting like this, you know."

I was standing on the doormat of Jaz's apartment. She stood in front of me. It was sari time, long black hair, mad colours and a smile that demanded manic love and an abuse of self-indulgence.

"Before you step over the threshold," she said as she took my hands in hers," allow me to give you a traditional Sikh welcome." With that she kissed me. This time it was the kiss of an expert. A full-blown snog which made my legs shudder and my stomach roll. Our mouths fitted like stilton to port. Our lips were the perfect combination. Eventually she pulled away. Not too far. We stood there for a moment, my arms around her narrow waist. Our eyes dug into each other. The pick and shovels were out again. Christ, did I want this woman.

"That's the first real kiss," I mumbled.

"Not the last though I hope," she said as her lips remained slightly parted. "Now come in or the neighbours will start enjoying themselves." Her openness was so attractive, so compelling. There were no hidden places with this woman. No secrets.

Her apartment was situated just off Baker Street, an expensive place to live. It was in one of those Edwardian jobs that were plastered all over London. Fifteen-odd apartments to a block and probably only two ever occupied on a regular basis. The rest were owned by rich Arabs and gassed-up Russians on the run from Putin. They all had to stick their tax-free money somewhere, didn't they? So bollocksovitch to Osborne, coalitions and hard-up Londoners.

"Now sit down Edwin, and make yourself comfortable. Whisky and water, no ice?" She remembered.

I sat down on an ocean-going settee. It was cream and neutral. This was no ordinary apartment. It wasn't furnished or decorated in the Asian style that I had so often encountered in the past. Integrated India abused brash colour and pattern with a loudness that deafened the unprepared, but here antique Persian rugs flew amongst genuine Indian artefacts that struggled to keep up. The whole place was subtle and elegant. The doctor had taste.

Jaz returned, drink in hand. She sat down next to me, leaning against the corner of the settee.

"A delightful home you have. Calming."

"Good, I'm glad you like it. That's how I've tried to make it. A place of calm and sensitivity. There's no thunder and lightening in here."

"That's a quaint way of describing it. There are storms every day in my house." I grinned these last few words; I wasn't about to spoil the moment by entering into a bitter diatribe of unhappy matrimony, "There are a few smells running about the place too. Food, you, incense."

"Me?"

"I don't mean you smell. Well, actually yes, you do smell, but it's all sex. What have you got cooking?" I quickly changed the subject but I was beginning to sweat. The woman was so close, we had kissed. I wanted to grab her there and then and bugger the peace and quiet. She leaned over me, kissed my cheek and stood up.

"All sex. That's interesting." She gave me a blast of her white teeth again. "Good sex is like good food, Edwin. It takes time. Anticipation also improves the quality." Her eyes and lips were speaking their own language and it wasn't Punjabi.

"What are you cooking anyway?"

"Chicken, prawn and coriander."

"Chilli?"

"Plenty."

"Good. I'm addicted to the stuff. I like things hot. Do you?"

"Very."

She then disappeared leaving me with my viciously rude imagination.

I knew precisely what she was doing. Building up the excitement. We both knew that before the night was over the pair of us would be enjoying a good romp. That's the thing about sex. Sometimes you don't have to say anything. Two people look, savour and know. I knew I would be in a for a pasting. The woman was a doctor. They were all the same these medico types. Nurses, doctors, physiotherapists, I had rogered them all in my time. Randy as hell. Must be all the physical stuff they deal with on a daily basis.

I could be wrong of course, but my experience still stands by the fact that if you have a medico on your hands, look out. Matrons? Now they really are in a class all of their own. Bossy buggers the lot of 'em. Get them into bed and it's 'do this' and 'do that' and make sure your willy has hospital corners on it before you put it away. Medicos? Randy harlots the lot of 'em, and so far I had no reason to believe Jaz was any different. It's all in the kiss after all. The woman had already fornicated me half to death on the doorstep. With her tongue anyway.

I heard some clanks and clatters coming from the kitchen. I have to admit there was a fine stench about the place. My appetite was beginning to bluster and moan. My Sikh doctor returned.

"How much longer?" I asked.

"Not long, about an hour."

"An hour? God, I'm starving."

"So am I, Edwin." She was standing in front of me. "By the way, do you like the sari?"

"You look magnificent."

"I don't often wear them. I felt a traditional evening would be different. A change. And from what I know of you so far you seem to consider convention tedious."

"Do I?"

"Yes. Not in any obvious way. You're traditional in your dress and manners, old-fashioned even. But this in itself is unconventional. Our conversations show me that there is the Marxist, the Capitalist and the Socialist in you. You're an enigma. You are not what you appear to be. Neither are you, I think, the pillar of the community that perhaps people are led to believe you are. You're a rebel Mr Hillyard, a closet militant. You are Edwin Hillyard and damn the whims and conventions of others. You play by your own rule book and no else's." She paused for a moment and then smiled mischievously, "Rather like me I suppose."

There was a sudden silence. Words stopped. We were in those moments of neither here nor there. The 'knowing' had absorbed us both.

Without saying another word or even giving me the chance to reply she took my hand and led me to the bedroom.

The bedroom, like the rest of her home, soothed and healed. Oriental rugs hung from the walls and candles spat their light across shadows that never died. The bedspread depicted Tiger hunts and sweating Maharajas wearing turbans that seemed to reach up to the skies, while ancient flintlocks pointed and sparked as elephants' trunks tried to keep out of the way. In amongst all this cushions splattered with colourful tapestry tried to calm them all down. The room both restrained and liberated. It was a place to live and a place to die. There was nothing in between.

We stood in front of her bed and kissed. This seemed to be enough in spite of my randy impatience. I could have kissed all night long and not wanted for anything more. I held her face in my hands. I nibbled, I licked. Believe it or not there was no fumbling. Saris and trousers floated away. Fingers plucked and tugged without urgency or aggression. This was nature at its best. I almost wished David Attenborough was in the room with his camera.

We fell onto the bed and for the next hour gorged ourselves. We ate, drank and consumed. Jaz knew what she was about.

Her grip was firm but soft. She handled my own body with an expertise that could only have been taught by a Master. Neither one of us became dominant. We both led. We both followed.

Our fingers and tongues went where they were bidden. She moved her hips over and across my lips. She soaked my hair with her passion. My tongue wandered without restraint as she forced herself into my mouth and leaned back so that her hands could fondle and touch me. After a while I turned her over. There was no inhibition.

Her buttocks glistened and shone in the candlelight. Her body narrowed at the waist and then expanded into two glorious ripe peaches. I wanted to bite. I wanted to eat. I wanted bits of them plastered all over my face. I tucked her waist under my arm, lifted her up slightly and pushed. I attacked. I lifted her up further.

"Jesus," I moaned. I wanted to soak her. She pushed back, her intimate muscles gripping me. We had both lost control. I was suffering. I dug my nails into her flesh. She shouted.

"Oh yes . . . please don't stop – oh God! Yes! Don't stop. Please don't stop!!" Her fingers squeezed. Milked as I rammed into her. Again and again. Her fingers reached down and played with her sex. Fast. Non-stop. This was love. This was human union at its best. At last I couldn't take anymore. I was bursting.

"Oh Christ" I managed to moan through clenched teeth.

"Oh God, I want all of you Edwin!" Jaz urged. "All of you . . . now! Please now!"

Our passion had gone beyond delicate touch. We gripped and pulled. When I was finally spent, she looked at me, her huge brown eyes, softened by her own climax. There was that post-coital look on her face. So intense. So unique. So female.

We lay back in each other's arms and stuck to each other for a while. Sex juices trickled around and between us. Neither of us seemed to mind. The room reeked of carnal play. Of love.

"You really are a slut, Jaz," I managed to whisper, "not what I would expect from a budding pillar of the medical community."

"You can talk, so don't complain." She reached for my willy. "God it's still a monster. It hasn't gone soft. Does it stay like that permanently?"

"With you around, the answer is probably 'yes'." She continued to stare at my manhood, fascinated by the fleshy monolith. I never quite understood what's so attractive about a throbbing blue vein myself, but there you are, that's the 'unhinged' nature of women for you. Never cease to amaze, do they? (And before all you female readers start yelling 'As if' and 'Bloody men and their willies again!', indulge my masculine insecurity if only for a moment.)

"It really is a bit of a beast you know," Jaz continued. "Not that I'm complaining. Any woman who says size doesn't matter is a liar. Either that or her man has got a small penis and she wants to delude herself."

"Come here," I ordered. "Kiss me."

We kissed and touched for a long time. For a first tumble this was the best ever. Remember my first bout with Clare? My fingertips wouldn't leave Jaz's smooth skin alone. Her body was so irresistible. She was a Marks & Spencer fresh fruit cocktail. Crisp to the bite, sweet on the tongue and bursting with variety. She wasn't just Jaz, she was now Edwin's Jaz (oh God, I'm getting carried away now). Her breasts were firm but plentiful and her nipples like cinnamon nougat – see what I mean, I'm beginning to sound like some self-indulgent celebrity cook now, aren't I? I'm damned if I'll actually name one, that would only give him or her some more richly undeserved publicity.

We were both lost. Time had stopped at her bedroom door.

I was dozing in that post-coital twilight zone when Jaz suddenly shot up.

"Oh no! The food! It's burning!" She leapt out of bed and ran to the kitchen. I woke up properly and smelt the death throes of chicken, prawn and coriander.

Later that evening we enjoyed a takeaway. It was the best one I had ever eaten. Jaz had been mortified at the destruction of her traditional cooking, but we had both ended up laughing. It was only a bit of chicken and prawn after all. She admitted that the takeaway variety tasted just as good, maybe even better. She insisted on paying for it though. This small gesture impressed me yet again. I had never known Clare to pay for anything. Her purse was for personal use only. In fact I didn't know if she had one; whenever we were out together she didn't carry a handbag, let alone a purse.

When we had finished eating Jaz put a bottle of good brandy on the table and two glasses.

"This is a special night Edwin, so let's enjoy a special drink."

There were more 'x's' on the bottle's label than the application forms for a dyslexics' convention. She poured the drinks. We both sipped.

"Rich and potent like you," I said and kissed her. The conception of love is like this – one becomes rather twattish and extremely tactile. We couldn't stop fingering each other. Everything was touch and feel. Urgent.

"Now, my Sikh medic, let's get down to basics. Where did you learn to fuck like that?" Jaz didn't bat an eyelid. That was another thing I liked about her. My foul mouth seemed to be quite acceptable. Hers wasn't bad either, when the weather roughed up.

"Straight to the point, Edwin, I'll give you that. What's happened to the perfect gentleman? The man who pampers me, opens doors, pulls out chairs?"

"Oh, I'm still a gentleman of the old school when I want to be, but since when do good manners intrude upon raw sex? You're a slut, woman. No two ways about it. Great for me. Every gentleman's dream-woman must be a slut in the bedroom, lady in public etc, etc. Best of both worlds. Now come on, I'm curious. Apart from anything else you haven't told me much about past loves."

"Do I have to? It's all very boring."

160

"Yes, you do. Please." I smiled and urged her on with a tweak of one of her brown nipples. They were still up like cobblers thumbs. We were both only half dressed.

"Oh God Edwin, don't do that, you'll set me off again. Now stop it!"

"Answer me then."

"Oh all right, if I must." I carried on tweaking her nipple. Funny things, nipples. Some like being pinched, others crushed or even clamped. There were also those that demanded the more refined approach. Licking, not chewing. Touching, not squeezing. I had even known a few nipples that enjoyed being sucked by a machine. Some women can orgasm with the right nipple manipulation and I soon discovered that Jaz was one of them. I got my tongue into action and my teeth – she obviously liked a bit of both – and before I knew it she was 'aahing' and 'oohing' and 'Godding' it. The woman had an orgasm there and then. Not a big one mark you, but enough to keep her going. Needless to say, when I had finished they remained hard and belligerent – the filthy houri. I allowed a few minutes for Jaz to recover,

"Now, where were we?" I said. "Ah yes, other men."

"Impatient aren't you. I've just had orgasm after orgasm and you are asking me about ex's! . . . Now if you must know, becoming a doctor didn't allow for many long-termers. There were boyfriends of course, but my determination to be a doctor got in the way. There was one serious relationship. We lived together for a few years. Even talked about marriage, it never happened though. He was a doctor too. We were both busy building up our careers, so you can imagine. . . ."

"You must have loved each other."

"Yes, we did in our own individual ways. We were together five to six years."

"What happened?"

"Oh, it died a natural death I guess. He got a job in America, I didn't want to go with him. As I told you in Claridges, I didn't really love enough I suppose. Anyway we parted on friendly terms. No bitterness. We still talk now and again. He's done very well."

"Was he white?"

"No, a Sikh. My father was very happy with the arrangement."

"I bet."

"Look Edwin, don't worry about it. I've told you I do my own thing. My father won't stop me. He never has done. I am not your typical Sikh girl, neither could I wear a mask of duplicity like so many of my friends."

"You've never gone for an arranged marriage then?"

"I thought about it once. We Sikhs don't force anyone to marry. The girl and boy make their own decisions. They're introduced to each other and then it's up to them. Many children just happen to believe that their parents will make a wise choice for them. In Asian culture age is revered, wisdom highly respected. You Westerners have gone very wrong in this area. For instance, how many Asians do you see in old folks homes? How many Asians do you see in the divorce courts? We must be doing something right."

"Oh, I agree with you entirely. But I have seen and experienced enormous hypocrisy in your culture. I thought Guru Nanak organised the first canteens where Muslims and Hindus of different castes could eat. Didn't he preach 'There is no Hindu, there is no Mussulman'? In other words he was all about toleration. Equal opportunities." Jaz laughed at my modern slant on the Guru, the blue and yellow specks in her eyes appearing to tease and tremble with humour.

"Well, since when was any religion without its hypocrites? Come on Edwin, what's new? Man has always poisoned and corrupted the originator of religious truth, whether it be Christianity, Islam or Sikhism. Mankind is religion's greatest tragedy, its most profound liar. When does any world religion practise what its birth preaches? I go along with Sikhi and its traditions to keep my father happy. We women are peacemakers, after all."

"And healers," I interjected.

"Quite," she smiled. "Be that as it may, I do not adhere to any particular dogma or path. It's unhealthy. I believe in me, at least my spiritual self . . . oh, and my karma."

"Well, that's a religion of sorts."

"Oh no, it's a philosophy. A belief but not a monotheistic delusion."

"You are a fatalist then? Or someone that believes in eventual freedom from the cycle of rebirth and the pain brought about by one's own actions or 'karma'?"

"Something like that, but I don't believe in reincarnation, just to confuse you." She laughed and then kissed me.

"So," I continued, unable to allow my exploration of her spirituality to stop. I wanted to know everything, "Freedom from rebirth can only be accomplished by a perfect union with God or in your case, Truth."

"I told you I don't believe in rebirth. I do a lot of yoga though. Both physical and spiritual. Some would say this is enough of a journey."

"Your body is certainly yogic; supple and firm."

"What about you anyway? I won't ask about a religion. You're too intelligent, I think, to believe in any God. There is a spiritual quest though. I can see that."

"Very perceptive of you. Yes, I am an atheist, it would be foolish to be otherwise. A spiritual quest? I'm not too sure about that. Religion is, for most, a necessity. A stretching of the imagination. Mankind is obsessed, preoccupied, with its own species. There will always be a primitive instinct to trust in a 'beyond'. The only one I've any time for is Buddha. Although sometimes even he irritates me. I mean what gave him the right to lecture everyone on self-discipline, the fat bastard?" Jaz hooted with laughter at my irreverence.

"Oh God Edwin, you really are too much! Is nothing sacred to you?"

"Not really. Life is too damned short. Piss-taking brings a reality to this tragic but fascinating fiasco we call 'life'."

We talked into the early hours.

Every minute that passed ticked a new discovery. I told her about my useless marriage, its impending dissolution. My frustrations. My unhappiness. My desire to get out of private practice permanently, I had had enough of it all. On this last point she had commented, "Well, with the willy you've got Edwin you'll never be out of work. You can always sweep the floors or wash windows!"

When sleep finally began to nudge us, I whispered, "Jaz, I think . . . I've a feeling that I'm going to love you. I can't help it."

"I don't need to think," she replied softly as she lay on top of me and kissed my lips. "I don't need to think at all."

Both of us knew that no more words needed to be said. There was that 'knowing' again. We allowed the silence to feel and tempt us. It gripped our hearts and moulded them together. After a few minutes her fingers began stroking my face and hair. "I can't stop touching you Edwin, I just can't. Has anyone told you what an interesting face you have?"

"No, can't say that they have. Wrinkled maybe, but never interesting."

"Lots of little scars. A bent nose that's had some stitches along the way. Lived in. A perfect face is boring."

"Schoolboy scrapping, and the nose was a result of intoxication, nothing dramatic I assure you."

"Yes, you look a fighter. Strong."

"I've had to be. There have been many times in my life . . . and one day perhaps I'll tell you."

"Good, because I want to know it all. Everything." There were a few more moments of silence.

"How are you on marriage and children anyway?" I asked. So much for sleep nudging us.

"Right man, who knows? As for children, I adore babies. Why do you think I'm specialising in obstetrics. Has to be the right man though." She kissed me.

"Point taken." I had tried not to show my relief. A few tanned little lions or lionesses running about the place was an interesting prospect.

"Talk me to sleep, will you? That voice of yours is better than any sleeping pill. I could listen to it all night and still be asleep."

"That doesn't sound much of a compliment. I thought it could give even the angels multiple orgasms."

"Oh I know, Edwin, I know." Her fingers moved from my face.

"Still twitching and throbbing I note."

This time our bodies spoke a different language. The sex was more cerebral. Lust and uncouth demand had been replaced by mindful care. There was a delicacy in our thrusts and orgasm. Carnal knowledge was creating its own wonders. Love was fine tuning and finishing its touch.

Even in the darkness of her bedroom the speckles of blue and yellow around her dark brown pupils made me love her. Her eyes. The compassion. The kindness. I knew all I needed to know. My lioness would protect, cherish and love me.

The following morning we went for a walk around Kensington Gardens. Some people stared at us and seemed to approve. A young couple actually said "You look nice" as they walked past holding hands. I didn't know whether they were referring to our clothes or our love. Either way it made no difference, the important thing being that we obviously looked happy and approachable, not a bad achievement for central London.

Jaz spotted a tramp curled up and forgotten sitting underneath a tree. People walked by trying not to notice, trying not to see their own jagged meanness with its facile excuse. It was hard to tell whether the tramp was male or female as a huge overcoat was covering the lump of human waste. The bundle wasn't begging, there were no grimy fingernails outstretched and waiting for deliverance or even a battered tin waiting for the tinkling tune of dropping coins. The bundle had obviously decided the milk of human kindness had curdled years ago and seemed to have given up on its own life in protest.

Jaz insisted we go over and give the bundle some money. I had no objections, neither did I care whether a few bob went on drink or drugs. If that was all the bundle had, then who was I to deprive? We dug deep, placed a note or two in the bundle's lap and walked on. The bundle didn't move, it didn't even twitch. Perhaps it had died after all.

We carried on walking and holding hands like the young lovers who had spoken to us earlier. We ignored all the precious activity that swirled and bounced around the Gardens. I thought of Jaz's charity to the bundle and wanted to love her even more. Sometimes I would unclasp my hand and put my arm around her waist. I wanted her close. A tailor had cut our cloth to perfection and we hung together as one. Even our seams were invisible.

At 11 o'clock we returned to her apartment. As we approached the house an Asian man jumped out of a Mercedes. The car was new. One of the luxury models. Expensive. The man walked up to us. Jaz immediately withdrew her hand from mine as her body stiffened.

"Jaspreet, where have you been?" The man asked. His words were abrupt. Demanding. "I've been waiting for you."

"I didn't know you were coming to see me this morning, Daddy. Nothing wrong is there?"

"No, nothing. Social call. Who is this?" Her father eyed me up and down. "Another boyfriend? I hope he lasts longer than the others."

I couldn't quite make out whether this was a warning for my benefit, or whether he was just trying to embarrass Jaz. Either way he looked formidable. Tall, slim and committed to a Spartan code of conduct no doubt, judging by his healthy appearance. No meat, no strong drink, no fags, no drugs, but plenty of prayer. A fundamentalist perhaps, and if so not very different from all the other fundamentalists really, Muslim, Christian or otherwise.

A closer inspection revealed the five Kalsa's (or K's) in all their orthodox glory, so this chap was definitely one of the chosen race of soldier saints. He was wearing a saffron turban and a steel bracelet, and I had no doubt that a comb was stuck in the inside pocket of his city suit. A blue strip of material was running across his chest; ah, I thought, the ceremonial dagger tucked behind his backside somewhere too. The only 'K' missing were the drawers (worn by the warriors of his history). This individual was on a crusade for '*dharmayuddha*' – a battle for righteousness – all right. His beard hung halfway down his chest, a bit like Mr J's really but not quite as grey, and cleaner too.

Jaz took the reins. She seemed wary of her father, but not frightened. Her body language was defiant.

"This is Edwin Hillyard. Edwin, my father Jagdish Singh Shemare." He looked as aggressive as a lion and that's a fact. The name 'Shemare' meant 'lion slayer' according to Jaz; a bit of a contradiction there I had thought at the time. 'Singh'– lion, 'Shemare' – lion slayer, see what I mean?

"How do you do," I said and held out my hand. He extended his hand as if I had just pulled out my willy for him to shake. His handshake was firm and fast. He obviously didn't appreciate physical contact with the likes of me.

"Do you two want to be left alone, family business or something? I asked. "I'll go down the road for a cup of coffee. Give you some privacy." Hostility was in the air and I didn't fancy having a dagger stuck up my arse – ceremonial or not.

"No, that's all right Mr Hillyard. There is nothing particularly important I need to speak with my only daughter about." He emphasised the word 'only'. He looked at Jaz. Disapproval. Warning. "I will see you next week, Jaspreet. Remember you are having dinner with your mother and I next Thursday. Your uncle Jasbir is over from Delhi with your cousin. They will be dining with us." Suddenly his voice changed, it was more threatening, stern, "Make sure you are with us by 7 o'clock sharp. No excuses."

He turned and went back to his car. Here was a man who had done well from his integration. His English was perfect. Hardly any trace of the Punjab. For all this, he retained his history, his culture. One had to admire him. He had succeeded without having to assimilate.

"Sociable chap, your dad. I thought you told me he was a tolerant soul," I said.

"Oh, take no notice Edwin. He's not all bad. Dotes on me really. Most Sikh fathers spoil their daughters to death. I'm no exception. That little display of paternal authority was for your benefit. He's always jealous of any man who comes into my life, boyfriend or otherwise. Making me out to be a loose woman is his way of protecting me. He doesn't mean it really."

"Glad to hear it. Will I last longer than the others do you think?"

"Oh, I think so," she teased, "a week or so longer anyway."

"Did I detect a whiff of 'arrangement' at this dinner party next week?"

"Don't miss much, do you Edwin? Yes, my father is still up to his old tricks. Trying to make some business alliance with a nice Sikh boy again I expect. He should have got the message by now, silly, stubborn man."

"What does he do anyway?"

"Just about everything. Property, imports, exports, textiles, you name it."

"Wealthy fellow then?"

"Oh yes. I think so anyway. He tries to buy me often enough, but I'm not for sale. Everything I have I have worked for. I don't own the apartment by the way in case you're wondering; my grandfather does and I insist on paying him rent. My father educated me, but that's it. God forbid that I should be beholden to or dependent on my father. If he had had his way I would have been married at eighteen with three children by twenty-one. No thank you."

Jaz was working in the evening so we spent the afternoon licking and eating each other. You know what it's like. Blossoming love. Can't leave each other alone. At least Jaz couldn't leave me alone. The woman was an animal. As I left the flat I considered stopping off at a sports shop for some knee pads. My knees were raw. Flayed. I had always thought that such knees were a product of youthful and surreptitious sex on the snatched but convenient carpet somewhere in the parents' house. There are some things then at least that middle age doesn't change.

CHAPTER 23

I travelled back to Suffolk all fingers, thumbs and a face that spoke a secret harmony. I was shining like an exotic glow-worm.

As I arrived home I knew there wouldn't be any awkward interrogations as to where I had been all night. Clare wouldn't care one way or the other.

Voices were coming from the sitting room. I recognised both. The unsavoury Jessica and my wife. I'll say that for Jessica, the woman was a stayer.

"Hello girls." I nodded at Jessica. The two of them ignored me. Ah, I thought, guess who's an unwelcome guest in his own house? I poured myself a drink, "Haven't you got a home to go to, Jessica?" I asked. The dimmer switch was being turned down on my previous glow. Clare's eyes gave me both barrels while Jessica looked straight through me. There was no mercy here.

"I'll be going in a minute, Edwin," the woman replied without looking at me.

"That's good, because I'm beginning to wonder whether or not you've become a sitting tenant. I am also beginning to wonder who the landlord is around here." I looked at Clare. Her face was a picture. Wished I had had a camera – I could have taken a photo of her face and stuck it to the seat of my leather armchair.

Jessica's hair looked as if its needle had gone into the red danger zone. I'll say that for her though, she didn't respond. Not verbally anyway. Before walking out I said, "A minute is too long. Now why don't you just get the hell out of my house Muz Howard, right now? You're getting right up my nose!"

I walked out and left them to it. I was about to put some music on when Clare barged into my hallowed space. "You bastard! You rude bastard! That's my friend in there. How dare you! What has she done to you?!"

"How dare I? Whose house is this? The woman is creeping up on me wherever I look. Dear God, she'll be in the en suite next watching me have a crap. I don't like her. Now get her out, sharpish! If you don't, I will!" Clare was quiet for a moment. Danger.

"You twisted, arrogant shit!" There was no shouting this time, Clare being at her most lethal when the volume was turned down. "You are going to regret this!" And off she went.

I have to admit I was impressed. Clare was brilliant. I hadn't seen her so seriously lathered-up for ages. Even her plate smashing exercises were eclipsed by this most recent outburst. I almost went back into the sitting room for another bout just to see her hatred for a second time. Damn, the woman was an expert. I had heard threats from Clare before. She usually carried them out too. I'll say that for Clare, she kept to her word. I had a feeling that an 'unreasonable behaviour' divorce petition would soon be arriving at my feet. Great. Clare would be doing me a favour. Sooner the better.

An hour or so later I heard a whispered departure. Clare hadn't carried out my wishes as instructed. So much for me being the master in my own home, eh? I hadn't really expected her to actually evict Jessica; I knew what a contrary harridan she could be. It has to be said though that Jessica must have known that her remaining was a massive affront to me. She must also have been aware of the risk she was taking. Had I been the more vengeful sort, I could have told Clare about the note her friend had written (funny how I still resisted hurting Clare unnecessarily, isn't is?) and thus the reason for my general hostility. Yet again I admired her nerve. They were both provoking me, but I wasn't going to respond. To hell with the pair of them!

Later that night I went up to bed.

Guest bedrooms were becoming a habit, but who was I to complain. It was only temporary after all. Before reaching my now permanent place of exile I poked my head inside our bedroom and asked the usual hopeless question, just to annoy.

"No chance of a shag then?"

I closed the door quickly. Clare might have calmed down into one of her throwing moods by now. No doubt some of you think my asking this question after every row is a trifle juvenile, even insulting, but at least it brought some humour into our dour marriage. There was nothing else in it after all.

I fell asleep nibbling the brown nipples of Jaz. Clare's nipples could rot in hell. I had forgotten what they tasted like anyway. In fact, sex with Clare had become a distinctly unattractive notion. That's love for you. There was Jaz, and I was not prepared to be unfaithful. Funny thing fidelity, it's always in the nether regions of the beholder.

The following morning we froze out the kitchen.

I sat on a stool smoking and drinking Assam tea. This was the only time I drank caffeine, and it had to be Assam. I was a man of discerning taste, or so I liked to think. One look at Clare scotched that notion though. I was fooling myself yet again. She was dithering around the kitchen sink, so something was up as Clare never went near the thing. Then she turned and gave me one of her special snarls. "I am going to see my solicitor this morning. Just for you to know I want you out of the house. As soon as possible please."

Hallelujah! Hallelujah! Hallelujah!

"Oh well, thank you for saying 'please'. Takes the bitterness out of things I suppose. Jessica moving in, is she?"

"Don't be stupid. I want a divorce, Edwin. That's all there is to it."

"And a divorce you shall have, my dearest. You can then screw Jessica to your heart's content."

Clare froze. Seconds passed.

"What? What did you say?"

"You heard. Do you think I'm stupid? Since that party you two haven't been out of each other's sight. You don't like cocks, you never have done. So it must be the other."

Clare stared at me. Mouth open. She despised me, but I wasn't about to stop. I was on a roll. I had become William Hill's Armageddon, a racing certainty. "Have you seen the pair of you? All eyes, touch. Christ, you must think I'm a complete fool. You're in love. You've swapped sides. You're—" I didn't get any further. Bang! I nearly fell to the floor. Thank God she had been too fired up to grab something. Her hand had done a good enough job though, all on its own. I reacted with a slap right across her caked-up cheek. God, did I enjoy the contact. I nearly went for another one. I was mad enough.

Up until this point I had remained calm. Apart from anything else the woman was trying to push me out of my own house. She stood in front of me now. The impact of my hand had set her back a couple of paces. The expression on her face was another one for the camera. I enjoyed every second of it. I had never hit her before. She was stunned. Shocked. For the first time in our relationship she realised I had my limits. I was human. There was only so much provocation and hurt a human being could take. I wanted to whack her again. And again. I admit it. I didn't though. Conditioning? Self-control? Who knows?

Clare's eyes killed me a few times over. There was total silence for a couple of seconds, then she turned and walked out.

CHAPTER 24

Clare cried as she drove her car to Bury St Edmunds.

"What is happening to me!" she shouted at the windscreen and passing glass faces that ignored her anguish. "What *is* happening to me?" she shouted again.

Tears were for childhood and stolen sweets, film sets and fools she kept telling herself as one hand gripped the steering-wheel and the other kept snatching at the gearstick.

"What *is* happening to me?" She couldn't stop. The tears continued to fall as the question kept thrashing her.

Were the tears a result of Edwin's hand? No.

They were tears of desperation and confusion. The dials, switches and buttons of her tin box ignored her pleas for answers. They were concerned only with her emotional driving; it was too early for the scrap-dealer's crusher. They were young with plenty of miles to go. Fresh and unused – like Clare in so many ways. Edwin's violent reaction had been coming for a long time. She had often wondered how he had always managed to exercise such incredible control. On many occasions she had actually wanted him to hit her.

These thoughts were kept deep in her hidden mind. Her own dark place. She remembered the time, not long after they had married, when Edwin had almost raped her. Well, rape was the wrong word. He had never forced himself on her. It had been close though. She had made it close. Sometimes pain and physical violence would stretch her mind into the erotic, her rare and lonely orgasms exploding on fingertips bent on punishment. These were the only orgasms she had ever known. They were hers. They were not for sharing. The punishment would always be meted out by a woman. A woman without a face or a name. A woman who lived to humiliate her: to beat her for betraying natural inclination. For corrupting nature.

For years Clare had fought her attraction to women. She had struggled and strangled herself with the complexities and conflicts of her undetermined sexuality. The violence of her hidden fantasies had instigated shame and disgust, and yet sometimes these overwhelming feelings of guilt would become a delicious adventure, an exploration into vivid sexual satisfaction. Her fingers could never resist the demanding moistness between her legs. A chance encounter with a stranger at a supermarket could sometimes stay with her for days. Until her fingers could resist no longer. The woman choosing vegetables became a manipulator. A sexual power-house. Clare would be unable to resist such strength. She would kneel and beg. Her imagination and fingers would do the rest.

Had Clare's mind been of a more liberated quality she may have celebrated her journey into the perverse. The unusual. Instead, she had been calibrated to love a man. To marry. To give birth. To be 'normal'.

She hated her prison. Her only release was fantasy and fingertip.

The players were always women. Strong and brutal. They would hurt her.

Her fictional foreplay would always begin in a benign way. A gentle touch. A gradual removing of clothing. Then her desire would take over. There would be no comic spanking, no plastic handcuffs. Her mind begged the real thing. Hard core. A woman would beat her into the abyss of pseudo-masochistic fantasy. She would always submit. She would always give in and suffer graciously. Her exquisite suffering could go on for ever. A clitoris never ejaculated and went limp. It didn't come and go. It could stay erect for hours. A man's penis was so pitifully unreliable. So useless.

Unknown to Edwin, Clare's bitterness had been her own creation, planned and constructed by Clare to protect herself against her own fingers of accusation and self-disgust. The word 'lesbian' terrified her. Sickened her.

Tears and blood-shot eyes swollen with shame and uncertainty ducked and hid from the irate frustration of crammed-in motorists. Had any one of them paused to think or look beyond their strengthened glass, compassion perhaps would have softened their motorised ferocity.

Clare thought about Jessica. Her friend from long ago. Even at the outset of their friendship she had felt an attraction. A bond. Jessica had once been a star in her fantasies. Then the fantasies had been less mature and more uncertain. Her frustrations were only just beginning to be realised at that time.

She missed Jessica when they were apart. She missed the understanding. The dependency. Whenever they were together Clare longed to touch and hold. She knew that her feelings had gone way beyond the platonic. That nonsense of friendship. The illusion. The torture of the unknown trampled on her desires. Her intuition told her that Jessica felt a mutual affection, but this was not enough for Clare. She wanted Jessica's love. She was desperate for it. She wanted Jessica.

All of her.

Did Jessica want her?

Her friend had no one important in her life, at least as far as Clare was aware. There had been no tell-tale signs of a man in Jessica's home. No razors, cologne or extra toothbrushes. She had never spoken of any man who was close to her. Had never married.

Could Jessica love another woman?

The question boiled away in Clare's mind.

She remembered an incident years ago when the two of them had had to share a hotel room on a stopover. It had been Spain, or at least somewhere hot. Their rota had allowed a few hours of afternoon sunbathing. Jessica had offered to massage some suntan lotion onto Clare's back. The oily hands had sent Clare into her dark place. The touch had not been impersonal or detached. Jessica's breath became slightly laboured as her movements coaxed and soothed. Clare had known. A sexual energy had passed between them – brief but certain. A colleague had interrupted their momentary thrill. Clare had never forgotten that brief encounter with lesbian excitement. Horror and bliss still pursued her memory.

More tears.

The unknown answers to all her questions were starting to mangle her grip on sanity. Where men were concerned, Clare had always been in control. They were always so easy to mislead, to manipulate. They were children lost in an adult world, and like children needed to be indulged and made to feel important. With Jessica she had ceased to be the mistress of her emotions. Her friend had taken away her will. Her power. She felt weak and helpless. How would Jessica respond to her devotion? Would she complete Clare as a person? Would she absolve the guilt and heal her destructive inhibition? Never before had Clare experienced such a total loss of initiative.

All these thoughts and conflicts raced through Clare's mind as she went to meet Jessica. Her friend had brought her to a new place. A place that promised both danger and fulfilment. Her impotence made her need all the more urgent.

CHAPTER 25

They met in the Angel Hotel.

Charles Dickens had stayed there once apparently, but no doubt it had been a lot cheaper then. It was a comfortable hotel, nothing really matched, but there was a feeling of 'home' about the place; it had none of the trite colour co-ordinating of modern monoliths, and you could find your way to the dining room and bar without much difficulty. In some ways the hotel caressed. This was an establishment that welcomed you as a human being rather than merely a faceless bearer of corporate plastic; it didn't push and shove,

Jessica had suggested they spend an hour together over coffee before going to see the solicitor. Back in control, Clare walked into the lounge of the hotel and couldn't resist the excitement she felt. It was always like this when she met Jessica. Her stomach would dip, her hands would shake, her heart would love.

Her friend was waiting for her on one of the sofas in the lounge.

"Hello, Clare. Come and sit down next to me. I'll order some coffee." She stood up as she spoke and gave Clare a hug and a kiss. The smell that was becoming so familiar almost made her swoon. It was Jessica's smell and always unmistakable. Natural and clean. Not bottled and created by someone else. Jessica ordered the coffee.

"Clare, you look awful. What's the matter? What have you done to your face?" Jessica noticed immediately the eyes drained of tears. The distress. The swollen cheek. She took her friend's hand. All of Clare's body reacted to the simple touch. "Edwin?" Jessica persisted.

"Yes, Edwin," Clare replied, "he hit me this morning." There was a hiatus of feminist outrage. Jessica's face turned grey, not red. Had it turned red the hotel's alarms would have gone off, what with her hair looking so combustible and about to explode.

"Hit you? The bastard! Are you OK? I mean physically?" Clare made a delicate snort. The blameless victim. Her efforts to hold back the sobs were downright courageous and even the gliding waiter was impressed. She had put some extra blusher on the swollen cheek.

"I'm fine Jessica, really. I'm fine."

"What happened exactly?"

"I told him I wanted a divorce. Like we agreed. That I was coming to see a solicitor this morning. I told him I wanted him out of the house. He made some horrible accusations . . . about you and me. God he was vicious."

"What do you mean about you and me? What did he say, Clare?"

"Awful things. Really awful. I can't repeat them." Jessica squeezed Clare's hand.

"You must, Clare. You are desperately upset, and it's no good keeping these things bottled up." Clare didn't need much persuading.

"He accused me of being your lover."

There, it was out. Clare had finally said it.

Her words had not been planned and yet she knew that a confrontation would have to arise at some time or another. Opportunity had forced her tongue to speak. As she said these words she looked at Jessica. Every part of her depended on Jessica's reaction. Her love would live or die in the next few seconds. Jessica looked Clare straight in the eyes.

"*Lovers*!" Jessica gasped, realising she was off the hook; for a few seconds there she had thought Edwin had spilt the beans about her advances. "What *is* the stupid man talking about? We haven't done anything, Clare. We are close friends that's all.

What is the matter with him? Jealous perhaps?" Jessica continued to look Clare in the eyes without letting go of her hand. Her voice was quiet now, soft. She was neither confirming nor denying. "He must know that you are a normal heterosexual woman, for heaven's sake." Clare didn't answer. She couldn't.

Silence prevailed for a few moments. An uneasy interlude filled with confusion. Then Clare spoke, at the same time hiding her disappointment at Jessica's lack of clarity.

"It's not the first time."

"What? Not more surely?"

"Yes. He has hit me before. Left me bruised, cut lip. There's been a history of it. He raped me two weeks after we married."

"Oh dear God, Clare. I'm sorry. So sorry. How have you put up with it? Why haven't you been to the police, had the bastard locked up? Husbands can't rape their wives any more. Men deserve their comeuppance. Why haven't you left him before? I had no idea. You've never said anything."

"I know. I feel so ashamed. I have always felt that it was my own fault. Edwin can be very demanding sexually. He's always very pushy. Won't take no for an answer."

"It's your right to say 'no', Clare. It's your body. Fucking men! They make me sick. They still think they own us!" There was genuine hatred in Jessica's voice, a critical anger. "You cannot go on like this, Clare. You really can't. I'm amazed that you have put up with it for so long."

Tears started to fall down Clare's cheek. "I know. I know. But what can I do? I'm not financially independent, am I!"

"You soon will be if I've got anything to do with it. How many credit cards have you got?"

"Three, why?" Clare had not expected such a question.

"Well, Edwin isn't short. I'll bet there are high credit limits on them. Start pulling out as much cash as you can before he realises. Start today. Now."

"Oh, I don't know. That's a bit dishonest." Innocent victim time again.

"No, it damn well isn't. You're an authorised user. Screw him for as much as you can. Make the bastard pay. Bleed him dry. Punish him!"

Clare was a little surprised at Jessica's frenzied solidarity and loyalty. She had expected support, understanding, she hadn't expected such anger. Had Clare known about the 'FUCK OFF' note, her love might have been more sensible. Or at least more restrained.

"OK, OK, don't worry about the finances," Jessica demurred. "Anyway Lesley will sort them out." Lesley was the solicitor they were going to see. "She will also deal with the property settlements and so on. The immediate problem is here and now. You can't put yourself at risk again. Edwin must get out of the house. Lesley will sort that out too. It may mean you staying in a hotel for a night or two. Or . . . well, I can put you up for a while."

"Oh I can't, Jessica. I can't impose."

Jessica touched Clare's cheek. "You are not imposing. Don't be silly. A friend in need and so on."

"Thank you Jessica. Thank you. I know I'll be safe with you." She sighed and turned a slow smile on Jessica, "I feel better already."

"Good. So drink up then, otherwise we'll be late – and if I know Lesley, she'll probably charge you for it. Solicitors. All the same."

Lesley Moresby & Co., Solicitors, poked out from a small side street located two minutes walk from the Angel Hotel. Moresby was a sole practitioner. She enjoyed an independence that allowed her to do what she liked in her fight for 'Welfare Rights', 'Debtors Rights' and 'Female Rights' generally. The press had dubbed her 'The Thinking Woman's Champion'. The woman was a zealot, a serious enemy, but most of all a boiler-suited, hard-hatted dyke with a chin capable of slicing men's hearts to pieces, not to mention solid granite.

They were met by a thin, frightened secretary, old before her time. Premature lines raced around her face fighting for somewhere to live. She was only thirty-five but looked sixty-five. She had worked for Moresby for ten years. Before this grave mistake where her choice of employment was concerned she had been a full-bodied and pretty example of womanhood. Men chased her short skirts, her make-up, her silliness. They adored her.

Moresby enlightened her and then seduced her. Being the charitable sort though, Moresby had kept her on as a loyal slave. Apart from anything else, manumission was appropriate only for those women who were loud and aggressive enough. Ugliness helped. Staff didn't count. Neither did spineless weaklings. Pam, the secretary, was both. Yet Pam remained puzzled: if men were so bad, why did Muz Moresby constantly try to be one?

Pam's persecuted femininity would sometimes rebel. The cold and impersonal office was occasionally subjected to the insult of a flower or two, but even they would wilt and dry up prematurely when attacked by the nasty contempt of her boss. Even so, a day or so of colour and beauty was worth the effort. The miserable grey walls and black furniture seemed to appreciate the diversion even if Lesley Moresby did not.

"We have an appointment for 11.30," Jessica announced.

"Ah yes," Pam looked at a diary. "Mrs Hillyard, is it not?"

"Yes," Clare answered. Being assertive was taking more of an effort with Jessica around.

"Please sit down, Muz Moresby won't be long. Would you like some tea? I'm afraid it's herbal; we don't keep coffee either. Muz Moresby is very health conscious, you see."

"No, thank you," Jessica answered, "we've just had some coffee." Neither Jessica nor Clare could make out whether the secretary was being sarcastic, facetious or matter of fact.

"Very well then. I expect Muz Moresby will come out when she is ready."

Clare was quiet. She had married a solicitor, lived with him for a few years and yet she still felt nervous. Her working-class roots engendered deference, even fear. She had been impressed by Edwin's sophistication, his urbane and cultured intelligence. It hadn't only been about money. Her marriage had ensured status, class. She could keep her nose permanently bent upwards. Her superior delusions had served her well. She would be a modestly wealthy woman in her own right before too long, she was sure of it.

"Are you all right?" Jessica asked. Her hand touched Clare's again. A look passed between them, a look that spoke a great deal more than Plato's musings on friendship.

"Yes, I'm fine. Just a little nervous. What's this friend of yours like anyway? If she's anywhere near as bolshie as Edwin, then God help him!"

"Oh, Lesley is a tough cookie, make no mistake. She certainly doesn't believe in kid-glove treatment. I've known her for quite a few years. Has a good reputation particularly when it comes to divorce settlements. You may find her a little . . . hard. Unfriendly even. Don't be put off. It's just her way. She's a babe in arms underneath the bullet-proof armour. She understands women and their side of things. She will fight to the death for you, believe me."

"She may need to, Jessica. I have no idea how Edwin will react to all this. Sometimes, in the past, I have often felt that I don't know him at all. He is very unpredictable."

"Well, don't worry. Lesley will sort it all out for you. I know she will. I have every confidence. You should too."

Lesley Moresby emerged from her office.

Cropped ginger hair shouted at everything she surveyed. She was a woman in her late thirties, tall, big boned, big jawed and big mouthed, in a long black dress with no sleeves. Freckles and ginger hair covered her formidable forearms. Her thighs couldn't be seen, but no doubt they were capable pieces of hard muscle. The woman wore no make-up or jewellery. Without the dress most people would have assumed she was a man. There were no obvious mounds of flesh up front to disabuse them either. She was the destroyer of family life, the rejection of husband and children, but more than anything else the promoter extraordinaire of lesbianism as the only way forward for equal rights, emancipation and opportunity for women.

Lesley Moresby was a mighty, if physically and mentally deranged, fanatic.

"Muz Hillyard, Jessica, would you like to come through?" She held open her office door for the briefest of moments and went back to her desk. Clare and Jessica were allowed to find their own way. Moresby saw marriage as an affront to female kind, thus the address of 'Muz'. Courtesy didn't come into it.

"Please sit down," Moresby ordered.

When all three were seated Moresby made sure that the air reeked of 'Let's all become lezzies and rule the world'. Yet her miasma of ridicule and contempt for heterosexual normality was no more than a passing atmospheric disturbance, since lesbianism, like gayness, racism and feminism had become old hat. They were now all part of society's lush tapestry, and most people with any degree of sense couldn't care less. And rightly so. The poor woman was yesterday's lesbian but had yet to realise it.

Clare was the most pathetic of the turbulent trio. She suffered. She did not celebrate her stubborn confusion. Her search for self-determination had been a bloody mutilation and nothing more. As she looked at the comical conundrum in front of her she became a traitor for a few brief moments. Perhaps she was better off with a man after all. At least Edwin knew which side of the fence to throw his balls over.

As requested, Clare did her assassination of Edwin competently and without flourish. When she had finished Cropped Hair expelled a convincing sigh of sympathy and understanding. As convincing as her manly jowls allowed anyway.

"Well, your spouse is a right bastard, no doubt about it." She was fond of the legal niceties this one. "I must advise you though that no doubt he will deny every word. Men are such fucking liars, you know." She frothed the last sentence. "From what you have told me he is obviously wealthy. In fact I have met him. He has done very well, at least that's the word amongst the local legal fraternity – I won't say brotherhood. There are a few of us women in there these days. This being the case, we will need more info about his finances and then get Counsel's opinion. We won't worry about a settlement for now. I presume a divorce is your main priority?" Clare faltered for a moment. Was this all going too fast, given that her security, her home and pampered lifestyle were at risk? Jessica noticed her friend's nervousness and spoke for her.

"Yes of course Lesley, it must be." The two pros eyed the amateur. Ineptness was frustrating.

"Er . . . yes, I suppose so." Clare finally confirmed.

"Good," Moresby said, "I feel that the best course is to have him for unreasonable behaviour. You have mentioned violence. That's a good start. First thing to do though is to get him out of the house. We don't want you at further risk. I'll see to an injunction. Will you be OK for a day or two? I can do an emergency job."

Finances? Violence? Injunctions? It was all flying straight over Clare's head. All she could think of was the woman sitting next to her and money. Why did divorce have to complicate things?

"Whatever you say, Lesley. Quite honestly I don't think Edwin will hit me again. He's not a violent man really—"

"Yes, yes," Moresby interrupted, not wanting to hear anything in Edwin's defence, "just leave it all to me."

She then went into the ins and outs of a matrimonial war, rubbing her hands to combustible levels as she tallied up her fees. Clare was a private client so it was open season. None of your Legal Services Commission crap here. No begging for some paltry Legal Aid.

The prospect of bleeding that arrogant bastard Edwin Hillyard dry made her mouth water. She hadn't forgotten the time he had called her 'a prickless bulldog who needed a shave' at that Law Society dinner.

This job would be a delight. A crusade even. The more of a mess, the more contention, bitterness and acrimony she inspired, the fatter her fee. After all, it was her job and she had been well trained. The Law Society prided itself on its training excellence. Clare was a victim. A female one. A kindred spirit, but let's not take loyalty to her sisters too far. Moresby had a 'partner' to keep and an expensive one at that. The clothes and make-up were costing a fortune. Moresby liked the sexy underwear, but did it always have to be silk?

A busy woman, Cropped Hair called the meeting to an end. She stood up.

"Right, well I know all I need to know for now, Clare. Leave things to me. Any problems, give Pam a ring. I'll need to see you again in due course, but let's get the priorities out of the way first. Mr Hillyard is in dire need of eviction. I'll be in touch." She leaned over her desk and stuck out a paw that could have crushed Clare with one squeeze. Clare's small hand nearly disappeared without trace.

As Jessica and her new client walked out, Moresby eyed Clare. The bum was something else, no doubt about it. She wouldn't have minded a bit of it herself. She loved cute femininity even when it cost her a fortune. Her partner wouldn't mind a sexy little diversion, tough if she did. Lesbian love was no different from the heterosexual variety. Moresby was a slut through and through. Proud of it. Her fidelity may have applied to women only, but which woman was irrelevant.

A few minutes later they were standing on the pavement outside Moresby's office.

"Are you OK, Clare?" Jessica asked. Her friend looked worn and tense.

"Just about. I never realised divorce could be so . . . er . . . dramatic. I feel a little overwhelmed."

"Yes, it must all be a bit of a shock. The violence doesn't help. Seeing you in there made me all the more determined to avoid marriage. At all costs. It just isn't worth it."

"No Jessica, it isn't."

"Well, you can't go home tonight. Come back to Norwich with me. Leave your car in Edwin's office car park." Clare held her enthusiasm in check.

"That would be nice I must admit. I don't want to be on my own at the moment. Some company would be appreciated. You've been so kind Jessica, you really have. I'm very grateful. I know you're busy and I appreciate all this."

"Don't be silly. You would do the same for me. Now leave Lesley do her job. Forget about Edwin. Let's enjoy some shopping therapy – on Edwin as I suggested. Don't feel bad about it for heaven's sake, he deserves all he gets, trust me." Clare didn't need much persuading as her previous pangs of guilt, even if counterfeit, had quickly vanished in Moresby's office. Besides, her magnetic strips hadn't seen daylight for twenty-four hours and soon they would start to complain.

"Yes, let's!"

Any semblance of regret, remorse, or any other of the more decent traits of human nature dissipated in the eyes of one obsessed with self, possession and purchasing power. For a while the two women searched. They were after the best. Clare coveted all the things she didn't need and therefore wanted. Eventually standing in an upmarket jewellery shop she decided upon a discreet but extremely expensive piece of jewellery. She produced her platinum card. The assistant smiled and took her card, Mrs Hillyard was a valued customer. When the assistant returned her face had changed. There was puzzlement and an embarrassed blush.

"Mrs Hillyard, I'm so sorry but the credit card company will not authorise the purchase. . . . I really don't know what to say." The woman held the card at arm's length. It had turned into a platinum excrescence.

Clare looked at the woman then glanced over her shoulder to see if anyone was looking, not that she cared much either way. "What? That's impossible! Not accepted? That's ridiculous! How dare you! There's a mistake. There must be."

"I really am so sorry, Mrs Hillyard. On transactions for this amount of money we always telephone the credit card company direct. They will not authorise the purchase. . . . Maybe they have some IT problems or something. It does happen." The assistant didn't want to experience the wrath of Mrs Hillyard. It was well known.

Clare fumed, "Don't be stupid! IT problems? Whoever heard of such a thing? Try this one instead. My husband has probably forgotten to make the monthly payment or something. Now hurry up will you?"

Relieved, the shop assistant disappeared again only to return looking even more fearful. This was not a good day.

"I'm sorry, Mrs Hillyard," she whimpered, "the card company will not authorise the payment."

"What?! Are you mad? That's just not possible!" Clare was beginning to lose control, and it wasn't due to divorce either. Jessica had noticed that her friend was attracting the attention of other customers. The situation was becoming tiresome. She took her friend's arm.

"Come on Clare, I think I know what has happened." She looked at the distraught assistant and said, "I'm so sorry. It's not your fault. Mrs Hillyard is a little upset at the moment. I hope you will understand. Come on Clare, let's go and have some coffee or something." She smiled at the assistant, took the proffered plastic and dragged Clare out of the shop.

As they walked to Jessica's car Clare swore and steamed. Coffee was out, so Jessica decided to head back to Norwich. After about half an hour into the journey Clare finally calmed down and moaned, "The bastard. He's stopped my use of the credit cards."

"He's quick Clare, I'll give him that." He knows you too, she nearly added but didn't fancy another outburst.

For the rest of the journey Clare grieved. She felt so alone, so bereft. Her life was in shreds. She had never known such horrendous loss. What would she do? Who could she turn to?

Without her cards she ceased to exist. This was worse than divorce! Perhaps some counselling was in order, it was the 'in thing' these days after all. Her brain sniffed as she looked across at the driver. At least there was Jessica.

The card humiliation was forgotten for the rest of the journey as Jessica constantly touched and held Clare's hand. She was Clare's only ally, only true friend. Each time Jessica's fingertip landed Clare shivered. She felt naked and exposed. They hardly spoke during the journey, tactile communication was enough.

The silence allowed Clare to wallow in both fear and excitement at the anticipation of what might be. She knew instinctively that their friendship had entered a new phase, a higher level, but again there was the unknown. The steps out of fantasy into reality frightened her. Her masturbatory journeys had been so harmless and secret, they had been simple dreams with no substance. She was always safe, anonymous. But consciousness and light pulled them apart. Now she was on the brink, an edge that she could not define or know. She felt a childish awareness of danger, a danger that existed when fantasy became tangible, when it could be touched and seen.

She could not stretch her vision away from Jessica's lips, her thighs, her breasts. Every time Jessica pushed down the clutch more thigh would be revealed. A muscle would murmur. Clare wanted to reach into herself there and then. She had never known such sexual urgency. Such primitive lust. Looking at Jessica, Clare knew that there could be no turning back. Here was her future. No man had ever made her body and will rage in such a way. No man had ever made her feel so weak and submissive. The contradiction titillated and intimidated all at the same time, yet even so she knew deep down that she was at long last finding herself. The real Clare.

CHAPTER 26

While Clare and Jessica were driving to Norwich, Tom's patience was beginning to wear extremely thin. Not only was this the third day he had had to take the children to school, it was also the third day he had had to leave the office to go and collect them. It wouldn't do, it really wouldn't.

Tom was a kind and understanding man by nature and not one to create unnecessary waves, but Lucretia was pushing it. Three mornings on the trot she had stayed in bed with a 'headache' and for three afternoons the 'headaches' had refused to abate. Pain killers had proved ineffective, as had his genuine sympathy. It was all getting too much. Now his wife wasn't even answering the telephone. At the moment he didn't know whether he should be worrying or getting angry.

Lucretia was fading, that was the only way he could describe it. The laughter had disappeared from her eyes and she was becoming so irritable that he was scared to open his mouth. Last night his crunching on a few Walkers crisps had been enough to set her off. Good God, the woman had blown a gasket over a couple of crisps. What the hell next?

He had tried everything. Doctors, not answering back, agreeing to everything, you name it. It had all got him precisely nowhere. For a moment the thought that she might be having an affair entered his head. After all the telephone wasn't being answered, so was she in bed – or, more to the point, was she in someone else's bed? No. Impossible. He was being stupid, he trusted Lucretia. Besides, each time he arrived home she looked such a mess that a blind deaf and dumb inebriate wouldn't go anywhere near her. Such a beautiful woman too. That was another thing, she seemed to have lost all pride in her appearance.

Dear God, what was he going to do? The woman was ill, he was sure of it. Seriously ill at that. But she just refused to do anything about it, kept blaming the menopause. Menopause his arse, she was too young – not that he was any expert on menopausal madness he had to admit. Since when did this mysterious change in female hormones completely poleaxe a woman anyway? Mind you, he had heard a few horrific tales about menopausal insanity from his friends, so maybe Lucretia was right after all.

When he arrived home, offspring in tow, Lucretia was sitting down at the kitchen table. These days it was either their bed or the kitchen table. Nothing in between. For a moment Tom sighed with relief. She was looking normal, dressed and made-up. Not that she wore a great deal of makeup, but the little she did wear made a difference.

"Oh hello. You're feeling better than?" Tom asked gently. All his words had to be gentle; anything else was likely to set off a nuclear holocaust.

"Yes I'm fine, thank you Tom. Feeling great in fact." Lucretia smiled and Tom nearly fell over. That's it. The woman's bloody mad. She's lost it. No other possible explanation. One minute bitch extraordinaire, the next lovable kitten. His friends had warned him.

"Well . . . I'm . . . er . . . glad to hear it. Headache finally gone, has it?"

"Oh yes, definitely. I feel great, I really do."

"Er . . ." Take it slowly now, Tom boy. You never know. "Er . . . I tried ringing you to see if you were OK, but no answer. I tried a few times in fact. Had you gone out or something?"

"What do you mean?" Lucretia straightened up. "What do you mean, Tom?"

"I mean, did you go out somewhere this afternoon? I'm only asking because it was a bit difficult collecting the children from school. I had to cancel a couple of clients . . . and being as your headache seems to be better I was just wondering why I—" Tom wasn't allowed to finish his sentence.

"Oh dear, Lord Denning had to cancel a couple of clients, did he?" The sarcasm was dripping from Lucretia's tongue like fat from a pig on a spit. "Well isn't that a shame! As it so happens, I did go out for an hour or two. A walk, not that that is any of your business. Stressful schools runs, aren't they? You know how you love stress. Thrive on it, so I didn't think you'd mind."

"Oh right. OK. Fair enough, Lucretia. I'm not going to argue with you. That's fine. Will you be taking them to school tomorrow?"

"I might." The smiles had disappeared now. There was nothing but spite in his wife's eyes. Even dislike. This was crazy. What had he done? What had he said?

"OK, well look, I have to go back to the office. Will you be all right with the children?" He wasn't too sure about this; was she safe with them? He never thought he would be asking himself these questions about his wife. Of course she would, now he was getting neurotic.

"What kind of question is that, Tom? Don't be silly. Now off you go, lamb chops for supper?" The smiles were back. Jesus Christ.

"Yes . . . yes. Fine. I'll see you later. About six."

"Don't work too hard, darling." Lucretia stood up and kissed him on the cheek. "I'm sorry for being such a bitch, take no notice."

Tom walked out of the house trying to come to terms with what had just happened and wondering who needed help the most, he or Lucretia.

CHAPTER 27

Jessica's home was a ground floor apartment in an old Victorian house. The building stood in its own grounds on the wealthy side of Norwich. It had been renovated and converted with no expense spared.

Jessica led the way through the front door.

Once again Clare was struck immediately by the space. The emptiness. There were no personal touches, no personality. Not even the odd photo or magazine out of kilter. Here was minimalism at its most extreme. 'Nothing' was the room's raison d'être. Their shoes echoed on bare floorboards. The walls of the sitting room had been painted white, the only two items of furniture were also white, a leather settee waiting to be pounced on by a crowd of people and a coffee table that virtually sat on the floor. Above the fireplace a square of black paint purported to be a picture.

There was no invitation for debate or discussion in the room. It was efficient, pragmatic and easy to clean. A cleaning lady would have been a waste of money.

"Sit down Clare. I'll get us a drink," Jessica said. "A decent one. Relax. It's been a long and tiring day. Let me take your coat." She removed Clare's coat from her shoulders. Her fingers lingered on the base of Clare's neck. Was it intentional or an accident? Clare felt the contact run right through her. Again she felt naked.

She sat down on the sofa. It made her feel tiny, even useless. The leather was cold and noisy so comfort had to be worked at. It reminded her of her past.

Here in Jessica's home she began to absorb the effect of white and black. The room started to warm up in a benign and subtle way. There were no quarrels here, no antagonism. The blankness was neutral in every way, as if the air around her required no explanation or hasty words. Slowly she began to understand, in her own small way.

Jessica returned and handed Clare a glass that seemed to have the same bold contempt for chaos as the rest of the room. It was wide, straight and deep. No pattern, no colour.

"Here you are Clare, it's an exceptionally large G and T. Don't rush it for heaven's sake otherwise you will be flat out. You're already tired and stressed, so go slowly." She smiled and handed the glass to Clare as she sat down next to her.

"This glass is huge. And heavy!" Clare exclaimed. "Wherever did you get them? I've never seen glasses like this before."

"Well, they're more tumblers, I suppose. They are different though, that's why I like them. They're so . . . functional. Hold plenty of alcohol too, which is more to the point."

Neither of the two women said anything for a few moments. They drank and enjoyed. Clare was the first to speak.

"You know, I am surprised at how easy all this divorce business is. That Lesley woman made it all seem so simple. At first I was so confused, but now things are beginning to make sense. I'm not so sure though whether Edwin will be too happy about things, particularly when he gets the bills!" They both laughed.

"God, yes," Jessica said. "I'd love to see the old bastard's face when he has to pay up. Being turfed out of his own precious house isn't going to make him too happy either, is it? Can you imagine the look on his face?" They laughed again. The room didn't enjoy the frivolity – the picture turned even blacker. It didn't like having its minimal equilibrium disturbed.

There were a few moments of silence. One of those lapses in conversation that for the insecure can be troubling. Clare, who was normally of the extrovert disposition and hated silences, for once felt at ease. It was the 'Jessica effect' again. She sipped her drink, thought for a moment and said, "You know Jessica, my divorce from Edwin will be a release. I don't feel any regret. Not even a sense of loss. I've read somewhere that divorce is worse than bereavement. For me it's a wonderful relief. I just want to celebrate. No more foul mouth, no more stinking farts. And the freedom. God, I feel great! You know I'm beginning to realise how little I feel for him. I never have loved him, you know. He's just been a passport if I'm honest. A passport to security. Perhaps I don't even know what love is." Her voice quietened. There was a sadness in her smile.

She turned to Jessica. Her eyes begged and implored. With enormous courage her finger reached out and touched Jessica's cheek. Jessica's eyes did not hesitate, did not detract. They lingered and held.

"Oh Clare," Jessica whispered as she took Clare's hand in her own, "Love can be many things. I will try and show you how beautiful it can be." She stood up and still holding Clare's hand led her to the bedroom. They both stood by the bed. Jessica's tongue met Clare's and a passion that Clare had only ever fantasised about erupted.

"Slowly," Jessica said, "slowly." They continued to kiss, pausing only to undo and unclasp. They remained standing, naked now, their breasts pushing against one another, their nipples reddened and taut. Jessica turned Clare around and placed her hands on the mattress,

"Open your legs," she ordered. The voice had changed. Clare had already left the only world she was familiar with. She did as she was told. Hands squeezed her buttocks. Left to right. Right to left. They stroked and touched. A tongue dug and pushed as fingers stretched and stroked and nails scratched and hurt. Jessica explored places that would have normally sickened Clare. Now she just poured and opened. There was no control.

"Do you like it Clare? Do you like me licking you? Touching you? Fucking you?" Clare could only just respond,

"Yes . . . oh yes!"

Jessica's voice had become more demanding. Coarser, more uncouth. She continued to probe with her tongue and fingers,

"Yes, oh God yes," Clare could only whisper. She was overcome by her own appetite. Jessica pushed her onto the bed and turned her over. She held down Clare's arms as she kissed her. There was more brutality.

"Clare, you're so wet. Soaking."

Jessica thrust again and again with her tongue as she sucked and bit. Deeper. Faster. All Clare could do was moan. Submit. She was lost. Before she knew what was happening she was lying on her front and her wrists were being tied to the corners of the bed. The helplessness increased her rate of orgasm.

"You've always wanted this, haven't you? Wanted to be fucked by another woman. Abused. I've known for years." Jessica hit Clare hard on the buttocks, again and again. The violence went way beyond soft spanking. Skin turned red. Livid. Clare howled with pleasure and pain. The sheets became wetter. As Jessica hit with one hand she masturbated furiously with the other. There was a pause as Jessica reached out to a bedside cabinet and withdrew her favourite toy. No oil was needed.

"I'm going to really screw you now, Clare." The phallic toy entered Clare. There was no warning, no finesse as she yelled and begged.

"Oh God, don't stop! Don't stop! I can't stop coming. Oh, please don't stop! Hurt me! Hurt me! Do what you like to me!"

Jessica lowered her head again. Tongue and dildo. In and out. Fast.

"Oh God . . . I'm being torn in two!" Clare almost screamed as the orgasms seemed to go on forever. .

"You love it though Clare, don't you? You really love it!"

Jessica's hand continued to play with herself. She was in control. Always in control. "Now it's my turn," Jessica said as removed the dildo. She untied Clare's wrists, turned her over and then straddled her face, "Lick me Clare, everywhere!" she ordered "Squeeze my breasts, you bitch! My nipples!" Jessica ordered again as she rubbed herself over Clare's face and tongue.

"That's it. Lick me. Lick until I tell you to stop! Oh God! Oh. . . . Oh. . . . Oh Christ! I'm coming . . . I'm coming!" She ground her pubis into Clare's face as her fingers gripped and pulled. Jessica was off on her own private journey as she soaked Clare who could only drink and love. Neither one of the women wanted to stop. Sex was all. Clare's was to do. To comply. To submit. At last she had been liberated and all her inhibitions demolished.

Hours later as dawn began to creep around the room the two women finally fell asleep.

Jessica had used and exploited. She had screwed Edwin Hillyard's wife, what sweeter revenge could there be? No-one ever rejected Jessica Howard. Ever.

And Clare? Well at least now she knew who she was.

She was also in love for the first time in her life.

CHAPTER 28

They were sitting in Jessica's office at the top of the building where she worked. Stuart McKenzie, the man from the Legal Services Commission, allowed Jessica to have her say as long as her words eventually led to the bedroom. She was trying to extort funding from him, but he wanted something in return for his good offices.

McKenzie was as much a player as she was. He also had the looks and disingenuous charm to match hers. The casework audit reports sitting in his briefcase were nothing to write home about. The file management systems had been below standard and some of the case work downright negligent.

Ms. Howard seemed confident enough, but unbeknown to her this confidence was going to cost. He held all the cards after all. The audit reports in his briefcase empowered him to pull the financial plug. This would not do Ms. Howard's self-esteem any good, of that he was certain. He had the edge and intended using it.

All the aces were in his briefcase.

If Jessica Howard thought she was smart, he was smarter. He knew her legs and bosom were being used to full effect, so let's see if she would put her body where her mouth was. Mind you, the other way around could be just as interesting. He continued to listen and to amuse his mind. Eventually, feeling that Jessica was truly spent he said, "Right then Jessica, I think we have explored all the main points. Obviously I will need to consider my recommendations and let you know in due course." He was purposely being uncommitted. Jessica took the bait.

"How long will that be, do you think? I do have to plan for next year. Development, budgets and so on, you understand."

"I really can't say at the moment. You are in competition with other bids, as no doubt you are aware. There is only so much money in the pot after all. We have to consider all bids fairly and impartially; I know you will understand." Give her some of her own bullshit, McKenzie thought. "We must look at each bid on its merits. Priority will be given to those areas in greatest need. It's fair to say I think that Norwich does not quite have the same need say . . . of an inner city like Birmingham, for example."

"Maybe not," Jessica was not going to let him get off the hook so easily, "but we are a large rural community, and there still are lots of problems out there. Real stresses and strains. Farmers going bankrupt and so on." To hell with that one. These precious farmers had been making a fortune from the Common Agricultural Policy for years. Sod them, let them stand on their own two Wellingtons for once, or Range Rovers for that matter.

"All these things will be taken into account I assure you."

"I must know as soon as possible Stuart, I really must." This was getting better by the minute. The woman was almost pleading.

"I will try to expedite things as quickly as possible, Jessica. Leave it with me. I understand your impatience, I really do."

Jessica smiled and caught his eyes. "It's nearly lunchtime," she said, deliberately looking at her watch, a delicate item designed for a female wrist. Jessica even changed watches according to who she was going to ensnare, her working watch being a ham-fisted affair, practical and no nonsense.

She turned to him. "Would you like to join me, Stuart?"

"Yes, why not."

"How about some authentic Norfolk sausages and mash?" He didn't look the vegetarian type, this one. She would have to suffer for the cause again.

"Sounds good to me."

"You're not in any rush are you?"

"No, Friday afternoons usually take care of themselves. If you want to get something done it's usually impossible to find anybody working anyway. So no, I'm not in any rush. All the time in the world in fact."

"Great. Let's go then."

They both knew that there was more on the menu than a Norfolk sausage.

Later that afternoon they arrived back at Jessica's flat. They hadn't finished their drinks when Jessica went to her bedroom and returned stark naked. Neither of them said a word. She knelt down on the floor in front of McKenzie and undid his flies. She pulled his trousers down to his kneecaps, ignoring how ridiculous he looked. There was no hurry. She used the tips of her fingers to stroke and play. Slowly. She then used her tongue to tease and tempt. He couldn't move.

After a few minutes Jessica looked up and said, "Do I get my funding then?" There was a pause as McKenzie composed himself.

"Oh, I think something can be arranged, Jessica."

CHAPTER 29

"But Jessica, I haven't seen you for ages!"

"Four days, Clare, to be precise . . ."

"Four days seems such a long time," Clare whined down the telephone.

"I know, but I'm very busy at the moment. Audits and so on. Please be patient, Clare. Maybe I can manage something on Saturday. Now calm down."

"Saturday! That's still five days away!"

"Yes, well that's the way it has to be, I'm afraid. Please understand."

There was silence. A resignation.

"All right, if you say so. Shall I come over to you?"

"Er . . . no . . . at least let me think about it." Jessica remembered a male date somewhere in her diary. While female flesh was fine as a diversion, masculine meat was usually more satisfying. McKenzie had been inventive she had to admit. They hadn't left things at a quick blow-job. He had been a repeater too. She had his number, perhaps a return match would be in order soon. "Look, I'll ring you tomorrow when I know where I am, all right?"

"It will have to be, I suppose." Clare was sulking. A spoilt brat and Jessica hated brats – of any description.

"Now, more to the point how is everything at home? No problems with Edwin?"

"No, none. Went like a lamb. Packed some things and disappeared. Probably sleeping in his office or something. I don't care either way. He wasn't difficult."

"Well, that's something – sensible man." Jessica would have loved to have seen Edwin creeping away from his own house like some disappointed thief on a lonely night.

"Clare, I must go now. I'll ring you tomorrow."

"Promise?"

"Yes, promise."

"Saturday?"

"I'll try. Now I have things to do. Must dash. Goodbye."

Jessica disconnected the line.

Clare was becoming a nuisance. Jessica hadn't mentioned the letter that had landed on her doormat that morning. She hadn't given Clare the chance. She had known from the expectant pauses in Clare's voice that the woman was almost biting off her fingernails with anticipation. Jessica hadn't been ready to discuss the contents of the letter that Clare had written. Her reaction needed to be measured, calculated.

Clare was in love with her.

For Jessica love meant commitment, which meant problems. Tears. Clare had been easy to manipulate and fool. Easy to abuse. She had seen this coming and cursed herself for allowing it to happen. Clare's touch, her kiss, pleaded with need and vulnerability. Two of the most dangerous ingredients required for love to prosper and intensify. Love sought out these conditions, hunted them down like the most voracious of predators.

"Love?" Jessica said the word out loud to herself. Its outrageous price always had to be paid in full as it never came with any arrangement for payment, settlement or less exacting monthly instalments. Its currency never changed, and tears and blood were always in surplus. Men and women wrecked and savaged their own humanity in an attempt to secure the unreal and unobtainable, when all 'love' really did was betray, commit treason and never take prisoners.

"Love." She said the word again, only this time she laughed. A laugh scented with tears long ago given and returned only with sickening mockery. For Jessica 'love' also meant fear, but most of all the handing over of who she was. Or who she had become. Now her soul was impregnable. Hers. There was no part of it left to give. She cherished its remnants and hoarded its precious debris. Nothing living would ever again take away the only gift left that she could truly honour and obey.

Herself.

She poured herself a large drink and drank most of it before sitting down in her cold sitting room. Her mind passed quickly from profound introspection to the more uncomplicated and mundane. It was easier. Stuart, the man from the LSC, had been fun. Straightforward. They had both known the rules. No illusions. No frills. Just sex and no questions or feelings, apart from those given to the carnal moment. She revisited the sex with Stuart. He had been good. Not the best, but good.

The simplicity of Stuart was quickly replaced by Clare again. The woman wouldn't leave her mind alone. The cerebral nagging and persistence never seemed to stop. Why couldn't Clare be as simple as Stuart? Why did she have to make all these mental demands all the time?

Jessica poured herself another drink. What was she going to do about Clare? The framed blackness above the fireplace stared at her. It wanted answers. It wanted her to look within at her own blackness, to seek out the truth of her own rarely revealed secrets. She was forced to confront the words as they drifted towards her. Choice? Independence? Strength? Compassion? The blackness impaled her brain as it chased her mind away from denial and deceit.

Admission, its cruelty.

Childhood agonies, parental suicide, a loneliness that intoxicated and inflicted, came to her as her hidden suffering was resurrected. Her eyes looked and saw. She submitted to the will of a blackness that gave nothing away.

In an instant she stopped looking and retreated.

Enough for one day.

She finished her drink as decisiveness arrived. Clare must be hurt, her love ruined before it found greater depth and meaning. Jessica and her 'self' must remain untouched, unscathed. She did not want a troubled mind. Clare was destined to be a victim in Jessica's arena, but at least the killing stroke would be executed with compassion. She would miss Clare's body but console herself with its memory. She also knew that Clare would continue to accompany her toys and fingers for some time to come. She would still use her friend, but in a less direct and kinder way.

Once again Jessica's compassion blended with her easy detachment. But at least there was compassion, and perhaps even a hint of contrition as well.

CHAPTER 30

The train lurched and brought me back.

I had been thrown out of my home and treated like a mass murderer for giving my wife a gentle tap on the chin – in self-defence I may add. Right now I was on my way to see Jaz. Sanctuary, peace and sanity.

On the divorce front the only satisfaction I had experienced so far was Clare's epileptic fit over her credit cards. That had been quite something. I was still waiting in anticipation for the 'how much?' bit. I knew my divorce was going to be expensive – but how expensive, that was the thing! Deciding that this was a particularly unedifying exercise I thought of Jaz instead and her lovely face. Divorce, irretrievable breakdown and financial settlements quickly vanished. They always did when Jaz entered my head.

Since my expulsion from domestic bliss I had been travelling back and fore to Baker Street. Jaz had been kind enough to share her bed, and on those occasions when the commute had been too formidable a prospect, I had used the vacant one-bedroomed flat above the office.

I didn't want to buy another house yet. Not in Suffolk anyway. Besides, any purchase would depend on how much the divorce cost me. More importantly were the living arrangements for Jaz and myself. I knew only too well that we were in the 'honeymoon' period. Things could well go tits up, so caution had to be exercised. This was the line I kept spinning myself anyway. The romantic spark in me said otherwise. Marriage, home, babies, this was my hidden agenda. I knew I had finally met my soul mate – oh God, now I'm sounding like one of those bloody silly presenters on daytime television.

'Soul mate', my arse. No seriously, I have to admit that I was utterly besotted with the woman; it can happen you know, even to me. Every time I saw her I wanted to slobber all over her.

I eventually arrived at Jazland.

I was greeted by her beauty and lips, more than enough for any man. Most evenings the idiots' lantern was ignored; we gave each other enough enjoyment without the dour bluntness of *Coronation Street* or *EastEnders*. We would sit holding each other and talking. Nothing important, just discovering who we were. We would touch and laugh, understand and delight each other. The nights with Jaz had become something worth living for.

Some nights I would wander and smoke. I would sit alone in her sitting room, the red cigarette-end the only light. Don't be fooled by my comic words, my casual safety nets. Divorce is a painful, extreme and horrible end. There are always tears, inside and out. Always crushing 'whys' and unanswerable 'what ifs'.

Often footsteps could be heard and Jaz would sit on the floor in front of me, her head resting in my lap.

"Can't you sleep?" she would ask.

"No Jaz, I'm restless. Sorry I woke you, go back to bed, I won't be long."

"Not without you," she would reply.

Sometimes we would stay like that until daylight pulled us apart. It had been many years since I had known such an honest and transparent love. It had been many years since love had created a tear of happiness.

During the weeks we had known each other our person-alities adjusted, flared and stroked. I had the edge – but only just. We fought to find each other's measure. We would argue about everything. Two blue-arsed and frantic flies buzzing up a window was enough to set off a battle for dominance. We were both strong willed. We clashed over many things but would always reach a truce before things became terminal – better than most 'happy' couples I suspect. We had our own way with each other. Our own kind of love.

With Jaz I came to rediscover the man I had forgotten. The one who knew how to give unconditionally and how to love. The skills of meaningful touch and eyes that were able to speak returned. The silent communication and gentle telepathy of love were handed back to me. The layers of thick dust that had covered the little things were blown away by my Asian woman. The sleepy words of concern in the troubled nights, a tailored cup of tea made just the way I like it. The food prepared in ways that only my palate enjoyed. All these thoughtful expressions of care brought me back to a life I had once known. A life that enjoyed the substance of love. With Clare there had been none of these simple things. The critical things.

Jaz was doing a night shift later that evening so I prepared the food. Pasta, pesto and punchy chilli. We both liked things hot. She dashed off to do her healing bit and left me alone to read and listen to Radio 4. At about 5.00 a.m. she returned and slid into bed. She tried not to disturb me but I felt her warm body all the same. I pulled her body into my own and felt an overwhelming peace. She was close and mine. She was all I needed.

Later on I felt a stirring next to me and opened my eyes. Jaz was kneeling on the bed looking at me. Neither one of us spoke. It was a serious moment. She touched my cheek and said quietly, "Don't ever leave me, Edwin. I love you so much."

I sat up and kissed her hand then her lips and said, "That's all I need to hear."

She still seemed agitated. Her eyes were intense and seemed to be struggling with something.

"Edwin, I must talk to you about Clare. I haven't interfered or intruded into your divorce but I would like to know what is happening. I don't want to be the 'other woman', neither do I want Clare to feel hatred. Please understand."

I looked at her and could see only kindness. She didn't want to hurt anyone. Bad karma. I knew that I had spoken little about my divorce. Not from any motive of deceit; I had merely wanted to keep Jaz out of things. Out of our own clean world. I had refused to use her as an emotional punch bag and was not prepared to place my burden on her innocent shoulders.

"I'm sorry," I said, "it's not my intention to exclude you. Never has been. Divorce is such a dirty business. It's rancid and cruel. It's not a place I want to take you."

"But Edwin, we love each other and love is all about feeling the pain and hurt of the person one loves. You cannot escape this. I feel your hurt during the night and during the day. I hear your words when you sleep. I smell your cigarettes when you sit alone. I feel, Edwin. You must understand. What kind of love would mine be if I didn't want to hold you and calm your fears? What kind of woman?"

"Not the one you are, Jaz. That I do know."

"Well then, tell me what is happening. Don't keep me away for fear of upsetting me. It hurts more when you don't share your anxieties. A lot more."

"All right," I sighed. Jaz deserved better. "I know when you put it like that that I'm not being fair to you."

"But Edwin, it's not about being fair. It's about you taking some help for once. From what I know of you, you have always gone it alone. Not good. There's me now. We are one. I'm here for you. It's no weakness to release what's deep inside. It's no weakness to share your problems. I know I can't solve everything and I know I can't tell you things I know nothing at all about. What I can do is listen. You can have my ears and my love for as long as it takes."

I kissed her. Her words touched me. She had the ability to destroy and demolish all the walls that I had built up around myself. I couldn't resist.

"Well, this isn't going to be easy and I don't want you to get the wrong impression so hear me out."

"Go on, Edwin." Those eyes of hers stretched into me and made the truth impossible to resist.

To a certain extent I had kept some of the truth away from Jaz. I wasn't prepared to risk losing her I suppose, even though in my view I had done nothing wrong. A woman, of course, might see things entirely differently, and Jaz was a woman after all. You can argue that there are always two sides to a matrimonial coin and I would have a hard time denying this, but no one enjoys broadcasting their exile and failure, even to the one they love.

"Clare doesn't want me in the house, as you know. I haven't been completely truthful about this. The fact is I slapped her during one of our . . . er . . . dramatic altercations. She hit me first by the way. Anyway, as you can imagine, these days a slap is enough to have you blasted out of your own home. Particularly where the victim is female. Of course male victims don't exist, do they? Anyway, she has filed a petition for my 'unreasonable behaviour'. Violence, drinking too much and being an out-and-out bastard all round, really."

Jaz touched my hand and looked down at the floor.

"I am not naïve Edwin, neither am I inexperienced in these things. Even so I don't believe you are a bastard. Not for a minute. Your fingers are too gentle, your eyes too kind. I trust my instincts."

"Thank you for the vote of confidence, but try telling Clare that. The real issue with Clare is money. She is out for as much as she can get."

"Nothing unusual then."

"No, not at all. Not these days anyway. I've often wondered when one hears of these ridiculous divorce settlements how much an individual actually needs. I've come to the conclusion that need doesn't come into it. There are only two factors – greed and punishment. Clare is out to wallop me. Well, frankly she can have whatever she wants. I really don't care. As long as I'm left with a modest amount of security she can bloody well have all the rest. I wouldn't like her karma though."

"No, I was just thinking that."

"In a funny kind of way the divorce will afford me the opportunity to change direction. I rather fancy the academic side of law. Wouldn't mind lecturing. No clients and no stress. Might even do some writing. How about a book called '*The Lawyer and the Sikh*'?"

Jaz laughed at this and said, "God, how would you write the sexy bits? On second thoughts, you have plenty of real-life experience." She looked at me and saw the expression on my face, "My God, you wouldn't!"

"Yes I would. I'm a great believer in true knowledge only coming from experience and so on. The empirical school of philosophy and all that nonsense. Besides, how could I not write about something or someone I didn't feel passionately about? That's where the writer's credibility comes in, surely. Makes me frisky just thinking about my pen describing you and me." She laughed again.

"Now, as usual Edwin, you are going from the sublime to the ridiculous. I mean what I have said. Don't close up. I won't judge. My karma, your karma is with us. I know it. I will always listen, and don't you forget it." Her voice had gone into a firmer mode. She meant every word. Her eyes searched my face for a few moments, then she said, "Violence? I do not think so."

I understood how all this might trouble her so finally decided to tell her the whole lot, smashed plates and all. To date I had avoided all the gory details – not for reasons of deception you understand, but purely to avoid boring her. I mean, who wants to hear hours of matrimonial discord for heaven's sake? No one in their right minds, surely.

At the end of my tale, she accepted. She trusted and rightly so; apart from anything else there was probably nothing unusual in my divorce anyway. Indeed the circumstances and 'unreasonableness' of mine were no doubt inordinately mundane and everyday as far divorces went.

CHAPTER 31

As soon as Clare opened the door Jessica's radar picked up a change in her friend. Clare seemed determined, strong. Two months had passed. The sex had deterred Jessica from her original intention to end things, but at last sense had prevailed. The sex had been so good and Clare had started to become quite accomplished. Clitoris against grey matter – there was no competition; same as men and penises really. Equality of the sexes was raging everywhere.

They were sitting in Clare's kitchen. There had been no soppy kiss behind the front door on arrival – Clare was still wary of unfriendly eyes and what people might think of her sexual revolution.

"I don't think Edwin is going to be awkward about anything," Clare said, for once without any self-pity. "At least Lesley doesn't seem to think so. He's accepted my petition and most of my financial demands. Apparently he's only arguing about his pension, but according to Lesley it will be a small price to pay. The house has to be sold, but I don't mind – it's too big just for me. Anyway Jessica, I've done some quick calculations. They're a bit rough but not far off the mark. I should come out of the divorce with a substantial sum of money, providing all the figures are correct. Although Lesley is waiting for confirmation of various accounts and investments and so on, she still thinks that if I invest my money wisely I won't have to worry about work for a long time, if ever."

Well, 'investing wisely' was soon going to go out of fashion where Clare was concerned, Jessica thought, but kept her mouth shut. Her friend was on full beam, bright and sharp. Clare suddenly jumped off the kitchen stool she was sitting on and hugged Jessica, "I feel so free. It's wonderful! You're wonderful! None of this would have happened without you. You have given me so much strength!"

She looked into Jessica's eyes. Love – new, just out of the showroom, sickening, pure and idiotic. Jessica remained calm. Clare had accepted her personality. The choice nature had made for her. She was a full-blown lesbian. Women only. Jessica had helped her along the road of self-realisation and honesty. There was just one problem. Jessica was a consummate trapeze artist. She could swing both ways regardless of danger and with or without a safety net. Her reserve went unnoticed by Clare, who spewed and gushed enthusiasm. Love scared the hell out of Jessica.

She had come to Clare's to end the affair.

Two months of sexual gluttony with her was enough. Her attempt at hurting Edwin in the process had been successful, or so she thought. Seduction, eviction and financial mutilation achieved. Job done.

Jessica wasn't greedy, neither did she enjoy hurting a relatively innocent party. Her original determination to stop things had wavered time and time again. Clare would smile and that would be it. Her resolve would disintegrate. She was wrong and she knew it. Men were so much easier to hurt. Most of them deserved it anyway. She had tried to stop Clare jumping into her own unique ocean without any oxygen tanks strapped to her back, but all to no avail. She had tried not answering phone calls, not seeing Clare – none of it had worked. Clare simply refused to see what her eyes were looking at. Every time Jessica tried, Clare would push the sex button. The one button that when pressed opened the door to the only weakness that Jessica possessed: sex. Even now, Clare's sexual attraction made her thighs twitch.

Jessica looked away and tried to ignore the overwhelming desire. She had to bring Clare back to the surface of her ocean with no stops on the upward journey. This would damage, perhaps even kill, but it was the only way. She was not responsible for other people's emotions or their love. She was just not responsible. The hidden part of her said that she was not a callous bitch either. She hated 'endings'. She loathed female tears. This was not going to be easy. If Clare had kept their affair casual, Jessica could have played it out until indifference and human nature stepped in to execute a natural death. A death with no tears. No mourning.

"I have been thinking, Jess," Clare continued. "I thought I would move up to Norwich. There's nothing here for me. Never has been really. I don't have any family so I'm free to go where I want to."

Jessica shivered, "Hold on now Clare—" She didn't get any further.

"We could buy a house together. I'll have plenty of money."

"What? Now look Clare, will you hold on a minute I—." Jessica was speaking as gently as her personality allowed. She took Clare's hand. It had to be now. Since when was there a right time?

"I think you're going too fast, Clare. Our friendship is only two or three months old—" She was careful to use the word 'friendship' before Clare interrupted.

"No, it's not! We've known each other for years. Don't be silly." This was getting nowhere. Clare was infatuated beyond reason.

"Yes, in a way for years I suppose, but we haven't had any contact during that time. People change, Clare. We mature as we get older. Our values, aspirations; they change."

"Yes I know all that, but these things don't matter, do they? As long as we are together, who cares? You and me Jess, that's all that matters. You and me."

Jessica looked at Clare. It was hopeless, the woman was on permanent transmit. This was love with both its eyes gouged out. She stood up and went to the sink for a glass of water. Keeping her back to Clare she said, her voice soft, almost pleading, "Clare, you're going too fast. Will you please listen to me?" Then she turned. "Look, you are vulnerable at the moment. Believe me, divorce, emotional upheaval, all these things can force you into the arms of someone. You may think you love, but honestly Clare, it's a false love. A momentary cry for help. You must see your feelings for what they are. You must. You may not have loved Edwin, but there must have been something. There always is. You were together for quite a while. You can't turn these things on and off like a tap. You need time, Clare. Time on your own to adjust. To find your way. I know it won't be easy being on your own but—"

"But I won't be on my own, will I?" Clare interrupted again. "I've got you, Jess. My friend . . . my lover."

Oh God, this was getting worse.

"OK, lover. Yes, we have sex, good sex, but Clare, even this doesn't last for ever. You can't rely on me to find your way through life. You can't." Jessica was getting annoyed. Impatience and frustration were taking over. This time there was no quarter given for interruption.

"I never intended things to go this far, Clare. Friendship, yes. Sex, yes. Love, no. I cannot enter into a committed relationship with you. At the end of the day I'm more for men than women, always have been and always will be, I'm just bisexual now and again. I'm *not* a full-blown lesbian like you Clare, for God's sake! You want only women. You have only ever wanted women. I could never be faithful to you any more than I could ever be faithful to a man. It's not in me. That's it, Clare, black and white. I cannot give you what you want. Accept it . . . please."

Her voice had shot up a few octaves. It was time for brute force. Ruthlessness, however crude. She didn't wait for an answer, "I never wanted this to happen. I have never wanted nor asked for your love. I don't want anybody's love, full stop. Fuck buddies, yes. Love, no!" Her voice lowered a fraction, it tried, "I know this is hard for you, but it's the only way. You will hate me for a while, but this will pass. One day you will hopefully come to understand that I am doing this for you. It's the kindest way. The only way."

Clare looked at Jessica, her eyes were clear, bright. Jessica continued, "We must stop seeing each other, Clare. We must." Clare seemed to be unmoved, so Jessica felt compelled to carry on without truly understanding why. "I am so very fond of you, Clare. You are a lovely person, but I am not for you." Jessica was surprised at her lying tongue. Clare was not a lovely person at all; she was a spoilt but bloody good lay, no more. For all this the woman was human and deserved some kindness, even if it was conditional.

Jessica waited for the explosion. Nothing happened. Clare sat calmly. There was no outburst of rejection. No drama. Jessica's words had been well rehearsed. In fact she hadn't really needed to rehearse, she had said them so many times that they usually popped out under their own steam.

Clare remained seated. Still no reaction. Silence. Jessica began to feel uncomfortable. Out of control of things. She knew of Clare's expertise with china missiles. Fear began to creep around her and the kitchen. Suddenly, Clare stood up and went over to her. She put her arms out. Jessica went to her. Thank God. No hard feelings. Her words had sunk in.

Clare whispered, "I understand Jess, I understand." They kissed. Clare pulled her mouth away and said quietly, "One last time?"

This time Clare led Jessica up the stairs. Clare was in control. Her body and sexual power laughed at Jessica's intentions. The woman was a fool. Jessica would love her. She knew it.

Women were no different from men after all.

CHAPTER 32

I arrived at my new 'home' having left Jaz that morning. 'Home' now was, of course, the office. Some home. She was working nights again for a couple of days, so it was back to the office. Well, it was my place of work I suppose, and at least I wasn't out on the streets, but apart from anything else, love or no love, I still had to earn the pennies. That's a good one I hear you readers moan, since when do lawyers only ever earn pennies?

I did my bit for clients, noticed that my 'quality time' – or is it 'leisure time' – was slipping away and decided to call it a day. I needed to collect some clothes and one or two items of a more personal nature from a building that was once my home. I still retained a key and as far as I knew Clare hadn't changed the locks. She had no reason to. Legally exiled I may have been, but she knew full well that I was no threat, her affidavit notwithstanding. She wanted nothing to do with me, but I could call now and again if I wanted to collect something, providing her car wasn't in the drive. I hadn't written the cheque yet, so she still needed an element of goodwill. I was in for a caning whatever I did, but I could have made a meal out of it or at least dragged it out for one hell of a long time just to annoy her or get my own back.

As I drove back to what was once my pride and joy, it occurred to me how unimportant it had become. How small. Jaz had become my home now and she was more valuable than any thatched brick. Divorce and Clare still saddened me, particularly in my quiet times. I couldn't help it, that's divorce for you. There were the odd happy times in our marriage. In the beginning, anyway. And how many people have said that as they trundle along to the divorce courts I can't help but wonder.

That's divorce for you. Love and hate in equal measure. Such a waste, all of it. There were times when I didn't know who to hurt and punish, myself or Clare. Money? That came and went, it didn't merit a tear. Mind you, with plenty of it I suppose that's easy for me to say. Home, hearth and heart? They are something different. As I drew closer to what my life had once been, regret at my folly in what seemed a lifetime ago jammed me into my seat. Regret and anger.

I pulled into the drive and saw Jessica Howard's car alongside Clare's. The damned woman has moved in, I thought. Now, I don't know how many of you readers have been thrown out of your own homes – for no justifiable reason I may add – but I can tell you this, when some sod – male or female, it makes no difference – moves into what was once your territory, bought and paid for by your own honest sweat and labour, then a feeling of utter outrage has a tendency to rear its apoplectic head.

My first thought was 'to hell with them'. It was still my house and Jessica Howard was also no doubt one of the main conspirators in my virtual bankruptcy (not quite, I'm not that bloody stupid) and homelessness. Anger was starting up in a big way. In the event, I remained in the car, rolled a cigarette, and allowed the lawyer to take over. Calm down, Edwin boy, calm down. Shouting and bawling will only result in an ignominious ride in a police car and no doubt another fifty-thousand pounds.

I sat, smoked, and conquered.

After about ten minutes of tobacco-assisted deep breathing, I clenched my testicles, made all kinds of noble resolutions and made my way to the front door. I was only collecting a couple of personal things after all.

I went into the house. It was quiet. Odd, I thought. I had expected to hear the usual female rubbish flying through the air. You know, skirts and tops, the latest dieting bullshit and so on, although I have to say I couldn't quite see Jessica Howard fitting into this category somehow. The woman was far too clever, I had to give her that.

I remained standing in the hallway for a few moments. Silence. No chatter, no laughter, nothing. Maybe the two witches had gone out for a flypast on their brooms. The French doors were slightly open in the sitting room, so I decided they must have gone outside to admire my horticultural genius. We were heading into summer and the sun had decided to show its arse for once. I immediately thought, right, collect my stuff and do a quick exit. Avoid conflict at all costs. I climbed the stairs and headed for the room that had once been my bedroom.

I opened the door.

My eyes viewed a scene that my brain would never have been able to imagine even if every single cell had been on full throttle.

Jessica was riding Clare's face faster than Red Rum at the Grand National. Even Lester Piggott would have had a hard time keeping up (had he still been alive, that is). I couldn't believe my eyes. Can you believe it? Four odd years I had been trying to get her to play the slut, no bloody chance. This Jessica woman comes along and wham bang, it's open sesame, no questions asked.

I stood in the doorway, dumbfounded, transfixed, shocked, paralysed and all the other novelistic descriptions you can think of. I remember thinking, Christ all those years of frustrating effort and here she was climaxing herself into oblivion with a woman! They were so far into each other's bodies they didn't even notice me standing in the doorway.

I stood there for a few seconds while my lower jaw almost hit the floor.

All the years of failure, the anger, and even the odd year or two of love came together in one fell swoop. The betrayal, the exploitation of my inherent kindness, and the humiliation that screamed at me from my own bed exploded.

I shouted, "You bitch!" and tried to drag Jessica off my wife's face. I wanted the woman out of my house – fast. In these moments I was unsure who I despised the most, Jessica or Clare. Either way I wanted to lash out. I tried to push Jessica off the bed but she fought back.

"You bastard! You bastard!" she yelled and punched me in the face. It didn't quite connect or at least I didn't feel any pain.

Next thing Clare was screaming, "You bloody animal! Leave her alone!"

She started hitting me and trying to drag me off her bed-mate. Can you imagine it? There I am, fully dressed, with two naked lovelies trying to tear me apart. You could have cut the hatred in the air into slices and flogged it to a group of manic fundamentalists. Clare was trying to give me a haircut, no scissors, while Jessica was attempting to blend my balls into her own special recipe for tomato purée. Clare was smaller than Jessica so I tried to get her off me first. At least I remember giving her a push; I was trying to save my scalp after all.

Jessica didn't give in so easily. She was a tough bugger, I'll say that for her. I clenched my fist and lamped her one. I'm not talking about a slap Clare-style, this was a fist with all the power behind it that I could muster. I think it hurt my hand more than it did her jaw. This was the first time in my life that I had belted a woman with bare and rolled up knuckles. It did the trick anyway and allowed my balls free to fight another day. She went flying off the bed and landed with a thump some-where or other. As you can imagine I wasn't in the mood for observing direction and landing sites.

Suddenly there was silence. Complete and total. Not even the violence could be heard.

A few brief moments of utter peace.

How long this hiatus of mercy lasted I will never know. Next thing Jessica was up and running to Clare who was lying on the floor. Silence re-appeared for an encore. I remember Jessica moving her hand about Clare's neck then her wrist while I knelt on the bed panting and dying for a fag.

Jessica looked up at me with a blank expression on her face and said, "She's dead."

CHAPTER 33

So here I am.

Unplanned holidays are always the best, aren't they?

That's what I'm having right now – and I don't even have to pay for it either.

It's ten days since that terrible fight and I remain in a condition of total disbelief. I don't even know why I'm in prison. Remanded in custody on a murder charge. Murder for God's sake? It was an accident. Clare fell the wrong way, banged her head in the wrong place and 'Goodnight Eileen' to all.

The trouble is that others seem to be of a different view, namely Muz Jessica Howard. According to her, upon my discovery of their sexual antics I lost the plot on a grand scale, frothed at the mouth and piled in screaming 'I'm going to kill you!' as I did so. I also grabbed Clare's head and gave it a good thump on the corner of the bedside cabinet for good measure.

What did I ever do to the bloody woman to deserve this? Insulted her once or twice I grant you. Even told her to where to go in no uncertain terms you will remember. Well so what? Not only was she screwing my wife, she was also trying to make it a threesome with me acting as the third party. Incredible. As if being a conniving whore wasn't enough, she was turning mendacity into an honourable profession as well.

I might not have liked Clare much, didn't like her at all in fact as things started to come to an end, but that doesn't mean to say I wanted her dead. That's a trifle extreme by anyone's standards. As for killing her even in the heat of a lover's row, well forget it. I didn't hate Clare. In fact I can safely say that I have never really hated anyone (on second thoughts the Howard woman is beginning to take away my virginity in this regard).

Clare was still young, and for all her faults deserved a bit more time on this planet. She didn't deserve to die.

Ours may not have been the greatest of love affairs, but there had been a depth of emotion – love even – in the beginning. At least for me. Clare? Well, who knows? Misery and mismatch seemed the only conclusion I could now draw, particularly now in light of Clare's support for the other team.

Surprisingly, I was beginning to understand Clare and to feel for her. This was the tragedy that I was now trying to come to terms with. You see, I would have understood her sexual confusion or at least tried to; in any event I would have listened, if possible helped, and certainly wouldn't have judged or condemned. Had she wanted to go I wouldn't have stood in her way. If only the stupid woman had come clean, I would have accepted and been her friend, the best friend she could ever have had, in fact. I struggled with this knowledge for hours. It was this that humbled me more than anything else. I could have prevented the circumstances that led up to Clare's death. I thought about the turmoil she must have gone through, the devastating realisation. Clare was such a bigot. A prude. She must have suffered.

Her short life had been a tragedy.

A lie.

I accepted that she had fallen awkwardly as a result of my violence. For this I make no excuse. There is none. But murder? No. Her death had been an accident. God knows, I could never have seriously hurt Clare. I'm not a violent man, but sometimes provocation can be so powerful as to turn us into something we are not. We lash out, fight, damage, without even realising it.

My prison bed continues to creak and mock me. It laughs at my compassion and then cries at my humanity. The *Sunday Times* hadn't arrived, so I rolled up an extra thin smoke instead. This was one place where the 'No Smoking' fascists were powerless. I'd love to see them come in here and start pontificating. Can you imagine it? A no-smoking nick. Now that would give HMP Inspectors a few sleepless nights and spoil their dreams of pretty prison boats simpering gently on the tranquil Thames. I would love to see the passive smoking brigade make a case in here. Passive? The cons would slaughter them.

I looked at the fingers holding my roll-up. They were starting to yellow. No pumice stones in here. My yellowing fingers made me sigh and realise how low I had become. My dignity and its death was all there in the yellow fingers. My unkempt hand began to touch reality and with it a brief sense of weakness. Jaz. My Jaz. I had managed to get a message to her through Tom. She would have been given a rough idea of what had happened. What a momentous balls-up I was involved in.

I hadn't spoken to her. I didn't want our conversation to be tainted by the obscene threats and impatience of other equally desperate men trying to use a telephone. I wanted to talk to her, to hear her voice and absorb her strength. I also knew that telephone lines could corrupt and distort, more so contraband mobile phones and their moronic text messages. Seeing her was out of the question. I wouldn't allow her to be degraded by searches and crude innuendo. I wouldn't be able to bear her seeing me in my present state. Pride is a powerful weapon to use against others, and oneself. My only option was pen and paper. Even this filled me with a strange trepidation. There were so many words to write. So many explanations and so many reasons, when all I really wanted to write was 'I love you'.

The following day my mind returned to law-student days and '*mens rea*' – intent. This was one of the critical elements in the commission of a murder. It still was, as far as I knew.

Tom did the criminal stuff, but short of a few brief consultations we hadn't got down to the details yet. One thing I did know was that I had never intended to seriously hurt Clare. I had thrown her off me in self-defence. Had she landed normally, all she would have suffered was a slightly bruised arse. This lack of intent would be crucial to my defence, that much I did know. This was assuming that I was even dragged into a courtroom. Actually, that's being a little too hopeful. I knew enough about criminal law to realise that if I was not had for murder, then manslaughter would be the prosecution's next best shot.

In my more sensible moments I believed I would be out soon. I knew Tom would be doing his level best. Jessica Howard was merely suffering from a bout of lover's pique and would come to her senses soon enough. The murder charge would be dropped and I would be released and bailed on a charge of manslaughter. I hoped so anyway. Jessica was an intelligent woman and not, I believed, a dishonest one.

Rejection does strange things to people, but I honestly believed Jessica would come to her senses. I kept convincing myself that all would be well. What else could I do? My green cell walls were not about to vomit any pearls of wisdom and advice, that much I did know.

I lay back on my musical bed and went into staring mode again. That's all you could do in this place. Stare and see nothing. At least in the physical sense. My mind on the other hand was exploring all kinds of panoramic vistas. One minute beauty, the next blaring tabloid headlines and comment.

I had experienced numerous smirks and upturned thumbs, not to mention an abundance of crude declarations of admiration. I was the pervy lawyer caught up in a rampant ménage à trois with two beautiful women. Actually perversion didn't seriously come into it; after all I had managed to achieve every man's sexual dream and fantasy. Or so they thought. No man would be enjoying the reality much if they were lying where I am at the moment, that's for sure.

All I know is that seeing my wife so tuned up, so sexually aroused by somebody else made me feel thoroughly inadequate.

Man or woman, it made no difference. It was a profound insult either way. I was still in a state of shock. I knew I had made angry accusations against Clare, but I hadn't really believed them. Reality again. Be careful boys, is all I can say. Keep two women or two men for that matter firmly in your dreams. If you care, watch out. Infidelity does not discriminate. I grant you threesomes enjoy their own fruits, but take my advice – keep them forbidden. Stick to one woman or man (if you prefer your own as it were) in all things; it's simpler.

My emotions were still doing their circus act. Jaz. Publicity. The national hate. My conviction without trial – the media were experts at this, after all. What was Jaz thinking about? How was she reacting? God help me if she was being influenced by the tabloids.

So far they hadn't got wind of our relationship. No one had, apart from Tom. Jaz was protected. Every time I considered the prospect of her being dragged into this I shuddered. All I could keep thinking about was keeping her out of this drama. I had to. She was an innocent. Neither of us had spoken to anyone about our relationship. Impending divorce had seen to that. Nevertheless, I also knew that where anything human was concerned, Lord Chance always had a card or two up his sleeve. It terrified me.

The thought of Jaz being made a victim of journalistic poison and editorial execution filled me with dread. I knew that I would have chosen a few years inside rather than see her being mutilated by our supremely ugly tabloid press. I could see the black headlines. They would torture until their sadism was satisfied and then ensure that the killing stroke was a slow and agonising one. The worst thing of all was that I was powerless. There was nothing I could do. My cell had totally emasculated me.

Apart from all this, would Jaz still want me?

This alone was my real hell.

CHAPTER 34

We were sitting in another green room. I swear to God that when I get out of here I will never wear anything green again.

Tom was interviewing me. We had already done the condolence and sympathy bit where Clare was concerned. There was nothing else to say. Her death would be with me for the rest of my life, and that was that. I just had to come to terms with it in my own way and in my own time.

My partner interviewing me, now that was a first. Junior partner at that, not that he would ever have countenanced such a vile denunciation of his professional status. Tom always claimed he brought in more fees than me. Utter nonsense. He was sitting opposite me now, suited up and looking all serious and pile free. His big brown eyes looked as if they were about to drop a few water bombs on some forest fire. The situation was crazy. Mad.

"Tom," I said, "what the hell are you looking so pained about? Piles still playing up or what? Good God man, I'm the one facing life imprisonment. Smile will you? Get a grip on that fat black arse of yours. I don't need grim faces right now, mine is enough for the pair of us. Now tell me what the hell is going on" He managed to raise a Domestos-toothed sympathy smile.

"Well Edwin, you haven't lost your lively and colourful approach to life, I see. Very commendable in view of your strained circumstances I must say. In the proverbial shit and still as objectionable as ever. Still, you can't keep a good man down as they say."

"Oh, cut out the crap Tom. What's happening?" I have to admit our Tom did look disturbingly serious. He normally ignored my insulting banter or at least returned like with like. This wasn't like him at all. Something was up. Something worrying.

"Edwin, the Crown Prosecution Service is going for gold. Murder."

"*What*?!" I couldn't believe what I was hearing.

"I'm afraid so."

"Tom, they can't! The bastards can't! I'm no murderer. It was an accident. I pushed Clare off me in self-defence, for Christ's sake!"

"Edwin, I know. I believe you. You don't have to convince me. You have my unstinting support, you know that. The CPS is after you for murder. Jessica Howard's evidence is the clincher. They're sticking to their guns. What the hell have you done to this Howard woman Edwin? Tell me."

I went through the whole story in biblical detail – improbable chapter, hysterical verse and miraculous parable. At the end of it I said, "Surely the CPS will eventually go for manslaughter. There *was* no intent, for God's sake! Even I can see the weakness of their case. It's Howard's word against mine."

"You can Edwin, but they can't as they obviously believe they have enough evidence for murder. So until all the statements are in, mainly Howard's, we have to wait and see. That's what's worrying me. What have they got?"

"Fuck all Tom, that's what. I've told you the truth. What would anyone have done if two strong women were attacking them? Christ, one was trying to scalp me and the other one castrate me!"

"I don't doubt it, Edwin. Anyway I've booked Jim Bowler. He's on board. No doubt we will work out the best strategy once all the prosecution bumph is to hand. You know how it works."

"Vaguely. Bowler's been a QC for quite a while now, hasn't he? Last time I spoke with him he was pissed. Good at his job though." I knew Jim Bowler personally. Had been plastered with him on many occasions. Could have been on the Bench years ago but had never fancied the monotony or reduction in income. Liked the drink, women and a dabble on the gee-gees too much. For all that he was as good as it gets. No doubt his fees would bleed me dry. There was no Legal Aid for me before all you readers start jumping up and down about bloody lawyers screwing the system, etc. etc. I was too rich, so bugger you.

"When will we be having a conference with Jim?" I asked.

"Next week."

"Good, sooner the better. Still no chance of bail I suppose?"

"I don't think so. You have too much money to skip the country, etc. Might threaten witnesses. Howard has been creating quite a scene. Must know some big hitters in the CPS too, if you ask me. Apart from all this there's the nature of the charge, the violence, and so it goes on. I have to say it doesn't add up. We've done all we can on the bail front as you know, but it's still no go I'm afraid. The Press are having a whale of a time, too. We lawyers are not a popular lot – but I don't have to tell you that."

I looked at my friend, the bare facts of my predicament beginning to pierce my delusions.

"Tom, you know all this is complete crap, don't you? Threatening witnesses? Jesus, who do they think I am? The fucking Godfather? Jessica Howard is lying. You do know that, don't you?" I was in a mess and I was starting to feel fear. I wanted allies.

"Of course I do, Edwin. You don't need to even mention it. Er . . . by the way, I spoke with Dr Kaur . . ." He paused. His face and eyes questioned. He wanted some answers. "A charming lady. Tough and on your side, she obviously loves you." I said nothing; the lack of response was killing him. "We had a long chat." Still no answers from me.

"Oh bloody hell, Edwin! I give up! What is going on? The woman was very concerned about you. I explained your side of things as instructed. Who is she, for God's sake? I have noticed that you haven't been spending every night in the office flat. I've also noticed that you've been spending a lot of time in London. Even you let the odd thing slip. Now tell me, what's happening? It could have an impact on your case."

I thought for a few moments then decided to come clean. After I'd finished Tom sat back.

"Well, I'm happy that you've found someone. I mean it. The trouble is your timing is all to hell. The prosecution could have a field day. There's a motive for a start."

"Yes I know, Tom. Don't you think I've already thought of that one? Not to mention the damage to Jaz. If you must know, I'm more concerned about that than anything else. If our relationship gets out, it won't do her career any good and that's just for starters. You know what the press are like."

"Don't worry, everything's under control."

"I'm being selfish here, Tom, I'm sorry. Never mind about me for the moment, how are you coping with the practice?

"Got a locum in to see to your current stuff. Seems to know what he's doing. Oddly enough the publicity doesn't seem to be doing us much harm. Quite the opposite, in fact. If anything it's pulling clients in, if you can believe that. Odd thing, adverse publicity. Your case certainly won't do my criminal practice any harm." He smiled one of his devious but lovable numbers.

"Glad to hear it, you mercenary bastard!"

"Anyway, don't worry about things, I'll manage."

"Easy to say."

"Now don't be stupid. Things will work out. I'll see to it. You just have to trust me. I will do all I can, you know that. Many of us know what a good and decent man you are. A cold-blooded murderer you are certainly not. You know as well as I do that the prosecution's case comes down to one thing. Your word against Jessica Howard's. I've already started digging on this Howard woman. You must be strong, Edwin. There are plenty of us in your corner and you know Jim is the best. He was booked up for God knows how long, but he has assured me that he will make the time for your case. They don't come any better and you know it. You are not isolated, Edwin, and don't you forget it." He looked at me, his face concerned and genuine.

"I won't and thank you," I said. His words helped but they could never remove the emptiness of a prison cell or the defeat of incarceration. I sniffed – a momentary lapse into my sensitive side. A tear or two were shimmering away on my pupils. "Tom, whatever else, look after Jaz, will you? Keep her informed. She must not be brought into this. She really mustn't. No one knows apart from you. Please keep it that way."

"Of course."

"Explain to her that I won't see her in here. You can understand why. You have given her my letter I hope, I don't trust sending anything through this lot?"

"Of course."

All this was starting to cause serious upset, I really wanted to be alone. Even in a cell, "Is there anything else, Tom? I'm tired."

"No . . . er . . . not for the time being." He fumbled with his hands for a few moments. I knew this gesture. It usually meant he was uncomfortable about something. "I'll be off then." He stood up and we shook hands "Come on now, Edwin. You can deal with this. We'll pull through. Trust me. I'll be back soon." He turned and headed for the door.

"Tom, just one last thing. Tell Jaz that I love her, will you? Just that." He looked at me, saw all he needed to.

"Of course, Edwin. Of course." The understanding that had paved the way to our close friendship passed between us. No words were needed. Abandonment was a danger. A risk. Prison exacerbated both.

Tom was about to knock the door for attention when he paused. "Oh damn!" he muttered and turned around. "It's no good Edwin, there is something I have to tell you. I was going to leave it for a bit, give you some time to absorb things. But I know you, you wouldn't thank me. You had better sit down." This was 'sit down in case the shock makes you fall down and hurt yourself' time. As soon as I saw the look on his chops I did a girding of my imprisoned loins.

"OK Tom, let's have it. Never mind the chairs. On the chin please." I was a great one for making harsh reality arrive fast and furiously. He sighed.

"Right. . . . Clare was eight weeks pregnant at the time of her death."

A few minutes later I was back on my disgruntled bed wallowing in a pungent stew of self-pity and guilt. Had Clare known she was pregnant? She must have done. She monitored her body like a scientist who has just discovered a cure for cancer. When? God knows, sex between us had been non-existent.

I vaguely remembered a drunken attempt at intimacy about two months before her death. It had been worse than a teen-ager's incompetent loss of virginity. I couldn't even remember ejaculating. Something must have happened though, unless of course Clare was having it away with another man. Somehow that didn't seem likely bearing in mind recent events. No, I was the father. No doubt about it. As if Clare's death wasn't enough. Now I was the killer of two people. Up to this point I had managed to maintain some semblance of balance. This latest revelation had blown my sense of proportion out through the cell window – bars or no bars. My exasperated desire for fatherhood had also been denied. I could hear Clare laughing all the way up to the most selective and expensive health club in heaven.

Why didn't she tell me? Why?

I knew the answer and hated for a while.

I even tried being a Christian for two hours and thirty four minutes. That's how desperate I was. I soon discovered that He or She didn't give a damn. I was on my own. Tough. All the gods out there were on leave enjoying themselves at a comedian's convention. Not one of them had the slightest interest in my time of need.

Surprise, surprise.

CHAPTER 35

Jaz was tired.

It was 8.30 a.m. and she had only just returned from doing a night at the hospital. Sleep escaped her. She seemed to drift between a hidden trance and an awareness of household creaks and whispers of the mind. Anxiety stopped a mental shutdown. It would not allow any rest. It was a selfish creature that demanded her constant attention, rather like many of the patients she spent her life trying to heal.

Edwin ran in and out of her mind, his face, his touch, his voice. The love. She missed them all. Even though she had read his letter countless times she continued to go back to it, she had to taste and swallow every word time and time again. She had developed an intimate relationship with the four prison-issue pieces of paper. These thin blue sheets were all she had, all she could love.

She was able to feel Edwin through every stroke of his pen as she handled the pages with care, not wanting to crease the elegant words or insult the character behind the pen. She had become used to Edwin's riddles. One minute the mouth of a drunken layabout, the next, refinement and subtle sophistication. He laughed and swore at the futility of social acumen and aspiration. He was a fur-lined communist one moment and a supercilious capitalist the next. His mind, incisive and quick, kept her on guard. Challenged. His strength warned her of secret lines that were not to be crossed – even by her.

She gave up the battle with tangled sheets that knotted about her legs and feet. It was hopeless; if her body wept for sleep, her mind wanted action, marathons even. She wanted to go to Edwin, to see him and try to heal his worry. She had come to know his innocence as she would a long and loyal friendship. Doubt did not exist. His letter had explained and clarified. The tabloids could vomit their last but she didn't care, she knew they had nothing to vomit except green bile. Jaz felt only pity for them. Karma would vent its own tears on them one day. Edwin's innocence would become their guilt. She was too gentle and forgiving to be angry with the bingo and bare-breasted celebrity press. They were an immature farce entertaining the mindless and dysfunctional.

But they could hurt.

She had dedicated her life to the healing of others. She gave herself to the sanctity of the living. Edwin's letter had told her that she must not come to see him. How could she help him if he wouldn't let her see him? Her helplessness, her inability to heal, frustrated and confounded her. He would not allow her to be exposed, yet she was like never before. She had given him her heart, her self. Her love must be his courage and his strength, she would see to it.

She decided to take a walk through the park. Her memories would bring some comfort. Edwin would hold her hand and touch her cheek again. Sleep perhaps would come later.

She opened the front door and was violated by an insane barrage of verbal cannonades and deadly electronic flashes.

CHAPTER 36

"How could you? How could you?"

The banks in Jaz's eyes hadn't quite burst. A few lonely tears had found freedom, if only for a short while. Her voice was calm, but her vocal chords were straining and shouting for help. She was sitting down on a chair, her face turned upwards. Jagdish Shemare stood before her. Imperious and unforgiving.

"For your own sake, Jaspreet. I am your father. I decide, whether you like it or not."

"You decide nothing, Daddy. Not where my heart is concerned."

"The man is a murderer. A white murderer. There are no choices."

"He is not a murderer! Isn't a man innocent until proven guilty?"

"In English courts perhaps, but we have our own laws, our own customs – and you know it."

"No, Daddy. No. Edwin has killed no one. You are no better than the gutter press who seek to judge and condemn. I have always respected you for your wisdom. I have obviously deluded myself."

"That's enough! I will not tolerate disrespect in my home!"

"Disrespect? Have you any idea how much you have hurt me by going to the press? I love Edwin. Whether you like it or not."

"Love? Don't be childish, Jaspreet. You are a grown woman. A professional woman. Although perhaps this is something to regret. I should have restrained your aspirations a long time ago. I have made a mistake."

"A mistake? Merely because I choose to live my life in my own way?"

"Loving a killer is not our way."

Jaz remained calm. She knew her father.

"You stole the last man from me. I know you threatened him with some of your thugs. I know. You have no idea how much you hurt me. How much pain you caused me. Now I have a chance of happiness and you will not allow me even this. What kind of father are you?"

"A good father, Jaspreet. One who cares for you." Not once had the man's voice expressed any true emotion apart from that of anger.

"Care? If you cared, why have you done this? You think all this publicity about our family is going to do your precious Sikh honour and reputation any good? Do you?"

"Headlines last for a day, Jaspreet. Shame and dishonour last for a lifetime. You have chosen to lay shame upon shame upon our honour. Upon our traditions, our religion, our caste!"

"Honour? Caste? White, black? For God's sake, we are in the twenty-first century. I am as British as Edwin is. Stop gripping the past. Please exercise some tolerance. We must all get on, all creeds, all races, all religions. Tolerate, Daddy. Understand. For God's sake, when are you going to tolerate?" Jaz was losing her calm. The fighter in her was starting to ready itself.

"That's enough! The honour of your family is greater than your infatuated love. What about the damage to your career? There are many Sikhs at the top of the medical tree! You can be one of them!"

"Career? Career? So you think you have helped my career? I've already been ordered to go and see my superiors in the morning. I'll be surprised if I have a job by lunchtime!" She was beginning to shout now, "You will not do this to me again, Daddy! You will not! Never again! I have had enough of your stupid extremes. Your vicious tactics and your even more vicious religion." She stood up and faced him, the lioness and the lion, "You will not hurt me again! Ever! I have had it with

234

you! Do not come anywhere near me or my home ever again! I warn you! You try any of your fanatical antics on with me again and I'll go to the police. Go near Edwin and I will do the same!"

Jagdish Kaur kicked his control out of the window. He raised his hand whilst his other hand reached for the dagger strapped to his waist. He didn't manage another movement. Jaz knew what her father was capable of. How far his fundamentalism could drive him. She hit him hard in the face and ran.

Ran for her life.

Later that night, after drinking a few extremely stiff gins, she knew there would never be a reconciliation with her father.

Their relationship was dead.

The following morning Jaz read the letter again. A week had passed since her love for Edwin had been flaunted and abused by the press. She sat on her bed and read his second letter for the umpteenth time that morning. Confusion. Loss. She had no idea how to react.

"Oh no Edwin, no," she murmured.

This time with only herself as a witness, she cried. Tears poured. She had confronted bereavement many times, had always said the right words in reply to sudden death. She had saved, stitched, won and lost. Young and old. Now her detached hands and heart were unable to walk down a cold white corridor of release. This time there was nowhere to go. No one else to heal. She had felt tragedy and the wordless pain of loss before. Now it had returned. This time it was more ruthless. More dedicated and passionate. Her tears dropped onto the words she held in her hands. Edwin's words.

He could not put her through this misery. He would not let her be punished. The letter had been for her. For her sake. All she could do was think of the agony that the man she loved must have gone through to write it. His loneliness and his fear. His unselfish courage fed her tears.

The hospital death she had come to know so well had always been complete. Final. There were no loose ends. The same could not be said for the loss of a living and healthy lover. Love was the intensive care unit that kept death at bay. It didn't breathe, it didn't eat. It continued to hold on, to live and to inflict. The conscious and unconscious mind would never give it up. The pain was far too exquisite. The words in his letter had told her to forget him, they reached into her and tore at her soul as they tried to demolish her heart. She must be happy the words had implored, she must pursue the vocation she loved. She must understand his wishes and the reasons why.

Edwin was blaming himself.

He loved her too much.

Once the shock had waned, Jaz dressed and went out for a walk. Her superiors had been sympathetic. There had been no threats or reprimands. No consequences of organisational ill repute. For now anyway. They had told her to take a week's leave. She intended using this time, using it for herself and Edwin.

Time to think.

The air brought balance as her footsteps tried to resolve. Edwin was wrong, they had to fight. Their love was strong, as was the truth. They would win. They must not give up. She had fought for other people's lives, had kept exploding hearts pumping blood; she had saved the love of so many others. Now she had to fight for her own and Edwin's. Regardless of his wishes she would not give in. She would stand by him and do whatever was needed. That was that. No argument. She had stood her ground against her father, she had stood her ground in her profession; now she would stand her ground against Edwin.

She would win.

As soon as she returned home she rang Tom.

CHAPTER 37

The indignity!

I am handcuffed and enclosed by a tight-fitting steel shroud. All the tiny window allows in is the odd shard of light. The naked eye is unable to penetrate it and see the outside world. I am being transported – that's what it feels like, Australia here I come – to trial and vindication, I hope. My modern transport ship stops and I hear shouts, screams and abuse. Someone manages to batter the side of the van. I jump. There are a few less pronounced thumps. Missiles, but harmless on impact. Eggs, bags of flour, faeces, who knows?

I am despised.

The media have done an admirable job.

All in the public interest, of course.

The courtroom itself has become a desire, a place of peace, common sense and sanity. I am placed in the cells below the court, my handcuffs are removed and I perspire. I force my belief in truth; no more negotiation with doubt. I see the arena above me as a forum to conclude fact, a place to make a wrong right. I start to feel confidence as anxiety is left with the violent ignorance outside. The unclean mob. The sorry multitude and wasted rejects of decency's quality controllers.

Jaz breathes and my mind turns over.

My letter to her and the words that I had dug out and used quickly. The letter was an end. For her. I had wanted to give my last as a sacrifice of the only valuable thing I had left – love. It can be so strong and priceless that its discarding is its own essence. My only gift had finally been given. The press had won, their revelation complete. They had hunted and found.

I sat and waited.

The bars around me were longer and more widely spaced. It made no difference.

CHAPTER 38

His Honour Judge Eamon Hawkins looked in the mirror and studied the red sash that ran across the black and violet colours of his legal status. The reflection pleased him, the mound of horse hair did not. The blasted thing had irritated his scalp for years. He had tried every remedy known to man, all to no avail. The wig had been responsible for many a harsh sentence – unbeknown to the hapless victims. He scratched and cursed for a few moments, gave up and reached for the papers on his desk.

He turned back to the full length mirror and read. He enjoyed looking at himself now and again. It reminded him of who he was and made sure that he didn't treat his position lightly. It also made sure that he didn't forget what the robes were all about: justice and humanity in equal measure. The wig and gown were mere trinkets of office. They did not deify – although some of his brethren were of the opinion that they did. Not so His Honour Judge Eamon Hawkins. He studied the papers in his hands and decided that this was going to be an interesting one, no open and shut job anyway.

He hoped the jury selection wouldn't take too long. He wanted a short day, the shorter the better. There was a twenty-nine-year-old solicitor waiting for his early evening attention, and God knows he would need all his stamina to keep her happy, the demanding little minx!

At fifty-nine, Hawkins had managed to retain both his hair and an erection of substantial girth and length. He was fit, handsome and distinguished. His voice was powerful and executed fools mercilessly. In judicial circles he was considered to be a fair judge and an extremely able one. He was on his way to the top. Few barristers standing before him would exercise the temerity to question his knowledge of law and procedure. He was a formidable man, both inside the court-room and out. A stickler for propriety in a court of law. Usually harsh on those who deserved it, he was kind where understanding and compassion were required.

It was well known that Hawkins had an adventurous male member. His peers tolerated, and most envied. He tended to be discreet and at least didn't mess around with youngsters – well, under twenty-ones anyway. His wife, a grey but extremely intelligent woman, had joined the toleration gang. She enjoyed a happy marriage, certainly in comparison with most of her friends, and even love from her husband. He always came home. He was wise enough to know the value of true love, its durability, its comfort and safety. He was a kind and caring husband who always satisfied her with accomplished sex when required. She was a content and happy woman.

In the barristers' robing room, Jim Bowler QC made a few brief notes in his blue legal pad. His client was innocent. Not that guilt or innocence ever played any games of conscience with his mind. Every client was entitled to the best defence he could muster – whether they did the crime or not was irrelevant. He acted on instructions only. His was to defend not to judge. Simple. If a client made an outright admission, that was different. Conflicts of this nature however were rare. Ethical gymnastics usually stayed in the gym where they belonged.

Bowler was a man of the world. As far as possible he avoided sympathy or enmity where his clients were concerned. Detached objectivity was his style and it had served him well most of the time. Hillyard was the exception. He knew the man personally. Not intimately, but they had spent some enjoyable evenings together. He liked Edwin Hillyard and understood his client. Usually he avoided any attempt at understanding those who fell foul of the law. The depths of the human condition and their unpredictable manifestations were for psychiatrists and philosophers to decipher, not him.

This time however, where Hillyard was concerned, he felt a degree of empathy. He knew all about betrayal. His wife had left him for America and another man, taking their two children with her. There had been no warning. He had come home one evening, wife and children gone. A note had been left reminding him that two of his suits needed collecting from the dry cleaners. There had also been a P.S. 'Sorry'. Just the one word. Six years later he had forgiven but not forgotten. He had adored his wife and his children. Now he saw his offspring once a year if he was lucky. He had come to know that he would never get over the loss; he would live with it until the day he died.

Through his own pain and the practise of criminal law he had learnt that sometimes people simply couldn't help themselves. He and Hillyard were of like minds on this front and had discussed this human riddle many times. Some people were just psychologically and physiologically incapable of resisting certain urges. They needed help, not punishment.

Bowler was a tall man. His long aquiline nose had sniffed the stench of human depravity and cruelty many times. He was not a handsome man, but there was a certain charming charisma about him. There was also humour in the intense eyes that rarely missed a trick, or for that matter a word. Both qualities had served him well where jurors were concerned. He had presence. He enjoyed a gamble and loose women, but since his divorce horses and women had become one and the same. Like horses, women only existed to be ridden when required.

Quite recently Bowler had turned down a place on the bench because it was too safe. Too uninspiring. He preferred the excitement of winning. The risk. That's why he enjoyed betting large sums of money on horses and women. The risk. A judge's salary would limit these excesses.

He straightened up.

His black gown hung straight and true. He looked attractive, even if his face was modest. There was also a belligerence in his eyes. Courage. He could be a frightening man when he wanted to be, his stare ferocious. This was the image he had perfected over the years. It was not Jim the gambler, womaniser and drinker. This was courtroom Jim. Underneath the threat was an astonishingly gentle and sentient man. He would forgive where most would kill.

Before leaving the barristers' robing room he thought about his client. He had attended a number of 'cons' with Hillyard. He remained impressed. The man would do well in the witness box. Bowler felt confident, but was experienced enough to know that nothing could be taken for granted. Even so, as he started walking to the courtroom his instincts told him there could be only one verdict. In some ways he wished the case was less predictable.

Uncertainty was far more fun.

He was stopped outside the courtroom doors by Jeffrey Evert QC for the prosecution – as expected. Evert's nose, what little there was left of it, seemed to oscillate with distaste as his facial muscles adopted one of their more insulting scowls. These scowls were notorious and many had tried to copy them – unsuccessfully. They were unique.

"What can I do for you, Jeffrey?" Bowler asked. His voice was deep. Demanding.

"More a question of what I can do for you, James, I think." Evert knew that his opponent loathed the formality of 'James', the name offending his liberal sensibilities. "My masters have had a change of heart and decided to be generous. Trials are a heavy burden on our ever suffering taxpayers as you know. A guilty plea will no doubt be looked on favourably by the Judge. I am assured—"

"Let me stop you right there, dear boy," Bowler interrupted. It was now his turn to demean, "My client will not compromise his innocence. The bargaining is done. The market place is closed. We are here for a trial for murder and a trial for murder we will have. Now good day to you." Bowler nodded his head a fraction and then swirled off through the courtroom doors.

"Arrogant bastard," Evert muttered. The man and his client were fools. The evidence was overwhelming. Evert shrugged. Bowler had never been renowned for his negotiating skills. He followed him into court.

Jeffrey Evert QC was short and fat. Huge tortoiseshell spectacles blocked out most of his face. This was just as well as he was such an unattractive man. His lips looked like two inflated red dinghies that had been tied together with the intention of saving no one. Either that, or he had been the victim of some Botox-demented cosmetic surgeon. His squashed nose only just managed to hold the specs in check. The nose itself had been the target for many a bullying fist during his public school days, so much so that some were convinced it was still trying to retreat inwards in order to avoid the blows. A few strands of hair survived at the back and sides of his head, otherwise he was as bald as a condom. His calling card was a green polka-dot handkerchief. It never left his hand. It mopped, wiped and soaked up the perspiration that flowed everywhere, from polished crown to chin. At times of stress his face poured.

The red lips and green polka-dots clashed as outrageously as the rest of his body. His voice assaulted ear drums as it shrilled at judge and jury. Evert's baggy trousers were another of his renowned features. When addressing the court his left hand was often seen scratching around in the cavernous left-hand pocket. It had been suggested that sweaty testicles the size of an elephant's were the cause of these constant and diverting meanderings, thus the outsized crotch. Certainly no-one liked Evert enough to speculate that his party piece may have had something to do with his being blessed with a monstrous penis.

All in all, Evert presented a comical appearance as he defied nature and gravity. In spite of all his physical challenges he was respected by his brothers in law. He was an able advocate and extremely effective, even if his voice sometimes rocketed to the ceiling through lack of manly weight.

CHAPTER 39

My most ridiculous dreams had never placed me in the dock.

I had been able to fly; I had been able to see through walls. I had even been able to fight fifty armoured cars. But the dock – no. Yet here I was, forced to sit on a bolted chair in a display case for one of the most recent and notorious 'True Crimes'. The whole court bustled with curiosity and sexual piquancy. Reporters struggled to keep their pens and mobile phones under control. Mine was a trial with all the right grubby ingredients to sensationalise their lifeless readers. Sex, murder, money and good looks were all here. This was 'Hello' time again. I was a 'Celebrity'. A wife-killing one, but nevertheless a celebrity.

I had arrived.

I was famous.

The courtroom was one of the more traditional affairs. All oak and dark, it appealed to me. Even soothed. It reminded me of earlier days when I had jotted down notes behind black gowns and wigs. Then, relaxed and enthusiastic, I was in one of the safest places in the world. In this court bright light, modern furniture and streamlined open space had not been used to expose legal secrets or betray the authority and dignity of justice. Here, richness prevailed to frighten and cow. This was a gallows court. The black cap had been worn in times gone by as Lady Justice deliberated and killed with glittering eyes.

I sat and watched strands of daylight barge their way through high windows. Again I remembered other days when I had been distracted by specks of dust rising and falling upon boredom and agonising lethargy. They would cavort and jive their way around the proceedings, ignorant of the seriousness of it all. My watching then had been uninvolved. My eyes would stray and close. Not now. I saw everything, I heard every sound. My future, my life in its mental form was on trial. I would not wander.

The jury was selected and the charge read.

I studied the twelve faces and the clothes they wore. Appearance can say it all. Never mind about 'appearances being deceptive'. The initial impact and a quick appraisal usually tells me all I need to know. 'Deception' doesn't come into it. Sovereign rings, tattoos and shaved heads tend to be reasonably reliable. White socks are a certainty. Throw jeans, trainers and short-sleeved shirts into the equation and you were away. 'Appearances deceptive?' I won't even start on how a suit is carried or a tie knotted.

The jurors were a cross between the *Daily Mail* and the *Sun*. No virtue in either, as you will have already gathered. Just my luck. It was a toss up between a self-serving middle class fascist with half a brain and a confirmed ignoramus with no brain at all.

There were four women and eight men. The women were more interesting. I gave them the serious eye. Not one above fifty and not one true-blue lesbian as far as I could tell. Anyway at least the 'butch' and 'manly' appeared to be absent, but this meant nothing. I had met some bloody good-lookers of the lesbian persuasion in my time. Hell, look at Clare.

The more prevalent bisexual types, although harder to distinguish, were not a worry; like everyone else in the jury box they could have swung any which way, which was fine by me. All women love a bastard, and right now I was a prime one with the looks to match. Unbeatable. I wanted their sympathy and understanding. I wanted their love.

As I peered and observed I decided the balance was about right. I couldn't detect any gays amongst the men – the lips are usually a giveaway, not to mention body language – which in my view would have meant neutrality. Who knows which way a rectum tickler would swing? I had received the odd male pass in my time. Right now though I didn't give a damn if I was fancied by a man or not. My freedom was far more important than any idiotic homophobic paranoia.

My jury-watching over I decided that they were all as good as it gets. There were no great thinkers in amongst them, but then it would have been crass for me to have expected otherwise. These days anyone with more than two brain cells stayed off the electoral role. As it happens, juries are notoriously capricious and unpredictable anyway. In fact it was a waste of energy trying to work them all out. It did pass the time though, and I received a couple of tongued lips and wanton eyes from some of the women. I knew I had a couple of 'Not Guiltys' in the pot if nothing else.

Hawkins had started to scratch and splutter. A sure sign of impatience. I had heard all about this learned lech. Decent old sod apparently, even if his penis reckoned it was still twenty-one. Don't know why I'm calling him 'old', I wasn't far off his age myself. Definite sign of ageing when judges start looking young, believe me.

At last the trial began. My release had started its journey, even though Jessica Howard had refused to help me with my heavy luggage.

The lying witch.

CHAPTER 40

Evert was up.

All fat, black and horse hair.

The pitch of his voice seemed to depend on the whereabouts of his infamous left testicle, which at the moment seemed to be eluding his left hand. His opening speech for the prosecution outlined the evidence he would submit in order to prove my guilt beyond all reasonable doubt. He addressed the jury eye to eye. Willing them to his own tortoise-shelled certainty. 'Guilty' was the new buzz word and they had better not forget it. Charm was not Evert's style. He was going to scare the hell out of the jury and bully them into submission.

In spite of his piercing voice, he was impressive. His, 'How now fat guts?' mimic of Falstaff outdid the image created by Shakespeare. This fat lump was a serious contender. Even I was beginning to believe that I had rammed Clare's head against the bedside cabinet.

The thrust of his case relied on three things as to why I wanted Clare up there with the angels, wings and all. Firstly, there had been a history of abuse and wife-bashing. Secondly, I was infatuated with a dusky maiden from the East and wanted Clare out of the way. And thirdly, I had loaded Clare with life assurance just before her death with the intention of a quick and handsome return on my investment. The money of course would ensure a happy release from my hatred of legal practise and a changed life sailing the Seven Seas with my new paramour. Means, opportunity, motive and a supreme load of bollocks were all here. Of course Evert had evidence, irrefutable, armour-plated and corroborated, to prove every single one of his insidious accusations and fancy fairy tales. Letters, witnesses and, of course, the jaundiced Jessica, would collectively confirm my guilt as a wife killer. All in all, and what with the domestic violence, this was a murder gritting its teeth in anticipation of its commission. In other words, me bumping off Clare was a forgone conclusion. Beyond all reasonable doubt.

I sat in the dock and seethed.

Actually I did a damn sight more than seethe. I wanted to kill. I wanted to wrench Evert's left testicle off and ram it down his unctuous throat. The things I could have done to him would have shamed a medieval executioner. In the event I checked myself. I had to keep in control. Angry passion would irritate Hawkins – outside the witness box anyway. I was beginning to understand the dramatic courtroom outbursts of innocent men. You sat there powerless whilst your life was torn to shreds. Not a pleasant experience I can tell you.

When Evert had finished his verbal tirade and execution by gob – he didn't need a noose – Bowler stood up to do his party piece.

Calm and good sense, this was Bowler. He seemed as surprised as me to be advocating this particular case. 'What were we all doing here?' 'How very inconvenient', etc., etc. He charmed the jury, held them to his bosom, they were all his best friends particularly the women. He was one of them. This whole thing was a charade he moaned. A nonsense. And in due course he would show why. Listening to him, my equilibrium and confidence returned. My innocence was in good hands.

The first witness to be called was a pathologist.

An expert on death.

His evidence had more or less been agreed beforehand, so there was no cross examination of the contentious kind. Clare had died from a sharp blow to the head. The pathologist enjoyed his discourse on cerebral intricacy and his fascination with a complicated language that only he had the brain power to understand. He concluded and left the stage. I wondered how full his back pockets would be after payment of his fee. Stupid, isn't it, how the little things in life can intrude upon your most dire moments?

Evert called his next witness. Dominic Brent.

I knew for a fact that this little shit wouldn't have a good word to say about me. Evert had chosen well. The last time I had seen Brent I had told him to 'Fuck off', remember? The colour of my garden fence was taking on a greater significance than I had originally given it credit for. It had to be Brent, didn't it? Payback time. Here was the local authority apparatchik in all his 'can't do' glory. 'Can't do', so work for a local authority or teach. In either case keep your mouth shut and don't tell anyone the truth. We paid Brent to attend countless 'meetings' that only met to decide that indecisiveness was inefficient and then appointed a sub-committee to exercise indecisiveness over the first meeting's indecision. Central government on a smaller scale, if you like.

Brent stood in the witness box, preened and official. He had arrived. His word would be taken seriously at last. The chief executive of insane bureaucracy and failure was dressed in a Marks & Spencer suit (top of the range), a checked shirt, striped tie and an uninspiring face that tried to convince everyone that he really did do a 'proper job'. In between this confidence trick he gave me a look of congealed spite. I smiled in return. No hard feelings, that's me.

"Mr Brent, you are a neighbour of the defendant are you not?" Evert asked.

"I am. We live in adjoining properties." Living 'next door' would have been far too mundane for this self-important twat.

"Could you be more specific?"

"Well, we are not side by side as it were, there is about half an acre of land between our two houses."

"How long have you known the defendant?"

"Three years, two months and . . . let me see, thirteen days. He moved into the adjoining property three years ago. March eighteenth just gone."

"Thank you, Mr Brent. Your accuracy is commendable." Wasn't it just? Evert made sure that the jury noted his reliability.

"How well do you know the defendant?"

"Not particularly well. He is not the most amiable of individuals it must be said. Unsociable if you like—"

"I object, your Honour! The witness has not been asked to provide a character testimonial." Bowler was pitching in early on. Make Brent nervous.

"I agree Mr Bowler," Hawkins said. "Will the witness please confine himself to answering the question?"

Brent was not the master of all those with fence posts stuck up their arses this time. He sank a few inches. Evert didn't push my little altercation with Brent over his garden fence and I knew why. Juries despised bureaucracy as much as everybody else. And Brent was bureaucracy right down to his toenails.

"Very well," Evert continued. "Mr Brent continue, but please desist from voicing an opinion on the defendant's personality and confine yourself to the facts."

"Right. . . . Well, my wife and I invited them to the house for cocktails a few times, but they were usually too busy. At least according to Mr Hillyard. His wife was a charming lady though. Always polite. Pleasant. She and my wife became quite friendly. It was Mr Hillyard who resisted our invitations, I think."

Clare and his wife? Friendly? News to me. Clare had always made jokes about the 'snobby' woman next door. This was a bit rich coming from Clare though I had to admit.

"Did your neighbours appear to enjoy normal matrimonial harmony?" What a question. Did such a thing exist?

"No. They certainly didn't."

"And why was that, Mr Brent?"

"Well, there were many occasions when my wife and I were disturbed by some of the goings-on at their house."

"Goings-on?"

"Rows. Serious rows. We used to be quite concerned. Sometimes we were genuinely worried if someone was being hurt. There was so much shouting, screaming even."

"Would you tell the court in more detail what exactly you heard?

"The rows were violent. That's the only way I can describe them. We often heard the noise of smashed glass, or plates. Crockery, that kind of thing. Of course I can't be sure about what exactly was being broken, but that's what it sounded like. Once or twice we considered calling the police. We feared for Mrs Hillyard. She was such a nice lady."

"You did not call the police? Or go round there yourself?"

"No. One does not like to interfere, but apart from this Mr Hillyard was an aggressive character. Who knows how he would have reacted?"

Bowler was up again. Too late though.

"Thank you, Mr Brent. That's all." Evert sat down.

Brent was enjoying this. He hadn't allowed the opportunity to vent his puerile malice in his search for revenge escape him.. All I wanted to do was strangle him. Not literally, I hasten to add. See what I mean? That's what being had up for murder does to you. Makes you defensive, paranoid. The slimy rat was after my blood. Now I admit Clare and I had had a few rows. She even threw some plates about, but what the hell – who didn't? Most of the time we ignored each other. Our home must have been one of the quietest places in Suffolk – and that's saying something, believe me.

"Mr Brent, you are a married man are you not?" It was Bowler's turn now. Calm and reason personified.

"Yes."

"A happily married man too, I will venture?" Bowler smiled, full of charm and understanding.

"Most definitely."

"And how long have you been married?"

"Twenty-six years."

"You are to be congratulated, Mr Brent. If I may be so bold, that is quite an achievement in these troubled times of matrimonial dissolution. A rare union one might even say." Brent was being honoured. He had just received his OBE. He stood in the box proud and self-satisfied.

"Thank you for saying so." All smarm now.

"My pleasure. Now Mr Brent, you have been married for twenty-six years. A successful marriage, correct?"

"Absolutely." Oh God that word, everyone and their bloody dog uses it these days.

"You have never had a quarrel then?"

"Well . . . er . . . no. Not a serious one anyway."

"And what would you consider a serious quarrel, Mr Brent?"

"My wife and I have our differences of course, but we always sit down and talk things through. We listen to each other. A marriage must be about give and take. And of course, communication."

"Indeed. And love too, surely?" Bowler didn't wait for an answer. "Love, Mr Brent. Passion. When there is love in a marriage feelings run high, do they not? Husbands and wives quarrel now and again. That is marriage, Mr Brent." Bowler turned to the jury and smiled, "For most of us mere mortals anyway, I suspect." The jury smiled with him. They knew all about matrimonial discord.

"I . . . er . . . I didn't say—" This was as far as Brent was allowed to go.

"You claim the defendant had violent quarrels with his wife. You claim smashed glass. You claim fear for Mrs Hillyard's life. Did you call the police, Mr Brent?"

"I . . . no. We didn't want to interfere. It was none of our business."

"Oh, I see. None of your business. That's a change from your previous view, I think. Who was doing all this shouting and screaming, Mr Brent?"

"I'm not—"

"Let me answer for you. It was Mrs Hillyard, wasn't it? . . . Wasn't it?"

"Well . . . er, yes. Most of the time I suppose."

"Most of the time? You suppose? Was it or wasn't it, Mr Brent? Yes or no?" There was a pause.

"Yes."

"Thank you. Would you also agree that a man with such an onerous civic duty – you are after all the chief executive of a local authority – would have little hesitation in reporting the possibility of a crime of violence to the police if such a man believed a crime of this nature was being perpetrated."

Silence.

"Mr Brent? . . . Silence again. "There were no such calls were there. Why?"

"Well . . . I . . ."

"I'll tell you why, Mr Brent. Because in the last three odd years you have never had any serious cause to report these so called 'violent rows' of your neighbours to the police. That is why, is it not? There were no serious threats to life and limb, were there?"

"That is not the point. I . . . er—"

"Mr Brent," Bowler was pushing hard, he didn't wait for an answer, "these violent quarrels are a figment of your imagination, aren't they?"

"I . . . I . . . well don't . . ." Brent was starting to splutter with anger. He hadn't come here to be made a fool of.

Bowler wasn't going to let him off the hook.

"A malicious imagination at that. You have come here today to exercise a grudge, Mr Brent, haven't you? A grudge that has festered for three years. A grudge over the colour of a garden fence no less."

"I . . . that's not true . . .!"

"I believe my client refused to paint his wooden fence in a colour to your liking and told you in no uncertain terms to, er . . . go away. Is that correct or not? We do have your solicitor's letters to hand if your memory is deserting you."

"Well I tried to . . . Hillyard was rude. Insulting!"

252

"Please Mr Brent, just answer my question."

"Well . . . yes, I suppose so, but he was—"

"Yes. Thank you Mr Brent." Bowler shuffled some papers for a moment then looked back up at Brent. "You have excellent hearing Mr Brent, I believe."

"What? What do you mean . . .?"

"It is true, is it not, that your individual houses are separated by about one half of an acre of land? Indeed I believe you have already confirmed this to the court." Bowler paused for a few moments to allow the jury to absorb his words. "Half an acre of land," Bowler repeated. "So, in spite of this physical distance, you were able to hear verbal argument and crashing glass? Yes? You were so close in fact to these imagined events that you feared for Mrs Hillyard's life. Yes?"

"No . . . it wasn't like that. I was often in the garden. Mowing the lawn and so on . . ." Brent managed to answer.

"Mowing the lawn? Does your lawn mower have a silenced engine then?"

"No, of course not."

"Then how were you able to hear all these goings on at the Hillyard household?" Bowler looked at the jury again and then turned back to face Brent. "Did Mrs Hillyard ever arrive at your home for protection? Did she ever complain to your wife, her friend, about a physically abusive husband? The answer is a resounding 'no' on both counts. I put it to you Mr Brent, that you have come here today for one reason and one reason only. To get your own back. To enjoy the bitter taste of revenge. And all over the colour of a silly garden fence."

Without giving Brent a second or two to reply Bowler said abruptly, "No more questions, your Honour" and sat down.

Brent looked suitably diminished.

I went back to my cell that evening knowing that Brent had been easy meat. I had a feeling that when the time came, Jessica Howard would put up far more of a fight.

CHAPTER 41

The following day Lesley Moresby was called.

Under normal circumstances a solicitor taking instructions would not have been able to give evidence due to confidentiality and client privilege, but since when was a corpse privileged? I watched as Moresby took the stand. Here we go, I thought, now Amazons have arrived in the twenty-first century (not the online shopping store by the way, but those women in the past of a more ferocious warrior inclination) and they haven't lost their arrogant spirit and determination to win at all costs either.

Moresby stood in the box and hated.

She penetrated faces, seeking weakness. The proffered bible was ignored. She affirmed instead. No doubt Jesus Christ, as far as Moresby was concerned, had been one of the main protagonists in the destruction of women's rights. The man had made women wash his feet for a start. If this wasn't male chauvinism at its most heinous, then what was? Of course the fact that Christ, a man, was prepared to return the compliment had nothing to do with it.

Evert stood before her. Small and insignificant this time.

It didn't help that the box was raised. She was a tall woman anyway, so she towered above the fat, little man. He looked relieved to be on her side. Her huge body could have crushed even his over-sprung girth. Her huge hands gripped the brass rail in front of her. She was dressed in black, her favourite and most threatening colour. Her hair had been cropped almost to the skull. Before opening his mouth even Evert must have thought, 'My God, what an unsightly wench'. He certainly appeared to be awed. On the other hand of course, perhaps he liked big, ugly women. You only have to walk round a few streets to realise how attractive some men find them. He coughed a couple of times and out came the green polka-dot handkerchief. The damn thing could have been taken on holiday and used as a tent. God knows why Evert used such massive handkerchiefs. Short man syndrome maybe.

"Miss Moresby?"

"Muz if you don't mind."

"Muz Moresby . . . you are a solicitor who has specialised in family law for some years, is that correct?"

"Correct."

"Indeed you are considered to be an authority in this area. You have had numerous articles and papers published and written practise manuals, is that not so?"

"Yes."

"Will you please tell the court how you came to know Mrs Hillyard?"

"Muz Hillyard came to see me on one occasion. She instructed me to begin divorce proceedings against her husband, the defendant, based on the fact of his unreasonable behaviour."

"Er . . . Miss . . . Muz . . . my apologies," even Evert hated this feminist hyperbole, "what exactly was the nature of the defendant's unreasonable behaviour?"

"Violence."

"Would you explain please."

"There had been a history of it. All fully documented. Times, place etc. All the details are contained in the late Muz Hillyard's affidavit in support of her divorce petition. The defendant had also sexually abused her."

"Thank you Muz Moresby." Evert looked at the Clerk. "The affidavit, that would be Exhibit 3. Please circulate to the jury."

Clare's affidavit specifying my violent behaviour and sexual abuse was passed from pillar to post. It was all a complete fiction. I remember at the time I had received it, I laughed. Someone had one hell of an imagination and it wasn't Clare. She didn't have the brain power. I knew only too well how solicitors could 'spin' an affidavit. Alastair Campbell hadn't invented the noble art, believe me – I'd done enough of it myself. Karma again.

Evert allowed an appropriate time for the jury's perusal and pre-judgement.

"Did you undertake any further action on behalf of your client?"

"Yes, emergency orders to remove the defendant from the matrimonial home. My client was at serious risk. I was not prepared to take any chances with her safety. The facts alone demanded immediate action. The defendant was a violent man—"

"I object your Honour," Bowler was up again.

"Yes, yes, Mr Bowler," Hawkins answered. "Will the witness please refrain from passing opinions unless specifically requested?" There was no reply from Moresby. She looked at the judge as if to say 'Get stuffed'.

"It is correct is it not that a decree nisi had yet to be obtained?"

"That is correct. The petition had been filed two weeks before my client's death."

Evert went through the affidavit word for lying word. He was making damn certain that the jury were left in no doubt about my violent and perverted sexual tendencies. He hovered and paused over my 'rape' of Clare two weeks after our marriage. The catalogue being read out shook me, and this time there was no mocking laughter. I was waiting for some glossy pictures to be exhibited next.

Evert finished with his examination of Moresby.

"Thank you Muz Moresby. That will be all for now." He sat down on his big fat arse and no doubt felt pleased with himself. This was going to be an easy one. He was one step nearer to the Bench and concluded ambition. The House of Lords and quintessential social achievement were in his myopic sights.

Bowler faced the witness who was defiant and unperturbed. Moresby was an unpleasant irritant and a distinctly unattractive one at that.

"Muz Moresby, does the ancient institution of marriage offend you? Is this why you insist on addressing both yourself and the late Mrs Hillyard as 'Muz'?"

"Your Honour," it was Evert's turn now. "I object, these comments are irrelevant."

"I agree. Mr Bowler, please refrain." Hawkins seemed disappointed. Bowler sighed.

"You are an experienced solicitor?"

"Yes."

"A specialist in Family Law?"

"Yes."

"An authority, no less."

"I try."

"Indeed. How many years have you been specialising in this area?"

"Ten."

"Then you will know that there are always two sides to a matrimonial cause. You do act for men as well I take it?" Moresby didn't answer, "Come, come Miss Moresby . . . my apologies slip of the tongue . . . Muz Moresby." Bowler looked at the jury as if begging their indulgence and it has to be said, their derision. "You do act for both men and women surely?"

"I only take instructions from female clients."

"Oh, do you? Why is that?"

"Choice."

"Really – it has nothing to do then with your general dislike of male kind?"

"Not at all."

"Very well. You agree that divorce usually involves both sexes."

"Of course. You are stating the obvious."

"Indeed. Then how can you be such an expert on this area of law if you discount the obvious by refusing to act for men?" Bull's-eye for Bowler.

"I . . . well, I—"

"Quite. I am sure the jury will be gratified to have learnt of your noble and commendable impartiality where divorce work is concerned." Bowler smiled at the jury; he was amusing them, drawing them into his arms, hugging them. They were all friends after all.

Suddenly Bowler changed tack. "In your statement you say that Mrs Hillyard had suffered physical abuse immediately before seeing you, the day in fact you applied for emergency non-molestation and occupation orders. Did you notice any physical damage to your client's person?" There was no reply, "I repeat, did your client look like a victim of physical and sexual abuse?"

"There were no obvious signs, no. But as you well know—"

"Yes, yes, Miss Moresby, just answer my questions."

"No, I will not! I will have my say Mr Bowler, whether you like it or not. Who are you to determine what physical and mental damage Muz Hillyard had suffered? You men are so clever with your fists! The defendant is a—"

"That's enough, Miss Moresby." Hawkins interjected. "Desist please!" Even the judge was forgetting his political correctness by addressing Moresby as 'Miss'. Either that or he thought it was all a load of old rubbish too, like everybody else. "Your response to the question is intemperate and ill-judged. I expect better from you." Hawkins was not one for amateur dramatics, however well-intentioned. Moresby shut up. The judge's fingers were twitching perilously close to his wig and she, like the rest of the legal community, knew that Hawkins' itching issues were not to be trifled with. Bowler continued.

"So Miss Moresby, you agree that there was no visual evidence of physical damage to your client? Cuts and bruises, for example?"

"No."

"Did your client seek help from her GP? A hospital?"

"No, but many women feel—" Bowler was not taking prisoners. He cut Moresby off.

258

"Did your client appear to be suffering from any mental health problems then? Depression, for instance? Excessive alcohol or drug abuse?"

"No."

"Imminent mental breakdown?"

"No, but that doesn't mean a thing and you know it. Muz Hillyard was distressed. Extremely distressed. I am not a doctor or a psychiatrist. All I can tell you is that the woman was frightened. Scared out of her wits, in fact. She told me that she had been a victim of physical and sexual abuse for some years. Judging by her emotional state in my office I had no reason to disbelieve her. The poor woman. Why else do you think I expedited her husband's removal from the matrimonial home?"

"I am indeed at a loss as to 'why', Miss Moresby. As far as this court is aware you undertook to remove the defendant from his own home in spite of not having a solitary shred of evidence to support his violent malfeasance. No police reports, no medical evidence. Nothing. How on earth did you manage to obtain an order in the first place?" That's it Jim boy, keep her off balance.

"I . . . I . . ." Moresby looked worried. I was enjoying myself. Bowler passed some bundles of paper to the clerk who then handed them to both Moresby and the jury.

"Members of the jury, will you please study the credit card accounts the clerk has just handed you. And you too, Miss Moresby." As she was scanning some of the sheets of paper Bowler said, "You will note that on the date of your consultation, Mrs Hillyard tried to purchase a . . . um . . . modest diamond bracelet for £19,300. The transaction was refused. Her authority to use the cards in question had been cancelled by the defendant the day before; he knew only too well his wife's capacity to . . . er . . . how shall I say? . . . self-medicate on plastic." Bowler turned to his friends in the jury box. " Forgive me members of the jury, but I believe 'self-medicate' is the latest term for avoiding directness. Put more bluntly, Mrs Hillyard was a profligate spendthrift of the first order." He turned back to Moresby. "Now then, this item is but one of many transactions undertaken by Mrs Hillyard. For the record, the bracelet was the only unsuccessful purchase in a long career of Mrs Hillyard's purchasing power. You will agree that her spending history does not lend itself to the proposition of a mean and penny-pinching husband, or for that matter, a woman pushed to the limits of her endurance due to poverty, social disadvantage and domestic violence. Judging by all the restaurants, clubs and so on that Mrs Hillyard attended, it seems quite hard to draw any other conclusion than that the lady enjoyed a thoroughly busy and happy existence, not to mention of course her enthusiasm for haute couture and personal trainers. I am confident that many a lady in this courtroom today would envy such a lifestyle. It is 'such stuff as dreams are made on' is it not? A celebrity lifestyle no less. Do you not agree Miss Moresby?"

"If you say so," Moresby was beginning to lose some of her zeal.

"I didn't quite catch that. Would you please repeat yourself."

"If you say so!" This time she shouted. Anger. Not good. The cool competent lawyer was on the run. She had already brought her professionalism into question by her previous outburst. Her arrogance remained intact though.

"Did the defendant breach your court orders? Did he cause any trouble for your client?"

"No. The defendant left the matrimonial home quietly. My client did not believe that he would be troublesome." A climb down.

"Really? Let me repeat what you have just said. In your own words, 'the defendant left the matrimonial home quietly' and Mrs Hillyard 'did not believe her husband would be troublesome'. This is a contradiction surely? One minute according to Mrs Hillyard's affidavit in support of her divorce petition the defendant is a cruel wife-beater, the next he is inclined to depart from his own home without so much as a whimper. I am sorry, Miss Moresby, but you are confusing me and I suspect the jury also. Your comments are at odds with the notion of the defendant being a deadly rapist and murderer. Do you not agree?"

"He's just clever. He's fooling the lot of you, but you just can't see it."

"So you say. Now, I come to this alleged rape four years ago or thereabouts. As a lawyer you would be fully aware of the need for proof. Did you encounter any from your client?"

"No."

"Once again, had this rape been reported to the police? Her GP?"

"No, not as far as I am aware."

"Well, let me assure you that no such reporting took place. Either to the police or to her GP. The deceased must have been extremely protective of the man she loved. This can be the only explanation. Would you not agree?"

"As you well know, hundreds if not thousands of women keep the abuse they suffer secret. Your sarcasm may impress the jury, but I find it rather juvenile." One up for Moresby; she was right too, and Bowler knew it.

"My apologies. If I may continue."

"You may." The belligerence was back.

"Are you married?"

"No."

"Have you ever married?"

"No."

"Do you have children?"

"No."

"You are a lesbian?"

"Yes."

"You have a reputation as a warrior for women's rights?"

"I believe so."

"Some would say you are . . . er . . . determined in your beliefs, is that not so? You did draft Mrs Hillyard's affidavit in support of her non-molestation and occupation orders?"

"Yes . . . I mean no . . ." Trapped.

Bowler looked at the jury.

"You seem unsure . . .?"

"Well . . . I think my trainee might have done some of the work." The woman was trying to pass the buck.

"So, you drafted the affidavit on your client's instructions of course, and your trainee helped you?"

"I'm not sure."

"You seemed certain enough a few moments ago. Could it be that your zeal for protecting women sometimes forces you into a somewhat cavalier approach to the drafting of important documents in support of applications to the court?"

No answer.

Silence.

Bowler turned to face the jury,

"So, members of the jury, we have a solicitor who will only act for women and who applies to the courts for emergency orders where the only evidence of violence is a quick one-hour appointment in her office, if that, and a questionable affidavit by her client. An affidavit that one assumes Muz Moresby, as the late Mrs Hillyard's solicitor, would have at the very least cast a discerning eye over. So distressed is her client apparently that immediately after the appointment she goes out and tries to spend £19,300 on some retail therapy. She must have been at her wits' end. The witness has now confirmed, in her own words, that she saw no evidence of physical abuse. Not a scratch. And what about this rape from the past? Where is the evidence . . .? You may well ask. Forever hidden in the mind of Mrs Hillyard no doubt. In her mind and her imagination. No more questions."

Bowler had finished his job of discrediting Moresby as a reliable witness.

Moresby stood down and continued to hate.

I had my doubts.

People were so neurotic these days that the jury may well believe that Clare's retail insanity was actually a cry for help. All a load of rubbish of course, but juries were renowned for swallowing it. Bowler had attacked Moresby's integrity and her legal competence. He had also exploited her sexuality and her unmarried status. She was the lesbian, childless feminist. He had hoped to exploit the middle-class jury and their aspirations for the 'back to basics' family unit and the 'harmonious fabric of family life'. Moresby was a traitor. A sexual pervert.

To be quite honest with you, I rather admired the woman. Hate to admit it. At least she had jumped off the fence and stuck two fingers up at everyone. It takes courage, if nothing else. She had kept her guns blazing too, apart from some momentary lapses. Bowler hadn't quite knocked her for six. She left the dock with a pointed snarl at the judge. She was proud of herself, her sexuality. Which was probably a damn sight more than could be said for most of the people knocking about the courtroom. Trouble is, if I could harbour a grudging respect for the woman then what about the jury? Hey, whose side am I on here? Lawyers – they always have to see all sides. Even so, I sat there and felt hellishly vulnerable. My future was in the hands of twelve people I didn't even know. An uncapped tube of toothpaste, a cold cup of tea, an objectionable youngster could all play a part in the verdict. These thoughts frightened me half to death. I didn't trust human nature, I never would. I had seen too much of it.

After Moresby had steamed her way out of the courtroom a few more witnesses were called. A GP, the jewellery shop assistant, a witness to Clare's outburst in the shop and so it went on. They all confirmed that there was no physical evidence to confirm that Clare had been beaten up on the day in question, but as Moresby had correctly pointed out this meant nothing. Female victims of domestic violence frequently hid their wounds both physical and mental. Regrettably I had to agree. I had done some divorce work many years ago and had encountered many such instances.

I knew that so far I couldn't count on anything. The main event hadn't turned up yet, and when she did I knew that my fate would rest on her evidence alone.

The venerable Jessica Howard could make or break my defence to the charge of murder.

CHAPTER 42

When Tom arrived home Lucretia was in the sitting room deep in thought. All the children were out, so 'thinking time' was never taken for granted. Such opportunities were rare, and when they arose they were grasped with both hands.

As Tom walked into the sitting room his wife's eyes appeared to be concentrating on her collection of porcelain figurines and dinnerware strutting around in a glass cabinet. Meissen, Dresden and Franz Wittwer had finally worked out how the Chinese had been doing it and now flaunted themselves in front of Lucretia's eyes on a daily basis. She loved her porcelain. She had started collecting when she was eighteen. Her purchases had graduated along with her career and pocket. It was now a fine and valuable collection. Something to be passed down the inevitable and deathly line of inheritance.

"Ah, you're in here. Are you all right?" Tom asked. "You seem quite engrossed."

"I'm fine, Tom. Just admiring my collection of porcelain. You know how its beauty and craftsmanship always affects me. It still amazes me how man can create such incredible art one minute and be so hideous the next. Odd lot, aren't we?"

"You can say that again. Although unfortunately I only tend to see the 'hideous' side of life. But there we are, my choice." Tom sat down next to Lucretia. She seemed calm today, her normal self. He almost breathed a sigh of relief. These days he never knew what would be confronting him when he came home. Laughter or anger, he never knew. He took her hand. "You seem very thoughtful, darling. What's up? Nothing bothering you is there?" Lucretia squeezed his hand and turned to face him.

"Tom, there is something I must tell you."

"What?" For a moment Tom wasn't sure whether he wanted to know. The recent changes in his wife's moods had led him to think all kinds of things, and there was a resignation in her eyes that he had never seen before. Or was it sadness? He couldn't be sure.

"Tom, I know I've been impossible to live with recently and I'm sorry. God knows I'm sorry. I've been blaming it all on the menopause and so on. Well, I assure you I'm not menopausal." She stopped for a moment and smiled. There was that awful resignation in her eyes again, resignation with a touch of sympathy, Tom was certain. Was it for him? Oh Christ, was it another man?

"Having said that I haven't been feeling right for quite a while. Miserable and dare I say it even depressed, not to mention snappy and irritable. My balance has been playing tricks on me as well, and there have also been these slight uncontrollable tremors and involuntary muscular movements. You wouldn't have noticed, Tom. I haven't told you any of this because I haven't wanted to worry you. I'm sorry."

"Well I . . . well." Oh God, what was Lucretia trying to tell him?

"Shush Tom. Please. Let me finish. I must finish, you must be strong."

"I haven't been lying about in bed all day as no doubt you have imagined. I've been going back and forth to the hospital. For tests. I now have the results. The doctor told me yesterday, but I needed some time to absorb things before telling you. Tom . . . I . . . I have Huntington's disease."

Tom looked at his wife. Saw the pain and strength. He knew about Huntington's, probably more than most people. He had once been involved in a legal dispute between some children over a Power of Attorney for their father who was dying from the disease. Huntington's was a fatal disorder of the central nervous system. Incurable. Tom took Lucretia's other hand and pulled her into his chest. He didn't know what to say or do. He just didn't know. He didn't even know what to think.

Eventually Lucretia pulled away from him. "Now there are some things you must promise me, Tom." Tears were starting to trickle down his cheeks, he couldn't stop them. He knew how debilitating and destructive the disease could be.

"Anything, my darling. Anything."

For a few minutes Lucretia told Tom that were drugs to manage the symptoms effectively. She could lead a relatively normal life for a good few years yet.

"When the symptoms get too much Tom, which they will, you must help me to die. I can't bear the thought of being unable to control my body at all, of not speaking properly, or of choking to death. Do you understand?" Lucretia was almost being matter-of-fact, but she still gripped his hands. "There is also the hereditary risk to my own children. Now is not the time to tell them. They are too young, but tell them we must when the time is right."

Tom had always known that she was stronger than he was, but her strength right now was almost frightening him. He quickly pulled himself together as he tried to come to terms with the shock of it all. "Tom, you must listen to me. I will die on my own terms and with dignity. The thought of our children and you seeing me in such a state is unbearable. By that time I will have no life. You must promise me that you will honour my wishes when the time comes and help me to carry them out. Will you do that for me?"

Tom looked down at his shoes. He was a lawyer, he knew the legal implications of what she was asking.

"I will be breaking the law Lucretia, and there is also a possibility I could go to prison."

"I know. I have already thought of that and I also know the enormous burden I am placing on you. But who else can I ask? Who else can I trust? Yours is the only love I believe in."

He looked into Lucretia's beautiful eyes and saw both fear and courage. He knew instantly that her request had nothing whatsoever to do with the law but everything to do with love.

Everything.

"When the time comes I will help you, I promise."

CHAPTER 43

Jessica Howard arrived in the witness box. My jaw dropped and I wasn't trying to lick a passing fly's arse either.

Who the hell was this? In another place and time I wouldn't have recognised the woman. The special beauty I had always observed in her had been unobtrusive. There had been no uncouth declarations. The woman in the witness box now was a ruthless man killer. The men in the jury sat up and dribbled. Their fantasies and internet porn lay a mere few feet away. As she had walked up to the box an unannounced silence arrived. Feet moved, muscles tensed and eyes strained. This woman knew how to perform. Her predecessors had all been tasteless starters. Howard was all the main courses on one plate.

Jessica had applied expertise to her appearance. She was so feminine I almost shook. Her makeup was restrained. No loud colours. Her black dress made sure the curves of her body were seen without full discovery. She looked elegant and refined. The mad hair had been tied up, but not too tightly. There had been no severity used in its pushing and pulling. It didn't offend. Her face carried gentleness, care. There was no aggression. No fight. Her eyes viewed the judge and jury with deep blue integrity and perfect credibility.

She read the oath.

Her words drifted in the air. No sharpness. She was here to tell the truth and nothing but. No one could possibly doubt the vision before them. As she read out the oath my stomach trembled. Bowler was going to have his work cut out for him. I already knew that Jessica Howard was a highly intelligent and streetwise woman. She was no Brent or Moresby. Worst of all, I also knew that she was the most crucial witness. The only witness that truly mattered. She had been in the bedroom. She had seen it all. Her word against mine.

I instantly regretted the male-dominated jury. Howard had already compromised them. Her beauty had damaged their brains and sense of proportion. I remembered thinking that a bit of fine tuning here and there would have turned Howard into a work of art. The woman had outflanked me. Even I was transfixed and regretting my 'Fuck off' note. Dear God, if I had accepted the goods on offer I wouldn't be where I am now, would I? Women again. We never learn. It would hardly have been an unpleasant experience either, would it? Even I was lusting and I loved another. Sex. God help us.

I thanked my good fortune that Bowler would be immune to the physical attack of Jessica Howard. Or at least he should be. Other briefs may well have been distracted. Not Bowler. I knew he was still getting over a wife who had gone colonial. I hoped his grief remained strong and true. Where Howard was concerned though, could I trust 100 per cent any man's responses to her?

The real shock for me was seeing something in Howard that I had never seen before – warmth. It was there, I'm telling you. Underneath the clever make-up and clothes it was there. Perhaps I was deluding myself, who knows, but I was feeling desperate, wasn't I? And I was sure there was more. Sadness maybe. I had noticed it before in the kitchen at home. It had been a brief shadow, a will-o'-the-wisp, but my instincts never let me down. There was more to Jessica Howard than the predatory feminist. There had been more to Clare too. I had always known; I had just been too lazy to find out – more is the pity.

"You are the manager of a Law Centre, a solicitor, is that correct?" Another one. The jury must be getting fed up with being inundated with lawyers. Probably didn't believe a word any of us were saying and who could blame them? Evert was on his feet and about to milk the do-gooding element. Before

Howard answered our eyes met. A collision. Our minds joined for an instant. It happened. It was over. Something.

"That is correct."

"What exactly does your Law Centre do?

"We provide free impartial advice to anyone who requires it."

"Anyone?"

"Yes. Usually we help people who are unable to pay for professional advice. Who can't afford solicitors. Who are stuck in poverty."

"And are you paid a high salary?"

Howard laughed slightly. It was charming.

"No, not that high. Enough though."

"You would say modest? Not the going rate say, if you were employed in private practice for instance?"

"Oh, definitely not. " Again the smile. Again the demure beauty.

"You must care about people, Miss Howard. You don't mind me calling you 'Miss'?"

"No, not at all. Yes, I care deeply about people. The disadvantaged." Not too many words. Just right. The woman was being someone else altogether. She had nearly castrated me for calling her 'Miss'.

"How long had you known the late Mrs Hillyard?"

"Clare? . . . Oh, about ten years." Evert's left hand was being unusually active in his trouser pocket, so much for professional detachment, "We met whilst working for the same airline company – air stewardesses. We liked each other from the start and became close friends. I left the company to go on to do other things before Clare. We lost touch, you know how it is."

"You met again though after some years?"

"Yes. We bumped into each other a few months ago. At a party of a mutual friend."

"Thank you, Miss Howard. How well did you know Mrs Hillyard?"

"Very well. As I have said, we enjoyed a close friendship in our er . . . younger days." Howard smiled and all the male jurors wished. Pin-up time. Disingenuous trollop. "We trusted each other. Confided in one another. Even though eight-odd years had passed with little if any contact, we were able to restart our friendship with little effort. Real friendship is like that, isn't it? No matter how many years go by without any contact you are able to resume the closeness as if only one day has gone by. Time merely suspends true friendship, it doesn't alter it."

"Quite, Miss Howard. Quite." Not that Evert would have known anything about true friendship. The only true friend he had ever known was his dog.

"So, Mrs Hillyard trusted you. Confided in you?"

"Oh yes. Absolutely." That bloody word again! Howard was beginning to go down in my estimation. Sharp she may have been, but she was starting to display a distinct lack of dexterity where her vocabulary was concerned, like all the other simple-tons who kept using that ubiquitous excuse for certainty.

"You enjoyed more than friendship did you not? It was more a loving relationship? Is that not so?"

"Yes."

"You supported each other?"

"Yes."

"Understood each other?"

"Yes."

Pens and eardrums started to jump. The juicy bits were about to be revealed, or so everyone thought.

Jessica continued, "I know this is hard to understand but we knew each other so well that we could almost read each other's minds. Love can be like that."

I was beginning to feel nauseous.

"Words are unnecessary, superfluous, there had been no physical relationship in our flying days. The sexual side of things just happened when we met up a few months ago. It was very natural. I had no idea that Clare was sexually inclined towards another woman, although once or twice in the past she had given me occasion to wonder. I have always been bisexual, but I believe Clare had come to realise that she was a committed lesbian. She wanted us to have a relationship. To live together. We were thinking about it when she was . . . when she died."

The woman's performance did not disappoint.

Evert was milking it for all he was worth. I did wonder why Bowler didn't get up and try to stop her maudlin soliloquies, but then I also realised that this could have gone against him. The jury was in love with her after all; at least all the men were. I wasn't so sure about the women: no doubt they were probably seething with jealousy. I was also beginning to wonder who the real victim was in this whole sorry mess.

"Mrs Hillyard was unhappy in her marriage?"

"Extremely so."

"Please go on."

"She felt she had made a terrible mistake marrying Edwin. Not only because of her confused sexuality but because of the way Edwin had changed. Before the marriage he had been charming, kind. But soon after he changed. Terribly so."

"Please explain."

"Well, Clare told me that he constantly beat her—"

"I object, your Honour! The witness statement is hearsay and cannot—"

"Sit down Mr Bowler." Hawkins ordered. "You are overruled. The witness testimony is relevant. Carry on Miss Howard, please."

"Thank you, your Honour," Jessica said, plenty of teeth and smiles again. "She told me that Edwin not only constantly beat her but also sexually abused her. That he was very demanding and would not take 'No' for an answer. She also told me he had raped her two weeks after her marriage."

The courtroom stirred.

272

Howard's testimony was effective. It was the innocent way she was telling her story, her lack of anger and disgust, her honesty – particularly about her own sexuality . It was almost as if she was blaming herself. The woman was inspiring sympathy. I was starting to fill my pants.

"Please go on."

"Well . . . she told me that he 'treated her like dirt'. Those were the words I think, if I remember correctly. She told me that he had beaten her on several occasions. The last occasion a few days before her death. I had witnessed evidence of the violence myself. The morning I took her to see Lesley Moresby. Clare was in a terrible state. Her cheek was red and swollen, in spite of the makeup she had used to try and cover it up. Edwin had beaten her upon being told that she intended to divorce him."

"Had she told anyone else about these violent episodes?"

"No, I don't think so, apart from Lesley, her solicitor. You see, Clare was very aware of Edwin's position. She didn't want to damage him professionally – his reputation. She knew what would happen if she went to the police. Edwin was well-known and respected in the local community. She was loyal, so very loyal . . ." I couldn't believe it but the woman's voice trailed off and she actually sobbed. The lying fucking harridan sobbed!

"Take your time, Miss Howard. Please, take your time. We understand how distressing this must be for you." Evert was doing his noble bit, but as if this wasn't bad enough, Hawkins, the lecherous old goat, nearly jumped off the bench to give the lying harpy a glass of water. Jesus, I was starting to blub with her – out of frustration.

"Are you ready to continue, Miss Howard?" Evert asked, all sweetness and light.

"Yes . . . I'm sorry. I am so sorry. . . ."

Silence for a few more moments. Effect again. Evert was enjoying every second. Jessica was squeezing the jury, imploring them to return a verdict of guilty.

She eventually managed to get a grip. "I tried to persuade Clare to leave Edwin. She was so frightened of him. She seemed to be in a constant state of fear. At long last I was able to take her to see a solicitor, you know – Lesley Moresby. The lady came highly recommended." That's it, let's hear a bit of sexed-up female solidarity.

"Why hadn't she tried to divorce the defendant before?"

"Money. Clare had no money of her own." (Plenty of mine though!) "None. She didn't work, so she was totally dependent on Edwin."

"Was there any other kind of abuse to your knowledge?"

"Yes. Verbal abuse. Clare wasn't well educated. She couldn't match Edwin. He frequently belittled her. Humiliated her. I had seen examples of this many times. At parties and in her own home. Edwin was always making her look a fool. His language was often crude and offensive. Clare hated it."

"What frame of mind was Mrs Hillyard in when you re-kindled your friendship?"

"Confused."

"Confused?"

"Yes, she seemed lost, diminished. She was not the vibrant young woman that I had known so well. Her sense of humour had gone. Her sparkle had vanished. I was deeply concerned for her. Oh God, none of this would have happened if I . . . oh God . . ." Sob, sob, sob again.

And then the women broke down!

I couldn't believe what I was seeing or hearing. I was speechless. I was the one who should have been a whimpering wreck, for God's sake! After a minute or two she took a swig of water, wiped the tears away, sniffed for England and then said in a wretched voice, "You see, Clare didn't want to hurt her husband. In a funny kind of way I think she still loved him. She just didn't want to hurt him. She couldn't help it."

The woman dabbed away at her eyes with a paper snot-rag and gave the men in the jury box an imploring look. She paused for a breath or two. Head bowed, nostrils sniffling. Hawkins was nearly falling off the bench, all tea, sympathy and 'I'll see you later in my chambers for a damn good rogering'.

I wanted to be sick. Everyone was falling for all this rot. Howard would have melted a fire-proof Oscar if one had been lying around.

"Miss Howard, are you able to continue?" Evert asked as he looked up at Hawkins who seemed to nod in agreement to something. "The court can adjourn for a short while if you need some time to compose yourself."

"No, no." Sniff, sniff. "I'm fine now, really." More sniffs.

"Very well . . . you er . . ." Evert continued, allowing enough of a pause to drag even more sympathy out of the jury, "received a letter from Mrs Hillyard about two months after your relationship had started. Exhibit 4, your Honour." Copies were given to Howard and the jury. "Will you please read out the contents of the letter, Miss Howard? Please take your time."

Howard cleared her throat. She was back in harness.

" 'My darling Jessica,

" 'I'm not a great letter writer as you know. Remember how you used to laugh at my postcards. Two words and that was about it. Anyway I was watching a programme on daytime telly that went on about the therapeutic – hope I've spelt that properly – virtues of writing things down. So I thought I would have a go. I don't know whether I need much healing now though – not since I've met you anyway. You have brought me so much happiness. So much love. For years I have struggled to find out who I really am. What I truly want to be. Can I ever thank you enough? Love you enough?

" 'All the wounds that Edwin has inflicted on me are beginning to heal. His violence, his mental cruelty. I really thought I would take my own life at one point. I just couldn't take any more of him. God Jessica, when

275

I think of how he has treated me. For so long. The sex, the abuse, he's such an animal but at least he's out of the house now. It's wonderful. The peace. No shouting, no rows. I know he can't hurt me any more. Bloody hell I'm writing about "him" now. Sorry. I'm actually writing to say I love you. I really do. I don't think I've ever said those three words to anyone in my life and actually meant it.

"'That's all I wanted to say Jessica. See you at the weekend.

"'I love you so much,

"'Clare x.'"

Howard finished reading, more loving tears. Less volume this time, but effective all the same. Her words had silenced any dissent. Her voice had delivered. The angels had spoken. Evert stood still. Quiet. Impact was everything. When the dramatic moment had finally died he said, "Will you please tell us in your own words exactly what happened on the afternoon of Mrs Hillyard's death. Please take your time. This is extremely important."

Howard did not pause. There was no need for a quick harvesting of thoughts. Her recollection of events could be written in solid concrete. I watched and felt my mouth fill with lead.

"Clare and I had been out for lunch. We returned to Clare's house for some coffee. I had taken the afternoon off knowing that Clare would need more than an hour of my time. In between the elation the divorce was causing her a great deal of stress and anxiety. Understandably so. Divorce is like that. She needed me. We drank our coffee and talked for a while. Eventually we went upstairs to her bedroom to make love. It was about 4.00 p.m. As far as I was aware we had the house to ourselves.

"I knew that Clare hadn't objected to Edwin calling in for his personal things provided she didn't have to see him. They had agreed apparently that if Clare's car was in the drive he would go away. Obviously on the afternoon in question Edwin had decided to ignore Clare's wishes. We were in bed together when the bedroom door opened. I looked up to see Edwin standing there. He was very still. I don't know how long he stood there. It could have been seconds, minutes. Everything just froze. Next thing he was screaming and shouting. I remember, 'I'm going to kill you,' quite clearly. I also remember the words 'slut' and 'bitch'. He rushed up to the bed and tried to drag me off it. I remember his eyes. I thought he had gone insane. There was no reason, nothing. Just blind hatred. I fought him for all I was worth. I was scared. Frightened that he would do serious harm to Clare. He was so mad; mad with anger. It was terrifying. I remember a heavy blow to my chin and I fell off the bed. I got up quickly. I saw him push Clare off the bed. He then grabbed her head with both hands and smashed it against the corner of the bedside cabinet, I don't know how many times. He was wild. Out of control. Clare's body seemed to go limp. He dropped her to the floor then he seemed to go rigid. He was standing above her looking down at her, breathing heavily, panting and sweating. I ran to Clare. I felt for a pulse. There was none. I tried some first aid, artificial resuscitation and so on. Nothing. The poor woman was dead. Edwin looked at me for a moment. I stared back and said 'She's dead'. He turned and walked out. The next thing there were policemen and ambulances. I learned later that he had dialled 999 as soon as he had left the room."

She stopped speaking.

More silence.

More suppressed coughs and verdicts of guilt.

Howard had cleansed herself. Her catharsis was total. The lying bitch! I had made a mistake. A massive mistake. Howard should have been the one on the floor about to meet her maker, not Clare. If I could have relived those moments. If. That's the dock again for you. Makes you think murder. It's the atmosphere, the courtroom. The history of the place.

What really disturbed me was the whole 'Howard effect'. There's me thinking earlier that I had seen some warmth in the woman. So much for my 'instincts'. The ruthless strumpet was in for the kill, no mistake. She had been calm. Her evidence given without histrionics, without hesitation or irrational passion. She had pitched her voice and words to perfection. There had been just the right number of tears, tremors and ripples of hesitancy. She had told the truth. Bowler was going to need a titanium-plated nutcracker to crack this one.

Jessica Howard was truth personified.

I could have wept.

Hawkins adjourned the trial until the following day. Bowler voiced his objection. He wanted to hit Howard with an immediate cross-examination. It would have been more effective had it taken place now whilst the jury had little time to absorb. Howard was showing signs of fatigue. Now was the time. Instead the jury would have all night to ponder Howard's side of the story and Clare's letter. One of the most damning pieces of evidence yet. The jury now had all night to prove me guilty. All night to believe. There would be no immediate opportunity to place doubt or conflict in their minds.

My night was going to stretch a damn sight further than theirs. That much I did know.

CHAPTER 44

Jessica lay in the hot water and breathed slowly.

She didn't dare move too quickly. The water had been heated to almost boiling point. Her skin had reddened. It was painful but this would soon become tolerable. In minutes her mind would transcend the hurt. It would find a unique level of peace. Her mind and self would become one. It had taken her years to perfect this state of beyond, of nowhere.

Nothing moved in the bathroom apart from the occasional flicker of flame from the candles that outraged the darkness and insulted the stillness.

She lay as silent as a corpse. Hardly breathing.

Her mind rejected 'self' as she followed her own path, not Buddha's; her meditation was her own. After thirty minutes to the second she opened her eyes and her breathing returned to normal. She turned a tap with her toe. She needed, wanted, more hot water. The minutes had turned the water cold.

As consciousness overtook her she realised something was wrong. She didn't feel re-vitalised. There had been too much activity. Her mind had refused to fully settle. She knew this feeling and it was rare. It couldn't be touched or explained. She knew that it meant uncertainty with herself. Disquiet. She remained in the water.

She was troubled.

The day had been demanding. She had lied. She had sought to devour Edwin Hillyard with her own special form of vengeance and pride. Pride: the sin, in all religions and in all philosophies. Even her own. She remembered his eyes. They had looked at each other above the wigs and black. In the briefest of moments there had been a kind of truce, a 'no hatred no man's land', even a distracted apology. The signal had been intense, brief and unnoticed by all except themselves.

She pulled herself out of the bath and dried herself, refusing to glance in a mirror as she did so. Normally she would examine her body, she was proud of it. It was a fine example of womanhood. A fine example of her. But not this time. Right now her own reflection would have overwhelmed and she would have been forced to remember who she really was.

A human being who felt.

A conscience that could be wounded.

CHAPTER 45

Howard was back in the witness box.

The chemicals and 'products' had lost some of their sheen. It was as if they had given up and gone off to some recycling plant. There was a difference in the woman's appearance, her demeanour. Fatigue? Worry? I didn't know, but something was up. Maybe she was recovering from a night of hard-core sex and heavy drinking, who knows? But there was a definite remoteness. A distance.

Bowler began his cross-examination.

I had spent all night thinking about this event. Revenge by proxy. Bowler was my knife, my hatchet. I hoped he had spent all night sharpening both. My God, did I not hope. I wanted to see the woman squirm, crawl and beg for mercy. My measured side told me this wasn't going to happen, so please humour me.

"You are a lesbian, Miss Howard?" Bowler was obviously in a 'straight to the point' mood.

"No."

"No? But you have sex with women?"

"Yes."

"A contradiction I believe, unless I am being exceedingly dim." There were a few sniggers around the court. A few sighs of expectation and certainly a bout of agitated writing.

"I am bisexual, as I have already said."

"Aaah . . . my apologies, I am being exceedingly dim after all, do excuse me. In modern parlance then, you 'swing both ways'. . . . Would you be so good as to explain to the jury what you mean by 'bisexual', as those in the jury of a less liberal nature may be a little confused."

"I object!" Evert was up. "Where is this questioning going, your Honour? Does my learned friend seek to lower the authority of this court by turning it into some back-street peep show?"

"I agree. Mr Bowler, where is this questioning taking us?" Hawkins enquired.

"To the truth, your Honour. To the truth."

"Very well, but please be quick about it. My court is not a place for common titillation."

"Thank you, your Honour. Now where were we, Miss Howard? . . . Ah yes, your confused sexual preferences. So you are bisexual . . ." he looked at the jury. "In other words, members of the jury, the witness is not particular as to whom she sleeps with . . . male or female. Are you married Miss Howard?"

"No."

"Have you ever married?"

"No."

"Do you have children?"

"No."

"So commitment, commitment that is to a permanent relationship whether to a man or a woman is not an item that is high on your agenda. Correct?"

"I wouldn't say that."

"What would you say then? You are an attractive woman – to both sexes it would seem – a young woman even, thirty-two is no age. You enjoy the best of both worlds as it were. I would have thought that your indifference to the gender of the recipients of your sexual favours would provide you with ample choice for a partner who would love, honour and obey, certainly more choice than we . . . how shall I say? . . . conventional individuals who are inflicted with the boring hum-drum of heterosexuality."

"Perhaps the right one hasn't turned up yet," Jessica replied, smiling. "In any event I would be loathe to 'obey' either sex." Bowler ignored the last few words.

"Ah, the right one. The perfect match. The illusion. Perhaps it has more to do with the fact that you will not commit. That would be far too much of a sacrifice, would it not? It would interfere with your career and sacred independence, would it not?" Bowler paused for a second only, "You wanted the defendant in your bed, did you not?"

Ambush time.

"Pardon?"

"I said you wanted Mr Hillyard in your bed. You wanted to have sex with him."

"I don't know what you are talking about."

"No? Then how do you explain making a brazen pass at the defendant on the 14th May. In his own kitchen and whilst Mrs Hillyard – your close friend – was upstairs getting dressed? Do you know what I am talking about now?"

"Again, no."

"Then let me continue to refresh your memory. You made physical advances toward the defendant on the 14th May last, in his kitchen. He did not respond to your sexual overtures. Being the determined sort you did not give up. Instead you slipped him a hand-written note without the knowledge of your 'close friend', Mrs Hillyard. Only this time she was actually in the room. The note said, 'Please ring me – and let's have some fun.' Your telephone number was written next to these words. But the defendant did not respond to your wishes, did he? In fact he returned your note to you as you and Mrs Hillyard were about to drive off. He had written on the back 'Fuck Off' had he not? How do you explain your bold advances, Miss Howard? How do you explain the defendant's immediate rejection?"

I'll say that for her, she remained calm. She wasn't going to be drawn.

"All this is fantasy. The defendant's fantasy. I made no such advances. None. I didn't like him. From the first moment we had met I had found him extremely unattractive. Both in looks and personality." Ah well, can't please them all. "Can you prove any of this nonsense? Where is the note?" Who needed Evert you may well ask? The woman was doing just fine all on her own. Bowler didn't respond – he couldn't. If only I had taken a copy of it. If only. Right now the 'if onlys' could go screw themselves. Howard was scoring. She continued, "We hadn't got on at all. In fact our brief conversations – if you can call them that – had been hostile. The defendant was writing a self-help book entitled 'How to insult'." There were a few titters around the courtroom. At my expense this time.

"Really." Bowler growled.

He was losing this one. He had hoped the accusation would have dented the women's confidence. She might even have feared that he had some irrefutable evidence to back up his allegations and made an out-and-out admission. Such things are not unknown in a court of law, particularly when a witness is in the witness box. Pressure and stress can do all kinds of things. No such luck with Jessica Howard, she was too cool and clever.

"Yes. He was always very rude. Clare had warned me. She had told me to ignore his bad manners. He was like it with everyone apparently." Here we go again. My directness and honesty upsetting people. "He threw me out of the house once. Told me to 'Get the hell out, that I was getting up his nose.'"

"So you deny ever trying to seduce the defendant?"

"Yes."

"You are a liar! An accomplished one at that!" Bowler's voice was rising. "Your primitive sexual urges did not stop at the defendant's wife, did it? You wanted her husband as well. Your bisexual appetite allows you to consume both sexes. Husband and wife. What is it to you? As long as your sexual desires are satisfied that's all that counts. One victim wasn't enough. You had to have two. In the same household. You are a sexual predator, Miss Howard. A ruthless, lying predator!"

"That's enough Mr Bowler!" Hawkins raised his voice too, a rare event, "You are shouting at the witness. I will not tolerate such tactics in my court. You will stop this bullying and vehemence at once!"

"Why, your Honour?" Bowler shouted back defiantly. "It is my duty to be vehement!"

The court fell silent.

Hawkins was not a judge to be so blatantly challenged. Seconds passed. The two men exchanged angry eyes.

"Mr Bowler, your impertinence is renowned as is your admiration for the late Marshall Hall," Hawkins said calmly with a few cubes of ice on top. "Nevertheless, I am the judge in these proceedings and you are a barrister, a Queen's Counsel, appointed to defend. Why do you suppose, Mr Bowler, that I am up here and you are down there?"

"Your Honour," Bowler replied, with a fine dollop of unctuous sarcasm in his voice, "*far* be it for me, a mere humble mortal, to attempt the *lofty* task of trying to fathom the inscrutable and *esoteric* workings of Providence. . . . Now, may I continue?"

Hawkins' wig nearly took off, but the dignity of his position prevailed – only just. He sneered a "Continue."

Bowler was a ferocious advocate, no doubt about it. For one moment there I thought he was going to join me in the dock! For the first time I was beginning to enjoy things. Well, 'enjoy' is perhaps too strong a word. Savour would be more accurate. Howard stood in the witness box. Her hands gripping the rail, tight. She must be fed up with being insulted and never being given a chance to fire back a few of her own. Her face had started to lose more of its chemical colouring.

Bowler pursued.

"Rejection is not a pill you are used to swallowing, is it Miss Howard? After all you are an attractive, if not beautiful, woman. Successful, accomplished. Men, women, they all fall at your feet. Except, that is, Edwin Hillyard. Here was one man unimpressed by your obvious charms. How that must have hurt for one who is so used to always winning."

Bowler looked at the jury, forcing them to see him as their best friend and understand. "In the arena of romantic endeavour, members of the jury, rejection can make even the most decent man or women extremely vengeful."

He turned back to Howard, "We are here today, Miss Howard, because of your fury at being rejected. You had been scorned. You had been humiliated. Thrown out onto the street. Revenge obsessed you. You couldn't have the defendant, so his wife would have to do instead. You would treat a personal snub with a far more lethal one. What could be more humiliating for a husband than to be cuckolded by another woman? You know your men, Miss Howard. I commend you."

This time I thought Howard was about to crack. Not so. She straightened up and said calmly.

"And I commend you . . . on your creativity. Everything you have alleged is nonsense. Pure nonsense. I can't even be bothered to react. That would only dignify your outrageous aspersions. As I have said before, where is your proof? Your corroboration? The defendant meant nothing to me. I repeat, nothing."

She looked at the jury. Her face was hard. 'Nothing,' she repeated.

This last word was said with just enough emphasis to be believable. She was not about to let go. "Must I remind you, Mr Bowler, that this is a court of law, not the set for a scene from *Hollyoaks* or some other equally torrid exercise in exaggerated and scurrilous gossip."

"Indeed, Miss Howard? Why then, would such a scene from *Hollyoaks* allow you more freedom to excel in your Thespian ambitions? You are, after all, a consummate actress."

"That's enough!" Hawkins was off again. "I am not going to tell you again, Mr Bowler!"

"My apologies, your Honour." An apology. Things were looking up. Bowler carried on, "Do you consider yourself in good health, Miss Howard?"

"Yes."

"Robust health? Fit?"

". . . Yes, I like to think so."

"Do you play any sport? Use a gym?"

"I play tennis and I use a gym."

"I believe Mrs Hillyard was a keen tennis player."

"Yes, she was, although we never got round to having a game. We planned to, though."

"I'm sure you did. Mrs Hillyard was a fit, strong woman too?"

"Oh yes. Didn't smoke or drink. Only the odd glass of wine. She went to the gym regularly."

"So, both of you were fit and strong?"

". . . Yes." I could see that Howard was wondering where all this was going. So was I.

"You were both naked in bed at the time of the tragedy. Is that correct?" He was chopping the testimony. Moving from point to point without there being any obvious connection. Such questioning created imbalance. He was trying to unnerve.

"Yes."

"Were the curtains drawn? I believe it was daylight outside."

"No."

"You were able to see all Mrs Hillyard's body then?" That was putting it mildly.

"Yes."

"And you had seen her naked before?"

"Yes."

"There was no fat? Her muscles were firm? Toned?"

"Well . . . er . . . yes."

"As are yours."

". . . Yes – I like to think so."

"I see. Er . . . by the way, did you happen to notice any bruising on your lover's body?"

"No." Howard had finally slipped up.

"Pardon?"

". . . No."

"How odd. I thought the lady was a victim of constant physical abuse?"

"Well . . . I . . ."

"So you didn't notice one scratch or bruise even when Mrs Hillyard's naked body was being used for your pleasure?" This time Howard did flounder. Bowler turned to the jury, "No cuts or bruises. No aches or pains. Nothing but fit well looked after bodies, members of the jury. Not quite what one would expect, I venture." He turned back to Howard. "In your evidence you say that you received a blow to your chin from the defendant. He hit you as you tried to defend his wife."

"Yes."

"In fact, he knocked you to the floor."

"Yes."

"Which side of the bed did you fall?"

"The left side."

"Are you sure?"

"Yes."

"What type of bed was it?" Howard was starting to look bewildered.

"A brass bed. A Victorian antique I think. It wasn't a four-poster or anything."

"Would you say the mattress was high off the floor?"

"High, low, I am not an expert on beds. It was just a normal bed."

"Hardly 'a normal bed' I think. Antique brass bedsteads are quite sought-after items, I believe. Expensive. The mattresses are certainly high off the floor by modern standards, would you not agree?"

"I suppose so."

"Good. Then the top of the mattress would have been two feet off the floor?."

"If you say so."

"I do. The distance has been measured. How did you fall?"

"What do you mean, how did I fall? I fell for God's sake, that's all there is to it!" Jessica was getting flustered.

"Well, did you fall on your back, your side, your front? How did you land?"

"On my front . . . I think. Look what is—" Bowler was not about to give up the advantage. He didn't give Jessica a chance to finish.

"Please think carefully, Miss Howard. In your statement you say you fell on your front. Are you sure of this?"

". . . Er . . . yes," she paused. "Yes, definitely."

"You are certain?"

"Yes, I remember using the mattress to pull myself up."

"You used the mattress to pull yourself up, you were that close to the bed, you are certain of this?"

"Definitely."

"Definitely. . . . The defendant hit you on the chin?"

"Yes."

"You are sure?"

"Yes."

"So, if I may summarise. You are in bed with the defendant's wife. The defendant walks in. He shouts at you and tries to drag you off his wife. You fight him. He hits you hard with a clenched fist. You fall off the bed landing on your front. Do you agree with me so far?"

"You are stating the bare facts, but yes, I agree with you."

"Good. It is gratifying to know that we can at least agree on something, Miss Howard," he smiled.

He looked at his blue legal pad and then his head shot up. "So, in those brief moments you fight with a man who knocks you to the floor. With a clenched fist. You fall face down close to the side of the bed. So close in fact that you are able to use your hands to grip the mattress and pull yourself up. In those brief, chaotic and violent seconds you are on the floor, dazed and in a state of shock if not unconscious. Yet in spite of all this you manage to obtain a calm, bird's-eye view of the defendant battering his wife's head against a bedside cabinet on the opposite side of the room.

"What did he do? Wait for you to have a ringside seat, or can you see through a two foot high bed? The medical evidence is agreed. Mrs Hillyard died from one blow to the head. One. How long do you think it takes for a normal man to commit such an act of violence? One second? Two? Are you so fit and healthy that you can withstand a blow to the chin, fall to the floor and still retain all your faculties? Can you recover in a split second? I think not. You didn't see anything, did you? If you saw anything at all it was the defendant trying to protect himself from an assault by his wife. A deadly assault from a woman caught in flagrante delicto. That's all the defendant did: protect himself and you know it. He acted in self-defence. He threw his wife off him. She fell. She hit her head. If you saw anything, which I doubt, it was this. Nothing else. There was no battering. The pathologist, an expert in these matters, has confirmed a single blow to the head. Unfortunately for you Miss Howard, and your tale of murder most foul, you were not allowed to attend the court whilst he gave his evidence. One blow, Miss Howard. One blow. I remind you that you said in your evidence that the defendant banged his wife's head against the bedside cabinet, 'I don't know how many times'."

Bowler looked at the jury again, "'I don't know how many times', members of the jury. There was one blow not, I repeat, 'many' blows . This has not been disputed by the prosecution. There was no murder."

He turned back to Jessica. "The defendant was being attacked by you both. Two fit and strong young women. More than a match for any man, particularly a middle-aged man. A man who attends neither gyms nor tennis clubs. A man considerably older than yourselves. One of you was trying to scalp him whilst the other one was trying to castrate him. What else was he to do? He acted in self-defence. He was trying to save himself and that's all."

"That's not true!" Howard yelled.

"Oh, it's true, Miss Howard. It's true."

"It's not true," she screeched again, all composure gone. Something had snapped. Bowler wasn't going to stop now.

"You are a liar, Miss Howard! You and Mrs Hillyard were incensed at being discovered; your passion interrupted. You hated the defendant. He had rejected you. Humiliated you. You saw no murder. You saw no battering. If you saw anything at all it was Mrs Hillyard being pushed off the defendant and receiving one accidental blow to the head as she fell. A blow that resulted from her being pushed away in self-defence. Your desire to hurt, to damage, to punish the defendant has brought you here today. By foul means or fair. The jury will not be fooled by your body, your make-up. They are too intelligent for that. Your deceit, your lies are known, Miss Howard. You fool no one!"

Bowler sat down exhausted.

The truth always drained him.

It was Evert's turn next. He stood up and used his cross examination to delve for substance and integrity. Howard recovered quickly and responded with courage. Bowler hadn't quite wrecked her. Her 'don't know how many times' I had bashed Clare's head had been a simple slip of the tongue, nothing more. There had been enough spirit left to leave me hanging to a rock face by my fingernails. Bowler's 'bed heights' was weak. I felt he was grasping at straws. I wasn't convinced anyway. Neither was the jury I suspected. Still, I gave him ten out of ten for trying. He didn't have much to go on after all.

I watched Howard step down from the witness box and wondered, 'Why?'

The court adjourned for the day.

It would be my turn soon.

My word against a woman I couldn't fathom.

My innocence against the unknown.

The untouchable.

CHAPTER 46

The only certainty in life is uncertainty. Dickens and the tax man have got it all wrong. Even death is uncertain; at least some would have us believe that there is no such thing. Eternal life. Paradise. Heaven, you name it.

So here I am. About to be called as a chief witness in my own defence. Charged and being tried for murdering my own wife. Not so long ago I was enjoying a rebirth of love, of hope. Now? Uncertainty was hammering me into the ground.

Jaz had visited me yesterday, against my wishes. She and Tom had conspired. Her face, the love, had unsettled me, as if I needed any more unsettling. At first anger had presumed its way in, anger and shame. She had seen me in my prison garb, my prison persona, the person I loathed and tried to refuse to see.

My eyes had flashed betrayal and demolished trust. Tom, Jaz, the traitors. She had queued with all the other reduced nicotine-soaked bodies on the 'Out'. She had sat down on a plastic chair, a clean body in a pit of lepers. When she had walked into the smoke-filled room, a room that had long ago said goodbye to honesty and deliverance, her eyes photographed and filed before she found me, lurking and ashamed. In that moment of silent frozen recognition a part of me committed suicide. Yet when she reached out her hand I took it, for what else could I do? Her touch neutralised my badness as we held hands and studied the tea-stained table top and cigarette burns. We tried to ignore the wild tears of resentment and outraged innocence that the convicted and beaten spilled into a room that was as hard as their hearts, their futures and their pasts.

We spoke few words, there was no need. The minutes passed and she finally left.

We both knew that we would go on.

CHAPTER 47

Somewhere in the flying dust of the courtroom my thoughts were dissolved by a name being called. A name I had once known so well. A name I had once been proud of. Edwin Hillyard.

Bowler stood before me. He had already squeezed as much goodwill as was humanly possible out of a few character witnesses so I was really his last chance – for an insane moment or two I wondered whether I should feel sorry for him.

"Mr Hillyard, how old are you?"

"Forty-five."

"Your occupation?"

"Solicitor"

"How long were you married?"

"Three years give or take a few months."

"How long have you been practising law?"

"Oh . . . it must be twenty years or so. Longer if you include the training, etc."

"Where did you read law?"

"London and Cambridge."

"Before these tragic events you were seeking a judicial appointment, were you not?"

"Yes." Now don't die laughing. It had been an avenue of exploration, nothing more. A way out. No more pressure. I had simply made some enquiries about being a district judge, that's all. Hypocrisy again, yes I know.

"Your initial application had been approved by the Lord Chancellor's Office had it not?"

"Yes."

"Rigorous vetting would have been carried out to get that far, correct?"

"I assume so."

"Your character, background, etc. would have undergone microscopic examination, so we may conclude that the august Lord Chancellor's Office itself had decided that you were a suitable individual to be considered for a judicial appointment?"

"I suppose so. Yes." I didn't feel flattered. My application had been a passing fancy, a whim. I hadn't relished the idea of messing about with small claims, possession orders and vindictive spouses.

"You are an honest man then. A man of integrity and decency."

"I would hope so."

"We have heard many observations about the nature of your marriage. It was unhappy, volatile, violent even. These observations have been made by those whom, of course, were not married to the late Mrs Hillyard or indeed shared the same home. Would you please tell the court, as a husband – the one man whom I must stress is in a true position to make observations on his marriage – whether or not your marriage was a successful one? A harmonious one?"

I had sat in that dock for hours listening to all these bastards lie, deceive and rip me to pieces. Well now it was my turn. The surprising thing is that I stayed calm. That's the lawyer for you. My delivery would be balanced. Fair. No bitterness. No name calling. I gave the court an account of a mistake. A mistake made by two people disillusioned by promises of physical and personality perfection. No one had been to blame. There had been no 'fault'. It was simple. We were unsuited. The marriage had been a sexless, childless fiasco. Full stop.

When I had finished Bowler continued, "These quarrels, Mr Hillyard, that we have heard so much about: were they violent?"

"No, definitely not, apart from one occasion when I slapped her in order to stop her hurting me further. She was out of control. I am not a violent man, nor have I ever been."

"Would you please tell the court about that one occasion."

"Yes, of course. We experienced tensions – yes. We were both unhappy with the marriage. And yes, we quarrelled – frequently.

But there was no violence apart from that one incident. Most of the time we just didn't speak to one another.

"A short time before her death things had come to a head. She had told me she was going to begin divorce proceedings. I accused her of having an affair with Jessica Howard. She hit me across the face, loosened a couple of teeth in fact – you have my dentist's confirmation. Date, treatment, etc. I am ashamed to say that I hit her back, slapped her. No fist. She had started to get hysterical, out of control. Slapping her seemed the only way to bring her to her senses. I had tried to use the minimum of force, that is to say I had not used all my strength. I exercised restraint. She was a woman and I had never hit a woman before – slapped one, that is.

"Clare had taken me by surprise, I simply hadn't anticipated such a crazy response to an accusation that had been made in a moment of irritation. I wasn't that angry about the divorce or even surprised. It had been coming for a long time. If Clare hadn't started proceedings, I would have done.

"At the time Clare's response to her having an affair with Jessica Howard shocked me. I hadn't really believed that they were actually having an affair. My words had been said out of childish spite. Nothing more. There may even have been some kind of belated jealousy, I don't know. I had struck a raw nerve though, even though my accusations had been made without any factual foundation.

"At the time I really had no idea that Clare was inclined toward any kind of lesbian relationship. She and Jessica had been seeing a great deal of each other, but so what? They had been friends for many years, and I certainly wasn't much company. We hardly spoke to each other, as I have already said. However, from the moment their friendship had been resurrected Clare changed. She became more distant, more remote. Even though our marriage was a total mess and the dying embers of any love between us would have needed a flame-thrower to re-ignite them, we had communicated to a limited degree.

When Jessica came on the scene even this stopped. Clare had become more hateful. More bitter."

"Why do you think your wife had changed so much?"

"She was in love. Not with me though."

"Mr Hillyard, did you care for your wife? Look after her?"

"Yes."

"She didn't go without?"

"Not as far as I am aware."

Bowler looked at the jury.

"Members of the jury, I ask you to remember the credit card statements. Mr Hillyard, you enjoyed a comfortable lifestyle. You and your wife?"

"Certainly. We were not short of cash. I earned a more than modest salary."

"And how much was that?"

"Oh, in a good year about one hundred and thirty thousand pounds. I had also inherited some substantial sums of money from my parents. Clare and I used to go on expensive holidays, eat out a lot. We had a delightful home and so on. We were more than comfortable."

"Did you have any mortgages, debts, etc.?"

"No, none."

"Was your wife an extravagant lady? Careless with her use of plastic?"

"Er . . . yes, I suppose she was. At least her spending never failed to surprise me."

"That is very modest of you, Mr Hillyard. I am sure that there are many husbands who would not be so generous with their answers." Bowler looked at his notes and added, "I for one," just within earshot of the jury.

"Indeed," he continued, "I would not be exaggerating when I say that your wife was extremely fortunate to have such an indulgent husband. I am sure that the ladies in the jury would relish such generosity of spirit." He gave them a smile and they returned it as if to say, 'Fat chance with the mean bastard I'm married to'.

Then he looked back at me. "Please tell us about your relationship with Dr Jaspreet Kaur Shemare?"

"We met by pure chance in the London Underground a few months ago. There had been a tragic accident. A suicide. Dr Shemare was one of those, along with me, standing right next to the man who killed himself. She was in a state of shock. Although she is a doctor and used to death it was the unexpected. The suicide was a particularly violent one. Very sudden and bloody. She seemed to faint, so I quickly caught hold of her lest she fall and hurt herself. I took her to the nearest bar for a stiff drink. We spoke briefly. A matter of minutes. I asked her for her telephone number and she gave it. We saw each other again. We . . . er . . . fell in love."

"You had not been going out of your way then to seek any extra-marital relations? Affairs?"

"No, definitely not. Quite frankly it was probably the last thing I wanted. My life was difficult enough at that time. The love that grew between myself and Dr Shemare just happened. It had not been looked for by either of us. These things tend to have a momentum all of their own as I'm sure everyone in this courtroom knows."

"Indeed. Please tell the court in your own words what happened on the afternoon of your wife's death."

"It was late afternoon, about 4.00 p.m. I had left my office early to go back to the house to collect some more clothes. At the time I was staying in the flat above my office premises. I was perfectly aware that legally I was not supposed to go near the house. However, Clare had behaved reasonably in allowing me to go there to collect whatever I needed provided she was not there herself.

"I arrived at the forecourt to the cottage and saw two cars. Jessica Howard's and my wife's. I know that I should have turned the car around and left, but I didn't. I just wanted a few personal things. The cottage had been my home for quite a few years after all. I had no intention of causing any scenes or trouble. All I wanted to do was to go in and out as quickly as possible.

"I had no desire at all to see Clare or her friend. It was over. There was also someone else in my life who meant the world to me. Conflict of any kind was the last thing on my mind. I went into the house. It was quiet. I remember at the time wondering why I wasn't being greeted by clinking wine glasses or idle chatter. There was no one in the sitting room, or anywhere else that I could see anyway.

"I noticed the French doors were open. It was a sunny day – warm. I assumed both Clare and her friend had gone outside to enjoy the garden. We had about an acre of it. Either this or they had gone out for a walk. I was rather relieved. It meant I could get my things and leave without any unpleasant confrontations. I went upstairs to what was once my bedroom.

"I opened the door and there they were, having sex in our bed. At first I couldn't believe my eyes. To put it delicately, Clare was obviously enjoying herself, as was Howard. They were having oral sex. I took one look. All the years of my being used, the frustration, the sexual rejection. It all came together in a few brief seconds. All I wanted to do was get Howard off my wife's face and out of the house. My house.

"I tried to throw the Howard woman off the bed. Off Clare. Howard fought back screaming, 'You bastard! You bastard!' and so on. She hit me in the face. A punch. I remember Clare joining in and yelling, 'You bloody animal!'

"Clare was tearing my hair out and Howard was trying to emasculate me. She was making a concerted effort to detach my testicles from the rest of my body. I was being overwhelmed. I am not a young man and neither am I particularly fit. Too much smoking and drinking. I am not a big man either. I only weigh about eleven stones.

"The two of them were trying to hurt me, kill me. I was trying to save my scalp. Howard didn't give in so easily. Out of the two, Howard was the bigger and no doubt the stronger. She kept coming. I hit her on the chin with my fist. I was desperate.

Frightened. I knew I had taken on far more than I could handle. I remember pushing Clare away, throwing her off me. In those violent moments I honestly believed that my life was at serious risk. The two of them were demented. I remember Howard falling to the bedroom floor. There was silence. I was kneeling on the bed – dazed – wheezing. I don't remember exactly how long this lasted. Seconds, I should think. The next thing I remember is Howard kneeling by Clare who had fallen to the floor. She looked up at me and said, 'She's dead'.

"I left the room and telephoned for an ambulance.

"Immediately after I rang the police. I did not grab my wife's head and smash it on the corner of the bedside table. I repeat, I did not. She must have hit her head on it after I had pushed her off me. Her death was a terrible accident. I myself didn't even see exactly what happened. I was too busy trying to fight off Howard. Clare's death had been an accident. God knows our marriage was over, but it had always been my intention to look after her. Her own solicitor can confirm that I was quite happy to make a generous divorce settlement. All I wanted for Clare was happiness. This was all I wanted for both of us. I did not want her dead. I did not want to harm her physically in any way at all. Her death resulted from pure accident. Nothing more. Nothing less."

I had given my evidence in as measured and as calm a way as possible. It had been hard. I wanted to scream the truth. I had wanted to cry. All those days alone in a cell. A cell with cruel, deaf walls. No one to hear, no one to listen, no one to believe. I had been given my audience and the chance to declare, to prove. Yet when the time finally arrived I had been cowed by a deep sense of loss. I had been unable to rage, unable to rant. All I had wanted to do was tell the truth. No bunting, no balloons, no fancy cards – just the truth.

Bowler had allowed a minute or so for my story to be properly absorbed. There had been the usual tailored and restricted sound of suppressed shuffling. My words had inflicted a temporary coma.

"Mr Hillyard, the post mortem confirmed that your wife died from one blow to the back of the head. Did you strike her head against the bedside cabinet?"

"No."

"Did it, even for the briefest of moments, enter your mind that you desired something more than the defence of your own person?"

"No."

"Did you want to hurt your wife?"

"No, never."

"You acted in self-defence?"

"Yes."

"Two healthy women were trying to mutilate you and you acted in self-defence?"

"Yes."

"You are certain."

"Yes, my love for Clare may have died but there was no hate. We were getting divorced. Why would I want to kill her? Why? What for? We were two people who had made a mistake. I was angry, yes. Who wouldn't be? I defended myself. What else was I supposed to do? What would anyone do in those circumstances?"

"Quite. Mr Hillyard . . . did you kill your wife?"

"No."

"Did you murder her in cold blood?"

"No, I did not."

"I ask you one last time. Did you grab her head and smash it against the corner of the bedside cabinet?"

"*No*, no—!" I had had enough now, my voice finally betrayed me, passion had pillaged my composure.

"*No!*" I shouted again, "for pity's sake, *why* would I want to kill her?! A part of me *died* with her, for the love of God! *Why*?!"

Silence.

"Thank you Mr Hillyard. That will be all for now."

CHAPTER 48

Bowler had been on my side. An ally.

Evert was an enemy. A capable one and not to be underestimated.

"Mr Hillyard, where had you been the night before your wife's death?"

"In London."

"With whom?"

"Dr Jaspreet Shemare."

"Your lover."

"She is more than that – but yes, if you want to put it that way."

"You freely admit your infidelity?"

"I rather think the media have admitted it for me."

"That's as may be. How long had you been having an affair?"

"About as long as my wife had been having hers, I suspect." This reply merited a grunt from Evert and a few grins from the jury.

"How long exactly?"

"Not long, a couple of months or so."

"A couple of months of deceit and lies then?"

"No. Both Clare and myself had totally lost interest in each other's lives. Neither of us really questioned the other's whereabouts. There had never been any need to lie about anything." I was wondering what Evert was up to. He could hardly play the outraged wife bit, could he?

"Are you committed to Dr Shemare? Is she committed to you?"

"Yes, on both counts."

"You were planning a future together?"

"Yes."

"Would you consider yourself a family man."

"I have never been given the opportunity to find out."

Suddenly I knew where he was going with this line of questioning. I intended to pre-empt him.

"I had wanted children from the first day we met. I was passionate about wanting to start a family. I wanted a house full of children. My wife had always adopted an anti-baby policy. The curves of her body were more sacred than child-bearing. However, in spite of this she was eight weeks pregnant at the time of her death. I was shocked to discover this. It didn't come to light until the post-mortem had been done. The conception must have happened by mistake. A fluke. As far as I was aware Clare was on the pill . . . not that she really needed contraception. Clare had always been passionately against having children. I doubt in fact if she would have had the baby. A termination would have seen to that. If she had known she was pregnant she certainly wouldn't have told me. She would have known that a termination would have gone against my wishes."

"A fluke you say? A fluke it must have been Mr Hillyard, particularly in view of your so-called sexless marriage . . ." Evert smiled as he turned to the jury and added, ". . . perhaps a few rampant fairies had managed to gain entry to your bed one night?" It was gallery time. He was mocking me, treating me with contempt. Goading. Prodding.

"Well, they must have had more luck than me then," I replied. I couldn't resist it, I'm afraid. A few sniggers shot round the court. Evert was becoming quite irritating, but I knew that I couldn't rise to his provocation. If I showed any temper it would go against me.

"You appear to be quite indifferent to your loss of fatherhood. An odd contradiction I think. Earlier you were passionate about your desire to have children. In fact Mrs Hillyard's incapacity to give birth had caused major difficulties between you and she. It seems to me that you were utterly indifferent to fatherhood. You were more interested in other women. Is that not so?"

"Very much not so. Neither you nor anyone else in this court can hope to have any idea how I felt upon the discovery of my wife's pregnancy. The loss. I cannot even begin to explain."

"You seem very certain about the fact that your late wife would have terminated."

My turn now.

"Clare had aborted twice before." That's got you, you fat four-eyed little shit. "Please refer to her GP's notes if you require corroboration." Evert must have missed this piece of evidence. Tut, tut.

So far Evert had been unable to hit any bull's-eyes. I knew this wouldn't last for long though. The man was too good. Up until now he had been playing, loosening me up. Hoping to draw me into a false sense of security. This wasn't going to happen. I had been in the law a long time. I kept hold of the initiative.

"Let me be quite clear," I continued." I had always wanted children, a family, still do. I had married quite late and knew that the hourglass was being turned quite quickly. I had wanted children desperately. Clare hated them. I had known nothing whatsoever about the two abortions. I had not been consulted. I found out afterwards, or at least Clare had goaded me with the information in one of her less endearing moments. Had my opinions and feelings counted for anything the terminations would never have taken place. Not in a million years. For Clare, babies were an impediment. A nuisance."

"I think the court is aware that your marriage was unsuccessful, Mr Hillyard. A violent one too, but unsuccessful nonetheless."

"That's not—"

"You battered your wife on several occasions, did you not?" Change of tactics now which was par for the course.

"No, I did not," my voice was firm. This lie was not up for negotiation.

"You are calling all of the witnesses liars?"

"Yes."

"You are saying your late wife was a liar?"

"Yes."

"She lied in her letter to Jessica Howard?"

"Yes."

"It would seem that all the people in this tragic affair are liars then . . . except you of course. Upstanding members of the community, professional people . . . they are all liars?"

"Misguided and fooled as well."

"And liars."

"I'm not . . ."

Evert interrupted, "Quarrelling, broken crockery. Screams. None of these things happened. Not in your deluded world it would seem. Not in your lying world. You have admitted that you hit your wife. You have admitted it to this very court."

"I slapped her—"

"A slap. A punch. A kick. What is the difference? Violence is violence. Fear is fear. You frightened your wife, terrified her. She lived in constant fear of your physical and sexual abuse. Is not this the truth? You raped her shortly after your marriage, did you not?"

"No. I repeat, I slapped her once after she had hit me, rather hard too – she nearly knocked my teeth out. Plates and things were smashed, yes, usually on my head. I am not a wife beater or even remotely violent. As for rape, that is complete fantasy. Your fairies must have been in the bedroom again."

Evert was not going to give up.

"Your wife was a brave woman. A woman who suffered. She did not seek help. And why? . . . To keep your reputation intact. You are a clever, educated man, Mr Hillyard, but you cannot fool everyone. We hear these words 'self-defence'. Here you are, a fit man. Strong in spite of the smoking and drinking.

Look at you. Not an ounce of fat. I believe you were a squash champion at one time. Your wife was a petite woman of eight stones and 5 foot 3 inches in height." He looked at the jury, "There was no competition was there? None! . . . Members of the jury one cannot help but wonder what on earth the defendant had to defend himself against?"

I had lost that one. I knew it. The bastard hadn't given me a chance. I told you he was good. He wasn't about to give up his advantage either.

"You had taken out a life assurance policy on your wife just before her death, had you not?"

"Yes. It had been a joint policy – equal cover. One million on each of our lives."

"One million pounds?"

"Yes."

"A substantial sum of money even by today's standards."

"That's debatable. Many people these days are 'millionaires', in bricks and mortar if nothing else."

"That may well be, but—"

"No 'buts', Mr Evert." My turn again. "My wife had been used to a solvent lifestyle. The policy had been taken out to ensure her security should anything happen to me. Frankly, a million pounds is not an amount worth killing for. You've probably earned a quarter of that from this trial alone." Couldn't resist again, but my own digs were getting the jury on my side which is exactly where I wanted them to be. Bowler wasn't the only one trying to strike up a solid friendship with the jurors. "My investments, properties, etc. are worth two to three times that." Careful here now Edwin boy, the credit crunch had lopped off a good bit of that. I suddenly felt that I had just put my foot in it. This is what happens when one takes one's eye off the legal ball and I didn't think Evert was going to let me forget it.

"Do you seriously think that I would have risked standing in this dock for a paltry million pounds? Wake up man!" In for a penny in for a pound, eh? Besides I enjoyed being contemptuous toward the man even though I knew it was going to cost me. The green polka-dots were out. He was sweating. Don't be fooled. This was normal.

"You were seeking to leave the law were you not?"

"Nothing definite had been decided, as I have already said."

"At forty-five you would need considerable sums of money to maintain your lifestyle until— say seventy-five or even eighty-five, without a substantial income. You agree we are all living much longer?"

"I believe so."

"This being the case, two to three million pounds to support your lavish lifestyle is not such a large sum of money, is it? Particularly when a large part of that is tied up in property.

"You are being silly."

"Am I? Am I really?" I didn't like this. Evert was the last person in the world to trivialise his cross examination. "You talk of investments. Well I have evidence here that shows that your Stock Market investments have reduced in value to a quarter of their original amount. About three hundred thousand pounds, in fact. Add this to the depreciation in property values of say 20%, plus the proposed divorce settlement you were being faced with and I would say you were in a rather strained financial position. Wouldn't you agree?"

He had a point and there was damn all I could do about it. The banks had played fast and loose with my money and I knew it; what I didn't know was by exactly how much. I hadn't taken much notice. That's financial smugness for you. I was a lawyer and book man after all, not a financial whiz kid.

Bowler was up, objections flew around. Discovery of documents, why wasn't the defence told? Etc., etc. All futile of course. The damage had been done and the jury had seen it being done.

Believe it or not, I didn't care that much about money. Besides I had Jaz. She was all I cared about. Anyway I was hardly a pauper for all that. The Stock Market and property may have taken a dive, but I was still worth a few bob in realisable assets alone. It was just a question of riding things out. The trouble is, I knew the jury wouldn't see it that way. I might not have cared, but they sure as hell would. Being a solicitor didn't help either. No doubt they were all thinking that my so-called millions had come out of their pockets. They were partially right too, at least as far as my corporate clients were concerned (not that they would appreciate the difference) which made my anxieties even more disconcerting.

I was worried.

"You have told the court that your wife's death was an accident. That you acted in self-defence. You would have us believe that these two women . . . these professional wrestlers . . . were tearing you apart. In self-defence you threw off your wife. She flies through the air and conveniently bangs her head against a passing bedside cabinet. It is not disputed that your wife died from a blow to the back of the head. However, once Jessica Howard had been removed from the fray as it were, you were free to do your will. Your murdering will, that is. You grabbed your wife's head with both hands, didn't you? You smashed it with all your considerable strength against the cabinet, didn't you? You killed her, didn't you?"

"I—"

"You wanted her out of the way. There was a new woman in your life. You were in love. You were fed up with your job. You wanted a new start. You needed money because your own funds had been drastically reduced. You wanted your wife dead. She was in the way, a nuisance. You wanted freedom."

"I did not kill my wife!" I shouted.

"Oh, you killed your wife all right. Of that there is no doubt. Violence upon your wife's person had become a habit. You enjoyed punishing her. Punishing her for being your wife. There was no accident. There was only opportunity. Your wife in bed with another woman. You, the pathetic cuckold. Anger, reaction – all these things played so well into your scheming. You saw an opportunity in those brief seconds to remove the most irritating and objectionable blight on your perfect life. You are an opportunist, Mr Hillyard. A deadly and vicious opportunist. You are a murderer. An inadequate one at that. You saw your wife being satisfied by another. By another woman, no less. You had been unable to satisfy your wife yourself. The humiliation. The degradation. You exploded. She had betrayed you and your pathetic ego. You were profoundly insulted. Your virility had been undermined. The great 'I am' brought to book. What else could you do? Revenge, Mr Hillyard. That was the only emotion in your heart on that afternoon. Revenge, sweetened by punishment and the chance to be free. Mr Hillyard, you killed your wife in cold blood, with brute force and without mercy. You murdered her. . . . No more questions, your Honour."

The jury was looking at me. Staring.

It was hard to find any compassion. Any understanding. I could see them all totting up the fees for probate and conveyancing they had paid over the years. The women were not responding to my cause. I struggled to find sympathy.

It was my word against Jessica Howard's.

Whose word would they believe?

For the first time since this awful journey had started, a long time in prison was becoming a serious possibility. As I left the dock that day my bones ached with fear. I looked up at the public gallery and saw a face as scared as my own.

Jaz.

CHAPTER 49

"Members of the jury, firstly let me thank you for your patience in listening to all the evidence that has been placed before you. Also the court would like to express its gratitude for you being here today. Sometimes public and civic duty can be an onerous and inconvenient pastime. We do understand." Evert was about to deliver his closing speech. He would bring all the prosecution evidence together into one foul delivery of my guilt.

"You have been brought here to this court to decide fact, fact beyond all reasonable doubt. This is why you are here. Please remember my words when you come to deliberate upon the evidence.

"What are the facts then of this tragic and sad case?

"A woman in her early thirties, an extremely attractive woman with everything to live for, had her right to life snatched away by the most brutal and ruthless of human hands . . . for no justifiable reason. Clare Hillyard harmed no one.

"She led a life that was full and content apart from the fact of a marriage that she no longer wanted to be part of. This was her only crime. A crime perhaps that many thousands of us commit every time we receive the Decree Absolute for divorce.

"The defendant will have you believe that his marriage, though unhappy, did not suffer from bitterness and violent outburst. This is a nonsense, a fantasy.

"You have heard the evidence of various witnesses, but I shall concentrate on the most important of those. I do not want to keep you here longer than I have to as I am sure you must all be very tired and want to go home.

"You have heard the chief executive of the local authority attest to screaming and smashed plates, broken glass, violence.

He and his wife feared for the safety of Mrs Hillyard's person. Why would this man, a man who reaches decisions upon many aspects of our daily lives, have come to this court to lie? Why? Anger at the colour of a garden fence as the defence would have you believe? A grudge? Ask yourselves, members of the jury, whether such a man would demean himself by an exercise in such mean pettiness. He came to this court to speak the truth. He had known that things in the Hillyard household were volatile. Had heard violent rowing. However, like many of us would, he felt unable to interfere. One does not tread into the matrimonial territory of others lightly. Mr Brent did what he felt was right. What most of us would have done is kept away. Allowed the parties to a relationship to sort their own problems out. But he had already been at the receiving end of the defendant's arrogant abuse. He knew what kind of response he would receive if he had interfered. He did the sensible thing. He avoided a confrontation. A confrontation that he felt could have become ugly, if not violent. Trust Mr Brent's words. He simply had no motive or reason to lie. If he was guilty of anything it was caring for his neighbour, Mrs Hillyard.

"I come next to Lesley Moresby. She took instructions from Mrs Hillyard to begin divorce proceedings. Moresby is a solicitor who has been specialising in Family Law for many years. She has written academic papers and practise manuals on this area. She knows her job. She is considered to be an authority on this particular area of legal endeavour. She is a professional; an expert. It was her experienced and professional opinion that there was enough evidence of abuse to apply for emergency court orders against the defendant.

"Let me remind you that such orders are not granted lightly. They have to be approved by a judge. They were approved. And why are such non-molestation and occupation orders sought? Because there is a serious and immediate risk of physical harm to the applicant. Further harm. A great deal of damage has usually already been done. These orders seek to prevent more abuse. They seek to keep the offender away from the home. Away from the victim of domestic violence.

"Muz Moresby exercised her professional judgement. Her expertise. In her view, Mrs Hillyard was at serious risk. Why?

"Lastly, members of the jury, I ask you to consider what possible reason an experienced and highly respected solicitor could have for lying about her own professional judgements? She has done nothing wrong. It is the defendant who is being tried, not her. Again, where is her motive for misleading you?

"I come next to Jessica Howard, the chief witness for the prosecution. The only eyewitness.

"She and Mrs Hillyard were lovers.

"They were planning on setting up home together. Jessica Howard is a responsible woman who works in the voluntary sector. Her organisation tries to help people who are disadvantaged. It also helps people who may not be so, it does not discriminate. It does not judge. Its advice is impartial. Indeed many of you may already be familiar with your own local Law Centre. If you are, then you will know of their lack of prejudice, their fairness.

"Jessica Howard earns a modest salary. Well below that which she would no doubt be capable of earning in the private sector. Would she have arrived at this position if her personal ethos had been one of deceit and mendacity? Would a woman whose whole working life is dependent upon integrity and fairness have come to this court today to lie to you? To fool you? Yet again I come back to motive. Why? Why would she want to deceive you? To what purpose? She told you what happened on that fateful afternoon. She was there in the bedroom. She was attacked by the defendant. She fought with him. Defended herself, as did Mrs Hillyard.

"By the defendant's own admission, there was a fight. She saw the defendant smash his wife's head against the bedside cabinet. Why would she lie?

"Members of the jury, you can do nothing but trust and believe the testimony of Jessica Howard. It is beyond all reasonable doubt. It is a statement of fact.

"I come now to the defendant himself. Mr Hillyard is an intelligent, highly educated man. A handsome, cultured and urbane man. A man that Mrs Hillyard could not possibly have hoped to compete with. To match.

"He has been successful in his chosen profession and has led a privileged and affluent lifestyle. He was a married man and yet he embarked upon an affair. He would have you believe that he had fallen in love. The only person the defendant is capable of loving is himself. Why did he marry Clare Hillyard? He certainly didn't love her, how could he? He himself has said it was a mistake. They were a mismatch. I'll tell you why he married. To satisfy his ego. It was essential to his image to have someone pretty. To have a woman on his arm that other men would covet. 'Arm candy' I believe is the common parlance.

"Clare Hillyard was a highly desirable women. The two had nothing else in common. Members of the jury, Clare Hillyard had become dispensable. She was no longer needed. She had become a tiresome nuisance. The defendant had recognised that even he could not turn back the clock. He wanted children. Not from any motive of love or kindness, I hasten to add. He wanted immortality. To leave something of himself behind. Ego again. He tells us that he knew nothing of his wife's two terminations. Can we believe that? The poor woman is not here today to answer; she is dead.

"Murdered by the defendant.

"The defendant met Dr Shemare. Here was his chance. A healthy woman, a doctor. Young enough to have a brood of children if necessary. Educated enough to compete. Socially adept. Financially independent. The ideal partner. On top of all this, she is a beautiful woman we are told.

"This time, past mistakes would not be repeated. He had learned. The defendant had to be free, members of the jury.

312

Free to ensnare another victim. Clare Hillyard was the impediment to his desire. She restricted, curtailed and prevented his ruthless intentions. She had to go. The defendant wanted a new life. No more private practice, no more Clare.

"He needed money for this enterprise. His own investments had taken a sound beating. He had to compensate for his losses. What did he do? The oldest trick in the modern annals of true crime. He loaded his wife with life assurance. He also knew that Mrs Hillyard would demand a substantial financial settlement on the divorce. Money was needed – substantial amounts. Where was he going to get it? We know that an opportunity presented itself on that afternoon in the defendant's bedroom. An opportunity to kill two birds with one well aimed stone. The death of Mrs Hillyard and one million pounds were the two birds – not to mention his release from financial provision for his wife.

"The defendant saw this opportunity in an instant. His clever, devious mind recognised the potential in that bedroom. On that bed. He took it. Freedom and financial independence were his.

"Members of the jury, you have heard of the violence that the defendant perpetrated upon his wife. A petite, pretty woman unable to defend herself. You have heard of the sexual abuse.

"His last act of abuse went too far. It was meant to. It was intended to. He wanted to kill, to murder.

"There was no accident. Do not allow him to persuade you with his obvious charm of anything other than this. He battered his wife's brains out. This is exactly what he wanted to do. He wanted her dead and his problems solved. None of the witnesses have lied. None of them have exaggerated or been spiteful with the truth. The evidence that has been put before you is unequivocal. There is no doubt.

"There is only one verdict you can return.

"Guilty. . . . Beyond all reasonable doubt."

CHAPTER 50

That night Evert's closing speech inspired black caps, blood-splattered oak and being 'taken from here to a place of execution'. So much for sleep.

Every so often Jaz would appear in my semi-conscious mind. Her face concerned one minute, laughing the next. She refused to leave me. Her surreal loyalty kept my mind alive as it helped me fight the hopeless tidal waves that were trying to drown me.

Evert had accused me of being a pervert, a psychopath, an ego-obsessed maniac, and last but not least, a violent bastard. There was no reasonable doubt about it, was there? Thank God we had done away with the noose. If Evert had had his way I would have been dragged from the court and strung up from the nearest lamp-post.

The next day Bowler addressed the jury. He was about to put the jury straight – at least this is what I hoped he would do. He stood before them. Tall, distinguished and eyes that said 'I defy you to challenge one word of what I am about to say'. He looked at them and demanded attention. His was the only voice and body in the court room; he dared them to even glance else-where.

"Members of the jury, you have heard all the evidence in this case. Evidence that the prosecution hopes will send Edwin Hillyard to prison for life . . . life, members of the jury." He paused, allowing the quiet to spice up the emphasis to his words.

"Marriage is a journey, members of the jury, a journey that seeks to discover uncharted and unknown territory. We begin our journey without knowing its true destination or where exactly it will end. This journey, like all journeys into the unknown, is often fraught with obstacles, unplanned problems and unforeseeable difficulties. I am sure there are many of us in this court today who know exactly what I mean. There are no maps, no directions or signposts for such a journey, nor perhaps should there be.

"In this case Edwin Hillyard married a woman whom he was to discover was sadly wanting. As time went by he came to realise he had made a mistake. Thousands of married people discover a similar mistake every day of every week. It is nothing unusual, nothing new; it happens. Indeed it has almost become a natural phenomenon; divorce has become as common as matrimony itself.

"The parties in the Hillyard marriage had realised their mistake. Divorce proceedings had been started. A parting of the ways inevitable. You have heard much from the prosecution witnesses of violence, quarrels, sexual abuse and suchlike. Some of these witnesses would have you believe that matrimonial discord is something unheard of. Well, we all know that is not true.

"How many of us in this courtroom today have not experienced a falling out with a partner during the past month? Very few, I imagine.

"Some witnesses have spoken of shouting, violent words, smashed glass, screaming even. Well, I put it to you members of the jury, those of you who are married or in a relationship, that such events are not unknown where the ordinary bonds between men and women are concerned. How frightfully boring a loving union would be without the occasional row or argument. I myself have been known to throw the odd cup. We men and women can be extremely frustrating and irritating creatures when we want to be, can we not? Particularly where the people we love are concerned.

"Can any of you deny that you never felt temper, anger, toward your partner? Have you never shouted or thrown things in the tumult of a row? Couples quarrel. They have fights. All rose bushes have thorns – even when the garden is filled with love. Couples do not however try to kill one another over a broken tea cup – rarely anyway. That would be taking the relief of tedium a little too far, I think." Bowler smiled at the jury, he charmed. I have to admit he was bloody good at it, and right now my life depended on it.

"The prosecution has tried to exaggerate and fantasise the conflict between the defendant and his wife. They would have you believe that the late Mrs Hillyard was living in a nightmare of sexual and physical abuse. The consummate, pitiful victim. Look at the evidence. What exactly is there to support these comical fictions? Gossip, members of the jury, gossip and trifles. I would remind you of some words from *Othello*,

> 'Trifles light as air
> Are to the jealous, confirmation, strong,
> As proofs of Holy Writ.'

Bowler paused, allowing the words to sink in. These days melodrama was often frowned upon, but he was old school and it had always served him well.

"What did Mr Brent give you?" Bowler continued. "I'll tell you what he gave you. A chance for him to exercise his childish, petty and officious grudge. His local authority mentality that we all know can be narrow, incompetent and overruns common sense. A garden fence? A different shade of brown? If he was so concerned about imminent grievous bodily harm, why did he not call the police? How did he manage to hear all these goings-on with a quarter of an acre of land in between his house and my client's? If the colour of a garden fence should cause so much insult and outraged reaction, then surely murder most foul would have at least prompted some kind of response? All Brent wanted to do was gossip in his local golf club, moan about a stubborn neighbour and come to this court to get his own back. Members of the jury, were a few of us believe what a local authority tells us, why then should we believe its chief executive?

"Next we have Lesley Moresby.

"An outspoken feminist and renowned warrior for women's rights. All very noble, I am sure you will agree. The problem is her testimony is tainted by her zeal and its lack of substance. Once again I refer you to the evidence. All we received from Muz Moresby were her opinions. Her views. Where were the hard facts?

"She received a story. A one-sided story, mark you, to matrimonial breakdown. We all know that in relationship breakdowns there are always two sides. Two sides, members of the jury. All Moresby gave us was a feminist slant on her fight for the emancipation of female kind.

"Where were the hospital reports? Where were Mrs Hillyard's GP's notes? Where were the police? The crime reports? Where were the cuts and bruises? Where was the hard evidence for her presumptuous conclusions? . . . There were none. None whatsoever.

"I come now to the only eye witness, Miss Jessica Howard.

"A beautiful and intelligent woman. Another fighter and warrior for equal rights and a feminist agenda. A law centre altruist and consummate protector of the weak and underprivileged. Miss Howard is also bisexual. Nothing wrong with that, except that it must sometimes cause a degree of confusion. One may well believe that a person with a bisexual inclination has the best of both worlds. This may well be so. But what happens when these two worlds clash?

"Miss Howard wanted the defendant. She wanted to have sex with him. Her verbal evidence would have you believe that she and Clare Hillyard were about to embark upon a loving life together. This is rubbish. You will note, members of the jury, that in her evidence nowhere does she mention her own love for Mrs Hillyard. I will tell you why. She did not love Clare Hillyard. She loved having sex with her, that was all.

317

"Whilst Clare Hillyard was giving away her heart, what was the subject of her desire doing? Giving herself to a man who was Clare Hillyard's husband and right under the tragic woman's nose. She made her advances in the Hillyards' house. Love? Jessica Howard is the sexual predator. Not the defendant. They exist. They do not know feelings or emotions. They know only sexual gratification. Not satisfied with Clare Hillyard, she wanted the woman's husband. At any cost. Did she care about the love Mrs Hillyard felt for her? I think not.

"Edwin Hillyard rejected her advances. He was faithful and honest. He had scruples. Howard was unused to rejection. A beautiful woman has few doors closed to her, but this particular door was unceremoniously slammed right in her face. She came to this court to lie, members of the jury, to lie and to punish.

"The prosecution has made much of a letter. The letter that was written to Howard by Mrs Hillyard. It is a letter that seeks to inspire sympathy and affection from the recipient. It makes sense, does it not, that Clare Hillyard would have been aware of Howard's lack of commitment? The woman felt insecure. She needed reassurance. She had struggled with her sexuality for years. It is not hard to understand that her new-found discovery had left her vulnerable. Even frightened. She would have exaggerated. Lied even, in order to win over Howard.

"One cannot help but wonder what has happened to a loving reply? Those who care and love each other usually reply to such declarations of affection. We heard nothing from Howard, did we? We heard no confirmation of her loving devotion in her evidence, did we? None.

"Howard tells us of Mrs Hillyard's fear, particularly in relation to rape and physical abuse. She tells us that Mrs Hillyard's cheek was red and swollen on the morning they went to see Lesley Moresby. The swelling must have receded extremely quickly for a so-called violent and ruthless attack – Moresby apparently noticed nothing out of the ordinary when questioned, neither did any of the other witnesses.

"The prosecution has presented us with observations only, together with the words of a married woman who was in the throes of infatuation, confusion and newly discovered lust. This is all. And none of it is reliable.

"Not one shred of medical evidence has been produced. Not one. Not one item of corroboration has been produced either from professional persons or even those who knew Clare Hillyard personally. Not one.

"Members of the jury, the only evidence you have been given to prove my client's guilt are the words of a vengeful, lying, nymphomaniac – a nymphomaniac I remind you who hadn't even seen Mrs Hillyard for the eight years prior to her death – intent on the destruction of a man who had the temerity to refuse and mock her sexual overtures.

"There she is. She has been knocked to the floor. Punched to the floor. She feels nothing, she would have you believe. Her chin is made of granite. Immediately upon receiving this blow and fall she gets up and sees my client battering the brains out of his wife's head. Not once but many times according to her own testimony you will remember. Yet she couldn't even get this right, as the pathologist confirmed. Death was caused by one blow to the head, and one blow alone. How can you trust the evidence of a woman which is proved in this very court to be so blatantly flawed?

"Your duty here today is to decide fact from fiction. The prosecution has given you fiction. Pure, undiluted fiction. My learned friend explores the fantastic world of fairies and goblins in his cross-examination, and even J. M. Barrie and his Peter Pan would have been impressed by his creative imagination, don't you think?

"I give you fact, not fantasy.

"Members of the jury, you must ask yourselves if the prosecution has shown you any evidence of constant abuse toward the deceased. They have not. Up to the time of her death Mrs Hillyard led a very comfortable lifestyle. She wanted for nothing. Her life would have been the envy of millions of people. You saw the credit card statements. You saw the factual evidence of this lifestyle. You must ask yourselves if this was the life of someone being cruelly battered and abused. Was it the life of someone with dark hidden secrets of violence and rape? Have you heard any evidence that confirms Mrs Hillyard's attempts to seek help? Confidential help. There are a countless number of agencies out there who provide advice and where confidentiality is assured.

"The prosecution has provided you with nothing to prove any of this, and why? Because Mrs Hillyard had everything she wanted. There was no abuse. There was no sexual cruelty. My client slapped her once. He admitted it to this court. It was a slap. A slap intended to bring his hysterical wife to her senses. That was all. Not one solitary shred of evidence has been produced to indicate any history of violence in my client's past. Nothing.

"He is not, and never has been, a violent man.

"The prosecution has made a feeble claim that financial gain was the motive for murder. Mr Hillyard is a wealthy man with or without one million pounds. His home alone is worth one million plus even allowing for the recent slump in house prices, not to mention the value of his practice which my learned friend omitted to mention, the premises he owns in his sole name, the antiques, classic cars, etc., etc. Money? Members of the jury, I think not.

"His other motive for wanting his wife dead was apparently his desire to be free to run off with Dr Shemare. Well, how many people in the middle of a divorce meet someone they fall in love with? Thousands. Do they all kill their spouses? It is not unknown, I grant you, that some do, but the vast majority certainly do not and the defendant is most certainly a member of that 'vast majority'.

"Divorce proceedings were underway. Mr Hillyard had contested nothing. He was happy to settle whatever was necessary on his wife to make sure she could have a fresh and comfortable start. The prosecution would have you believe that this was yet another reason for the defendant wanting his wife out of the way. He is a generous man, however. Remember the credit card statements. Believe it or not, members of the jury, his love for Dr Shemare was more important to him than money. Even in these cynical times there are some who do not treat money as their god.

"Members of the jury, the defence does not challenge the fact that the defendant threw his wife away from him in an attempt to defend himself. It does not challenge the fact that he punched Jessica Howard. It does not challenge the fact that Clare Hillyard died from a blow to the back of the head.

"What we challenge is the prosecution's assertion that Edwin Hillyard took hold of his wife's head in cold blood and smashed it with all his force onto the edge of a bedside cabinet. This did not happen. There is no evidence to prove that it did happen. My client told you that he threw his wife off him. He was being attacked by two strong, healthy women. He acted as any normal human being would act. He defended himself. Fought back. He believed his life was in danger, or at the very least that he was at risk of immediate and serious physical harm. He acted in self-defence, members of the jury. I repeat, self-defence.

"Mrs Hillyard hit her head against the bedside cabinet. It was an accident. My client never had any intention of seriously hurting his wife. None. And there has been no evidence, no reliable evidence at all that you can trust implicitly to prove otherwise.

"An accident, yes. Murder, most definitely no.

"There had been no intent. No cold blood. Without 'intent' there can be no murder. All you have heard from the prosecution is the pitiful evidence of those who would delight in the defendant's misery. Of those who desire revenge for their own juvenile and spiteful ends. Look at the evidence. Search for it.

Consider its scantiness. Its lack of fibre. Its integrity – or lack of it.

"Ask yourselves if everything you have heard in this court-room can bring you to believe that this man Edwin Hillyard murdered his wife. Can you all satisfy your common sense, your intelligence, your consciences . . . beyond all reasonable doubt that this man intended his loss of temper, loss of reason even, to result in the death of the woman he was married to? That he took her head in his hands and ruthlessly battered her to death?

"Perhaps, members of the jury, you will look into your-selves. Your own hearts; your own minds. Here was an accident of the most horrible kind. Has not my client suffered enough? He still felt for his wife. He had simply learnt to love again. Not only is his wife dead, but so is his unborn child. A child that he would have moved heaven and earth for, had it survived. A child that he would have loved without restraint or condition.

"Members of the jury, my last words to you must be these. . . . I humbly accept that I neither have the pen of Tolstoy nor the pencil of Doré; they alone could truly describe the defendant's horror at the discovery of his wife's death. A cold-blooded murderer . . . a psychopath . . . would have felt noth-ing. Does my client look like such a man? Does he have the eyes of a brutal calculating killer?" Bowler looked at me and then back at the jury, "I think not."

He paused for a few moments as he looked directly at the jury. He challenged and implored.

"I demand a verdict of 'Not guilty', members of the jury. I defy you to find otherwise . . . I demand it!"

CHAPTER 51

I was back in my cell.

It was a Monday night. The jury had been sent out after the judge's summing-up. Hawkins had been fair and unprejudiced. He had outlined the case against me with an objectivity that deserved my admiration. How had the jury taken it? I simply didn't know. Had I been a betting man I wouldn't have known where to put my money.

Bowler had done an efficient job. He couldn't have done any more. The evidence was in my favour. At least I believed it was, but was my lawyer's objectivity still intact? Would the jury believe me? They had been sent out at 4.30 p.m. that day. They would be accommodated, watered and fed. Tomorrow they would decide my fate. Tonight I would tear at my hair and finish the job that Clare had started.

The morning came quickly. For once I hadn't noticed time.

My journey to court had gone without my hearing even a car horn. I was placed in my usual home – the cells underneath the courts. I waited. Dear God, did I wait! Forget airports and train stations, this was the real thing. This was 'waiting' on a supernatural level.

The hours went by. Each time a security officer moved, I jumped and my stomach grabbed my throat. Each time a key turned, my nerves turned over with it. Each time a voice echoed, my life ran in front of it.

1 o'clock, 2 o'clock, 3 o'clock. Nothing. Movements, but none in my direction. 5 o'clock, time to go home, back to my permanent residence.

Another night.

Another hell.

The jury was struggling.

Another day went by – no verdict.

They were more than struggling.

On the third day the court is told they can't agree. The judge instructs them that he will accept a ten to two majority verdict.

A fourth day.

Now everyone is getting seriously angry. I am close to mental shutdown.

11.00 a.m. Friday morning. I am hauled up to the dock. I don't really see or hear anything. My brain has detached itself. By this time all the reality has become too much. It doesn't want to know any more. It doesn't even care.

The courtroom is full of anticipation as I am asked to stand. I hardly hear the polite request. Did I detect a note of sympathy in the clerk's voice? Does he know something I don't?

There is a shuffling of shy feet. A man stands, well shaved and clean. White shirt, red tie. I couldn't miss the tie.

The clerk says something to the man. I think it's a question. The clerk wants an answer.

I hear only 'Not guilty'.

There is Jaz.

Her lips, cameras and questions. People pushing, shoving, and squeezing. I am in the back of a car.

There is speed.

There is light and air.

I see a brown arm around my shoulder. Black hair rests against my lapel. Sleep.

Freedom.

EPILOGUE

Two years have gone by.

This morning I received a letter from the Probation Service confirming that I was no longer the subject of a supervision order. I had served my sentence. Hawkins had been lenient. Not guilty of murder, but of manslaughter. Two years probation and his eye of understanding. Sympathy, even. The man knew all about women.

Jaz and I have survived.

We live in a quiet part of the country where the people have short memories and even shorter curiosity. Jaz left her ambitions to consult in London. She now spends her days seeing to mothers with small children in a busy general practice. I have spent the last two years writing this book. My inspiration has always started at 9.00 a.m. and finished at 4.00 p.m. My little brown doc is expecting her own bundle of hell in about two months time. I am looking forward to it. The challenge. The old against the new. The different kind of love.

I have heard that Jessica Howard left her job soon after the trial. She went off to Thailand, so the story goes, to meditate and to find truth. I wish her well. I still feel that there was more to her than malice and moral bankruptcy. A lot more. Maybe one day we will talk. I would like her to explain, to help me understand.

Maybe one day.

I learnt about Lucretia. There were tears in Tom's eyes as he told me. I placed both my hands on his. I would always be there if he needed me. We speak at least once a week and see each other every month or so. Lucretia is responding well to the medication he tells me. The practice, which I handed over to him without strings is still doing well. He lives and fights along-side his darling wife.

Before I go, there is one last thing that I must tell you. In confidence and strictly between you and me. The formidable Muz Moresby was right, the only one, you have to hand it to her. Remember when she told the court how clever I was and that I was fooling everybody? Well, the punch to Jessica's chin did knock her out. She was on the floor – face down, out cold. She had obviously been unable to remember. It had all been so quick. Those seconds – or it could have been a minute, possibly two – provided me with an opportunity I simply couldn't resist. An opportunity, as Evert himself put it, 'To remove the most irritating and objectionable blight on my perfect life'.

How right he was.

So now you know for certain. All lawyers are lying bastards, so never ever trust a bent brief.

Cheerio!

THE END

PS. The life assurance helped as well!

xxx

Also by the same author:
THE RAGGED CLIFFS TRILOGY . . .

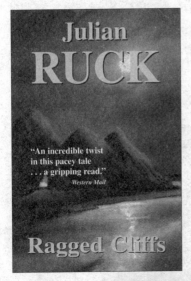

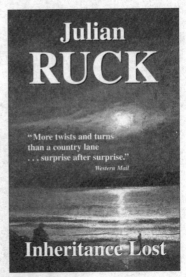

www.julianruck.co.uk

ABOUT THE AUTHOR

Julian Ruck trained as a lawyer in London before spending some time in both Denmark and Israel. On his eventual return he entered the world of Academia, lecturing law. This was not to be a lifelong commitment as some years later he found himself managing Legal Services Commission contracts in the Not For Profit Sector.

www.julianruck.co.uk